Please return/renew this item by the last date shown.

To renew this item, call **0845 0020777** (automated)
or visit **www.librarieswest.org.uk**

Borrower number and PIN required.

Libraries**West**

lowered his mouth to hers.

Dear Reader,

This is one of my most ambitious books ever! These characters got inside my head and heart and demanded that I deal with subject matter I've never attempted before. In my mind, there are two she-ros in this book, but don't worry! Only one of them is the "romantic lead." And what a woman she is. A shy bookworm princess with bad hair who is known for not making waves is thrust into a situation that challenges her to be stronger than she ever dreamed she could be.

The second she-ro is the hero's mother. I pictured her as an older but still gamin Audrey Hepburn determined to savor every moment of life. The dreamy forbidden hero comes from a long line of pirates. I see Nic Lafitte looking like a slightly rougher-edged version of Antonio Sabato, Jr. I love the way shy Princess Pippa turns worldly Nic's head and heart around in ways he would have considered impossible.

Throw in a long-standing family feud and a crowd of Royals, and our hero and she-ro are in for the journey of their lives. I hope this story will be a "heart-warmer" for you...

Wishing you love and joy,

Leanne

THE PRINCESS AND THE OUTLAW

BY
LEANNE BANKS

First published in Great Britain 2012
by Mills & Boon, an imprint of Harlequin (UK) Limited,
Eton House, 18-24 Paradise Road, Richmond, Surrey TW9 1SR

© Leanne Banks 2012

ISBN: 978 0 263 89464 6
ebook ISBN: 978 1 408 97141 3

23-0912

Harlequin (UK) policy is to use papers that are natural, renewable and recyclable products and made from wood grown in sustainable forests. The logging and manufacturing processes conform to the legal environmental regulations of the country of origin.

Printed and bound in Spain
by Blackprint CPI, Barcelona

Leanne Banks is a *New York Times* and *USA TODAY* bestselling author who is surprised every time she realizes how many books she has written. Leanne loves chocolate, the beach and new adventures. To name a few, Leanne has ridden on an elephant, stood on an ostrich egg (no, it didn't break), gone parasailing and indoor skydiving. Leanne loves writing romance because she believes in the power and magic of love. She lives in Virginia with her family and a four-and-a-half-pound Pomeranian named Bijou. Visit her website, www.leannebanks.com.

This is dedicated to the family members and friends who hang in there for the long haul when a loved one is terminally ill. May the special people in your life who have passed on continue to inspire you, make you laugh, make you wise and make you love forever…

Prologue

"**W**hat is *he* doing here?"

Phillipa was wondering the same thing. At her sister Bridget's gasp, her other sister, Tina, leaned toward Bridget. "Zach says he's a huge contributor here. Everyone loves him," Tina said distastefully.

"They clearly don't know him," Bridget said and nudged Phillipa. "Why can't we escape him?" she whispered. "Maybe it's because he's the devil and that means he can be everywhere at once."

At that moment, Phillipa almost agreed with Bridget. Nic certainly seemed to have some kind of dark power over her.

Phillipa had tried to slow things down with Nic Lafitte, but persuading the man to move at anything other than warp speed had proven impossible. He was a force of nature with a will that rivaled every kind of powerful destructive weather. Typhoons and tornadoes had nothing on him. She'd successfully avoided him for the past three weeks and she had been certain that fleeing her home country of Chantaine to visit her sisters in Texas would buy her even more time.

Who would have ever thought she would be caught staring at him at a charity social ball in Texas as he accepted an award for philanthropy? Phillipa knew that Nic had ties to Texas, but with his extensive business dealings, he had ties to many places.

The ballroom suddenly felt as if it was shrinking. Panic squeezed her chest. She had to get out. She had to catch her breath. Feeling her sister's curious gaze, she swallowed hard over the lump in her throat. "I'm not feeling well," she said. "Please excuse me."

When Bridget offered to come with her, Phillipa had to remain firm. "I'll be back in a little bit."

Sticking to the perimeter of the room as she fled, she kept her head down, hoping she wasn't drawing attention to herself. If she could just get out of this room, she would be fine, she told herself. Out of the room and away from Nic. Away from how he affected her.

She stepped out of the ballroom and held the door so it would catch softly as it closed, then took a few more steps away and leaned against the wall, which felt cool against her skin. Her sisters hadn't been exaggerating when they'd told her Texas summers were hell.

Phillipa took several deep breaths, willing her heart and mind to calm. How had she gotten herself into this? Why? Among her siblings, she'd done her best to maintain a low profile. As number five out of six strong personalities, it hadn't been that difficult. Her oldest brother, Stefan, had been born and bred to rule—everyone except his siblings anyway. Phillipa had found refuge in academia. It was much easier pleasing a few professors than being a princess and constantly making public appearances and dealing with the media. By nature, she'd always been an introvert. She'd never enjoyed crowded gatherings, hated posing for photographs and had little patience for all the effort it seemed to take to make her presentable.

When her first two sisters began to focus on their new husbands instead of royal duties, Phillipa had plunged herself into graduate studies to avoid being in the public eye. Her sister Bridget had seen through her plan and it had clearly irritated her, although Bridget had bucked up and done a fantastic job. The trouble now was that Bridget was determined to get a break and she had earned it. Phillipa cringed at the prospect of all the public appearances she would be forced to make.

"I'll be damned," a familiar male voice said, making her eyes pop open. "If it isn't the missing Her Highness Phillipa of Chantaine."

Phillipa stared into the dark gaze of Nic Lafitte and her lungs seemed to completely shut down. "I didn't know you would be here."

His mouth twisted in a half smile. "Why doesn't that surprise me?" he asked and slipped his hand around her arm. "Lucky for both of us that I am. We have unfinished business. You're coming with me. I can have my car delivered in seconds."

Her heart pounded. "I can't. My sisters expect me back for the rest of the event. They'll call the authorities if I go missing," she said.

"It wouldn't be the first time your family has tried

to get me in trouble with the law." He glanced around and tugged her down the hallway. "If you won't leave with me, then I'll take my moment somewhere else."

"Where are you taking me?" she asked. "This is crazy. I need to go back to my table. I need—" She broke off as he pushed open the door to a room marked Coat Closet and dragged her inside.

He pulled her to the back of the small room and gently, but firmly gripped her shoulders. "Tell me what you really need, Pippa. What do you really want?" he asked her in that dark, sexy voice that made her feel as if she were turning upside down.

A half-dozen images from the stolen moments they'd shared shot through her brain. The time they'd gone swimming at night. The afternoon she'd spent on his yacht. The walk they'd taken on the opposite side of the island when she'd learned so much about him and he'd made it so easy for her to talk about herself. Despite the bad blood between her family and his, Phillipa had never felt so drawn to another man in her life.

He lowered his head, holding her gaze until his mouth took hers. His kiss set off a riot of reaction and emotion inside her. He made her feel alive and out of control. She pulled back and whispered. "This is insane. It will never work. That's what I tried to tell you before."

"Why not?" he challenged her. Nic was always challenging her. Sometimes gently, sometimes with more strength. "If I want you and you want me, what is most important?"

Pippa bit her lip and struggled to remain rational. Members of her family had caused a lot of trouble by giving in to their emotions. She didn't want the same kind of trouble. "Want is a temporary emotion. There are more important things than temporary emotions."

"If that's true, why did you kiss me back? Why are you here with me right now?"

Pippa heard a gasp from the doorway and terror rushed through her. "Someone is here," she said. "We've got to get out of here," she said, stumbling toward the door. Nic helped to steady her as they stepped outside the closet.

Her sisters Bridget and Tina greeted them with furious disapproval stamped on their faces. Pippa inwardly cringed.

"Get away from my sister," Bridget said.

"That's for her to say, not you," Nic said.

"You're just using her," Tina said. "You only want her because she can redeem your terrible family name."

"Not everyone finds my family name reprehensible. Some even respect it," he said.

"That's respect you've bought with money," Tina said. "Leave Phillipa alone. You can never be good enough for her. If you have any compassion, you'll at least protect her reputation by leaving now."

Nic tightened his jaw. "I'll leave, but Phillipa will make the ultimate decision about the future of our relationship." He glanced behind him and met Phillipa's shocked, pale face. "*Ciao,* darling. Call me when you get some courage. Some things are meant to be," he said and strode away.

Chapter One

She'd started running for exercise. That was what Pippa told her security detail anyway. She knew the truth. She was running from memories. Memories and the possibility that there was only one man for her and he was the one man she couldn't have.

"Stop it," she told herself, staring at the empty beach in front of her. Azure waves dappled onto white sands. By noon, there would be quite a few more bodies enjoying the beach. At six in the morning, however, she was the only one around. She debated turning on some music via her smartphone. She usually welcomed the noise, hoping it would drown out some of her thoughts. Today, she was searching for a little peace. Maybe the sound of the waves would help, she thought, and started out.

One foot in front of the other, she ran for two min-

utes, then walked for three. It was called interval training and the different paces suited her. Pippa had never
been athletic. From the time she'd learned to read, she'd
always been happiest with her nose stuck in a book.
Her nanny had been relieved because her brothers and
most of her sisters had been more demanding in one
way or another.

Running again, she inhaled the scent of the salt air.
The humidity was low today and she could feel the
moisture on her skin begin to evaporate. Slowing after
three minutes of running, she took a swig of her water
and trudged onward.

Along the shore, in the distance, she spotted a long
figure walking. She would wave and be friendly. Pippa
was a royal and Chantaine royals were not allowed to be
snooty. Other runners might be able to put their blinders
and zip past everyone in their path, but not a Devereaux.

As she drew closer, she saw that the figure was that
of a woman. Short white hair crowned her head, and a
sundress that resembled a nightgown covered her pe-
tite frame.

Pippa nodded. "Good morning," she said.

The woman looked away and stumbled.

Curious, Pippa vacillated as to whether to approach
her. Perhaps she was longing for solitude just as Pippa
was. The woman stumbled again and Pippa felt a twist
of concern. She walked toward the woman. "Pardon
me, may I help you?"

The woman shook her head. "No, no. I'm fine. It's so
beautiful here," she said in a lilting voice that contrasted
with the lines on her face and the frailness of her frame.

Something about her seemed familiar, but Pippa

couldn't quite identify it. The woman stumbled again, and Pippa's concern grew. Was she ill?

"Yes, the beach is lovely. Are you sure I can't help you? I could walk you back to where you started," she said. "Or perhaps you would like some water."

The woman's face crumpled. "No, no. Please don't make me go back. Please don't—" She broke off and collapsed right in front of Pippa.

Alarm shot through her. "Oh, my God!" she exclaimed and bent over the woman. This was *one* time when she would have loved to have had her security detail close by. Pippa put her arms around the woman and lifted her, surprised by her light weight. Glancing around, she pulled her toward a small stand of palm trees.

Frantic, she held the woman and gently shook her. "Please. Miss. Please." She spilled water from her bottle onto one of her hands and gently patted the woman's face. "Please wake up. Please."

Terrified that the woman was dying, she reached for her cell phone. The woman clearly needed emergency medical attention. Just as she put her finger over the speed dial for her security, the woman blinked her eyes. Huge and full of emotion, her eyes captivated Pippa.

She held her breath. "Are you all right? Please take a few sips of my water. It's clearly too hot out here for you. I'll call for help and—"

"No," the woman said with a strength that surprised Pippa. "Please don't do that." Then the woman closed her amazing, mesermizing eyes and began to sob.

The sound wrenched at Pippa. "You must let me help you."

"There's only one thing I want," she said and met Pippa's gaze again. "I just want to die in Chantaine."

Pippa gasped. Then a lightning flash of realization rocked through her. She looked at the woman and saw the resemblance of Nic in her eyes. His bone structure was a stronger, more masculine version, but his eyes were all Amelie. "Amelie," she whispered. "You're Amelie Lafitte."

The woman reluctantly nodded. "How do you know?"

"I know your son Nic." Pippa also knew that Amelie was in the final stages of cancer. Her time was drawing painfully close.

Amelie looked away. "I just wanted a little walk on the beach. I bet he's quite peeved that I left the yacht."

Peeved wasn't the word that came to Pippa's mind. "I'll call him for you," she said.

"Then all my fun will be over," she said with a cute pout. "He's such a worrywart."

Stunned at how quickly Amelie's spirit had returned, she hesitated a half beat, then dialed his cell. Despite the fact that she'd deleted it from her phone records months ago, every digit was engraved on her brain.

Five minutes later, a black Mercedes came to screeching halt on the curb of the road above the beach. Pippa immediately identified the dark figure exiting the driver's side of the vehicle. Nic. As he strode swiftly toward her and Amelie, she could see the tension in his frame. Seeing him after all these months set off a visceral response inside her. Her stomach clenched. Her heart beat unevenly.

"Hi, darling," Amelie said, remaining seated on the sand under the tree as she sipped Pippa's water. Pippa was still surprised at how quickly the woman had recovered after fainting. "Sorry to be a bother, but I woke up early and I just couldn't resist the chance to go for a walk on the beach."

"I would have been happy to walk with you," Nic said and turned to Pippa. What she wouldn't give to get a peek behind his dark sunglasses. "Thank you for calling me. I'll take her back to the yacht now and you can continue your run. I didn't know you were a runner."

She felt her face heat with self-consciousness. "I'm more of a combination walker and runner."

He nodded and glanced back at his mother. "Dad's beside himself with worry. It was all I could do to keep him from tearing after you."

"Paul can't hobble with crutches let alone tear after me with that broken foot of his. The doctor said it will be ten more weeks before he can put any weight on it at all," she said, then turned her head thoughtfully to the side. "You know what I'm in the mood for? Crepes. There used to be a wonderful café on the edge of town. They made the most delicious crepes."

"Bebe's on Oleander," Pippa said. "It's still there, and Bebe's granddaughter helps makes the crepes."

"Oh," Amelie said, clasping her hands together. "It's still there. We must go. And we can bring one back for Paul." She turned to Pippa. "You must come, too."

Pippa blinked at the invitation and slid a quick helpless glance at Nic.

"Mother, do you know who Pippa is?" he asked as he extended his hand to help her rise to her feet.

Amelie studied her for a long moment and frowned. "She looks a bit familiar. I can't quite." Her eyes widened. "Oh, dear. You're a Devereaux. I can see it in your eyes and your chin. Oh, dear. This could get a bit messy."

"Just a little," Nic said in a wry tone. "But let's give her the choice. Would you like to join us for crepes, Your Highness?"

Pippa heard the hint of goading challenge in Nic's voice. She'd heard it before, but it seemed to hold more of an edge than ever. The truth was she didn't want her photo taken with Nic and his mother. To say it could cause problems was a huge understatement.

"That's okay," he said before she could respond. "Thanks again for looking out for my mother. Ci—"

"I'm coming," Pippa said impulsively. "Unless you're rescinding the invitation," she tossed back at him in her own challenging voice.

He paused a half beat and tilted his head as if she'd taken him off guard. The possibility thrilled her. "Not at all. Would you like to ride with us in my vehicle?"

"Thank you, but no. I'll drive myself and meet you in about fifteen minutes," Pippa said and turned her gaze to Amelie. "I'll see you soon. Please drink some more fluids."

"Thank you, darling. Isn't she delightful?" she said to Nic. "She fusses just like you do."

"Yes," he said in a dry tone. "Delightful."

Fifteen minutes later as Pippa put a ball cap on her head and adjusted her large pair of sunglasses, she wondered if she'd lost her mind agreeing to join Nic and his mother, the notorious Amelie, for crepes. Glancing in the rearview mirror, she could easily imagine the horror on the face of the royal advisers. Running on the beach at 6:00 a.m. in her current state was one thing, but walking into a public place of business was quite another. She thought of Nic's goading attitude and made a face at the mirror. Well, she couldn't back down now. Stepping from her car, she could only hope she wouldn't be recognized.

Because she'd spent far less time in the public eye than her siblings, that was on her side. Her hair, however, was very distinctive and not in a good way. Wavy and brown with a tendency to frizz, she hoped she'd concealed it adequately by pulling it back in a ponytail and covering it with a cap.

She walked into the old but elegant eating establishment that featured every kind of crepe one could imagine. As soon as she stepped inside, she spotted Amelie, who also saw her and lifted her hand in a wave. Nic, sitting opposite Amelia, turned his head around to look at her and also waved. His gaze said he was surprised she'd shown up, which irritated Pippa.

She walked to the booth where Amelia and Nic sat and sank onto the red vinyl seat.

"Lovely that you joined us," Amelie said and smiled as she lifted a menu. "How shall I choose? I want one of everything."

Enchanted, Pippa picked up the menu. The array of choices was vast and mind-boggling. "What are you in the mood for?"

"Something sweet," Amelie said. "Sweet, fruity. Oh, no, chocolate, too." She shrugged helplessly.

The waitress approached. *"Bonjour.* How can I help you? Coffee?"

"Yes," Amelie said. "Café au lait."

"Tea," Pippa said.

"Coffee, black," Nic said. "Ladies, any idea what you want to order?"

"Apricot crepes. Strawberries and cream. Chocolate hazelnut. Banana cream." Amelie paused.

Wondering how the woman could possibly consume that many crepes, she exchanged a quick glance with Nic, who shook his head and rubbed his jaw. She glanced back at Amelie. "Do you want anything with protein?"

"Not particularly," Nic's mother said.

"And you?" Pippa asked Nic.

He shrugged. "I'm here for the ride."

"Can you please also bring us the crepe suzette and some carryout boxes?" Pippa asked the server.

"No problem, ma'am," she said and stared at Pippa for a long moment. "Pardon me, you look familiar."

Pippa fought a sliver of panic and held her breath. *Please don't recognize me.*

"Are you a newscaster?"

Relief rushed through her, making her almost giddy. She shook her head and smiled. "Nope, I'm just a university student. Thanks for the compliment, though."

The server's face was sheepish. "No trouble. I'll have your order up as soon as possible."

"Thank you so very much," Pippa said and after the server left, she felt the gazes of both Nic and Amelie.

Amelie sighed, lifting her shoulders and smiling with a charm that lit up the room and Pippa suddenly realized who the woman resembled. Gamin with super-expressive eyes, Amelie could have been a white-haired twin of Audrey Hepburn. "It's so wonderful to be here again. Magic. The smell is divine. I should have come back sooner, so I'll just make up for it today."

"You don't want to make yourself sick," Nic said.

"Of course not. I'll just take a bite of each, and we can take the rest back to Paul." Amelie's smile fell and she made a tsking sound. "Poor Paul. He's in such pain with his foot."

She said it as if she suffered no pain herself, but Pippa knew she did. She took a quick glance at Nic and caught the tightening of his jaw. She was struck by Amelie's determination to grab at every experience in life and Nic's struggle to hide a myriad of the emotions he was experiencing.

"I've heard the recovery from a broken foot can be a bear," Pippa said.

"Oh, and trust me, Paul is a being a complete bear," Amelie said. "He doesn't like being restrained. Never has." Amelie glanced at Nic. "It runs in the family." She turned back to Pippa with an expressive, interested gaze. "But enough about us. Tell me about you, your interests, your life. Over the years, I've read a few stories in the news about the Devereauxs, and I must confess I wondered about Edward's children. I'm sure he must have been proud of all of you."

Pippa paused. The truth was her father hadn't been very involved with any of his children. He'd given the most attention to her brother Stefan because he would be the heir, but her father was mostly pleased that he had enough children to do the work, so he could spend more time playing on his yacht. Often with women other than his wife.

"I've always been a bit of a bookworm. I'm working on my doctorate in genealogy with a specialization on the medical impact on the citizens of Chantaine. My brother Stefan is determined to improve the health care of our people, so he has approved my path of studies."

"That's fascinating," Amelie said. "What have you learned so far?"

"Like many countries, our people are more susceptible to some diseases and conditions than others. These can be traced back hundreds of years to the introduction of different immigrants, new foods and changes in our environment. The neurological disease that struck down my father can be traced back to his great-great-grandmother's family. There are also certain cancers that became more common such as when Chantaine experienced a large immigration from Iceland."

Amelie gave a slow nod. "I wonder if—" She glanced up and broke off with a smile. "The crepes are here."

Just as she'd said, Amelie only took a bite of each crepe. She savored each bite, closing her eyes and making a *mmm* sound. "I'm tempted to eat more, but I know it would be a mistake." She leaned toward Pippa and extended her hand. "Dear, I must tell you that even though I couldn't marry your father all those years ago, I wished him only the very best after we parted. I hope he was happy."

Pippa tried to think of how to respond to Amelie's words. The story about Edward and Amelie's courtship was the stuff of tabloids. Before he'd taken the throne, Prince Edward had fallen for Amelie and Amelie had been entranced by him for a short while. When she'd met Paul Lafitte, from the States, however, she'd fallen for the tall, dark Texan hook, line and sinker. The Lafittes descended from pirates and even Pippa had to agree the Lafitte men held a dark, irresistible charm.

When Amelie tried to break off her engagement, Prince Edward had refused. Paul had intervened on her behalf and there'd been a terrible brawl. Her father the prince had been humiliated and Pippa wasn't certain he'd ever truly given his heart away again.

"I think he enjoyed his life," Pippa finally said. "He loved his yacht and the sea and we always felt glad that he was able to indulge his passion."

Amelie patted Pippa's hand. "You're a lovely girl. As they say in Texas, you do him proud. Now, if you'll both excuse me while I powder my nose," she said and stood.

Nic also stood. "Need an escort?" he asked.

"Not this time, darling. Maybe you can talk Pippa into nibbling on some of those crepes," she said and walked away.

"Is she okay?" Pippa asked when he sat down.

He shrugged. "For the moment. The next moment could bring something totally different. She knows her time is short and she's decided to make the most of it. The only problem is she's turned into an eight-year-old. Impulsive, runs off without thinking. With my father down due to his broken foot, I've become her keeper."

Pippa swallowed over the knot of emotion in her throat and began to put the crepes in the carryout boxes. "I'm sure it's difficult. On the one hand, you want to give her everything she wants. On the other, you want to keep her safe. It's an impossible situation. She told me," she said, biting her lip, "that she wants to die in Chantaine."

His gaze narrowed. "That's going to be a tough wish to fulfill given the fact that my father isn't allowed to set foot on Chantaine."

Cold realization rushed through her. "I forgot all about that. I can't believe that would be enforced after all these years."

He gave a rough chuckle. "After all these years, your family still hates me. I can't take the chance that your family would lock him up in prison."

"It wouldn't be my family. It's a silly law," she said.

"Same result. It sucks, but Amelie can't have every wish on her bucket list. I'll do my damn best to make sure she gets as many as I can," he said and stood as his mother arrived at the table.

Amelie met his gaze and sighed. "We should leave, shouldn't we?"

He nodded and placed the boxes in a bag.

"Let me look around just one more moment," she said, surveying the room as if she wanted to savor each detail, the same way she'd savored each bite of the crepes. "I've already spoken to Bebe. She's lovely as is her granddaughter. *Ciao,*" she whispered and picked up the bag, then led the way to the door.

A terrible helplessness tore at Pippa as she followed Amelie out the door. She felt Nic's presence behind her and tried to tamp down the painful knot in her chest. Seeing him again had been like ripping off a bandage before the wound was healed. She'd thought the longing she'd felt for him before was awful, but now it was even worse. Knowing that he was facing some of his darkest days and that she shouldn't, couldn't, help him, was untenable. Meeting his magical mother face-to-face and seeing her courage and joy made her feel like a wimp. Her biggest challenge to date was writing her dissertation.

Amelie stopped beside Nic's Mercedes and turned to Pippa. "I hope we meet again, Your Highness. You're the nicest princess I've ever met. I'm sorry I frightened you with my annoying fainting spell. But then you gave me water and helped me remember Bebe's. I certainly came out the winner in this situation."

"I beg to differ," Pippa said. "It was my great pleasure to meet you."

"*Ciao,* darling princess," she said and Nic opened the door for her.

Pippa should have turned away, but she couldn't resist one more look at his face. It was the worst kind of craving imaginable.

He turned and met her gaze for a heart-stopping moment that took her breath away. "*Ciao,* Princess."

Still distracted by her encounter with Nic and his mother after she'd returned to the palace, Pippa started down the hallway to her living quarters. She would need to set the Lafittes' situation aside if she was going to make any progress on her research today, and heaven knows, progress had been very slow coming since she'd made the insane mistake of getting involved with Nic. The problem was that even after she'd broken off with him, he still haunted her so much that she struggled to get her work done.

Just as she turned the corner toward her quarters,

she heard a shrill scream from the other wing. *Tyler,*
she thought, easily identifying one her sister's toddler
stepsons. He was going through a screaming stage.

"Tyler, darling, you're not dressed," her sister Bridget
called, her voice echoing down the marble hallways.
"Don't—"

Pippa heard Tyler cackle with glee. She also heard
the sound of her sister's heels as she ran after him.
Chuckling to herself, she wondered when Bridget would
learn that toddlers and high heels didn't go together. She
rushed down the hall and turned another corner, spot-
ting Tyler running toward her in all his naked glory.
Bridget followed with Travis in her arms.

"Oh, Pippa, you saved my life. Can you grab him?
The little beast thinks it's funny to run all over the palace bloody naked."

Tyler shrieked when he saw Pippa and skidded to
a stop. Glancing over his shoulder at Bridget bearing
down on him, he knew he was caught. Pippa scooped
him up in her arms before he had a chance to get away.

"What are you doing? Did you just get a bath?" Pippa
asked and buried her nose in his shoulder, making him
laugh. "You smell like a deliciously clean little boy."

"Thank you so much," Bridget said breathlessly. "At
least I got a diaper on Travis."

As soon as she stepped within touching distance,
Tyler flung himself at her. "Mumma," he said and
pressed an open mouth kiss against Bridget's cheek.

Bridget squeezed him against her and shifted Travis
on her hip. "Now, you get all lovey-dovey," she said and
gave him a kiss in return.

"Where are the nannies?" Pippa asked and held out

her hands to Travis. He fell into her arms, then stuck his thumb in his mouth.

"I gave Claire the morning off and Maria had to take care of an emergency with her mother," she said. "I had planned to check on the ranch Ryder and I are having built." Bridget rolled her eyes and laughed. "I never dreamed Stefan would permit a ranch to be built on Chantaine."

"I never would have dreamed you would live on a ranch with twin stepchildren."

"They're not steppies to me," Bridget said. "Ryder and I are in the process of making it all legal. The little perfect, gorgeous beasties will be mine just as much as they are his."

"Would you like me to watch the boys while you go check on the new house?" Pippa offered. Because Chantaine was an island, new construction was a long process and she knew both Bridget and Ryder were eager for their own place.

"I feel like I take advantage of you far too often. I know I'm not helping you get caught up on your studies…."

Pippa felt a sinking sensation in her stomach. Bridget and the boys weren't the real reason she'd had a difficult time focusing on her studies. "It's not as if you'll be gone all day," she said.

"True," Bridget said. "Only an hour or two. You're the perfect sister," Bridget said, leaning forward to give Pippa a kiss on the cheek. "Let's go back to my quarters so I can at least get my little nudist dressed before I leave."

Pippa smiled as she followed Bridget down the hall

and into her family's suite of rooms. "I think it's your outlook that has changed. Since you got married to Ryder, everything's close to perfection."

"That just goes to show the power of having a good man in your life," Bridget said. "As soon as I have more than half a moment, I must get to work on finding one for you."

Alarm shot through Pippa. "Oh, so not necessary. I still have to finish my work for my PhD."

"That won't be forever," Bridget said as she dressed wiggly Tyler.

"I can only hope," Pippa muttered.

"It won't be," Bridget said emphatically. "Besides, you can't wait forever to move on, romantically speaking. I can help with that."

"You seem to forget that our family is dreadful when it comes to matchmaking," Pippa said. "How much did you enjoy Stefan's attempts at matchmaking?"

Bridget waved her hand in a dismissive gesture. "That's different. I won't be trying to match you up with someone who can contribute to Chantaine. I'll find someone hot and entertaining."

"Lovely intentions," Pippa said. "Don't strain yourself. The boys and I will have some fun in the playroom."

"Perfect. If I'm late they can have lunch in an hour."

"Will do," Pippa said. "Are you truly going to have cattle at this ranch?"

"If Ryder has his way," Bridget said with a sigh. "If we have to take the man out of Texas, we'll just bring Texas to him. *Ciao.* I'll be back soon," she said and kissed both of the boys.

As soon as Bridget left, the twin toddlers looked at her with pouty faces. Travis's lower lip protruded and he began to whimper. Tyler joined in.

"Absolutely none of that. She'll be back before you know it." Bridget set both of them on their feet and took them by the hand. "To the playroom," she said and marched them into the small backroom. If there was one thing she'd learned about caring for toddlers, it was that it helped to be willing to make a bloody fool of herself. She immediately turned on the animal sounds CD and followed the instructions to make honking sounds. The boys dried up and joined her.

Just over an hour later, Bridget returned and Pippa could no longer escape her studies. She retreated to her room with a half sandwich for lunch. She thought of the crepes and her stomach clenched. Her mind kept wandering to the time she'd spent with Nic and his mother.

She told herself not to think about it. It wasn't her responsibility. These genealogy charts required her complete and immediate attention. She'd used every possible device to procrastinate doing her work entirely too long. Inputting her second cousin's name to the chart, she forced herself to focus. Whenever she conducted her research on people whom she knew, she often thought about their personal stories. Her second cousin Harold had moved to Tibet and his sister, Georgina, had married a man from England and was raising her children in the countryside. Pippa had always liked Georgina because she'd been such a down-to-earth sort of woman. It was a shame she didn't see her more often.

Harold and Georgina's deceased parents had owned a lovely cottage on the other side of Chantaine that was now left vacant because neither Harold nor Georgina visited Chantaine very often. Why, in fact, Pippa was certain it had been nearly eight years since either of her second cousins had set foot on Chantaine.

Pippa stopped dead, staring at the cursor on her laptop. *Vacant lovely cottage. Nic's parents.*

"Stop it," she hissed to herself. It would be incredibly disloyal. If her brother Stefan ever found out, he would never forgive her. And there was no way he wouldn't find out. Not with her security haunting her. She was lucky she'd escaped discovery today.

Back to work, she told herself sternly and worked past midnight. She finally crawled into bed, hopeful she would fall into deep sleep. Thank goodness, she did. Sometime during the night, she sank into a dream where a black limo crawled through a beautiful cemetery. Cars and people dressed in black but carrying flowers followed the limo. Everything inside her clinched with pain. A white butterfly fluttered over the black limo, capturing her attention. It could have been the spirit of...

Pippa suddenly awakened, disoriented, the images of the limo and the butterfly mingling in her mind. She sat up in bed, her heart slamming into her chest. Images of her brother Stefan, Nic, his mother, Amelie.

This wasn't her business, she told herself. Her heart ached for Nic and his mother, but she couldn't go against her family to make his mother's dream come true. She just couldn't. It wouldn't be right. It would be a terrible betrayal.

She tried to catch her breath and closed her eyes.

She tried to make her brain stop spinning. How could she possibly deceive her family for Nic? For Amelie?

But how could she not?

Chapter Two

It took most of the rest of the day to catch up with her cousin to get permission to use the cottage. Georgina was so gracious that it made Pippa feel guilty. Oh, well, if she was going to go through with providing the cottage for Nic's mother and father, then her web of deception was just getting started. The choice to deceive her family was unforgivable, but the choice to turn her back on Amelie was more unacceptable. Her stomach churned because she wasn't a dishonest person. The prospect of all the lies she would have to tell put a bad taste in her mouth.

She would normally try to reason with Stefan, but Pippa knew her entire family was unreasonable about the Lafitte matter. She would have to learn to push aside her slimy feelings about this and press on. The first task was to call Nic.

* * *

Nic studied the recent reports from his and his father's business on his tablet PC while he drank a glass of Scotch. He took a deep breath of the Mediterranean night air as he sat on the deck of his yacht anchored close enough to shore for his mother to catch a glimpse of her precious Chantaine whenever she liked. He just hoped she didn't do anything impulsive like jump overboard and swim to shore. Rubbing his chin, he shuddered at what a nightmare that would be. He couldn't put it past her, though, especially after she'd sneaked off the other morning.

Nic was caught somewhere between genie and parent, and he wasn't equipped to be either. The reports on both his father's businesses and his own looked okay for the moment, but he knew he would have to go back to the States soon for his father's company. With Amelie's illness, Paul Lafitte had understandably been distracted. Despite the fact that they'd separated on two different occasions, Amelie was the light of Paul's life and Nic wasn't sure how his father would survive after his mother… Nic didn't even want to think the word, let alone say it, even though he knew the time was coming.

Sighing, he took another sip of his Scotch and heard the vibrating buzz of his cell phone. The number on the caller ID surprised him. After his surprise meeting with Princess Pippa the other morning, he figured he'd never see her again except for public affairs.

He picked up the phone and punched the call button. "Nic Lafitte. Your Highness, what a surprise," he said, unable to keep the bite from his voice. Pippa had turned out to be the tease of his life.

"Hello. I hope I'm not interrupting anything," she said, her voice tense with nerves, which made him curious.

"Just a perfect glass of Scotch and rare solitude," he said.

A short silence followed. "Well, pardon the interruption, but I have some news that may be of interest to you."

"You called to tell me you missed me," he said, unable to resist the urge to bother her. During and after their little interlude last year, the woman had bothered the hell out of him.

He heard her sharp intake of breath and realized he'd scored. "I called about your mother."

His pleasure immediately diminished. "What about her? Have you discussed the situation with your family, and now they won't even allow her and my father in the harbor?"

"No, of course not," Pippa said. "If you would just let me finish—"

"Go ahead," he said, the semi-peacefulness of the evening now ruined.

"I found a cottage for your parents where they can stay," she said.

Nic blinked in sudden, silent surprise.

"Nic, did you hear me?"

"Yes. Repeat that please."

"I found a cottage for your parents on Chantaine," she said.

"Why?" he demanded.

Another gap of silence followed. "Um, well, I have these cousins Georgina and Harry and neither of them live in Chantaine anymore. They haven't even visited in years, and they inherited a cottage from their parents. It's been vacant, again for years, so I thought, why not?"

"Exactly," Nic said. "Why not? Except for the fact that my father has been banned from setting foot on Chantaine. I don't suppose your brother experienced a sudden wave of compassion, or just a rational moment and has decided to pardon Paul Lafitte."

"You don't need to insult Stefan," she said. "My brother is just defending my father's honor."

"Even though Stefan wouldn't have been born if your father had married Amelie," Nic said.

"Yes, I know it's not particularly logical, but the point is I have found this house. Your mother wants more time in Chantaine. Staying there can make it happen."

"You still haven't addressed the issue about my father," Nic said.

"Well, I thought we could work around that. Your mother mentioned that he broke his foot, so it's not as if he'll be able to tour much. When he does, perhaps he could wear a hat and glasses."

"And a fake mustache?" he added, rolling his eyes. It was a ludicrous plan.

"I know it's not perfect," she said.

"Far from it," he said.

"But it's better than nothing."

"I can't take the chance that my father will end up in jail."

"Perhaps that's not your decision to make," she countered, surprising him.

"What do you mean by that?"

"I mean shouldn't he be given the choice?" she asked. "Besides, your father's presence may never be discovered. It's not as if there are copies of his photo posted everywhere the way you do in the States."

"It's called a Wanted Poster, and they're mostly just displayed in post offices and convenience stores these days. We've progressed since the Wild West days," he said.

"Exactly," she said. "And so have we. No one has been beheaded in over one hundred and fifty years, and we haven't used the dungeon as a prison for nearly a hundred."

"Why don't I feel better? I know that Chantaine doesn't operate under the policy of innocent until proven guilty. Your judicial system, and I use the term loosely, moves slower than the process of turning coal into diamonds."

"I didn't call to debate my country's judicial system. I called to offer a place to stay for your mother and father. If you want it, I shall arrange to have it cleaned and prepared for them. Otherwise…" She paused and he heard her take a breath.

"Otherwise?" he prompted.

"Otherwise, *ciao,*" she said and hung up on him.

Nic blinked again. Princess Pippa wasn't the rollover he'd thought she was. He downed the rest of his exquisite Scotch, barely tasting it. What the hell. She had surprised him. Now he had to make a decision. Although his father had caused trouble for the entire family, Nic felt protective of him, especially in his father's current state with his broken foot and his grief over Amelie.

Nic closed his eyes and swore under his breath. He

already knew how his father would respond if given the choice of risking prosecution in Chantaine. Paul Lafitte was a blustering bear and bull. He would love the challenge...even if he was in traction and confined to the house.

Raking his hand through his hair, he knew what he had to do. He walked inside to the stateroom lounge where his father dozed in front of the television. A baseball game was playing and his father was propped in an easy chair snoring.

Maybe he should wait until tomorrow, Nic thought and turned off the television.

His father gave a loud snort and his eyes snapped open. "What happened? Who's ahead?"

"Rangers," Nic lied. The Rangers were having a terrible season.

"Yeah, and I'm the Easter bunny," his father said.

Nic gave a dry laugh. His father was selective with the use of denial, and apparently he wasn't going to exercise that muscle with the Rangers tonight. "Good luck hopping," he said. "You need anything to drink?"

"Nah. Take a seat. What's on your mind? I can tell something's going on," he said, waving his hand as if the yacht belonged to him instead of Nic.

Nic sank onto the sofa next to his father. "I got an interesting call tonight."

"Must have been a woman. Was she pregnant?" his father asked.

Nic gave a short laugh. "Nothing like that. I've been offered a cottage where you and Mom can stay. On Chantaine."

His dad gave a low whistle. "How did you manage that?"

Nic shrugged. "Lucky, I guess. The problem is you still have legal issues in Chantaine."

His dad smiled and rubbed his mouth. "So I do, and punching Prince Edward in the face after he insulted your mother was worth it ten times over."

"Easy to say, but if you stay in Chantaine, there's a possibility that you could get caught." Nic shook his head. "Dad, with their legal system, you could be stuck in jail for a while."

"So?" he asked.

"So, it's a risk. You're not the young buck you once were. You could end up stuck there while Mom is..." He didn't want to say the rest.

His father narrowed his eyes. It was an expression Nic had seen several times on his father's face. The dare a pirate couldn't deny. He descended from wily pirates. His father was no different, although his father had gotten caught a few times. "Your mother wants to rest in Chantaine. We'll accept the kind offer of your friend. To hell with the Devereauxs."

"Might not want to go that far," Nic said, thinking another glass of Scotch was in order. "A Devereaux is giving you the cottage."

"Well, now that sounds like quite the story," his father said, his shaggy eyebrows lifted high on his forehead.

"Another time," Nic said. "You need to rest up for your next voyage."

His father gave a mysterious smile. "If my great-

great-grandfather escaped the authorities on a peg leg, I can do it with a cast."

Nic groaned. "No need to push it, Dad."

The next morning, he dialed the princess.

"Hello," she said in a sleep-sexy voice that did weird things to his gut.

"This is Nic. We'll accept your kind offer. Meet me at the cottage and I'll clean it. The less people involved, the better."

Silence followed. "I didn't think of that," she confessed. "I'm accustomed to staff taking oaths of silence."

He smiled at her naïveté. "This is a different game. Too many people need to be protected. You, my mother and father. We need to keep this as quiet and low-profile as possible."

"Okay. I'll meet you at the cottage mid-morning," she said.

"What about your security?" he asked.

"I'll tell them I'm going to the library," she said.

"Won't they follow you?"

"I'll go to the library first. They'll get bored. They always do."

"Who are these idiots on your security detail?" he asked.

"Are you complaining?"

"No," he said. "And yes."

She laughed, and the breathless sound made his chest expand. He suddenly felt lighter. "How do you end up with the light end of the security detail?"

"I'm boring. I don't go clubbing. I've never been on

drugs. I babysit my nieces and nephews. I study gene-alogy, for bloody's sake."

He nodded, approving her M.O. "Well done, but does that fence ever feel a little too tall for you? Ever want to climb out?"

"I climb out when I want," she said in a cool voice. "I'll see you this afternoon around 1:00 p.m. The ad-dress is 307 Sea Breeze. *Ciao,*" she said and hung up before he could reply.

Nic pulled the phone away from his ear and stared at it. He was unaccustomed to having anyone hang up on him, let alone a woman. He must have really gotten under Pippa's skin to affect her manners that way. The possibility brought him pleasure. Again, he liked the idea of *bothering* her.

Just before one, he pulled past the overgrown hedges of the driveway leading to an expansive bungalow. Looked like there was a separate guest bedroom. Dibs, he thought. He could sleep there and keep track of his parents while keeping on top of the businesses.

He stopped his car behind another—Pippa's. He rec-ognized it from the other day. Curious, he stepped from his vehicle and walked to the front door and knocked. He waited. No answer. He knocked again.

No answer again, so he looked at the doorknob and picked the lock. Pirates had their skills. He opened the door and was shocked speechless at the sight in front of him. Pippa, dressed in shorts and a T-shirt with her wild hair pulled back in a ponytail, was vacuuming the den.

The princess had a very nice backside, which he en-joyed watching for a full moment…okay, two.

Pippa turned and spotted him, screaming and dropping the vacuum handle. She clutched her throat with her hands. The appliance made a loud groan of protest.

"Did you consider knocking?" she demanded.

He lifted two fingers, then pulled up the vacuum cleaner handle and turned it off. "Twice. You didn't answer. I would have never dreamed you could be a cleaning fairy. This is a stretch."

"I spent a couple summers in a rustic camp in Norway. Cleaning was compulsory. We also cleaned the homes of several of the camp leaders."

"You didn't mention this to your parents?" he asked.

She laughed. "I didn't speak to my parents very often. I mentioned something about it to my nanny after the second summer and was never sent back after that. The cleaning wasn't that bad. The camp had a fabulous library and no one edited my reading choices. Heaven for me," she said.

"Will clean for books?" he said.

She smiled and met his gaze. "Something like that."

He held her gaze for a long moment and saw the second that her awareness of him hit her. Breaking the visual connection, she cleared her throat. "Well, I should get back to work."

"Anything special you want me to do?"

"Mop the floors if you don't mind. I've already dusted the entire house, but haven't touched the guest quarters outside. I think it would also be a good idea for you to assess the arrangement of the furniture throughout the house for any special needs your parents may have, such as your father's foot problem. We don't want him tripping and prolonging his recovery."

"I don't know. It might be a good thing if my father is immobile. He could cause trouble when he's full strength," Nic said. "He's always been a rebellious, impulsive man. I hate to say it, but he might just take a trip out of the house so he can feel like he's flying in the face of your family."

Pippa winced. "He wouldn't admit his name, would he?"

"I hope not. That's part of the reason I wasn't sure this was a good idea," he said.

"What made you change your mind?"

"You did. My father will be okay if he's reminded that his responsibility is to make this time for my mother as trouble-free as possible. I'll make sure he gets that message in multiple modalities every day."

"Thank you very much," she said.

"If you're so terrified that your family will find out, why did you take this risk for yourself? Your relationship with your brothers and sisters will never be the same if they know you did this."

She took a deep breath and closed her eyes for a half beat as if to bolster her determination. "I hate the idea of disappointing my brothers and sisters. I hate it more than you can imagine, but I wouldn't be able to live with myself if I could help your mother with this one wish if I had the ability. And I have the ability."

"I'll do what I can to make sure the rest of the Devereauxs don't find out. I haven't told my mother yet about the cottage. She's going to be very excited."

Pippa smiled. "I hope so."

"Thanks," he said. "I'll go check out the bedrooms."

An hour later, after Pippa finished vacuuming and tackled the kitchen, she found Nic cleaning the hall

bathroom. It was an ironic sight. Hot six-foot-four international businessman scrubbing the tub. Just as he
wouldn't expect to find her turn into a cleaning machine, she wouldn't expect the same of him, either. She
couldn't help admiring the way his broad shoulders followed the shape of a V to his waist. Even in a T-shirt,
the man looked great from behind. Bloody shame for
her. *Get your mind out of the gutter.*

He turned around before she had a chance to clear
her throat or utter a syllable. She stared at him speechless for a second, fearing he could read her mind. *Not
possible,* she told herself as she felt her cheeks heat with
embarrassment.

"Can I help you?" he asked.

In too many ways, she thought, but refused to dwell
on them. "I'm almost finished with the kitchen, and it
occurred to me that it might be a good idea to arrange
for some groceries to be picked up for your parents before they arrive."

"Groceries?" he echoed.

"Yes, I was hoping you could help with a list."

He made a face. "I don't do a lot of grocery shopping. My housekeeper takes care of that."

"I have less experience with grocery shopping that
I do with cleaning. That's why I thought we could send
someone."

"Who can we trust?" he asked.

She winced. "Excellent point."

"After we move them in, I'll just arrange for a member of my staff from the yacht to take care of house and
shopping duties," he said. "But unless we want to delay

their move-in, it looks like we'll need to do the initial run ourselves."

"We?" she squeaked.

"I didn't think it would be nice to ask you to do it by yourself," he said.

But it had clearly crossed his mind. She frowned.

"Will that put you a little close for comfort to the plebeians?"

"No," she told him, detesting the superior challenging expression on his face. "I was just trying to remember if I'd left my cap in my vehicle."

"I have an extra," he said. "I'll take you in my car."

"What about the list?"

"We'll wing it," he said.

Moments later, she grabbed her cap from her car and perched her oversize sunglasses on her nose. She didn't bother to look at her reflection. After spending the afternoon cleaning, she knew she didn't look like anyone's idea of a princess. Nic opened the passenger door for her and she slid into his car.

After he climbed into the driver's side, the space inside his Mercedes seemed to shrink. She inhaled to compensate for the way her lungs seemed to narrow at Nic's proximity, but only succeeded in drawing in a draft of the combination of his masculine scent and subtle but sexy cologne. He pulled out of the driveway.

"Which way to the nearest market?" he asked.

Pippa blinked. She had no idea.

"Here," he said, handing her his phone. "Find one on my smartphone."

It took a couple moments, and Nic had to backtrack, but they were moving in the right direction.

"I'm thinking eggs, milk, bread and perhaps some fruit," she said, associating each item with one of her fingers. It was a memory trick she'd taught herself when she was young. The only problem was when she ran out of fingers.

"Chocolate, cookies and wine," Nic added. "A bakery cake if we can find it. My mother's priority for eating healthy went down the tubes after her last appointment with the doctor. My dad will want booze and carbs. His idea of health food is a pork roast with a loaded baked potato."

"Oh, my," she said, trying to wrap her head around Nic's list versus hers. "I hope we can find—"

"They'll be happy with whatever we get for the first twenty-four hours," Nic said as he pulled into the parking lot. "Let's just do this fast," he added and pulled on a ball cap of his own. "The faster we move, the less chance you have of being discovered."

"I think I'm well-disguised," she said as he opened the door and helped her out of the car.

"Until you open your mouth," he said.

"What do you mean by that?"

He led her toward the door of the market. "I mean you have a refined, distinctive voice, PD. A combination of husky sweet and so proper you could have been in Regency England."

"PD," she echoed, then realized PD stood for Pippa Devereaux. "Well, at least I *look* ordinary," she huffed.

He stopped beside her. "And I don't," he said, tugging on his ball cap.

She allowed herself a forbidden moment of looking at him from head to toe. He could have been dressed in rags and he would be sexy. She swallowed an oath. "You don't know the meaning of ordinary," she said and walked in front of him.

Hearing Nic grab a cart behind her, she moved toward the produce. "Surely, they'd enjoy some fruit. Your mother seemed to favor fruit crepes the other day."

"They were wrapped in sugar," he said as she picked up a bunch of bananas and studied them. "In the basket," he instructed. "We have a need for speed, PD."

"I'm not sure I like being called PD," she said, fighting a scowl as she put the bananas in the cart.

He pressed his mouth against her ear. "Would you prefer PP instead? For Princess Pippa?"

A shiver of awareness raced through her and she quickly stepped away. "Not at all," she said and picked up an apricot. "Does this look ripe?"

"It's perfect," he said, swiping it from her hand and added two more to the cart. "Now, move along."

She shot him an affronted look but began to walk. "No one except my brothers or sisters would dream of speaking to me that way."

"One of my many charms, PD," he said and tossed a loaf of bread into the cart.

Moments later, after throwing several items into the cart, they arrived at the register. Pippa picked up a bag of marshmallows.

"Good job," he said.

"I thought they could make that camping dessert you Americans eat," Pippa said. She'd read about it in a book.

"Camping treat?" he echoed.

"Some More of something," she said.

His eyes widened. "S'mores," he said. "We need chocolate bars and graham crackers. Get him to hold you," he said and strode away.

"Hold me?" she said at the unfamiliar expression and caught the cashier studying her. He was several years younger than she was with rings and piercing in places that made her think *ouch*.

He leaned toward her. "If you need holding, I can help you after I finish my shift," he said in a low voice.

Embarrassment flooded through her. She was rarely in a position for a man to flirt with her. Her brother usually set her up with men at least twenty years older, who wouldn't dare make an improper advance, so she wasn't experienced with giving a proper response. "The grocery order," she finally managed. "I was repeating what my, uh, friend said. He misspoke, as he often does. The grocery order need holding."

The cashier looked disappointed. "The customer behind you is ready."

Pippa considered pulling royal rank, but knew it would only hurt her in the end, so she stepped aside and allowed the person behind her with a mammoth order go first.

Less than a moment later, Nic appeared with chocolate bars and graham crackers. He glanced at the person in front of her and frowned. "How did that happen? I told you to hold the cashier."

"There was a mix-up and he thought I wanted, uh, him for reasons other than his professional duties. When I refused his kind invitation, he felt spurned and allowed the customer behind me to proceed." She sighed. "Do all men have such delicate egos?"

Nic lifted a dark brow before he pulled his sunglasses over his eyes. "Depends on how many mixed messages we get. Poor guy."

Chapter Three

"Are you sure you want to read to Stephenia tonight?" Eve Jackson Devereaux, the wife to the crown prince of Chantaine, asked in her Texas twang as she walked with Pippa to her stepdaughter's room inside the royal master suite. "You look a little tired."

"I wouldn't dream of missing it. You and Stefan enjoy a few extra moments this evening. You deserve it."

"You are a dream sister," Eve said.

Pippa felt her heart squeeze at how Eve left off at the in-law. "As are you," she said and studied her sister-in-law. "You look like you could use a long night's rest yourself."

Eve frowned and pressed her hands to her cheeks. "Oh, no. Maybe I need one of those spa boosts Bridget is always talking about."

"Or just rest," Pippa said. "You may be Texan, but you're not superhuman."

Eve laughed. "If you say so. I didn't want to ask, but I have a routine medical appointment tomorrow. Can you backup for the nanny?"

It wasn't convenient, but Eve so rarely asked that she couldn't refuse. "No problem. You're sure it's just routine?" she asked.

Eve smiled. "Nothing else. Thank you. I knew I could count on you. But Stefan and I were talking the other night and we both realized how much you do for all the nieces and nephews. You're due some happy times of your own and we're going to work on that."

"Work?" Pippa echoed, fighting a sliver of panic. She definitely did not want to become the object of her family's attention. Especially now. "How?"

Eve shot her a sly look that frightened her. "You'll find out soon enough."

"There's no need to work that hard," Pippa said. "I'm busy with my dissertation and—"

"Don't worry. Just enjoy," Eve said.

"Right," Pippa said nervously. "Don't work too hard."

Eve opened the door to Stephenia's room where the three-year-old sat playing with her toys. "Steffie, I thought you wanted Pippa to read to you tonight. You're not in bed."

Stephenia immediately crawled into bed with an innocent expression on her face, her ringlet curls bouncing against her flushed cheeks. "I'm in bed," she said in her tiny voice, which never failed to make Pippa's heart twist.

Eve tossed a sideways glance at Pippa and whispered, "She's such a heart stealer. We're so screwed."

Pippa laughed under her breath. "Thank goodness Stefan has you. I'm lucky. She'll fall asleep by the time I finish the second book."

"Or first," Eve said in a low voice. "She's been a Tazmanian devil today. I have to believe she's spent some of her energy."

Stephenia lifted her arms. "Mamaeve."

Pippa knew Eve had felt reluctant to take on the name of Stephenia's mother even though the woman had perished in a boating accident. Out of respect, Eve had taught the child *Mamaeve*. Eve rushed toward the child and enveloped her in a loving hug.

"Daddy?" Stephenia asked.

"In the shower," Eve said. "He'll kiss you good-night, but you may already be asleep."

Steffie sighed and gave Eve an extra hug. The sight was heartwarming to Pippa because she'd mostly been raised by hired nannies. She knew it could have been much worse, but it gave her such relief to know that her nieces and nephews would have such a different life than she'd experienced.

"Pippa," Stephenia said, extending her arms, and it occurred to Pippa that she would fight an army to get to her niece.

"I'll let you two go to *Where the Wild Things Are*," Eve said, backing toward the door and giving a little wave. "Sweet dreams."

"Good night," Pippa said.

"'Night Mamaeve."

Eve smiled and left the room closing the door behind her.

Pippa sank onto Stephenia's twin bed and pulled the child against her. *Where the Wild Things Are* was especially appropriate for Stephenia because the child had been such a bloody screamer when she'd first arrived at the palace. Stephenia was the product of a relationship between her brother Stefan and a model who'd never bothered to tell Stefan about his child. He'd only learned about Stephenia after the mother's death. It had been a shock to the family and the country of Chantaine, but everyone had taken Stephenia into their hearts. How could they not? She had Stefan's eyes and spirit and she was beautiful.

Pippa began to read the book and before she was halfway through, Stephenia was slumped against her, sleeping. She felt the warmth of sleepy drool on her shirt underneath the child's face. Pippa chuckled to herself and carefully situated Stephenia onto the bed. She brushed a kiss onto her niece's head and slid out of the bed, leaving the book on the nightstand. Pippa turned off the light and kissed Stephenia once more, then quietly left the room.

As she walked down the hall, she wondered, not for the first time, if or when she would have children of her own. Pippa knew she'd been shielded from normal relationships with the opposite sex. Every date, and there'd been few, had to be vetted by Stefan, the advisers and of course, security. The only relationship she'd had that approached normality had been her brief *thing* with Nic. She supposed she couldn't really call it an affair because they hadn't done the deed, but Nic hadn't bowed to her unless he'd been joking. He'd treated her like a desirable woman. Pippa couldn't remember another time when she'd felt genuinely desirable.

She rolled her eyes at herself as she entered her small suite. She had far more important things to do than worry about feeling desirable. Thinking back to what Eve had said about how she and Stefan were planning to work on her happiness, she cringed. This was *not* the time.

Nic moved his parents into the cottage. The activity exhausted both of them, so they were taking naps, his mom using her oxygen. She'd begun to use it every night. Nic had adjusted the bed so that her head would be elevated. Many days his mother hid her illness well, but lately he could tell she'd had a harder time of it. She resisted taking too much pain medication, complaining that it made her sleepy. Amelie was determined to get every drop of life she could, and she was giving Nic a few lessons he hadn't expected along the way.

He'd brought over a few members of his crew to clean the pool and jacuzzi and get them operational as soon as possible. He dug into the labor with his men, hoping that expending physical energy would help relieve some of his frustration. Even though he mentally knew that he couldn't make his mother well, he had a bunch of crazy feelings that he spent a lot of effort denying. It was important that he continue that denial because his parents sure as hell had enough on their own plates without his crap.

As he cleaned the side of the pool wall with a brush, he spotted Pippa coming through the gate carrying a bag. She was wearing a skirt that fluttered around her knees and a lacy cotton blouse. As usual, her wild hair was pulled into a topknot. He'd always thought her hair was a sign that she wasn't nearly as proper as she seemed. He knew she considered herself the plainest of the Devereaux sisters, but during that brief period they'd spent time together, he sure had enjoyed making her fair skin blush with embarrassment or pleasure. She was the most sincere and sweetest woman he'd ever met.

Appearing intent on her plan, whatever that was, she walked right past him as if she didn't see him. Just as she lifted her hand to the door to knock, he gave a loud wolf whistle.

His men stopped their work and gaped at him. Pippa stood stock-still, then lifted her hand again to knock. "Hey, PD," he called, climbing out of the pool. "What's the rush?"

Hearing his voice, she whirled around to look at him. "I didn't see you." She glanced at the pool. "You were working?" she said as if such a thought was impossible.

"Yes, I pitch in with manual labor every now and then. It's good for the soul, if I have one, and it usually helps me get a good night's sleep." He liked the way her gaze skimmed over his shoulders and chest, then as if she realized, she was looking where she shouldn't, her gaze fastened on his nose. "My parents are both taking naps. They're worn out from the move."

"It's already done," she said. "You move quickly."

"When it's necessary," he said, thinking perhaps he'd given Pippa too much wiggle room all those months ago.

The door suddenly opened and his mother, wiping

sleep from her eyes, blinked at the sunlight. "What—" She broke off when she saw Pippa and her lips lifted in a smile. "Well, hello, fairy princess," she said.

"Mom," Nic said. "Don't use the P word. Remember this is all on the down low."

"Oh, sorry," she said with a delicate wince. "I'm just so grateful and you made it happen with the snap of your fingers."

"My cousins made it easy," Pippa said.

"But you made the call," Nic's mother said. "I must leave them something in my will."

Pippa bit her lip.

"TMI, Mom," Nic said. "What's in the bag?" he asked Pippa.

"Gelato," she said. "I know we got ice cream yesterday, but this is from one of our favorite gelaterias."

"Let me think of the name," his mother said. "It's on the tip of my tongue."

Pippa opened her mouth, then closed it.

His mother's eyes widened. "Henri's."

"Yes," Pippa said, clearly thrilled. "You have a great memory."

"Bet you brought hazelnut chocolate," his mother said.

"Yes, and a new flavor from the States. Rocky Road. It has marshmallows, chocolate and nuts. Worth a try," Pippa said with a shrug.

"I'll say," his mom said. "Let's taste it now or I'll have to fight the mister for that one."

Nic chuckled at the interchange between his mother and Pippa.

"What are you laughing at?" his mother asked. "Be careful or you'll get no gelato."

"No gelato for me. Water now and beer later," he said.

"Spoil sport," his mother said and he guided Pippa and his mother inside the house.

"I didn't know you were going to fill the pool," his mother said. "Could be a waste," she warned.

"If you enjoy it once, it won't be," he said, heading toward the kitchen. "If you enjoy thinking about taking a dip in the pool or Jacuzzi, then that's enough, Mom," he called over his shoulder as he went to the kitchen and grabbed a bottle of water.

"You're such a good son," she said.

"Does that mean I get some of that gelato?" he asked as he reentered the room.

"And you are the very devil," she said. "Just like your father."

He glanced at both his mother and Pippa. "And you know I'm not anyone but me," he reminded her.

"True," she said. "But he is a scoundrel," she said to Pippa.

"I agree," Pippa said, her eyes swimming with emotions that reflected the drama of the moment. "Well, I can't stay, and I must confess I thought you might not even move in until tomorrow, but I clearly underestimated your son."

"It's not the first time I've been underestimated," he said, meeting Pippa's gaze.

She gnawed on her lower lip and he felt a tug toward her. He'd made a mistake with that before, but something about her got under his skin. He'd known a few women. Some as beautiful as beauty queens and world-class models. Why did she affect him this way?

"I'll try not to do the same thing again," she said.

He shrugged. "We'll see."

"I want gelato," his mother said.

"Then you shall have gelato," Nic said.

Pippa met his gaze, then looked away and walked to the kitchen. "Let me scoop it for you, Mrs. Lafitte. I hope I didn't overdo the chocolate."

"Call me Amelie," she said as she followed Pippa into the kitchen. "And you can never overdo chocolate."

"That's good to know," Pippa said and searched through several drawers for a scoop. "There we go," she said and dipped a scoop of both flavors into a bowl. "Enjoy," she said with a smile on her face.

She shot an uncertain glance at Nic. "Would you like some?"

"I'll wait until later," he said, noting the way Pippa pressed her lips together.

She nodded. "I should go," Pippa said.

"Oh, no," his mother said. "You just arrived."

"You need to rest. You've had a busy day," Pippa said.

His mother frowned. "Promise you'll return."

"Of course I will," Pippa said. "Don't let your gelato melt."

"You're so right," his mother said and dipped her spoon into the treat.

"I'll walk you to your car," Nic said.

"I can do that myself," she said.

"No," he said and escorted her to the driveway. "You need to know," he told her. "It's going to go down from here. She was good just now, but she's struggling and it's just going to get worse. A lot of people wouldn't be able to handle it...."

She stopped and turned, looking offended. "I'm not a lot of people. I'm not the type of person to abandon someone when—" She broke off and realization crossed her face. "You said that because I broke off our relationship."

He shrugged. "If the shoe fits."

"That was a totally different situation," she said. "It was a temporary flirtation. You and I are not at all well-suited."

"Because your family hates mine," Nic said, feeling a twist of impatience.

"That's part of it. There's no good reason for us to continue a relationship when we know there's no future. It was sheer craziness on my part."

He laughed. "Good to know. You're saying you weren't really attracted to me. You were just temporarily insane."

"I—I didn't say that," she said.

Nic watched the color bloom in her cheeks with entirely too much pleasure.

"And what if my last name was not Lafitte?" he had to ask because the question had dug at him at odd moments.

Her expression changed and a hint of vulnerability deepened her eyes. She opened her mouth, then closed it and looked away. "I can't let my mind consider that because you are who you are. I am who I am." She shook her head and turned toward her vehicle. "I need to leave. I'll check on your mother la—"

Nic saw her foot catch on a tree root and instinctively caught her as she tripped. He pulled her against him and inhaled her soft, feminine scent and felt her body cling to him. For about three seconds. Then she pushed at his arm and moved away from him.

"I should have been watching. Sorry," she said and met his gaze.

"No big deal. You're okay. That's what matters," he said.

In that moment, in her gaze, he saw the same tug and pull of feelings that he had inside him about her, about them. There was so much she wasn't saying that she looked as if she could nearly pop from it. "Thank you," she finally said.

"Ciao," he said and watched her as she got into her car and drove away. There was unfinished business here for both of them, he thought. He'd tried to leave Pippa behind, but something about her nagged at him like a fly in the room he couldn't catch. He needed to find a way to get her out of his system.

That night Pippa dressed for the family dinner her brother Stefan had called. With her youngest brother playing soccer in Spain, and her oldest two sisters and their families out of the country, that left Bridget, her husband, Ryder, the twins and Stefan and Eve and Stephenia. She was extremely bothered from her visit with Nic and his mother this afternoon. Amazing how such a brief time in the man's presence could disrupt her so much. She'd suspected he would get over her in no time. He was far more experienced than she was. There must have been a dozen women ready and willing to soothe his ego.

Yet, he acted as if he was still irritated by the fact that she'd ended things. It wasn't as if she'd truly dumped him. They had never had a public relationship, just a few furtive meetings. She couldn't deny he'd made her knees melt with the way he'd looked at her, and the connection she'd felt with him had made her breathless. She also couldn't deny that he'd acted as if he were attracted to her, as if she meant something to him.

The truth was part of the reason she'd refused to see him again was because her out-of-control feelings frightened her. If ever a man was unsafe, it was Nic Lafitte. Yet she'd found him irresistible which only proved that she must have some sort of self-destructive tendency inside her that she hadn't known existed. Now that she knew she had this tendency, she had to beware of it and fight it if it ever reared its head again.

Pippa looked into the mirror and adjusted her top-knot of out-of-control hair. She called it her curse. Every once in a while, the humidity lowered and her hair was almost controllable. Not today, though. Putting on a little lip gloss, she dismissed it and her other thoughts and headed toward the royal dining room.

Stefan had instigated the "family dinners" a couple years ago. Ever since Bridget had gotten married, she'd felt the odd man out at the dinners. She'd worked around those feelings by focusing on her nephews and niece. But still…

Entering the dining room, she spotted Bridget and Ryder holding the twins while Eve chased Stephenia.

With the three high chairs, the palace looked far different from last year.

"Stefan will be here any minute. No need to put the darlings in the high chairs until then. How was your day?" Eve asked Pippa.

"Good," Pippa lied. "Made a little progress on my research."

"Good," Ryder said as he held Tyler and shifted from foot to foot. "Your genealogy studies could really help me with medical plans for Chantaine. I'm working on health prevention at the moment, and I'd like to see a better developed hospice plan in space."

Pippa's stomach clenched at the mention of hospice, although she wished Amelie could have access to such a program. "Both of those are vital. We're very fortunate Bridget brought you to us."

Bridget held Travis and smiled up at Ryder. "I can't agree with you more," she said as she jiggled the boy. "I hope Stefan doesn't take much longer or this family dinner is going to turn into a family scream-in."

Eve winced. "He said it would be just a moment."

"Yes, but we all know it's tough being crown prince and we're glad he's doing it and not us."

Seconds later, Stefan entered the small room with a broad smile. "You're all here. And healthy. This is good."

"And rare," Bridget added. "Given the twins' on-and-off sniffles. We'd better get on with the family dinner. I can't promise how long they'll last."

"No problem," Stefan said. "Sit down and relax. The food will arrive immediately. My assistant advised the chef."

The small group situated the children and sank into their chairs as staff poured water and wine for the adults and juice for the young ones. Before too much fussing, a server brought Cheerios for the babies.

"Takes them longer to pick up," Eve said with a smile.

"Well done," Bridget said.

"The main course will arrive in just a moment. I'd like to take this moment to share some good news. Eve and I are expecting our first child."

"Second, including Stephenia," Eve added.

"Oh, how wonderful. Another baby," Bridget crowed. "Takes the pressure off me."

Pippa laughed at her sister's reaction. "And me."

Bridget and Eve gasped at the same time. "You wouldn't dare. You're the good sister."

"Oh, no," Bridget corrected herself. "That's what we said about Valentina and she got pregnant before she was married."

"I was just joking," Pippa said.

"Thank you," Stefan said as he lifted his glass of wine and took a hefty sip. "One heart attack at a time, please."

"Besides," Bridget said as the staff served filet of sole. "We have plans for you."

Pippa felt a sliver of nervousness and took a sip of her own wine. "You and Eve keep talking about plans. You're making me uneasy."

"They're good plans," Bridget said as she set a plate of cheese, chicken and vegetables on Tyler's tray.

"We know you've been cooped up working on your degree," Eve added.

"Chantaine has several celebratory events scheduled during the next few weeks," Stefan said.

Pippa took a bite of the perfectly prepared fish.

"And we're going to set you up with some of the most eligible bachelors on the planet," Bridget said gleefully. "How exciting is that?"

Pippa's bite of fish stuck in her throat. "What?"

"It will be fun," Bridget said.

"No pressure," Eve said. "We just want you to enjoy yourself. You work hard with your nephews and niece and your studies."

"It's occurred to me," Stefan said, "that you haven't had many opportunities to form relationships with men. You've been protected. Perhaps overprotected."

Pippa's stomach tightened. "How lovely of you all to decide it's time for me to have a relationship. Without consulting me, of course."

Silence descended over the room. Even the children were silent as they munched on their food.

"We thought this would make you happy," Bridget said. "You work so hard. We wanted you to have some fun."

"Would you want your sisters and brother to make decisions about men you would date?" Pippa challenged.

Bridget winced. "When you put it that way…" she said.

"I am," Pippa said. "I don't need or want you to find dates for me. It's embarrassing," she said, her appetite completely gone.

"We don't intend it to be embarrassing," Stefan said. "Your position in the royal family makes it difficult for you to socialize with men. We'd like to make that easier."

"The same way the advisers tried to make it easy for you," Pippa said, setting down her fork.

"There's no call for that," Stefan said.

"And there's no call for matchmaking for me," Pippa said.

"Pippa, you haven't been the same since the incident with—" Bridget cleared her throat and lowered her voice. "That horrible Nic Lafitte. We just want to help you get over it."

"I'm completely over it. I know he was only interested in me to make a point with his ego." Even as she said the words she knew her family wanted to hear, she felt as if she were stabbing herself. "I may be naive, but I'm not a complete fool." She debated leaving the table, but knew her family would only worry more about her. She lifted her drink. "We have more important things to celebrate. Cheers to Stefan and Eve's new baby. May your pregnancy be smooth and may your child sparkle with the best of both of you."

Ryder lifted his glass. "Here, here."

"Here, here," Bridget said.

Tyler let out a blood-curdling scream, and the tension was broken. Soon enough, Travis joined. Stephenia followed.

Most important the focus was no longer on Pippa. She took another big sip of wine and knew she wouldn't be able to eat one more bite of food. With the children providing a welcome distraction, she gave a discreet signal to one of the servers, who immediately removed her plate. As she looked at each face of her family, she felt a combination of love and sheer and total frustration. She wished she could scream just like Tyler did.

Chapter Four

Two days later, Pippa mustered the time and courage to visit the Lafittes. The name Lafitte was like pyrotechnics as far as her family was concerned. Perhaps she should mentally give them another name so her stomach didn't clench every time she even thought it. Instead of Lafitte, she could think of them as the LaLas. Much less threatening. No unnecessary baggage with LaLa.

The idea appealed to her and Pippa smiled to herself when she thought about it, which was entirely too often. It was difficult not to become impatient with her sisters and brothers over the feud with the Lafittes. After all, the Lafittes were human, too. Look at their current situation with Amelie trying to make it through her dying days and poor Paul with his broken foot. And poor Nic trying to manage all of it.

Sighing, she pulled into the driveway and stopped the car. She glanced over her shoulder even though she was certain her security guy had been dozing when she'd left. That was Pippa. She knew well how to bore a man to sleep. She glanced in the mirror and bared her teeth at herself.

Grabbing the flowers from the passenger seat, she got out of the car and braced herself for the possibility of seeing Nic in workman mode in a tight T-shirt and slim-fitting jeans. Walking into the courtyard, however, she saw no workers around and the pool and Jacuzzi were full of fresh clean water. The sunlight glinting on the water made it all the more enticing, but she suspected the water was frigid.

The house was so quiet and peaceful she wondered if Amelie and Paul might be napping again. She hesitated as she stood in front of the door, not wanting to disturb their rest.

"Hey."

Pippa turned at the sound of Nic's voice as he walked from the guest quarters closer to the driveway. "Hello," she said. "I was afraid to interrupt. It's so quiet."

"I heard your car in the driveway," he said. "Last I checked both my parents are napping again, although I think my mom is getting restless. She'll need a field trip soon. Nice flowers. Come on inside," he said and opened the door to the cottage. He paused, cocking his head to one side. "I'll check to see if the bedroom door is still closed. Just a minute."

She watched him walk down the hallway. Seconds later, he returned, his face creased with concern. "She's gone."

Pippa bit her lip, feeling a quick spurt of apprehension. She couldn't help remembering how Amelie had fainted the last time she'd gone out on her own. "Are you sure she's not somewhere else in the house? Taking a nice long bath. Maybe she's in the kitchen."

He shook his head as he walked toward the kitchen. "I could see the open door of the bathroom." He glanced in the kitchen. "Not there. This isn't good."

"Maybe she went for a little walk in the neighborhood," Pippa suggested hopefully.

"The problem with my mother is that she doesn't take little walks. She probably escaped when I was working and the new house staff went to the market. I thought she was sleeping," he said and swore under his breath. "I have to go look for her."

"But where?" Pippa asked, watching his muscles bunched with tension even as he rolled his shoulders.

"I don't know, but I can't sit here waiting. I'll leave a note for Dad and Goldie. He'll be helping out here at the cottage for the time being."

Wanting to help, she impulsively offered, "I'll go with you." She suspected she surprised herself as much as she'd surprised him.

He gave the offer a flicker of consideration, then shook his head. "There's nothing you can do. I'll call or text you when I find out anything."

His easy dismissal of her irritated her. "I do know Chantaine better than you do."

"What's to know? The island isn't that big," he said.

"Did you know about Bebe's Crepes?" she asked.

"No, but—" He broke off and raked his hand through his dark hair. "Okay. But my first priority is finding my mother. If you're afraid someone may be able to identify you, you'll just have to duck behind the seat."

"Yes. Just let me put the flowers in water and grab my baseball cap," she said.

"I'll go ahead and call Goldie and ask him to come back now. I don't want my dad freaking out here by himself."

Pippa quickly placed the flowers in a pitcher she filled with water because she couldn't find a vase. Hearing Nic's low voice in the background gave her a sense of urgency. She raced to her car to grab the baseball cap. She'd put her hair in a topknot again, refusing to fight with it this morning. Pulling it down, she looked for an elastic band so she could put it in a ponytail and slip it through the back of the cap.

Hearing Nic's feet on the gravel of the driveway, she glanced up and pushed her fingers through her hair self-consciously.

"You should wear it down more often," he said.

"Oh, so I can look like I put my finger in an electrical socket?" No one had ever pretended to like her hair. She'd heard of a treatment that might tame it, but the idea of the hours it would take to accomplish it put her off.

"I like it," he said with a slow grin. "It's kinda wild. Makes me wonder if you have a wild streak underneath."

"I don't," she assured him and stuffed the unruly mass through the back of the ball cap as best as she could. "Shall we go?"

"I'm ready," he said and tucked her into the passenger side of his Mercedes.

"Has your mother mentioned any particular places in

Chantaine that she wanted to visit?" she asked as soon as Nic pulled out of the driveway.

"Since she moved into the cottage, she's just talked about how happy she is to be here, how beautiful it is."

"Hmm. Where are we headed first?" she asked.

"The beach," he said.

"That's a bit to cover. I don't supposed you've heard her talk about any specific beaches," she said.

"I've heard her talk about Chantaine a lot," he said, narrowing his eyes in deep thought. "She used to tell us bedtime stories about Chantaine before we went to sleep at night when my father was gone."

"Gone?" she asked.

"In prison," he said. "His conviction was overturned on a technicality. For a while there, she wouldn't let him come back."

Shocked by his revelation, she blinked. "I'm sorry. I didn't know. That must have been difficult."

"It was the gift that keeps on giving. My older brothers never forgave him. My younger brother just withdrew."

"But they've been in touch with your mother since she's been ill," she said.

"They won't talk to her if there's any chance they have to speak to my father," he said.

"Oh, my goodness, they're as bad as my family," she blurted. "If not worse."

He shot her a sideways glance, but kept his focus on the road. "Yeah."

"I'm sorry, but I'm just shocked. You never told me about all of this. Of course, I'd heard things about your father from my family, but you just said his conviction was overturned."

"Yeah, well, everyone's got a few skeletons in their closet. Even Stefan with his surprise daughter," he said.

Pippa bit her lip. It had been both scandalous and traumatic for the entire family and country for Stefan to learn he'd fathered a child fifteen months after the fact. "As soon as he'd learned about her, he'd done his fatherly duty. He's been a wonderful improvement over the example he had, let me tell you."

"Does that say more about your father or Stefan?" he challenged.

"My father wasn't involved with us. He procreated so that there would be children to carry on the work of the Devereauxs. The more he procreated, the more he could stay on his yacht and the less he would have to do." Her heart was slamming against her rib cage. She'd thought she'd settled all this as a child. Heaven knew, it was old news. "Stefan *reads* to his daughter most nights."

"Okay, okay," he said. "No need to yell."

"I wasn't yelling," she said, then reviewed her words and felt a slap of embarrassment. "Was I?"

"Just a little, but I probably deserved it," he said and pulled the car alongside the beach. "Let's check here." He opened the door for her and they scanned the beach from each direction.

"Did she mention this as one of her favorite beaches?" she asked, staring past rows of hot bodies.

"No. It's just the closest to the cottage. Why do you ask?"

"Well, Chantaine's beaches may share sand and

water, but they each have their own personalities," she said.

"Such as?"

"This is more of a singles scene, a pickup beach. As you can see from the demographics, a younger crowd frequents this beach. Farther north near the resorts, you'll find the celebrities and international visitors. Even farther north, there's a family beach where you'll see more children."

His hair whipping in the wind, he narrowed his eyes. "What's the name of the family beach?"

"St. Cristophe," she said.

"It was on the tip of my tongue," he said. "Let's go there. She went there often as a child before her parents died. She talked about eating fruit, cheese and crackers at the beach. I just hope she didn't decide to go into the water."

They both got into the car, traveling in silence up the coast. Pippa could sense Nic's tension. "If you could just persuade her to leave a message before she leaves..."

"Tell me something new. Maybe she'll listen to you if you say something to her," he said.

"Me? Why would she listen to me?" she asked, surprised at the suggestion. Amelie had only just met her.

"She's grateful to you for the use of the cottage and you're female. She thinks I'm just being overbearing and protective," he said.

"I'll give it a try," she said, full of doubt. "Maybe we could get a list of things she wants to do."

"Like a bucket list?"

She cringed. "That's morbid."

"But part of the program at this point," he said, clenching his jaw.

Pippa's heart twisted. She hated it for all of them, but Nic was only speaking the truth. "St. Cristophe Beach is just a few more kilometers north. We should be there soon."

As soon as the sign for the beach greeted them, Nic again pulled onto the side of the road and helped her from the car. Pippa scanned the beach. "Do you see her?"

He shook his head. "Let's split up. I'll go south. You go north. Call my cell if you find her and I'll do the same. Okay?"

She nodded in agreement and walked northward. The breeze was picking up and the clouds were rolling in, bringing the air temperature down. With Amelie's slight frame, Pippa feared the woman could become easily chilled even though it was summer.

Walking along the beach, she looked from one side to the other. Chantaine's beaches had their share of rocks and trees. Going barefoot could lead to serious discomfort. One more thing to worry about if Amelie had impulsively removed her shoes.

"Look! Isn't that Princess Phillipa?" a woman's voice called.

Pippa froze. Bloody hell, now what could she do.

A woman and several children raced toward her. Oh great, her security detail was going to kill her.

"Your Highness," the woman said, making an awkward curtsy. "Boys, take a bow. Girls, curtsy."

Pippa couldn't help smiling at the woman's delight and friendliness. "It's not necessary. I was here just taking a little walk. St. Cristophe is such a lovely beach. Are you enjoying your day?"

"Very much," the woman said.

The children echoed, "Yes, ma'am."

"Even more so seeing you here," the woman said. "Is there any chance you would give me an autograph? It would be a dream come true."

Seeing a small crowd forming, Pippa knew she'd better make the best of it. "Now, I didn't want to make a big production of this, so you're going to keep my little escape to the beach a secret. Won't you?" Fat chance with Facebook and Twitter alive and well.

She began to shake hands, sign autographs and make pleasant conversation. It really wasn't that difficult. The people were so lovely and kind. Her cell phone rang in the small purse she carried. "Excuse me for just a moment," she said and drew back slightly from the crowd.

"I found her," Nic said. "She was sitting beside a tree sleeping."

"I'm so relieved for you," she said. "But I've been discovered. Go ahead and take her home."

"How will you get back?" he asked.

"I'll figure out something. Or someone will alert security and it won't be necessary. I just wish my car wasn't in your driveway."

"I'll have Goldie take care of it. Where do you want it?"

"Close by, but he doesn't have the key."

"Goldie won't need it," he said. "I'll text you when he's close. He'll grab a cab ride back. *Ciao.*"

Pippa opened her mouth to protest, but she knew Nic had hung up, so she turned back to the crowd and continued to chat, sign autographs and even pose for a few photographs. Yes, there was going to be an inquisition in her very near future. Several moments later, her cell signaled a text. Certain it was from Nic, she didn't bother to look and began to say her goodbyes.

"It was lovely meeting all of you," she said. "But I really must go. *Ciao.*"

She climbed the sandy hill to the road and after walking south a short distance, she spotted her vehicle. Unfortunately she also spotted the vehicle belonging to her security man Giles. Dread tightening her stomach, she walked toward the man. She really didn't want to lose Giles as her personal security guard. He was, after all, the oldest security member on the force. With the exception of her secret meetings with Nic nearly a year ago, he regarded her as a sweet but boring student who posed very little security threat. Plus he was given to taking nice long naps in the afternoon.

"Your Highness," he said wearing an extremely displeased expression. "You didn't inform me of your plans to visit the beach today."

"I know," she said. "I'm terribly sorry. It was an impulse after lunch. I mentioned my plans to pop into a café for lunch, didn't I?"

Giles shook his head. "No, ma'am, you didn't."

"Oh, it must have slipped my mind. You know I usually pack a lunch, but I forgot this morning. My recent studies have been a bit depressing, detailing the causes of deaths of all our ancestors. I just felt a walk on a family beach would clear my head," she said, hoping she was boring the bloody stuffing out of him.

"But you usually prefer the more isolated Previn Beach," he said.

"I know. I guess I just wanted to see happy families playing on the beach. I do apologize. I would never want to trouble you."

"I know you wouldn't," he said. "But you must apprise someone of your whereabouts. If something happened to you, I would never forgive myself."

"You are absolutely correct and I'll never do it again," she lied and felt guilty, but she couldn't change the course she'd started and she wouldn't if she could.

"But you should have informed your Giles or someone," Frank, the head of security said to her. Because one interrogation wasn't enough.

"I know," Pippa said. "But I also know that Stefan has said that he wants us to make more impromptu public appearances."

"Impromptu to the public, not to security."

"So sorry," she said, and tried to conceal her insincerity. It seemed to be growing easier. She hoped she wasn't becoming a lying wench.

Frank sighed and began to pace across her public den. "Your Highness, except for your lapse with *Mr. Lafitte,* you have been an easy royal to protect. Since then, your studies and family have dominated your life. We don't wish to intrude, but if you continue to be unpredictable, then we will need to provide further security."

"I apologize again for not giving you more information today. I will do my best to be as predictable as possible in the future," she said.

Frank gave a sideways tilt of his head. "Perhaps I wasn't clear. We need you to be transparent."

Pippa gave a slow nod. The last thing she wanted to be was transparent. "Of course. And that's exactly what I shall be. Transparent. Predictable," she quickly added.

"Thank you very much, Your Highness," Frank said. "It is only our desire to protect you."

"I know," Pippa said. "And I'm very grateful," she added, exaggerating.

Frank smiled and nodded. "Thank you, Your Highness. I knew we could count on you."

Pippa lifted her lips in a smile as he left her suite. She'd just bought herself a couple more days of freedom. She hoped.

The following day, Pippa skipped visiting the Lafittes and even texting Nic. She felt as if she needed to stick to being predictable and transparent for at least one full day. That next night, however, she tossed and turned as she tried to sleep. She couldn't be what she needed to be for her family. She couldn't be what she wanted to be for the Lafittes.

She finally fell into a fitful sleep full of images of Nic and Amelie. Strong, strong Nic who would never admit pain or vulnerability, yet his dark eyes said something far different. Unable to sleep, she paced her bedroom and tried to work. She finally gave in and sent a text to Nic. *I'm going to need a different disguise.*

When a civilized time of day finally arrived, Pippa took a shower and got ready to go to the library. She sat down to work, and even though she had the concentration of a water newt, she forced herself to focus. Some time later, a package was placed beside her.

Glancing up, Pippa caught sight of a big bald man walking away from her. She lifted her hand. "Sir?"

The man didn't turn around. Pippa frowned, staring at the package. She glanced around her, then turned it over. The package bore the initials PD. Curious, she eyed the package with a sideways glance and slid it onto the chair beside her. Nic Lafitte was crazy. Who knew what scheme he had in his wicked mind?

She glanced back at her own laptop and with her heart racing, she tried to stare at the screen. Forget concentration. She would just like to be able to *read* the words on her screen. After seven tries, she gave up, grabbed the package and walked to the ladies' room. She went into a stall, ripped open the package and pulled out a gray-haired wig. Pippa couldn't help snickering. Her curiosity shooting upward, she pulled out the rest of the contents of the package. A hat, an ugly gray dress, tennis shoes and a key to a car.

She fished out a scrawled note at the bottom of the package. "The car is old, gray and rusty. In America, we call it a POS mobile. More later."

POS mobile? She couldn't wait to hear his explanation, she thought as she changed into the ugly gray dress. After she finished dressing, she carefully folded her other clothing and placed it into the package. Walking out of the restroom, she looked into the mirror and gaped. She looked at least thirty years older if not more. Pippa snickered again. *Well done, Nic.*

Following her instincts, she walked out the back door of the library and looked around for an old gray, rusty car. She immediately spotted it. The car was the most hideous vehicle she'd ever seen. Pippa walked to it, unlocked the door and got inside.

She turned the key and pressed the accelerator. The engine coughed to life. The summer heat combined with her wig and droopy dress made her feel as if she were suffocating. Pippa pushed the button for the air-conditioning, but only hot air blew from the vents.

"Bloody hell," she muttered and drove out of the parking lot.

Nic heard the sound of an engine backfiring outside his window. Glancing away from his tablet computer, he saw a gray-haired woman in a black dress exit the car and felt a ripple of pleasure. She'd come. He hadn't been sure she would. Pippa was an odd mix, and he'd already learned the hard way her first loyalty was to her family. She'd probably endured some pressure from her security guy and maybe even her family if they knew about it.

He was surprised she continued to visit. After all, her conscience should be clear. She'd made a dying woman's wish come true. Heading for the door of the guesthouse, he wondered why Pippa clearly felt the need to do more.

He stepped outside and caught sight of her walking toward the back door. "May I help you, miss?" he called, relishing the opportunity to tease her.

Whirling around with her hands on her hips, she stared at him, the gray curls of the wig so stiff they didn't move. "Very funny," she said. "As if you didn't handpick this lovely disguise."

"It worked, didn't it?" he asked as he strolled toward her.

She gave a reluctant nod. "Yes, but the car is another matter."

"I'll get Goldie to do something about the engine backfiring. We wouldn't want to call attention to you."

"The car may be a little over the top," she said. "It's distinctive and there's no air-conditioning."

"That must be hard on a woman your age," he said and bit back a grin. Lord, he felt like someone had turned on the light for the first time in two days. His mother had been alternately ill and sleeping. "I wasn't sure you'd come."

Her expression of contempt waned slightly. "You made it easy." She sighed. "How is she?"

He shook his head. "Not good. Sick or sleeping for close to thirty-six hours. It seems she gets a burst of energy and uses up all of it, then she can barely lift her head for days. I never know when one of these dips is the beginning of the—" He broke off. "Something bad."

"I'm sorry," she whispered. "I'm really sorry."

Feeling as if he'd revealed too much, he looked away from her and shrugged. "Part of the program. I'll deal with it. Good thing I've got Goldie. He's a licensed practical nurse, too."

Pippa blinked. "Goldie appears to be a man of many skills. Where on earth did you find him?"

"He and my father were in prison together. Goldie's record wasn't expunged, but he was a good guy. I hired him and he developed a hobby of educating himself. I paid for all the courses, but they've ended up benefiting me."

He felt her gaze on her for a long moment.

"I would like to meet him, please," Pippa said. "So far, I've only caught glimpses of his talents and abilities."

His gut tightened with something strange he almost couldn't identify. It took several seconds. Jealousy? He racked his brain to remember when he had felt this way before and couldn't. He led the way to the house. "Sure, I'll introduce you to Goldie. He's in the main house probably putting together a gourmet meal for dinner."

"He's a chef, too?" she asked.

"Oh, yeah, that was another one of his certificates. It's paid off in spades."

"The palace would *love* to have someone like him...."

"Don't even think about it. But if you do, he'll turn you down flat. He's the most loyal ex-con ever," Nic said.

"That remains to be seen," Pippa said. "The Devereauxs have seduced more than a few of the best of the best."

He stopped at the front door and turned around to meet her gaze. "I know that better than most."

Her cheeks heated and her eyes darkened. She cleared her throat. "Um..."

"Yeah, um," he echoed, saving her a response and opened the front door. "Let's go inside."

He guided her past the foyer into the kitchen. "Goldie," he said in a low voice.

The multitalented man appeared within two seconds, wearing an apron around his waist. "Yes, sir."

Goldie was sixty, but looked fifty because he worked

out. He was bald, muscular, with a gold hoop in his right ear. He usually wore a black T-shirt and black pants. He looked intimidating, but Nic knew he had a heart softer than that of a teddy bear. "Her Royal Highness, Princess Pippa Devereaux, this is Gordon Goldwyn."

Goldie gave a solemn bow. "Your Highness, my pleasure," he said.

Pippa smiled. "My pleasure," she said. "You're a man of many talents. Thank you for delivering my car to me at the beach and also leaving the envelope and car for me."

"I'm honored to serve," Goldie said respectfully.

"How is it that you are talented in so many areas?" she asked.

"I'm a lifelong student. Some things I learned got me into trouble. I'm fortunate that Mr. Lafitte encouraged me to explore my interests. Would you care for a drink or something to eat?"

"I'm fine. Thank you very much."

Goldie nodded, then turned to Nic. "Can I get something for you, sir?"

Nic waved his hand. "No, thanks. Any sign of my mother?"

"No, but your father is getting restless watching her," Goldie said.

"You're saying he could use some TV time. Sports Central," Nic said.

Goldie nodded. "A game would be even better."

"I got a million on DVD," he said.

"Then you've got what he needs," Goldie said.

At that moment, his mother walked into the room, looking gray and gaunt. "I'm thirsty," she said.

Nic rushed to her side. "What are you doing?"

She leaned against him. "I'm Lazarus rising from the dead. Hopefully, I'll do it a few more times," she said and stared at Pippa. "You look familiar. Are you someone who went to school with me?"

"Not quite," Pippa said with a smile. "But I would have loved that."

His mother frowned. "Were you in the orphanage with me?"

Pippa shook her head. "No, but you and I went to Bebe's Crepes together."

His mother stared at her for a moment, then smiled. "Princess Pippa," she crowed. "I love the look," she said, stretching out her hands. "You're my old best friend Rosie."

Pippa nodded and he saw that she was holding back her laughter. "Thank you so much. I'm sure Rosie is a most excellent person."

His mother nodded. "She is, but you are, too." Her eyebrows furrowed. "May we please have some refreshments?" she asked.

"What would you like, ma'am?" Goldie asked.

"Something fruity," she said. "Orange juice or lemonade."

"I'll bring both," he said. "Please take a seat in the den."

Nic assisted his mother to sit on the sofa. "There's no need to treat me like an invalid," she complained.

Nic gritted his teeth. Every other day, if not more often, his mother *was* almost an invalid. Yes, he was happy as hell that she didn't want to be treated like

one. In his mind, that meant she might be around a
little longer.

Pippa put her hand over his and met his gaze as if
she knew everything he was feeling. Still dressed as a
gray-haired lady wearing a baggy dress, she looked like
an angel to him. An angel he wanted more than he'd
ever wanted anyone else.

Chapter Five

Pippa concealed her alarm at how weak Amelie appeared. Just two days ago, she'd seemed an entirely different woman, going off by herself for a jaunt to the beach.

"I want to go on another adventure soon," Amelie announced as she sipped lemonade. "I'd like to go today, but I'm too bloody tired. Tomorrow will be a different story."

Pippa caught sight of Nic rubbing his forehead and face. She could see his shoulders bunch with tension. "Just let someone go with you so we don't have to call out a search team."

"A search team isn't necessary," Amelie said with a stubborn tilt of her chin. "I was fine."

"You were asleep on a public beach. You overestimate your energy level," he said.

She waved her hand in a dismissing gesture. "Plenty

of people doze on the beach. It's one of the pleasures of life. You wouldn't understand because you don't know how to relax."

"If you would agree to a GPS monitoring anklet…"

Amelie's eyes widened in indignation. "I'm not on house arrest. I refuse to be treated like a prisoner during my last days."

"It's just for tracking. Safety. It would give me some peace of mind," Nic added.

"Well, it wouldn't give me peace of mind walking around in public with an anklet designed for criminals."

Nic sighed. "I'm worried about you. What if you collapse and there's no one there to help you? Is that really the way you want to go?"

Pippa cringed at his bluntness, but she could tell he was feeling pressed. She honestly wouldn't like to be in his situation.

Amelie lifted her chin. "I don't get to choose the way I want to go. If it were up to me, I'd transform into a butterfly and float away, but the doctor says that's not possible."

A tense silence followed. Pippa felt it inside her and took a deep breath to ease it. "Well, I can see that the genes for independence and outspokenness are quite strong in both of you. I'm sure both of you enjoy those qualities in each other."

Nic glared at her, but Pippa forced herself to smile. "Mrs. Lafitte, perhaps you and I could go on an outing tomorrow or the next day, depending on how you're feeling. With my new disguise, I believe I'm safe to go anywhere."

Amelie smiled in delight. "Call me Amelie. And you

don't look a thing like yourself. That wig is so horrible, I think you may look even older than I am."

"Thank you," she said and shot Nic a wry look.

"I've been thinking I'd like to learn a new hobby. Years and years ago, I learned to knit, but I've forgotten everything. Do you know of any knitting shops on Chantaine?"

Ignoring Nic's astonished expression, she nodded. "I know of one downtown. If you feel like it, we could also have lunch."

Amelie seemed to brighten at the suggestion. "Lovely. This will be wonderful. I like having something to look forward to." She paused and glanced at Nic. "Have you heard anything from your brothers?"

"No," he said, and Pippa noticed the slight clench of his jaw. "You should let me call them again."

She shook her head. "You did that last year when I had my last treatments and they all visited then. It was a disaster with your father. I was just hoping things could be different now." She sighed. "There are some things we can't change. Best not to focus on them. I'll look forward to my outing with you tomorrow," she said to Pippa. "I think I'll sit outside by the pool with a book and this lovely lemonade."

"It's a beautiful day," Pippa said. "I think you'll enjoy it."

Goldie appeared in the doorway. "Can I get you something to eat?" he asked.

Amelie made a slight face. "If I tell you I'm not hungry, you'll tell me I need to eat something to keep up my strength. Crackers," she said.

Goldie's face fell. He'd clearly hoped her appetite had improved. "Yes, ma'am."

"Are you sure I can't join you outside?" Pippa asked.

"No, thank you, darling. I just want a little Chantaine sunshine," Amelie said and carefully rose from the sofa.

As soon as Amelie left, Pippa turned to Nic. "What is wrong with your brothers? Even my terribly dysfunctional family came together at the end of my parents' lives. Surely your brothers could do the same. It's the only humane, compassionate choice. You must make them come here at once."

Nic leaned toward her and gave a short laugh. "Here's a news flash, Princess. There's no royal decree available for the Lafittes. Besides, we don't respond well to attempted force or manipulation. My older brothers are holding on to a mile-wide grudge against my father. My youngest brother makes sure he's too busy to be contacted."

"But you must have some influence with them," she said, appalled at the situation.

"My oldest brothers would make the trip if they didn't have to face my father," Nic said. "My mother won't allow that. She refuses to turn her back on my dad even though she's earned the right more than once."

Frowning, Pippa rose and paced across the lush burgundy carpet placed on top of the ceramic tile floor. "There's got to be a way. Perhaps Goldie or I could take your father for a drive—"

Nic shook his head. "Not gonna happen. My mother wouldn't allow it."

"Well, we will just have to figure out another way," she said.

"We?" he echoed, rising to walk toward her.

Her stomach dipped as he moved closer. She kept trying to forget his effect on her, but every time she felt she was successful in staying focused on Amelie, Nic did something to upset her equilibrium. Unfortunately, it took very little. Seeing him stand and breathe was apparently problematic for her.

"I'm still not sure why you feel my mother's problems have anything to do with you," he said, looking down at her and resting his hands on his hips.

"Technically, I suppose they don't, but I would think any compassionate person would want to help," she said.

"Including Stefan?"

She bit her lip. "If Eve had anything to say about it, yes, he would help. I know you believe Stefan is a monster, but he's not. Just as he believes you are the very devil, and you're not."

"Good to know you don't think I'm the devil," he said.

She opened her mouth to retract her statement, then decided against it. "I will try to come up with a solution for your mother and your brothers. In the meantime, I can take Amelie shopping tomorrow, but I'll be busy the day after. I'm supposed to escort some soccer player around the island, then accompany him to a charity fundraiser that evening."

He lifted an eyebrow and his eyes glittered with something that gave her pause. "Is that so? Is the fundraiser at the St. Thomas Hall?"

"Yes, as a matter of fact, it is."

"This should be—" His lips twitched. "Fun. I'm invited to the same fundraiser."

"Oh," she said, her stomach taking a downward plunge. "You probably weren't planning to attend, were you?"

"I hadn't decided, but I could use some entertainment. May as well."

"But what about your mother?"

"It will just be for the evening," he said. "Goldie can call me. I'm not glued to Chantaine. I'll have to leave for business commitments within the next couple of weeks." He paused. "I'm at peace with my mother, and she's at peace with me. We have no unfinished business."

Pippa felt the oddest sense of calm and excitement from Nic. She'd never, ever felt that combination before. She took a deep breath and pushed past her feelings of panic about her feelings. That peace Nic had just mentioned, that was what was important. She felt it and knew it deep inside her. "I'm so glad that you have a good relationship with your mother. It will help you after—" She broke off, not wanting to say the words.

"After she's gone," he said.

Pippa nodded slowly.

"Because you didn't have the best relationship with your mother," he said.

"It wasn't horrible," she said quickly. "It was just distant. Our family was different. We weren't raised the way most other children are raised."

"It's different being royal," he said.

She nodded.

He reached out to take her hand in his. His fingers felt strong and sure wrapped around hers. "Most people don't have perfect childhoods. You take the good and screw the bad stuff."

His simple words gave her the biggest rush. They reverberated inside her. She wanted to be that person who could *take the good and screw the bad*. Every once in a while, though, she felt caught between herself as the chubby preteen who didn't feel worthy of her parents' attention and a grown woman who was on her way to earning her doctorate. The touch of his hand just made her want more… At that moment, Nic made her feel she was capable of anything she wanted to do and be.

A loud cough sounded. Mr. Lafitte stood on crutches at the entrance of the room. "Where's Amelie?" he asked, looking more than a little rough around the edges. His hair stuck up in a wild Mohawk and his jaw was heavily whiskered. "Is she okay?"

Pippa automatically pulled her hand from Nic's while Nic turned to his father. "She's fine. Outside by the pool."

Mr. Lafitte slumped forward slightly. "Good. As long as she's not swimming."

Nic winced. "Good point. Goldie," he called, "can you see my mother?"

"She's in a lawn chair, sir."

"Good." Nic took a quick breath. "Can I walk you to your car, Great-Auntie Matilde?"

Pippa felt a flash of realization. She'd forgotten she looked thirty years older. She smothered a laugh at herself. She'd been concerned that she was giving Nic mixed signals.

Well, she would have if she didn't look like his grandmother. Walking out of the cottage, she waved at

Amelie and strode the rest of the way to the horrid vehicle she would drive to the library, where she would change out of her outfit and return to her identity as Princess Pippa.

Nic opened the door for her.

"I hope it's cooler now. I burned up on the drive over here," she said.

"Goldie did a little magic. You should be more comfortable now."

"Thank you," she said.

"Thank you." He leaned toward her slowly and pressed his mouth just next to hers. It could have been a kiss on her cheek, but it just missed the mark. It could have been her mouth, but it wasn't. He almost made her forget that she was dressed like his grandmother.

Nic watched Pippa putter away in the POS mobile. She continued to make him admire her. He tried to name a woman who would be willing to disguise herself as a woman thirty years older and drive a wreck of an automobile just to check on a dying woman who was not related to her. Pippa was different. He'd known that from the beginning.

He returned to the front door.

"Nic, darling, come sit with me for a moment, please," his mother called. "Ask Goldie to bring you a Scotch. Or whatever it is that you drink."

"No need," he said. "It's early for that."

His mother glanced up from her wide-brimmed hat. "Haven't you heard? It's five o'clock somewhere." She rang the little bell Goldie had given her, insisting that she ring it anytime she wanted anything.

Goldie immediately appeared. "Yes, Miss Amelie."

"Please fix a drink for Nic. His usual," she said.

Nic sank into the chair beside her. "How's the book?"

"I fell asleep, so I don't know," she said. "But I'm loving the sunshine. You will have many stars in your crown for bringing me to Chantaine."

"That was Pippa's doing," he said.

"And you're quite taken with her," his mother said and sipped her lemonade.

"I wouldn't say that," he said, irritated at her suggestion.

"No, but I'm dying, so I can speak the truth," she said and shot him a knowing glance from the top of her sunglasses. "I would never ever suggest going after a royal especially because Paul and I made a bit of a mess with the Devereauxs back in the day. That said, I can tell the princess is also taken with you."

Goldie delivered his Scotch and Nic took a long drink. "Yes, that's why she dumped me like garbage several months ago."

His mother waved her hand dismissively. "Family's a tricky thing. You ought to know. I'm quite impressed that she's made such an effort to please a dying woman. Especially when her family wouldn't approve. I can't help believing some part of her is trying to help you."

"If so, then that part is buried very deep," Nic said dryly.

"You have to find your own way. I'll just tell you that some people are worth fighting for. Some people are your destiny," she said.

"You're speaking of Dad," he said, always stunned by the fervency of her devotion to his father.

"I am. He would steal for me. He would die for me. He would go to prison for me. He would do anything for me. I hope you'll know that kind of love," she said and leaned back against the chaise longue.

After a lovely lunch and bit of shopping spent with Nic's mother, Pippa prepared herself for her afternoon and evening scheduled with Robert Speight, the world-famous soccer player from England.

"Aren't you excited?" Bridget asked as she *helped* Pippa get ready for an afternoon outing. "He's so hot. Stefan protested. He wanted to put you with a count from Italy, but I insisted. You deserve a treat after all the academic work you've been doing along with being such a good auntie. Good Lord, don't you ever go shopping?" Bridget continued. "All I see are long skirts and blouses."

"I haven't had a lot of time for shopping," Pippa said, wishing she didn't feel such a strong sense of dread about the setup with the soccer player. She feared he was going to be quite disappointed and bored.

"Well, there's always catalogs and online shopping. For that matter, the palace stylist would be happy—" She broke off as she whisked through the hangers of clothing in Pippa's closet. "Don't you even own a cute little pair of shorts?"

"I'm sure there are some in there somewhere. I just prefer skirts. They're more comfortable," Pippa said and reached for a beige linen skirt that flowed to her calves.

"Absolutely not," Bridget said, scooping the skirt back from her. "If you insist on wearing a skirt," she muttered, pushing through a few more hangers. "Ah," she said, pulling out one of Bridget's few above-the-knee skirts. "Here, this one will work."

"I'm not sure it fits anymore," Pippa murmured, holding the pink skirt against her. "And I think I may have stained the blouse that goes with it."

Bridget pulled out a white scoop-neck cotton blouse. "There. It will be perfect with sandals. Why did you cancel the salon appointment I made for you yesterday? I told you about the new treatment. Smooth, shiny hair and because you're Miss Practical, you won't have to spend so much of your time styling it every day."

"I don't spend that much time, now," Pippa said. "I either pull it back or put it on top of my head."

"Hmm," Bridget said and studied Pippa for a long uncomfortable moment. Bridget took her hand and led her to the sitting area of Pippa's suite. "I'm not sensing a lot of enthusiasm about your outing with the soccer player." She sighed. "Please tell me you're not still pining for that terrible Nic Lafitte."

Pippa looked away. "Of course I'm not pining for him. But I'm not pining for a setup, either. Think about it. Did you like it when Stefan set you up with men hoping for a romance or marriage?"

"I hated it," Bridget said. "Fought it with every bit of my strength, but most of those men were at least ten years older than me. Robert is your age. And he's regarded as one of the most eligible bachelors in the world. I'm not trying to arrange a marriage. I just want you to have a little fun. You're due."

Pippa gave a slow nod. "I appreciate the sentiment. You're sweet to want me to have some fun."

Bridget met her gaze and groaned. "But you're not

at all interested. Well, at least give the poor man a try.
Trust me when I say I didn't have to do any coaxing to
make this happen. He was more than happy to spend
the day and evening with you. And who knows? You
may have a fabulous time. Promise me you'll *try* to
have fun."

"I'll do my best and I'll also try to make sure that
Mr. Speight is entertained," Pippa said.

Pippa treated the date as if it were a project. She
planned to take the soccer player on a tour of the island,
stopping at a few of the famous beaches. If time permitted, she'd arranged for a brief turn on the royal yacht.

Robert Speight was an impressive specimen. He
stood over six feet tall with a well-muscled body. His
hair was red and skin extremely fair. The exact opposite of Nic, she thought, and immediately wished she
hadn't made the comparison. Their date started out well
enough with Pippa giving a running commentary on
the history of Chantaine as she showed him points of
interest. It was only when she saw his head rolling back
against the headrest, his eyes closed and his mouth open
that she got her first clue that she'd begun to bore the
poor man.

Thank goodness she'd arranged for a picnic lunch
at a private beach. She and Robert sat on a large blanket and ate food from a gourmet basket prepared by the
palace chef. Robert asked for photos, but kept fighting
the yawns.

"Sorry," he said sheepishly. "Late night last night
partying," he said waggling his bushy red eyebrows
suggestively. "If you know what I mean."

She didn't, so she just made a vague little sound. "I

thought it was very generous of you to lend your name to the charity fundraiser this evening. So many people are looking forward to meeting you."

He shrugged. "I have to do a few of these every now and then for the sake of my image. It helps me get other endorsements. This one included exotic beaches and a date with a princess. What's not to like?" He leaned toward her and placed his hand over hers. "I've heard Chantaine has some nude beaches. You want to take me there?"

Pippa blinked at the proposal and tried not to laugh. She'd spent a lifetime trying not to be photographed in a bathing suit. A nude beach was totally out of the question. "I'm not really permitted on the nude beach," she whispered. "Photographs live forever. If you have time tomorrow, I can arrange for a driver to take you."

"But it would be much more enjoyable with you," he said.

"I'm so sorry," she said and took back her hand. She was going to have a chat with Bridget tomorrow, she promised herself.

Later that afternoon, Pippa received a visit from the palace stylist, Peter, to make sure she was properly dressed and coiffed. Dressed in a designer gown that reminded her of a pink cocktail napkin, she bit her teeth. Peter applied more makeup than she wore in a year. He sighed and swore over her hair. "A keratin treatment would change your life."

"It takes too long," she said.

"It's not as if you would have to sit in a salon like the rest of the world. We would bring the cosmetologist to the palace. Your hair would be straight for three to four months after one treatment."

Pippa stared into the mirror at herself and made a face. "I don't know if I want it straight."

Peter lifted one eyebrow. "As you wish, Your Highness."

"Your way of saying I'm crazy," she said.

Both of Peter's eyebrows flew upward, which was quite an accomplishment given the Botox he regularly had injected into his forehead. "Pardon me, Your Highness if I offended you."

"It's true. You think I should get the treatment and have straight hair. Straight hair is more fashionable than crazy, wavy hair."

Peter seemed to work on his restrained. "It's my job to keep the royal family informed of current fashion. Your hair…" He began and moved his hands, but couldn't seem to find the words.

"I hate my hair and love my hair because it's different," she told him. "You have to admit, it's not like anyone else's hair in the family."

Peter tilted his head to one side. "You make an excellent point, Your Highness. We shall begin to capitalize on your hair," he said. "We shall make your hair a new trend. We can name it the Princess Pippa hairstyle. Perfect."

Alarm shot through her. "No need to go that far," she said.

He lifted his hands. "I can see it now. Magazine shoots, commercials. It will be fantastic publicity for the royal family."

"Not in my lifetime," she said quietly.

He sighed. "Begging your pardon, ma'am, you give this impression of being a people pleaser, yet you somehow stop me in my tracks when I try to expand you."

"And you like me for that, don't you, Peter?" she said more than asked, unable to hold back a grin.

Peter shook his head but smiled. "I do. Let me spray you one more time," he said lifting a can of hair spray.

She lifted both her hands to block him. "I'll die if you do."

"An exaggeration," he said.

"You would know because you're the master of exaggeration," she retorted, her hands still braced to shield herself from the hair spray.

Peter groaned. "You make this difficult for me, ma'am. What if this man is your future husband?"

"No worries," she said, adapting a phrase she'd learned from Bridget. "He pushed hard for me to take him to a nude beach."

Peter frowned. "A cad. In that case, perhaps I should give you sea salt spray. It will take your curls to a new level."

Pippa laughed. "No need. Thanks for your help tonight."

"Someday, a man will sweep you off your feet."

Pippa laughed again, and her mind automatically turned to thoughts of Nic. She clamped down her thoughts and feelings. "I prefer my feet on the ground."

Thirty minutes later, she joined Robert Speight in a limo headed for the charity event. "Nice dress," Robert said, staring at her cleavage. "Are you sure I can't talk you into a trip to one of your nude beaches tomorrow?"

Pippa refused to honor the subject, let alone the question. "Did you know that I'm working on a doctorate in genealogical studies? I had some extra time this afternoon while I was waiting on alterations for my gown. Did you know that you may be distantly related to Attila the Hun?" The truth was just about anyone could be distantly related to Attila.

Robert shot her a blank look. "Attila the Hun?" he echoed.

"Yes, he's quite famous."

"I'm drawing a blank," Robert said. "Can you refresh my memory?"

"He was a ferocious warrior. The Romans were terrified of him. He was excellent with a bow and an amazing horseman. Quite the sportsman," she said.

Robert stuck out his chest with pride and smiled. "Like me."

"Exactly. He was known as a conqueror." *And barbarian.*

"I've got to make a little speech tonight. Maybe I could mention him," he said. "Maybe spice things up for people interested in history."

She opened her mouth to correct him, but couldn't quite make herself do it. "Just as long as you understand that I said that you *may* be related to Attila. I would need to do an in-depth study to verify the possibility."

"Hey, it's a good story. That's all that counts to me," he said, leaning toward her as if he were going to kiss her. "You're cute. Let's make some private plans after the event."

"Oh, I—" The limousine pulled to a stop. She glanced out the window, thankful for the interruption. "We're here."

"Yeah," Robert said as the driver opened the door. "First time with a princess. In more ways than one," he added against her ear as he folded his hand around her waist.

Pippa's stomach rolled.

She stepped out of the car and felt a thousand camera flashes as she strode toward the entrance of the building. Robert grabbed her hand and she struggled to free it. She pointed at a camera and she took advantage when he loosened his grip. Clasping her hands firmly together, she walked inside and smiled at the crowd that applauded.

"Pippa, Pippa!"

She was surprised to hear so many call her name. She'd always thought of herself as the anonymous Devereaux.

Robert put his arm around her and whispered in her ear, "Give me a kiss. They'll love it."

She bit her lip and turned her head. "I see some of your fans," she said.

"Where?" he asked.

Moments later, they entered the ballroom and Pippa waved to the crowd. There, several people screamed out loud. "Rob, Rob!"

"There you go," she said, but she needn't have. Robert was fixated on the crowd, waving and throwing kisses.

They were led to the head table and Pippa took her seat. The rest of the guests took their seats. Instinctively, she glanced around and her gaze landed on a man with broad shoulders, dark eyes and dark hair. Tonight he wore that Stetson as if to proclaim to all of Chantaine and her family that he didn't give a damn.

She liked him even more for that.

"This is fun," Robert said. "Just tell me it's not another rubber chicken dinner," he said.

"Lobster," she said and barely managed not to roll her eyes.

She felt Nic's gaze on her. He was silently laughing.

"So that guy's name is Atowla?"

"Attila," she said. "Attila the Hun." She was caught between a barbarian and a pirate. She wasn't sure which was worse.

Chapter Six

A server discreetly handed Pippa a piece of paper with her sorbet. Putting it in her lap, she opened it and glanced at it. *Meet me on the second floor in 5. N.* Pippa took a quick sip of water and briefly met Nic's gaze. She shook her head.

Her so-called date whispered in her ear. "It's time for more pictures," he said. "Stand up and I'll give you a passionate kiss. The press will love it."

Pippa nearly choked. "I was just going to tell you that I need to, uh, powder my nose. I'll be back shortly."

Robert's face fell. "Well, damn."

"I won't be long," she said and stood. She gave her security man a wave of dismissal and quickly walked to the hall outside the ballroom. Restroom was to the right, she remembered. Pippa had attended several events at this venue. The second floor offered a lovely view of the beach. Her stomach took a dip. Nic clearly remembered that fact, too.

She headed toward the restroom.

"Pippa."

She automatically paused, her heart leaping at the sound of Nic's voice. Pippa sucked in a quick, sharp breath and forced herself not to turn around. She didn't need to because Nic was at her side in seconds. "This is not a good idea. Go away," she whispered.

"Your Highness," a woman called. "Princess Phillipa."

Pippa frowned and turned at the distress in the woman's voice. She stared into the lovely heart-shaped face of a very young-looking woman. She was dressed in a miniskirt and tank top.

"You can't have him. I'm having his baby."

Pippa dropped her jaw. "Pardon me?"

"You can't have Robert. He belongs to me. He's all excited about being with a princess, but it will pass. He'll come back to me. He has to," she said and began to sob.

Pippa instinctively gathered the girl into her arms and glanced searchingly at Nic. "You're getting too upset," she said.

"He belongs to me. I'm having his baby," the young woman continued to sob. "He belongs to me."

"Darling, I wouldn't dream of taking Robert from you. This was just a charity appearance for both of us."

The girl pulled back, her baby blues filled with tears. "But he was so excited about being with a princess. He told me he couldn't make a commitment. Big things were coming in his future," she said, her voice fading to another sob. The woman buried her face in Pippa's shoulder again.

She met Nic's gaze again. "Please ask a server to give Robert a note. Robert's friend and I will be upstairs. He should join us immediately."

Nic lifted a dark eyebrow and dipped his head. "As you wish, Your Highness."

As soon as he turned away, she felt a rush of relief. "Let's go upstairs," she said. "I didn't hear your name."

"Chloe," she said and sniffed and swiped at her cheeks as Pippa led the way upstairs. "You're much nicer than I thought you would be. I was sure you would steal Robert from me."

"Oh, Chloe, I wouldn't dream of that," she said with complete and total honesty. She wouldn't take Robert if he was handed to her on a silver platter. She guided Chloe into a room and propped open the door.

Just a couple moments later, she heard voices coming from the hall. Nic's and Robert's. The door swung open and Nic and Robert stepped inside.

Robert's eyes widened. "Chloe, what are you doing here?"

Chloe bit her lip. "How could you leave me, Robert?"

Looking incredibly awkward, Robert shrugged his wide shoulders. "It was just temporary." He shot a quick glance at Pippa. "The princess required my presence for the charity event."

"I did not," Pippa said, unable to contain herself. She wanted to punch the scoundrel. She clenched her fists.

"Okay, well, I had to show for the charity event. The princess was just a bonus," he amended.

Nic cleared his throat. "I think Chloe has some important news to share."

Chloe gulped and appeared to force a smile. "I'm having your baby," she said.

Pippa looked at Robert and saw the tall, strong athlete turn as pale as ghost. "Baby?" he echoed.

"Yes, I'm having your baby," Chloe said and walked toward him.

Robert fainted backward. Nic caught him just before he would have hit the floor.

Pippa sighed, crossing her arms over her chest. "Are we going to have to call the medics, too?"

"Let's try something a little more basic," Nic said. "Can you get a glass of water?"

She glanced around the room and saw a stack of paper cups and pointed at them. "There's a water fountain in the hall."

"I'll take care of it," Chloe said.

"Get two cups," Nic said and gently lowered Robert's head to the carpeted floor.

Chloe ran out of the room. Seconds later, she returned.

"I think you should have the honors," he said to Chloe.

"What do you mean?" she asked, clearly confused.

"Throw the water in his face," he said.

Chloe's eyes widened in alarm. "In his face."

"It's the best thing for him," he said.

"Are you sure?"

"Couldn't be more sure," he said. "If you don't do it, then I will."

Chloe took a deep breath and threw a cup in Robert's face.

The athlete blinked and shook his head.

"It worked," Chloe said with a delighted smile. "You were right."

Nic nodded and extended his hand. "Can you give me the second cup?"

"Of course," she said and gave it to him.

"You coming around, Speight?" Nic said as the man lifted his head.

"Yeah," he said, rubbing his hand over his face. "Why am I wet?"

"So many reasons," Nic said. "You okay? Are you conscious?"

Robert lifted himself up on his elbows. "Yeah, I'm good."

Nic nodded and dumped the second cup of water on Robert's head.

Robert scowled and swore. "Why the hell did you do that?"

"In Texas we would say you need a good scrubbin'," he said in his Texas drawl. "I just thought I'd get you started. Pops."

After Robert pulled himself back together and dried himself with some paper towels, he returned to the ballroom and Nic arranged for a car to take Chloe back to her hotel.

Pippa felt the pressure of passing time. She knew her absence would be noted if she didn't return soon, but she wanted to thank Nic for his help. After stepping just outside the door, he returned and strode toward her.

"You okay?" he asked, his dark gaze intent on her.

She laughed. "Of course I'm fine, thank you. I wasn't the least bit enamored of Robert from the beginning."

Nic walked closer. "Are you sure about that?"

Pippa frowned. "Of course I'm sure. Do you really think I could be so easily won over by a man just because he's a world-famous soccer player?"

"You fell for me pretty quickly in the beginning," he said, lowering his mouth to half a breath away from hers.

Her heart skipped. "I was young and foolish."

He laughed, and the deep, hearty sound echoed inside her, making her feel alive. "It was six months ago."

"Eight months," she corrected.

He lifted a brow. "I didn't know you were counting."

She opened her mouth, but at the moment, she couldn't deny... Anything.

His mouth brushed hers, and the sensation made her felt as if she were melting and blooming at the same time. His mouth searched, plundered and empowered hers. She felt sensual, womanly, and it sounded crazy, but she felt as if she could fly. It was such an amazing, euphoric sensation that she didn't want it to ever end. During a moment that felt like centuries or seconds, she slid her arms around Nic and reveled in the strength of his body. It seemed to flow into hers.

She craved more of the feeling. There was more, she thought. More...

Nic pulled back slightly. "Let me take you away," he whispered. "For just a while."

Every fiber of her wanted to say yes, but her duty and obligation screamed no. "I want—" She took a breath and tried to clear her head. "They're expecting me for the end of the dinner. After twelve minutes, people start to notice when a royal is gone." She swallowed over the craziness rolling through her, but she fought the drowning sensation she felt when she stared into his eyes. "They actually notice before that, but if there's a distraction such as a famous soccer player, we get a bit more time."

"After the dinner, then," he said.

Her stomach dipped as if her amusement park ride had abruptly plunged and risen and plunged again. "Oh," she said. "Uh, I—" She broke off and shook her head. "This is crazy. We tried it before. It didn't work out."

"Why?" he asked, his gaze wrapping around hers and holding it.

She opened her mouth to answer, but the words stopped in her throat.

"What's the problem, Princess Pippa? Cat got your tongue?" he asked and kissed her again.

Pippa melted again, feeling as if she were having an out-of-body experience. His arms felt better than chocolate, his mouth, the same. She felt as powerful as the ocean. She clung to him, but duty tugged at her. It was so ingrained that she couldn't quite forget it.

Pippa pulled back. "I have to go."

"Chicken," he said.

Something inside her wanted to prove him wrong. "Blast you," she whispered, and wiped her mouth as she ran from the room.

Although she was bloody distracted, Pippa finished the interminable evening. With photos, but no passionate kisses. She took a separate limo to return to the palace, all the while consumed with thoughts of Nic. What if she could have met him? Where? She felt a terrible aching need to be with him, but she knew she couldn't. For a thousand reasons. She arrived to find Bridget waiting in her quarters, bouncing with excitement.

"Tell me all about it," Bridget said. "How hot was he?"

"Too hot for me, given the fact that a, he pushed to go to a nude beach."

Bridget's jaw dropped.

"B, he wanted to French kiss me in public for the sake of getting photographs with a princess."

"Oh, my—"

"And c, congratulations are in order. The very young mother of his baby showed up at the charity event."

"He has a child?" Bridget asked, her eyes wide with horror and shock.

"He is a father-to-be. I believe the popular term is baby daddy."

Bridget gave an expression of pure disgust. "Oh, how horrible. I don't know what to say."

"Just say you won't set me up again," Pippa said. "Please."

Bridget winced. "I'm so sorry." She lifted her hands. "I just wanted you to have a little fun."

"I know your intentions were good," Pippa said. "They always are. You have a good heart and you love me. I know you love me. I just need to find my own way in this area." She decided to make a bigger push. It was her moment. "As you know, my birthday is right around the corner. Everyone is pushing for the palace to make budget cuts. I've decided I want a little more control over where I go. I'm going to request more limited security."

Bridget shook her head, fear filling her eyes. "Oh, no, you can't do that. Not after what almost happened to me. Not after what happened to Eve."

"If you recall, you actually had security when you were leaving that charity event when you were almost stampeded by that gang. I think it makes sense to follow what other royal families are doing. I'm *way* down the list to take the throne and heaven knows I have no interest. Current practices suggest I be given security for official events with a panic button for my use at all times. Do you know how much the head of security grilled me because I took a walk on a family beach last week?"

"It's the social media," Bridget said. "People with camera phones are everywhere, tweeting, taking photos. You can't possibly expect anonymity or privacy, Phillipa."

"It doesn't help to have security nipping at my heels every minute," Pippa said.

"I thought you had a soft spot for your security man. You seemed to have an easy enough relationship with Giles before, well—" Bridget broke off. "Before the Lafitte incident."

Pippa felt her irritation grow. In the past, she would have just sighed and fallen silent. "All of you made entirely too much of a fuss. Can you honestly say you never dated someone Stefan would have considered inappropriate?"

"Stefan considers any man he doesn't choose to be inappropriate," Bridget scoffed and began to pace.

"He almost didn't approve of Ryder until he figured out Ryder could be the new health minister. But Lafitte was different. His family—" Bridget shook her head. "There's just too much bad history between his family and ours. Plus his father had to have been a terrible influence on him."

"Some people might say the same about the influence our father had on us," Pippa muttered.

Bridget shot her a sharp look. "What are you saying?"

"I'm saying I want my personal business to be my business. I'm saying I want to make my own decisions about security and dating."

"We just all adore you and we don't want you to be hurt," Bridget said.

"I realize that, but I'm not four years old. I'm a grown woman. I may be the youngest daughter, but I don't need all of you looking after everything in my life. I want you, Tina and Stefan to stop it. Now." She barely kept herself from stomping her foot for emphasis.

Bridget blinked, then sighed. "You may be able to persuade Tina and me, but good luck with Stefan."

It was a good thing she didn't care what the tabloids said about her, because she would have become extremely depressed the following day. Princess Phillipa Dumped by Soccer Player the headline read with photos from the charity event and her impromptu visit last week on the beach. Not cover-girl shots. Pippa had always shrunk from any potential emphasis of her image. She was no fashion leader, that was certain. Her sisters Fredericka and Bridget had seemed to do enough of that for everyone, thank goodness. It had taken the focus off her. Her other sister, Valentina, had been a bit less fashionable, more normal in her figure and ultimately more concerned with relationships than her image.

That was probably the reason the weight of royal appearances had worn heavy on Tina's shoulders and she'd become the wife of a Texas businessman rancher. Tina made occasional appearances for the family and attended to a few royal duties, but her focus was happily fixed on her marriage and young daughter. Over the years, Pippa had filled in the gaps on the schedule or substituted when one of her siblings couldn't make an event.

She hadn't spent a lot of time thinking about what she truly wanted for herself because she'd been so busy finding ways to avoid causing trouble or being in the spotlight. Ever since she'd gotten involved with Nic all those months ago, she found herself fighting a restlessness that seemed to grow worse every day. She wished it would go away. She'd thought once she'd broken off with Nic that she could go back to normal, but normal didn't fit anymore. Sipping a cup of tea and sitting inside the small suite where she'd lived since she was a teen, she stared outside her window to one of the palace courtyards and felt like a caged bird. She didn't like the feeling at all.

Taking a deep breath, she prepared herself for her meeting with her brother Stefan. He'd requested the meeting first thing this morning. She suspected he had something on his mind and she intended to do what she'd heard Eve say on more than one occasion. Pippa was going to give her brother, the crown prince of Chantaine, a piece of *her* mind.

She walked down the long hallway to the opposite wing of the palace, then up the stairs to the office where her brother worked. On rare occasions, her father had also worked here.

Her brother was a working prince and he'd spent most of his adult life living down their father's yachting playboy prince image. All the Devereaux children had been raised to understand that duty was first and foremost. Some had accepted the duty more easily than others.

Pippa lifted her hand to knock on the door.

Stefan's assistant immediately responded with a slight bow. "Good morning, Your Highness. His Highness is ready for you."

"Thank you," she said and walked through the outer office into Stefan's office.

Stefan stood and smiled. "Thank you for coming on such short notice," he said and moved from behind his desk to embrace her.

Pippa hugged him in return, noting he wore a suit, signaling he had other official meetings today. "As if you would let me refuse you," Pippa gently teased him, taking in the office. The decor combined the history of the Devereauxs with Stefan's interests in horses, his studies in leadership and economics and a few of Eve's homey touches from Texas.

She also noticed a wooden toy on the corner of his desk and pointed at it. "For Stephenia?" she asked, smiling as she thought of his toddler daughter.

"Eve and the nanny bring her to visit. I like to have

at least a couple things in the room that she's allowed to touch. I don't want her to remember my office as the no-no room," he said.

"I like that," Pippa said. "It's a lot different than the way we were raised."

Stefan nodded. "That's the plan. Please have a seat."

Pippa sat on the edge of one of the leather chairs. She would have preferred to remain standing. Standing somehow made her feel stronger. "How is Eve?" she asked.

His eyes lit at the mention of his wife's name. "A bit of nausea and I think she's more tired than usual, but she's trying not to let me see it. I've asked her assistant to limit the number of invitations she accepts. We'll see how long that works. She can be as stubborn as—" He broke off. "As I am."

Pippa laughed. "One of the many things we love about her."

Stefan nodded, then turned serious and she could tell he was going to start discussing the reason he'd invited her to his office. "I'd like to go first, please," she said breathlessly.

His eyes flickered in surprise and he paused a half beat, then gave a slow nod. "All right. Go ahead."

Pippa took a teeny, tiny breath and clenched her hands together. "My birthday is next week," she said.

Stefan smiled. "I know. That was part of the reason I asked you here."

"Really," she said. "Well, I've been thinking about this a lot and I believe I'm ready to drop my security back to official events only."

Stefan stared, again in surprise.

"It's really the current trend among royals and I know you're trying to keep us up-to-date. All of our expenses are being scrutinized by the government and the press, and I think it would be an excellent way to show that we can be economical."

Pippa sat back and waited for Stefan to respond.

"I'll take it under advisement. However, my first response is no. With the brawl Bridget and Eve faced last year, we've learned that we can't count on all our citizens behaving in a welcoming or even civil manner."

"If you'll recall, that was an official event and security was present."

His eyes narrowed with irritation and dark memories. Pippa understood the dark memories. Stefan had been falling in love with Eve when she'd been injured. "I said I would take it under advisement, but you must understand that I regard your protection as a very serious responsibility."

"I appreciate that very much," she said. "But I'm insisting."

He tilted his head to one side in shock. "Pardon me?"

Pippa's stomach clenched. She knew that expression. He'd used it far more often with Bridget because her older sister had felt perfectly free to argue with Stefan. Pippa, on the other hand, avoided arguments like the plague. Except this time.

"I said I'm insisting. I don't do a lot of insisting, but I am this time. And I think you should also know I'm considering moving out of the palace."

Another shocked silence stretched between her and her brother.

"And how do you plan to pay for this apartment?" he challenged.

"I earn a small stipend with the research I do, and I have a savings account. It's true most of my clothes have been provided by the palace, but I don't need a different dress every day. It's not as if everyone is watching every move I make."

"You underestimate how interested our people are in you," he said. "As evidenced by the crowd you drew during your impulsive walk on the beach last week."

Pippa winced. She wondered who had ratted on her. It wasn't as if Stefan spent a lot of time on internet social sites. "Yes, and everyone was perfectly polite."

"You'll be entirely too vulnerable if you were to move away from the palace," he said.

"Entirely too vulnerable to what? I would still have a panic button and I could have alarms set up in an apartment. Admit it. Jacques will be of age soon enough and you would allow him to live away from the palace."

"That's different," Stefan said. "He'll be a young man and would feel trapped here."

"The same way I feel trapped," Pippa said.

Stefan looked as if he'd been slapped and she felt a stab of regret. "I thought you liked having access to the family, the twins and Stephenia, the family dinners."

"I do," she said. "I love my nieces and nephews. I love my family. There's no reason I still can't babysit and attend family dinners. I just need some space."

Stefan sighed, then straightened his shoulders. "Perhaps you just need a break. When I tell you what I have planned for you, I know you'll be pleased."

Pippa felt her stomach twist with dread. There was

always a catch involved when Stefan had a *plan*. "No, really," she began.

He held up his hand. "You've had your turn. Now it's mine. I've arranged for you to take a holiday to the coast of Italy for your birthday."

Pippa immediately thought of Amelie and shook her head. "That's a lovely thought, but this isn't a good time for me to take a holiday. Due to my studies," she added.

"It's only for a few days and the break will be good for you. You'll have only two appearances to make during your trip. One celebrating the anniversary of a museum and the other will be a christening ceremony for a new cruise ship that will be making stops in Chantaine. I've arranged for an escort for you. Count Salvatore Bianchi. He's a bit older than you, but his family is considering opening several wineshops here, so we'd like to further that relationship. And who knows? Perhaps the two of you will hit it off," Stefan said, wearing his most charming smile.

Pippa felt a twist of suspicion. "Just how much older is Count Bianchi?"

Stefan shrugged. "I'm not sure. He's a widow with children. I believe one of them goes to school with Jacques." Jacques, her nineteen-year-old brother.

"So what you're saying is he could be my father," Pippa said.

"Age is just a number, Pippa. I assure you that you'll have more in common with the count than the soccer player Bridget arranged as your escort. My assistant will give you your itinerary later today and the palace stylist will help you with your attire for the trip."

"And if I don't want to go?" Pippa said.

"The arrangements have been made. People will be expecting you. Besides, I can tell by our discussion today that you need this holiday. You *will* enjoy it," he said and stood.

"Because His Royal Highness decreed it," she muttered and also rose.

A flicker of irritation passed over Stefan's face. "I've always counted on you for your sweetness."

She felt a quick surge of pain at the prospect of disappointing Stefan. "I'm sorry. I'll go on the trip, but Stefan you need to understand that it won't change my intentions regarding my security and moving out."

"We'll see," he said.

Chapter Seven

Two days later, Pippa managed to make her way to the Lafittes' temporary cottage. She drove the rickety car from the library wearing the terrible disguise over her clothes and pulled off the wig as soon as she pulled into the cottage driveway. Unbuttoning the too-large matronly blouse, she stepped out of the car and pushed down the hideous skirt.

She heard a wolf whistle and glanced up to see Nic smiling at her as he leaned against the guest quarters door wearing jeans and a black T-shirt that outlined his broad shoulders and muscular arms. "Don't stop now," he said, referring to her awkward striptease.

She bundled up the disguise in her arms and rolled her eyes as she walked toward him. "I despise this outfit."

"But it gets the job done," he said.

Unable to argue his point, she pushed open the gate. "How is your mother?" she asked.

"Restless. She may need an outing," he said. "A short one. Any ideas?"

"I'll think of something. Have you made any headway with your brothers?"

"Heard from one and I'm hounding the others. I may have to resort to unconventional methods of getting their attention."

She shot a sharp glance at him and he shook his head. "You don't want to know."

"Actually, I do," she said. "I may need to use subversive tactics with my own family at some point."

She felt his glance at her, but didn't meet his gaze. "Okay. I'll send a fake officer to stop them on their way to work. This officer will deliver a message."

She met his gaze. "That's drastic."

Nic shrugged. "Drastic times…"

She couldn't help smiling at his creativity. "Well done."

He shot her a half grin. "It's only the first step. I have others planned if this doesn't work."

She nodded. "What are we doing with Amelie this afternoon?"

"I don't know. Depends on her mood."

"How is her appetite?"

"Temperamental at best," he said.

"Maybe she'll take a few bites of gelato."

"You'll have to put on your disguise again," he reminded her.

"I know. I want to cool off until then."

Nic opened the door for her and she stepped inside

the cool foyer. Pippa walked toward the den and saw Amelie and Paul cuddling on the sofa and watching television. She hesitated to interrupt, but Paul glanced up at her.

"Hey, y'all come on in," he said.

Amelie glanced up at her. "It's Pippa!"

The delight in Amelie's voice grabbed at her heart. "Yes, I'm here for just a while."

"We should have another adventure," Amelie said.

Nic gave a low groan from behind her.

Pippa smothered a smile. "We should plan something."

"I want to do something now," Amelie said. "Paul is feeling better tonight."

Pippa remembered her earlier suggestion. "Would you like some gelato?"

Amelie's face lit up. "Perfect." She turned to Paul. "Do you think you can manage a ride in the car?"

"I can do anything for you," Paul said. "And gelato sounds good, too," he said with a rough chuckle.

Pippa's heart twisted at the obvious love that flowed between the two of them. Reluctantly, she put on her costume again. The four of them got into Goldie's SUV and drove to Chantaine's best gelato shop. They ordered ten flavors. Amelie took a teeny bite of each of them. When they returned, both Amelie and Paul were worn out.

Pippa stripped off her disguise again. "I hate this disguise," she muttered to Nic as they sat by the pool. "I think I hated it from the beginning," she said. "Do you think your mother enjoyed the outing?"

He nodded. "My father did, too. They won't admit it, but it helps if the trip is a short one."

"How do you think your father is dealing with your mother's illness?" she asked.

"Depends on the day. Sometimes he's in denial. Other days he's trying to grab the moment. He's definitely not fit for making business decisions."

"So you're doing that for him?" she asked.

He nodded, his head still resting against the chair, his eyes closed.

"He's lucky to have you stepping in for him," she said.

"Someone has to," Nic said.

She stared at Nic as he sat in the chair, in his jeans and T-shirt, his head tilted back. "But why you?" she asked.

He cracked open an eyelid. "Because no one else would."

"Does that mean you would have preferred to let one of your brothers take on this challenge?"

"I would have preferred to have just about anyone take on the challenge, but I knew no one would. My father is an ex-con. Trust in his business is precarious at best. I have to both check behind him and authenticate his company to his customers."

"If his business is so precarious, how are your mother and he surviving so well?"

Silence settled between them, making Pippa wonder about the mysteries of Nic's family. Suddenly, it dawned on her. "You're taking care of them, aren't you?"

Nic sighed. "His business has huge potential, but with the economy and his reputation, it's a struggle."

Pippa thought about all Nic was trying to do for his parents and felt an overwhelming sense of admiration and something deeper, something she couldn't quite name, for Nic. "You're quite the amazing son."

"You would do the same in my circumstance," he said.

Pippa shook her head. "I wouldn't know how to do everything you're doing," she protested. "Plus my relationship with my parents wasn't half what yours is."

Nic pulled his head from the back of the chair and met her gaze. "But you were there at the end."

Pippa took a deep breath, remembering both of her parents' deaths, and nodded. "Most of us were. Stefan and Valentina pulled us together. It wasn't easy. I think they suffered because of it."

Nic nodded. "It's a tough time. If there are more people, there's a bigger cushion."

"But you have none," she said.

He shrugged and cracked a grin. "I'm from tough stock. We've had to scrabble for everything. No royalty in my blood."

"Hmm," she said. "Bet there is. Just about everyone has a bit of royalty in their background."

He chuckled. "You would know. Your Highness genealogist. Bet you can get me that information by next week."

Pippa's feeling of lightness sank. "Not next week now that Stefan is sending me on a trip," she said glumly.

"Where?"

"The place isn't the bad part. It's my escort."

Stefan's eyes widened. "Another escort?"

"Yes, that's what I said. I also told him I want to

ditch my security and move into an apartment away from the palace."

"Bet that went over well," Nic said in a dry tone.

She laughed. "Not at all. He ignored me."

Nic nodded. "You may have to go ahead and make your move before he has approved. And be prepared to be have your title taken away. Stefan is known for his priority on loyalty."

Her heart twisted at his words. He'd described Stefan perfectly. "I hate the idea of disappointing him. He's always counted on me not to cause any trouble."

"Sometimes you have to cause trouble if you're going to be who you're meant to be," Nic said.

His words vibrated through her. "When did you learn that?"

"When I was about eight years old," he said.

She smiled. "Wise words."

"Children are wiser more often than not. Where are you headed and when?"

"Capri, Italy, in three days. This is supposed to be a birthday gift, but I have to make two appearances and I have an escort who has a child as old as my youngest brother."

"Stefan's idea?" he said more than asked.

"Yes, they're trying to make a match. Bridget was trying to give me a hot, young sports guy. Stefan is always about the man who can bring added value to Chantaine. Ultimately, he was thrilled that Bridget fell for a doctor who became our medical director."

"But you have to live with the choices," Nic said.

She nodded. "I do."

"My mother will be crushed if we don't get a chance to celebrate your birthday," he said.

Pippa racked her brain for a time she could break away. "Friday afternoon."

"Night," he said.

She blinked at him. "Night?" she echoed. "How am I supposed to do that?" she asked.

"Creativity, ingenuity," he said. "You're a Devereaux," he said in a slightly mocking voice. "You can do it."

Pippa sighed. "I'll try to figure it out," she said. "I need to put on my disguise so I can return to the library."

"Unless you want to stay here," he said, his tone seductive.

Pippa wanted to stay far more than she should admit to anyone, including herself.

Nic told his mother about Pippa's birthday and she immediately asked Goldie to make a cake and instructed him to get ice cream and noise-making toys. At seven o'clock on Friday, Pippa arrived in a rush, wearing her horrid costume, and he'd never seen a more welcome sight. Greeting her at the gate, he helped her disassemble her disguise.

"You have no idea what I had to do to make this happen," she said, ripping off her wig and raking her fingers through her hair. She pulled a band from her wrist and pulled her hair up into a ponytail.

"We'll make it worth it," he said and led her toward the front door of the cottage. He knocked first.

She frowned at him. "Why are you knocking?" she asked.

"Don't discourage me. I'm being polite."

"Oh," she said, realization crossing over her face.

"Come in," a female voice called.

"Amelie is awake," she said.

Nic opened the door and Pippa walked inside.

"Surprise!" the small group cried. Streamers filled the air.

Pippa gaped. "Oh, my goodness." She clasped one of the streamers in her hand. She clearly couldn't help grinning. "How cool is this. You shouldn't have done it. I didn't expect it."

"We wanted to celebrate," Amelie said. "You deserved a party. Bring the cake, Goldie."

Seconds later, Goldie carried in a birthday cake with lit candles.

"Is that a fire hazard?" Nic joked.

Pippa frowned at him, then returned her gaze to the cake. "Oh, wow," she whispered.

Nic felt a ripple of pleasure at her obvious delight. "Ready to blow out those candles, Princess? Make a wish," he coached next to her ear.

"Just one?" she asked.

He chuckled. "As many wishes as you can fit in while you're putting out the candles."

"Okay," she said and bit her lip. She inhaled deeply and blew out the candles. Milliseconds after they were snuffed out, she looked at him and smiled. "I did it."

"So you did," he said.

"Time to cut the cake, eat the gelato, open gifts," Amelie said.

"Gifts," Pippa echoed. "There weren't supposed to be any gifts."

"Why not?" Amelie asked. "If there are birthday parties, there should be gifts."

Goldie served the cake and gelato, along with champagne. Mr. Lafitte then presented Pippa with a wrapped box.

"It's from me," Paul said.

"Really?" Pippa said and unwrapped the gift which held a box of chocolates and a bottle of champagne, along with a gift certificate to one of her favorite local shops.

"You did too much," she said, clearly surprised and delighted. "I didn't expect this."

"We Lafittes like the element of surprise. Don't forget that," he said with a broad wink.

"Thank you, Mr. Lafitte," she said and brushed a kiss over his cheek.

"Call me Paul, sweetheart," he said.

"Thank you, Paul," she said and another gift was given to her. She opened it to find a long knitted scarf.

Her eyes filled with tears, Pippa looked at Amelie. "Oh, no, you didn't."

"I fear I did," Amelie said with a laugh in her voice. "I realize it's not the best handiwork, but hopefully my effort will warm your heart."

"I will treasure it," Pippa said through a tight throat. She tried to remember when she'd had a birthday that had made her feel more special. She couldn't. For various reasons, her birthday had often been overlooked. There had been conflicting schedules. Her brothers and sisters had been busy. There were always more pressing obligations.

Tonight, however, she was the most important part of the Lafittes' evening. "I don't know what to say. You are—" Her voice broke and she swallowed hard over the lump of emotion lodging in her throat. "You have no idea how special this is for me."

"Bet you had gourmet cakes and birthday balls," Paul said.

"I had birthday cakes and birthday balls, but only a couple of times. My parents were rarely around for my birthdays. It was also sporadic for my brothers and sisters. Everyone was so busy," she said and shrugged, fearing she'd revealed too much. She bit her lip and smiled. "But this is fabulous. You've made me feel so special."

"That's because you *are* special," Amelie said and reached to embrace her.

Pippa hugged the woman and Amelie's gaunt frame frightened her. She was so thin. She felt so fragile. At the same time, Pippa had learned that Amelie was a strong, strong woman.

Goldie poured her another glass of champagne, but Pippa asked for water. She had to drive back to the palace.

"This has been delightful," Amelie said. "But I'm pooped. Tomorrow I'll be stronger, though, I promise," she said, wagging her finger.

"Of course you will," Pippa said. "I would expect nothing less. I have to go away for a few days, though, so I'll check in when I return."

Amelie frowned. "Away? We'll miss you."

"I'll miss you, too," Pippa said, hating the prospect of leaving the Lafittes behind. With Amelie in such fragile health, Pippa wondered if something would happen to her when she was gone on the Italian holiday.

"Good night, darling. Happy birthday," Amelie said. Paul followed, giving her a kiss on her cheek.

After they left, Pippa turned to Nic. "I should probably go."

"You didn't finish your cake," he said.

How could she? she wondered. She could barely breathe, let alone swallow Goldie's cake.

"You're gonna hurt Goldie's feelings," Nic added.

She winced. "I can't eat that entire cake," she whispered.

"Let's take part of it to the guest quarters. That should help," he said. "Bring your champagne."

She shook her head. "I have to drive back to the palace," she said.

"I'll handle that," he said.

"How?" she asked.

He shrugged. "Trust me."

Pippa decided, for once, to trust him. Heaven knew, she'd seen an entirely different side of him with the way he was dealing with his mother's illness. "Lead me on," she said, lifting her glass of champagne.

She followed him out the door and he led her into the guest bungalow. A breeze flowed through the window, more delicious than any central air-conditioning could ever be. "This feels nice in here. Have you had a hard time adjusting to the small quarters?"

"There are interruptions from my parents when I'm

working sometimes, but for the most part, I've liked it. I don't need that much space," he said.

She laughed. "I'm thinking of your yacht. It's huge."

"That's different," he said.

"And your ranch in Texas?" she asked. "Your big, big ranch? Is that different, too?"

"And your big, big palace?" he returned.

"I live in a small suite in the big, big palace," she said. "And I'm prepared to live in a small apartment."

"Why are you making the big move now?"

She shrugged and moved around the small den of the bungalow. "It's overdue. It just took me a while to see that."

"Have a seat," Nic said from behind her.

Too aware of his presence, she felt a dozen butterflies dancing in her stomach. She sank down onto the sofa and took a sip of her second glass of champagne. Nic sat beside her holding the plate with her piece of cake and soft gelato.

"It was better a few minutes ago," he said, scooping up a bite with a spoon and lifting it to her mouth.

She opened her mouth and swallowed the sweet treat. "It really is delicious. Goldie could be a bakery chef."

"Goldie is a lot of things," Nic said. "Bodyguard, medic, mechanic, cook. Hell, he would make a great nanny."

She smiled. "He's so big and brawny. That's a funny image." She took another bite of cake.

"All packed for your holiday?"

The cake stuck in her throat and she coughed. Nic handed her the glass of champagne. She took a quick sip, then shook her head. "No, I've procrastinated. The palace stylist chose some things for me, so I'll take them. I hate to admit it, but I'm dreading it, which is ridiculous. Who wouldn't be happy with a trip to Capri?" She made a face. "But with those appearances and the fact that I'm supposed to spend time with the count, it doesn't feel like a holiday. It feels like an assignment."

"Do you have any free time?"

"The last day," she said.

"I could meet you," he said.

Her heart stopped, then started at his suggestion. "Oh, that would be—" *Fantastic,* she thought before she stifled herself. "We shouldn't. I'm sure my bodyguard will be there."

He shrugged. "We could get around him," he said. "But if you'd rather not—"

"Are you sure you can leave Amelie?" she asked.

He nodded. "She's been fairly stable. It would be just a day or two. To be honest, I have business with a colleague in Rome. I've been putting it off. I could take care of business, then meet you in Capri."

Although she knew it was insanity to even consider a secret rendezvous, Pippa could not make herself say no. She opened her mouth to try to form the word and her lips refused. Her whole body and being wanted to be with Nic and she was bloody tired of denying herself. "Yes," she finally said and closed her eyes. "But this could be messy. You know that, don't you?"

Nic laughed. "I've been dealing with messes since I was six years old."

She wondered what it was about Nic that made her feel stronger. When she was with him, she felt as if she could do almost anything.

He met her gaze and he must have read her feelings in her eyes. Pulling her slowly toward him, he gave her a dozen chances to turn away, but she didn't. She couldn't. But she couldn't help wondering why he continued to pursue her. He was experienced. He could have any woman he wanted.

"Do you want me just because you can't have me?" she whispered, the fear squeezing out of her throat.

"No," he said. "Besides, we both know I can and will have you. The question is when," he said and lowered his mouth to hers.

Pippa melted into him. She was afraid to trust him, afraid to trust her feelings because she never really had before, but her fear of missing him was bigger than her fear of trusting him.

She kissed him back with all the passion in her heart and felt his surprise and pleasure ripple through her. He paused just a half beat before he kissed her more thoroughly.

She slid her fingers through his hair, craving the sensation of being as close to him as possible. He leaned back on the sofa and pulled her on top of him. She felt his arousal, swollen against her, and the knowledge made her even more crazy. She squeezed his shoulders and biceps and shuddered against him as he took her mouth in yet another kiss that took her upside down.

Pippa couldn't remember feeling this way. Even though she and Nic had been involved before, they'd never gone all the way. Now she wondered how she could possibly fight how much she wanted him.

She felt his hand tenderly rub her back. "Hey, you

know where this is headed, don't you?" he asked against her mouth.

Pippa moved her mouth from his and buried her head in his shoulder, taking desperate breaths.

"Pippa, are you sure you're ready?" he asked.

He wasn't going to make it easy for her. He was going to make her choose. And maybe that was part of the reason she wanted him so much. It was time.

She lifted her head to meet his gaze. "Yes, I am."

He sucked in a quick, sharp breath and chuckled. "I'm ready, too, but I want you to think about it a little longer."

Pippa blinked. "Pardon me, are you refusing to be with me?"

He rose to a sitting position with his arms still around her. "I don't want you to do something impulsive and regret it."

Anger flickered through her and she narrowed her eyes. "You sound like my family. You sound like you don't trust me to make my own decisions."

"It's not that. I'm protecting you," he said.

"That's what they say, too," she said. "No one trusts me to make my own decisions. No one," she said and pushed away from him.

"I'm going home," she said.

"I have to drive you," he said. "You've had too much champagne."

Pippa stood, wrapping her arms around her waist, feeling humiliated. "Goldie can take me."

"I will take you," Nic said, rising.

Pippa bit her lip, feeling rejected and vulnerable. She wanted to hide.

"Pippa, you know I want you," he said and cupped her chin with his hand. "How much of a demonstration do you need?"

She swallowed over the desire pulsing through her. "It seems so easy for you to turn it off," she whispered.

He took her hand and placed it over his chest where his heart thundered against her palm. "Does that feel easy? I can show you more," he said as he moved her hand to his hard abdomen.

"S'okay," she said breathlessly.

"What do you want?" he asked.

"You've confused me," she said, clinging to him.

"Well, damn," he said. "Why would I do that?"

She looked up, studying his face. "I thought you would be the ruthless type when it comes to sex."

He held her against him for a long moment. "I am, but for some reason just not with you," he said.

Confusion and a half dozen other feelings swarmed through her like bees. The part of her that knew she was no beauty queen stabbed her with self-doubt. Pippa had made it a practice not to think about image, but all the criticism she'd received from the press over the years suddenly bombarded her. Maybe she wasn't sexy enough. Even though he'd been aroused, he'd been able to stop without a great deal of effort. At the same time, she'd lost all sense of time and place and could have gone much further without a second thought.

Self-conscious, she pulled away. "I really should get back to the palace," she said.

"Pippa—"

"I don't want to talk right now, if that's okay. I have

so much I need to do in a short amount of time to get ready for this trip."

With Goldie following in another vehicle, Nic drove her to the palace, and the silence between them was so uncomfortable that Pippa could barely stand it. Yes, she knew she'd told him she didn't want to talk, but now she would be leaving for her holiday, and she would just be full of doubts. Maybe it was for the best. Maybe this had been a close call and she could get her head back on straight with this trip.

He stopped a block away from the palace. "Can you make it the rest of the way?"

"Of course," she said. Overwhelmed by all the feelings tugging her in different directions, Pippa bit her lip. "Thank you for the birthday celebration and the ride to the palace. Listen, there's no need for you to make a special trip to Capri. I'll be there only a day and—"

"Are you saying you don't want me to come?" he asked, his gaze dark and penetrating.

She took a deep breath. "I'm saying you know my situation. I may not be able to spend time with you. The decision is completely up to you. *Ciao,*" she said and got out of the passenger side of the car.

Chapter Eight

Pippa arrived in Italy the next day. Count Bianchi greeted her at the airport. He was nearly bald with a paunch, but she tried very hard not to compare him to Nic. It was difficult because she had begun to compare every man to Nic.

"A pleasure to meet you, Your Highness," he said.

"And you, Count Bianchi," she said.

"Please call me Sal," he said. "You're such a lovely young woman. I'm pleased to have you by my side."

"Thank you very much, Sal," she said. "Tell me about your children."

During the ride, to Sal's chateau, she learned that Sal's oldest child was, in fact, older than her by five years. Sal also had several grandchildren. He showed her several photos and mentioned his wish to marry again.

Pippa rode the fence by praising his children but not

encouraging any discussion of her interest in him. After
a quick respite in her room, she shared dinner with him
in his formal dining room. Finally, they made the trip to
the museum where Pippa made a brief speech encouraging historical and genealogical research.

Pippa begged off when Sal invited her to join him
for a nightcap.

The following day, she geared up for a ride on a
yacht, complete with photos. Afterward, she helped
christen a new cruise ship with the count by her side.
Every second, she damned Stefan for arranging this.
Someone had clearly given the count entirely too much
hope and she had to find a way to let him down easy. A
chauffeur drove them back to his estate after the event.

"Have you enjoyed yourself?" the count asked, leaning toward her.

Pippa discreetly scooted away. "It's certainly been a
long day. I'm more than ready for a good night of sleep."

"I understand you'll be in my country tomorrow
night," the count said. "I would love to show you Capri.
I know several restaurants and beaches that might
please you."

"I couldn't trouble you," she said. "You've already
done too much for me."

The count sighed.

"Sal, may I ask you? How long has it been since your
wife passed away?" she asked.

He looked at her in surprise. "Ten months and three
days."

She smiled and took his hand. "You're still counting days," she said gently. "I don't want to be presump-
tuous, but I don't think you're ready for a new wife. I

know you're lonely, but I encourage you to take your time. You're a good man. You deserve a good woman."

He inhaled and smiled at her. "I'm an old fool to think I could attract a young princess like you."

She shook her head. "It's not that," she rushed to assure him. "I can tell that you're still not over your wife. I'm sorry for your pain, but at the same time, I know you're fortunate to have experienced that kind of love."

"Yes, I am," he said and began to talk about his former wife. Nearly an hour later, they arrived at his home. He appeared startled by the passage of time.

"I'm sorry if I've bored you," he said, clearly chagrined.

"No apologies necessary. I treasure a good love story, and that is what you and your wife had," she said.

"You're such a warm, lovely person. I wish I were at a different place in my mourning," he said.

"The right time will come," she said and pressed a kiss against his cheek. "The right woman will come."

He gave a soft chuckle. "Funny how the young can teach us so much," he said and helped her out of the limousine. "If I can ever do anything for you, it would be my pleasure," he said and kissed her hand.

"Thank you, Count Sal. My biggest wish for you is someone who will provide comfort to your heart. In the meantime, enjoy those grandchildren."

Sal gave a light laugh. "I'll take your advice."

The following morning, Pippa left the count's estate. After her last meeting with Nic, she wasn't sure he would meet her. She'd been so temperamental. He'd been so calm. His calmness infuriated her. She felt as if she couldn't control her passion. She didn't want to feel alone in her feelings and wanted to know that he felt the same way.

As she walked into her room with a lovely view of the ocean, Pippa stood in front of the open windows and inhaled the sea air. Her resort was located just outside the busy section of the beach, so she was able to enjoy the view without the crowds thronging to the pebbled beaches. Although Chantaine had its share of rocky beaches, Pippa had to confess Capri offered breathtaking vistas of steep cliffs, narrow gorges and limestone formations.

The sight was so beautiful she thought it might just clear her mind, and that was exactly what she needed. She refused to wonder if Nic would show or not. She had one day to truly relax and enjoy herself and that was what she intended to do. Pulling on the bathing suit the palace stylist had purchased for her, she glanced in the mirror and shrugged. Not too bad, she thought, then slathered herself with sunscreen from head to toe and grabbed her cover-up.

Situated on a hill, the hotel offered several decks with lounge chairs for sunning and enjoying the gorgeous views. Pippa accepted the assistance of staff to position an umbrella over her as she reclined in a chaise longue. She stared at the rocky coastline, willing it to clear her head. It occurred to her that Amelie would have loved this. The thought made her unbearably restless. Perhaps a magazine or book, she thought, rummaging through her bag. She pulled out the book on French history she'd been reading just before bedtime during the past month.

A shadow fell over her. Another waiter, she thought. Pippa had never been one to overindulge, especially when it wasn't even lunch yet. But perhaps a mimosa... She glanced up to see Nic standing over her.

Her heart lurched and the rush of pleasure she felt was so powerful that she couldn't squeak out a sound, let alone a word of greeting. He was dressed in jeans, a shirt and a ball cap, and his expression was gently mocking.

"Still pissed?" he asked.

She could argue that he was the basis for her *irritation* and confusion, but she was so bloody glad to see him that she knew it would be a waste. "Not too much."

"That's good. You want to chill here on the deck or are you in the mood for a little adventure?"

"Adventure," she said without waiting half a beat. "I'll tell my security I'm taking a tour."

Within a half hour, she was riding on the back of a motorcycle, clinging to Nic for her very life as he zigged and zagged around the curvy streets. If Stefan or Giles knew, they would have her head. Nic took another curve and she burst out laughing at the thrill.

"What's so funny?" he yelled at her.

"I'm terrified. I've either got to scream or laugh," she yelled back.

He nodded in approval. "We're just getting started."

After a lovely but terrifying ride, Nic pulled into the driveway of a chateau with stairs descending to a dock where several boats were moored. "What now?" she asked.

"We're going for another ride, this one on the ocean. You don't get seasick, do you?" he said, taking her hand.

She shook her head. "I'm a Devereaux. It's not allowed. My father never would have permitted it," she said as she walked down the steps with him.

"What trait would he have chosen over seasickness in his children?"

"Oh, I don't know. Two heads," she joked.

He stopped and looked at her and laughed. "You ought to get out more. I think it's good for you."

"And you?" she asked.

"Haven't had a lot of time for that lately," he said, his smile fading for a second. "But we've got today and a boat at our disposal."

"How did you arrange it?" she asked.

"My friend owns this chateau. He's out of town and he said I could use the house, the boat and the pool. I have access to a ski lodge in Switzerland he has used, so it all evens out." They walked across the dock and he helped her into a boat.

"Where are we going?" she asked.

He shot her a mysterious smile. "Places you can reach only by boat."

Joining him on the motorboat, Pippa reveled in the wind in her face. Nic didn't coddle her with a slow speed or by taking it easy on the curves. The wake made the ride bumpy enough that she had to sit down a few times.

"You're a fast pilot," she shouted to him. "Have you ever raced?"

He nodded. "But now we need to get to a special place."

"What special place?" she asked.

"You'll see soon enough," he said. He glanced over

his shoulder toward her. "Come here," he said extending his hand. "Wanna drive?"

Surprised by the offer, accepted his hand and he pulled her onto the seat next to him. "We have to slow down just a bit," she said.

He lowered the speed and she took the wheel. It was her first time because heaven knew her brother wouldn't have ever permitted it, let alone security. She gripped the steering wheel with her hands and turned it away from a huge yacht headed for the port side of their craft. The wake of the yacht created ripples, making the boat bounce against the waves.

Pippa laughed at the bumpiness but held tight.

"Doing good," Nic said, placing his hand at her back. It was a steadying sensation. Supportive, but not controlling. "Head this way," he said, pointing left.

She drove several more moments, then turned the wheel over to him. "Thank you. That was glorious," she said, unable to wipe her smile from her face.

"Glad you enjoyed it," he said, then revved up the speed again. "Hold on, Your Highness."

After several minutes, Nic slowed as they drew close to a series of rocks jutting from the ocean. "Where are we going?"

"Guess," he said, slowing the speed even more.

In the distance, she saw a rowing boat. Realization hit her. "The Blue Grotto," she said, so excited she could hardly stand it. "I know it's supposed to be a huge tourist spot, but I've always wanted to see it."

"I was hoping," he said.

"But it's supposed to be incredibly crowded." She glanced at Nic. "Why is it deserted? Is there a problem?"

"I bought an hour for us. No other boats during that time," he said.

She blinked. "That would be obscenely expensive," she said. "Stefan would throw a fit if he knew."

"He doesn't have to know," Nic said with a smile. He pulled closer to the rowboat and dropped anchor. The guide from the rowboat pulled right up next to their motorboat. Nic and the guide assisted her onto the rowboat.

"Buongiorno," the man said. "I'm Roberto. I will be your guide."

"Buongiorno and *grazie,* Roberto. I'm very excited to see the Blue Grotto," she said.

Nic hopped aboard. "Just tell me you've got a great singing voice," he said and shook Roberto's hand.

Roberto's mouth lifted in a wide grin. "The best. When I tell you, you must lie down in the boat." He turned to Nic. "Hold on to your sweetheart."

Pippa sank to a sitting position. Nic sat behind her and wrapped his arms around her. "Just following orders," he said.

She laughed, feeling the same terror and exultation she'd felt on the motorcycle and the speedboat. As they drew closer to the famous cave, she and Nic reclined in the boat.

"Prepare to enter the Blue Grotto, a spectacle providing thrills since the Roman times. Statues of pagan gods rest on the floor of the grotto. Once inside, you will see a surreal view that will make you feel as if you are floating through a clear sky. The reflection of the sunlight produces a unique transparency. There is no bluer blue," Roberto said. "Stay low, then you may sit up for a few minutes."

Sitting cradled in Nic's arms, Pippa stared in wonder at the blue universe on which they floated. They could have been riding on the sky if not for the lapping sound of the ocean against the cave walls.

"Put your hands in the water," Roberto said.

Both Nic and Pippa dipped their fingers into the cool water.

"It's so beautiful," she said.

"As are you, *signorina,*" he said, and began to sing *"Bella Notte."* The acoustics were amazing. She almost didn't want to breathe because she didn't want to miss a nuance of the experience. Surrounded by Nic's strength and the wonder of the Blue Grotto, Pippa wanted to absorb everything. This was the kind of magic she wanted to store up inside her for sad, bad days.

When Roberto sang the last note, she glanced up at Nic. "This was amazing," she said.

"Quite a show," he said and took her mouth in a kiss.

After they boarded the motorboat, Nic took them back to the chateau. "Are you starving?" he asked. "My friend offered me anything in his pantry and refrigerator, but I thought we'd order takeout. The view is great and I thought you'd just as soon skip a public restaurant."

"That sounds perfect," she said and joined him as they climbed the steps to the chateau. Chugging her water, she sank onto a chair on the patio which overlooked the sea and sighed in contentment as she heard Nic call in an order to a restaurant.

Nic sat down across from her, lifting a bottle of beer to his lips. "You like Capri?"

"How could I not?" she said and shook her head. "I've never had a day like this."

"It was pretty good, wasn't it?"

"That's an understatement, and you know it," she said.

He chuckled at her response.

"Perhaps you do these kinds of things on a far more regular basis," she said.

"I've had some thrills, but the person you share it with can make a big difference," he said. "You need to make any calls to your security guy?"

She made a face at the reminder. "He said for me to call him when I returned to my room." She drummed her fingers on the table. "I suppose I could tell him I've returned and I'm safe and sound."

"Your choice," he said and took another drink from his beer.

Her stomach dancing with a combination of anticipation and apprehension, she placed the call. Her security man seemed satisfied. "I'd like to freshen up," she said and Nic pointed her to the toilet.

When she looked in the mirror, she nearly didn't recognize herself. Her cheeks and lips were flushed a deep pink. Her eyes looked so blue against the contrast of her skin and her hair was wilder than she'd ever seen it. Pippa chuckled and shook her head. It was hopeless. There was no use trying to tame it.

Dinner arrived and she and Nic enjoyed a meal of pasta, seafood and wine. Pippa knew Nic joked to diffuse tensions and cover his feelings, but she knew underneath it all, he had his share of stress. She'd never seen him this relaxed since she'd met him.

"You enjoy the sea. It's therapeutic for you," she said, touching his arm.

"It can be. It's not always." He shrugged. "What about you? Do you enjoy boating?"

She shrugged. "I haven't always. When I was a child, my father was known for spending as much time on his yacht as possible. He missed birthdays, appointments so he could escape on his yacht. In retrospect, he must not have been a very happy man."

"Tough being crown prince," Nic said with a wry grin.

"Perhaps. Some are better suited for the job than others. Stefan takes it very seriously, sometimes too seriously in my opinion. He's very controlling. I remember once when I was a teenager, we were on a family outing on the yacht and I asked if I could take the wheel just for a moment."

"Let me guess," Nic said. "He refused. There are plenty of men who can't give up the wheel."

"Why did you let me?" she asked. "For all you knew, I could have wrecked the boat."

"You're excessively responsible, Pippa. If you'd been concerned, you would have asked for my help. Plus, you underrate your abilities," he said in a matter-of-fact voice as he took another sip of red wine.

"You can't know that. I could be a total klutz," she said. "For all you know, we could be in a hospital from my flipping that boat."

He shot her a sideways glance full of humor. "I have excellent instincts."

She sighed and took a sip of her own wine. "Well, I can't argue with that."

"Anything else you want to argue about?" he asked, swirling his wine in his glass.

She couldn't help chuckling. She had been a bit contrary. "No."

"Good," he said. "Want to go for a swim in the pool? We can turn out the lights."

Pippa was still wearing her swimsuit under her clothes. The invitation for an evening swim was irresistible. She stood. "I'm ready."

He chuckled at her immediate reaction. "I should have asked earlier. I'll grab some towels. Let's go."

Cutting the lights, Nic grabbed some towels and led her down to the pool with a flashlight. Pippa tripped on a step, but he caught her against him. "Okay?" he asked.

"Yes. It's so dark," she said, laughing nervously.

"That's the idea," Nic said and led her the rest of the way to the pool. Clouds cast a filmy cover over the moon, but there was some light reflected against the water of the pool.

"It's beautiful," she said.

Nic jumped into the pool, the splash spraying over her legs. "It is," he said, with a wicked smile on his gorgeous wet face. "Come on in."

She paused half a second and jumped in. Two seconds later, she felt Nic's arms around her. "It's a little chilly."

"You'll warm up in a minute. Trust me," he said, pulling her against him.

She looked up into his face, feeling a crazy joy at the sight of the droplets on his face. "You're not warm," she said. "You're hot."

"I'm that way every time I get around you," he said and dipped his mouth to hers for a quick kiss.

The brief touch of his mouth on hers made her sizzle and burn deep inside.

She instinctively wrapped her legs around his waist.

"I like that," he said, pressing his hand at the back of her waist.

Everything that had been brewing between them for months tightened so much that she could hardly breathe. "Whew," she breathed.

"Take it easy," he said. "You okay?"

"Yeah," she breathed.

"You look like you need another kiss," he said with a half grin and lowered his mouth.

She sank into his mouth, feeling him, inhaling him. She couldn't get enough. His tongue slid past her lips and she savored the taste of him, the feel of him wrapped around her. The buoyancy of the water only added to the sensuality of the experience.

Nic slid his hands over her thighs and cupped her hips as he gave her a French kiss that made her feel as if she were turning upside down. She felt the same excitement race through her that she'd experienced earlier today when she'd driven the boat.

He squeezed her against himself. "I love your laugh," he muttered against her mouth.

"Good thing," she said. "I can't remember laughing more than I do with you."

"Hold your breath." He kissed her again, twirled her around again and sank, inch by inch underwater. It was a crazy, sexy, amazing experience kissing Nic that way. Seconds later, he rose, bringing her to the surface. She sucked in a quick breath of air, staring into his face. His strong, sexy face was covered with droplets of water. His eyes bored into hers.

The electricity between them sizzled and burned. She lifted her hands to cradle his face. "You're quite an amazing man."

He stopped dead. "That's quite the compliment," he said.

"I'm just telling the truth," she said.

"Good to know," he said and untied the top of her bathing suit. His hands slid over her breasts.

She inhaled quickly.

"You want me to stop?" he asked.

She hesitated a half beat. "No," she whispered.

He leaned his forehead against hers. "Pippa, I'm not gonna wanna stop," he said.

Her heart slamming against her ribs, she bit her lip. "Neither am I."

They played and frolicked in the pool. He kissed and caressed her, coaxing her out of the bottom of her bathing suit so that she swam nude with him. They got each other so worked up that he almost took her in the pool. Instead, he dragged her from the pool, wrapped a towel around her, another around him and half carried her up the stairs to the house.

Carrying her to the master bed and following her down, he seemed to devour her. And Pippa wanted him to consume her.

"Are you sure you're okay with this?" he asked, clearly reining himself under control.

"Yes," she said and stretched her arms out to him.

Nic slid his hand between her thighs, testing her

readiness. He rubbed and caressed her, making her wet with wanting. Sliding his finger inside her, he drove her even further. He made her want deep inside her.

"Nic," she said, squeezing his arms.

"You want me?" he asked, his voice raspy with his own desire.

"Yes," she said, close to pleading.

He slid his lips down to her breast, taking one of her nipples in his mouth. The sensation electrified her. She felt the instant connection between her breast and lower, deeper inside her.

"I want you inside me," she said. "In me."

In some corner of her mind, she knew he was putting on protection. Seconds later, he pushed her thighs apart. He thrust inside her and she felt a rush of shock and burning pain at the invasion. "Oh," she said.

Nic stopped, staring at her in surprise. He swore under his breath. "You should have told me."

"I wasn't thinking about it," she said. "My mind was on—" She wiggled as she grew more accustomed to him. "Being with you," she said and wiggled again.

His gaze darkened and he fastened his hands around her hips. "You're gonna make this tough on me," he said in a rough voice.

"Hopefully, it won't be all bad."

Nic groaned and began to move in a slow, delicious rhythm. Pippa felt the beginning of exquisite sensations sliding throughout her.

"You okay?" he asked in a low, uneven voice.

"Yessss," she said. "This is sooo—" The twist of tension growing inside her took her breath.

The pulsing rhythm continued, and she clung to him,

staring into his dark gaze, taking and feeling taken. His jaw tightened with restraint, he reached down between her legs and sought her sweet spot, sending electrical impulses through her. The combination of his possession and his caresses were too much.

She jerked and rippled in response. Suddenly, her body clenched in indescribable pleasure and she arched toward him. "Nic," she called, feeling as if her voice were separated from her body.

He held her tight and she felt and heard his own climax ripple through her.

It was the most profound experience of her life and she knew she would never, ever be the same.

Their harsh breaths mingled in the air. The sound was as primitive as what she'd just experienced. At this moment, she felt Nic inside her body, her mind, her blood. She wondered if she would ever breathe without being aware of him again.

Chapter Nine

Nic lay on his side and pulled Pippa against him. She was half asleep. He tried to take in the impact of what they'd done. Nic had known it was inevitable. He had known they would make love. He had known she would be his.

He just hadn't known how much it would affect him. Months ago, when he'd first met Pippa, he'd wanted her, reluctantly felt a need for her. Something primal had driven him toward her. He'd hoped it had all been about sex, but now he knew he'd been wrong.

Something in his psyche was tangled with this woman, and he wasn't sure how in hell he could untangle himself from her. Aside from the fact that she felt so soft and right nestled against him, he felt himself wanting more. Wanting something he hadn't known was possible.

It didn't make sense. Other women had made themselves available to him. Sometimes he'd accepted their overtures. Sometimes he'd refused. Now, he felt himself falling deeper than he'd ever expected.

He frowned as he luxuriated in her naked body against his. He'd thought that once he took her, he would be okay. He would be rid of the itch that plagued him day and night for her. But it hadn't worked. Now that he'd taken her, it was almost as if he was more committed. He wanted her more.

That was strange as hell.

He slid his hand over her crazy, curly hair. She sighed and the sound did something crazy to his gut. He felt incredibly protective of her. More so now. He knew she was mostly asleep, but her hand closed over his, as if she were protecting him. The notion was amusing, but the gesture stole his heart.

The rude ping of his cell phone awakened Nic. It took a few pings, but he finally recognized the sound. Grabbing his cell phone from the bedside table, he pulled it up to his ear. "Yes," he said.

"Nic," his father said. "Your mother's in trouble. She needs help. The regular doctor can't be reached."

Nic sat up straight in bed. "What's wrong?"

"Her belly's distended. She's in pain," his father said.

"I'll take care of it," Nic said. "I'll be there soon."

Pippa opened her gloriously blue, groggy eyes. "What's wrong?"

"Amelie is having problems. Her belly's distended."

Pippa frowned, rising in the bed. "Oh, no. Your doctor isn't available?"

Nic scowled. "He should have been. She may need

to have some sort of draining from fluid buildup. I may have to find another doctor."

Pippa blinked, then frowned again. "If it takes too long, maybe I can find another doctor."

"Who?" he asked.

"My brother-in-law, Ryder McCall," she said.

"Won't that cause problems for you?" he asked.

"What's more important?" she asked. "My problems, or your mother's?"

Two hours later, they were on a plane, in different rows, to Chantaine. Even though she wasn't sitting next to him, Pippa could feel Nic's tension reverberating throughout the jet. She wished she could help him, but ultimately, she knew she couldn't. Ultimately, she knew Amelie would die. And she would die soon. The question was how could they make Amelie's passing easy. The jet landed in Chantaine and she exited the plane ahead of Nic.

Needing to get away from the watchful eye of Giles, her security man, she made a quick trip to the ladies' room.

Nic called her on her cell. "I can take her to a clinic, but that won't guarantee her privacy. The news could get out that she's here."

"Wait," she said. "Let me see what I can do."

She took several deep breaths, then dialed the number for her brother-in-law, Ryder. He immediately answered.

"Ryder McCall," he said.

"This is Pippa," she said. "Don't reveal who you're speaking to. It's an emergency."

He paused a half beat. "How can I help you?"

"There's a cancer patient who needs some kind of draining. I'm hoping you can help."

He paused again. "Where can I meet you?"

Pippa gave him the address. An hour later, she arrived at the cottage and met with Nic. "Ryder is coming."

"Can he help?" he asked as they stood in the den. Amelie was in the bedroom, bloated and suffering.

Paul banged his crutch on the floor. "She's in pain. What's taking so damn long?" he demanded.

"Ryder will be here any moment," Pippa tried to reassure him.

"Ryder?" Paul echoed. "Who the hell is Ryder? What kind of doctor is named Ryder?"

Seconds later, Pippa's brother-in-law strode into the house. He met Pippa's gaze. "How sick is she?" he asked.

"She's terminal," she said in a low voice. "We want to keep her as comfortable as possible," she said.

Ryder met her gaze. "You should share this with your family," he said.

"My family wouldn't understand," she said. "You know how much they hate the Lafittes."

"I don't understand the grudge," Ryder muttered.

"I need your help and your confidence," she said.

"The first is easy. The second is not. Soon, you must tell your family about this," he said.

Pippa felt her stomach twist. "There's enough trouble today," she said. "Please help Amelie."

Moments later, Goldie drove Amelie to a local clinic

where Ryder performed the procedure that would bring her relief.

Just a few hours passed and Amelie was brought home.

"Thank you," Nic said, clearly weary from the whole experience. "How much trouble will this cause you?"

Pippa shrugged. "Ryder will give me some time. It's more important that Amelie is okay."

Nic's gaze grew shuttered. "You know it's only a matter of time for her," he said.

"I know that," she said. "But I want her to be as comfortable as possible."

He took her hand and clasped it for a long moment. "How did I get so damn lucky to know you?"

She smiled. "That's an excellent question. I feel the same way about you."

In the middle of the night, Pippa returned to the palace. Happily enough, she didn't have to endure a screening from her security detail. Unfortunately that didn't extend to Bridget. Her sister could out-snoop any P.I., and Pippa was doomed to face her questions.

"How was the count? Was he a prick? Was he determined to get into your pants?" she asked as Pippa gulped down her first coffee of the day.

"He was lovely. Just older. We both realized that he was still in love with his wife and he should take his time before getting involved with anyone else even though he was lonely."

Bridget blinked. "Really?"

Pippa nodded. "Really."

"So what did you do for the rest of your trip in Capri?"

"I took a tour," Pippa said.

"A tour?" Bridget echoed, chagrined. "The least the count could have done was to give you a proper tour of Capri."

"I didn't want him to do it," Pippa said. "He was a sweet man, but I used up all my patience during the two days I spent with him. I just needed to take a break after that."

"I suppose I can understand that. I feel bad that you've experienced such bad matchups from Stefan and me," Bridget said.

"There are worse things," Pippa said.

"True," Bridget said. "Ryder went out last night to help a terminal cancer patient."

Pippa's stomach clenched. "How terrible."

Bridget shook her head. "He has a difficult job."

Pippa nodded. "Yes, he does," she murmured.

Bridget shrugged. "Well, did you enjoy Capri? I hate to think the whole trip was a waste."

Pippa nodded again. "Yes, I got to see the Blue Grotto. It was amazing."

"Did you really take a tour?" Bridget asked.

"Yes," Pippa said. "The sight of it was amazing. Worth the crowd."

Bridget shook her head. "Better you than me. I would love to see it, but I couldn't stand the crowds."

"It wasn't that crowded when I was there," Pippa said. "I guess I got lucky."

"Did the guides sing for you?" Bridget asked.

"'*Bella Notte,*'" she said with a smile.

"How romantic," Bridget said. "A shame you didn't have a handsome man accompanying you."

"It was beautiful," Pippa said.

Bridget sighed. "You're a saint. You know how to make the best of everything."

"I would never call myself a saint," Pippa said.

"That's because you don't know what demons the rest of us are," Bridget said with a dirty giggle.

"You overstate your evil," Pippa said. "Most of us just do the best we can."

"That attitude is what makes you a saint," Bridget told her.

Guilt stabbing at her. She was lying to her family. "Please don't call me a saint. I'm not worthy of that," Pippa said.

Bridget tilted her head, studying Pippa's face. "If you insist," she said. "But if anyone ever deserved saint-hood—"

"It wouldn't be me," Pippa said in a flat voice.

Stefan wouldn't meet with her the following day. His assistant said he was too busy. After soldiering through her brother's romantic aspirations for her with the count, Pippa was more than peeved, so she took a rare move. She sent him an email and text. In general, the family was instructed not to bother Stefan with personal texts. She usually respected the instruction. After all, she knew he had a terribly demanding schedule and she didn't want to add to his burden. Today, her patience wore thin.

Happy birthday to me. I'm moving out and ditching my security. Cheers, Pippa.

Seconds later, she received a text from Stefan. I order you not to make any changes before you and I have an opportunity to talk.

She sent a return text. Apologies. You used up your orders when you tried to match me up with a man nearly the age of our father. *Ciao.*

Then she turned off her phone. Pippa felt a rush of adrenaline race through her. Her heart hammered against her rib cage. She was so rarely defiant. She exulted in the feeling. For a moment. Then she realized she needed to find a place to live. Immediately.

She spent the morning making calls to apartments, eliminating those without a security gate. By afternoon, she had a list of properties and made visits. At five-thirty, she signed a lease for a one-bedroom apartment. It cost a little more than she'd hoped, but the situation was perfect for her. Now if she could just ditch her security detail.

Pippa finally turned on her phone again, dreading the incoming voice mails and messages. She was immediately deluged by messages from Stefan, some of which had been written in all capital letters. She deleted them without reading and sent one last message regarding her security and the fact that she was ready to make a press release regarding her status change in security.

A half beat later, her phone rang, and her stomach immediately tightened. Pippa saw that it was Stefan and considered pushing the ignore button. *Coward.* Scowling at the truth in the accusation, she picked up the call. "Good evening, Your Royal Highness," she said.

"What in bloody hell has gotten into you?" Stefan demanded. "I realize getting you together with the count was a stretch, but your overreaction is totally unnecessary."

"It's not an overreaction. I just turned twenty-five," she said.

"But you've never complained before," Stefan said. "I can't allow you to move out and dismiss your security. Are you sure you're not having some sort of women's issue?"

If his pompous attitude weren't so offensive, she would have laughed. "Pretend I'm male and this will all seem overdue," she said.

"But you're not. You're my youngest sister and it's my duty to protect you."

Her heart softened. "That's so sweet, Stefan, and I do appreciate it, but I will die of suffocation if I stay at the palace. It's time for me to go."

"I don't understand this. You've always been so reasonable," he said.

"Acquiescent," she corrected. "I feel like Rapunzel, but with bad hair."

Stefan sighed. "At least continue your security."

"No. My security is a leash. It's unnecessary except when I make appearances assigned by the palace. Trust me, the citizens of Chantaine will cheer when they see another expense deducted by the palace."

"They won't know about it until after the fact," Stefan said and swore. "Promise you'll still attend family dinners," he added.

"I will," she said, her heart softening again. "You're so busy you won't notice that I'm gone."

"I already notice," he said.

Pippa felt her eyes burn with tears. Her emotions

caught her off guard, but she refused to give in to them. "I promise to babysit your new child," she said. "None of the new generation of Devereauxs will escape my terrible singing voice."

Stefan laughed. "I love you, Pippa."

Pippa's heart caught. For her hardnosed brother to admit such feelings aloud was monumental. It was all she could do to choke the words through her throat. "And I love you."

They hung up, and Pippa began to weep.

The following day, she enlisted the help of security to help her move into her apartment. She was able to make her move under the radar of Bridget because her sister was busy with the construction of the new so-called ranch. Pippa didn't want her security man to get a hernia, so she insisted he get help.

By noon, she was moved into her apartment. Surprisingly enough, she had more room in her new quarters than her previous suite at the palace. She felt a strange combination of relief and anxiety.

Sinking down onto the antique sofa that seemed so out of place in her new surroundings, she took a deep breath. She was free. That was what she'd wanted. Right?

A knock on the door startled her. She rose, looked through the peephole and saw Nic standing outside her door. She whipped the door open. "How did you find me? And how did you get through security?"

"Goldie," he said with a shrug. "You gonna invite me in?"

Fighting a sudden, strange awkwardness, she nodded. "Of course."

He stepped inside and glanced around. "Downsizing?" he asked.

"Actually the apartment is larger than my quarters at the palace," she said, folding her arms over her chest.

"Really," he said more than asked as he glanced around the apartment. "Did they put you in the palace dungeon or something?"

She laughed. "No, but I had no children, so I didn't need a larger suite. How did Goldie find out about my move?"

Nic shrugged. "Goldie has his ways. I don't question him. He just gets the job done. Why didn't you tell me about your plans for the big move?"

"Besides the fact that I didn't know if it would all work out, I don't owe anyone an explanation about my plans," she said.

He gave a low whistle and dipped his head. "As you say, Your Highness."

She wrinkled her nose at his response. "Truthfully, would you feel the need to make explanations about your own living arrangements?"

He met her gaze and gave another shrug. "Touché. I'm just curious what inspired all this."

"It's been a long time coming," she said, walking toward the balcony window. "Stefan fought it every inch of the way. I know he means well, but it will take him a long time to understand what I said about feeling like Rapunzel with very bad hair."

"I like your hair," Nic said.

She laughed, her heart warming at his comment. "That's not the point. I must confess I'm a bit worried that it was so easy for Goldie to find me. If he can get through the security, others could, too."

"Not likely," Nic said. "Many foreign nations could learn a lot from Goldie."

"But how did you get through?" she asked.

"I'm interested in buying the entire complex," he said.

Pippa blinked. "Pardon me?"

"It's just a story, but you never know," he said. "Have you ordered pizza?"

"What do you mean?"

"It's a tradition. Whenever you move, you order pizza for dinner because you're too tired for anything else," he said.

"I hadn't thought of it, but—"

"It's on me," he said with a sexy smile. "Because I didn't get here fast enough to help you move in."

Her heart softened. "That's very nice," she said.

"I have ulterior motives," he confessed. "I want you to share it with me."

"I can do that," she said.

Forty-five minutes later they sat with their feet propped on the boxes, munching on a loaded pizza. "I would have chosen vegetarian," Pippa said, but took a bite of her second slice anyway.

Nic shook his head. "No. Moving day turns everyone into a carnivore."

"If you say so," she said, smiling at him. "What made you put Goldie on me?"

"When I didn't hear from you, I got worried. I didn't know how hard your family would be on you once they learned about your relationship with the Lafittes."

"They still don't know," she said, taking a long draw from her glass of water.

He shot her a look of disbelief. "You sure?"

"Reasonably sure. I can't believe neither Stefan nor Bridget would be able to hold back their opinions if they knew. They're both extremely outspoken," she said.

"Bet Stefan hated that you moved out. I don't think he thought you would go through with it," he said.

"Hate is a mild term for it," she said, smiling at him. "And you're right. He didn't believe I would go through with it even though I'd warned him."

He grinned at her in return. "I'm surprised the palace didn't disintegrate from his temper tantrum."

"The palace has endured temper tantrums over the course of several centuries," she said. "I must confess I wonder if Stefan has cracked a few walls."

"Well, he's turning the tide. He's no playboy prince," Nic said. "That kind of will is going to shake some foundations."

Pippa nodded. "That's a good way of saying it. Stefan has fought to overcome my father's reputation."

"I'd say he's doing a pretty damn good job."

"He is. I've tried to support him, but I had to move away from the palace. I couldn't stand the restraints anymore."

"The timing's interesting. Did the Lafittes have anything to do with your decision?"

"Perhaps," she said. "You're all such independent sorts, even Amelie. You made me aware of how trapped I feel."

"And how do you feel now?" he asked.

"Great," she said, reluctant to reveal even her tiniest regret.

"And a little scared," he said.

"I didn't say that," she said.

"Your mouth didn't, but your eyes did," he said and cupped her chin. "You're gonna be okay, Pippa. You're stronger than anyone thinks."

"What makes you so sure?" she asked.

He gave a dry chuckle. "You've already proven yourself ten times over."

The strength in his gaze both empowered and aroused her. The combination of feelings was strange but undeniable. She leaned toward him and he took her mouth. The room began to spin.

The kiss turned into another and another. Soon enough, he'd removed her blouse and skirt. She pushed away his shirt and jeans, and he was inside her. This time, slowly.

"Okay?" he asked, his restraint vibrating from his body.

"Yes," she said, drawing him into her.

The rhythm began. She took him and he filled her. More than ever, they had more in common. She was a rebel just like him, and their joining was more powerful with the knowledge of it.

The next morning, Nic awakened before dawn on the mattress on which they'd collapsed on the floor. Pippa breathed in a deep, even sleep. She'd been exhausted and he could still feel her tiredness against him. But Nic had tasks calling him, even at this time of day. His businesses, his father's business, his mother's illness.

He tried to make himself slow down and relax for just a few moments.

"You're awake," Pippa whispered and turned her face into his throat.

His heart stuttered. "How did you know?"

"Your whole body is tense. I can almost feel your mind clicking a million kilometers an hour," she said.

He felt the slightest easing inside him. "I thought you were asleep."

She gave a soft chuckle that tickled his throat. "Not."

He tugged her fabulous, curly hair with one hand and slid his hand low between her legs. "As long as you're awake."

She gave a soft intake of breath. "Oh, my."

"Oh, yeah," he said and began to make love to her.

An hour later, they took a shower together and had to hunt for towels. They dried off with blankets instead which provided even more of a distraction.

Nic dressed in the clothes he'd worn the day before. Pippa stood before him with a damp blanket wrapped around her.

"Will you be okay?" he asked.

"Of course," she said. "I have a dozen boxes to unpack. My biggest fear of the day is a visit from Bridget or a call from Tina."

He rubbed her shoulders. "You can handle them."

"Yes, it just won't be fun," she said and made a face.

"Call me if you need me to break any legs," he said.

She laughed. "Now that would go over well."

"I'll check in on you later, but seriously, call me if you need me," he said.

"I will," she said. "And I may take a break from unpacking to visit your mother."

"She would like that," he said. "She did okay physically after the procedure to drain extra fluid, but I can tell it bothered her to need it."

She sighed. "I wish I could change this for her."

"You already have," he said.

"Have you been able to reach your brothers?" she asked.

"Two down, one to go," he said. "They said no the first three times I talked to them. I've got them up to a maybe."

"You're amazing and they're stupid," she said.

"It's complicated with my dad," he said. "If I hadn't been successful on my own so young, I may have shared their attitude. The weird thing about that success is that it freed me to forgive him."

Pippa loved him even more for his ability to express how he'd grown. Not every man could do that. She reached for his hand. "You're a good man."

His hand enclosed hers. "Careful. Never forget that I come from pirates."

Chapter Ten

Nic chewed through another two antacids as he stared at his electronic tablet and tried to figure out when he could break away for a two-day business trip. His mother had seemed more tired than usual lately, sleeping more during the day. He didn't know what in hell to do. If he left and she passed, he would never forgive himself.

He had thought that spending the day and night with Pippa in Capri would rid him of the increasing edginess he'd felt 24/7. Being with Pippa calmed a part of him, and he'd thought just a little time away with her would give him the break he'd never admit to needing.

He'd known going into this that it would be no picnic, but he would never have predicted the effect the situation would have on his body. He had begun to feel like a caged animal, rarely sleeping longer than three hours at night. The knowledge of his mother's impending death seemed to squeeze his throat tighter and tighter every day. He was always running out of antacids. He'd been determined to keep his emotions under strict control, but his frustration at his inability to change his mother's pain and the ugly progress of her disease wore him down.

He heard the sound of his mother singing outside his window and immediately glanced outside. He stared in disbelief at the sight of her as she approached the pool. It was 1:00 a.m.

Alarmed, Nic raced out the door. "Mother, what in hell are you doing?"

Amelie glanced over her shoulder. "Oh, hello, darling. What are you doing up so late?"

Nic felt a sliver of relief. At least she was lucid. He let out a half breath. "Finishing up some work," he said, moving toward her. Although she was still eating, she looked thinner.

Amelie tilted her head, sympathy creasing her brows. "You're not sleeping well, are you?" she said more than asked. "Come here and sit with me for a few minutes. I was going to go for a swim, but it can wait," she said as she sank into a chair.

Nic shook his head, but joined her. "You can't go swimming. Dr. McCall said you have to wait for five days after the procedure to swim or take a tub bath."

She frowned. "I could have sworn it's already been five days." She waved her hand. "My memory's not the best lately. The pain meds help the pain, but they make me sleepy. Makes for a difficult choice." She sighed. "But enough about me. I'm sick of it all being about me. How are you and Pippa?"

"What do you mean me and Pippa?" he asked, rubbing his jaw.

"Well, there's obviously something between you. It's a wonder the sparks don't burn down the cottage. What are you going to do about it?"

"It's complicated," he said.

She laughed. "You think I don't understand complications?"

"She's very devoted to her family. They hate me. It's an impossible situation for her. I can't ask her to give up her family," he said.

"Pippa is a very strong woman. You're a strong man. The two of you together, you may be able to achieve something that seems impossible," she said.

Nic couldn't see it. He couldn't see asking such a thing of Pippa after all she'd already done for him and his mother.

"You have no faith," she said. "You'll have to find your way. But remember what I said."

"I will," he said.

"And I wish you wouldn't suffer so much about the fact that I'm dying. I'm going to be fine. I'm a bit worried about your father, but I think if you get him a dog, it will help."

Nic blinked. "A dog?"

His mother nodded. "He'll need the blind adoration and companionship. Trust me on this."

His stomach knotted at the direction of their conversation. "We don't have to talk about this."

"Yes, we do," she said and put her hand over his. "I'm worried about you."

He clenched his jaw. "You don't need to worry about me. You raised me to be strong."

"Yes, but you don't have superpowers. Deep inside, you think you should be able to save me, and the fact that you can't is ripping you apart. If I'd known it would be this hard for you, I would have stayed in the States and worked with hospice. This has been too much of a burden on you."

"I wouldn't have it any other way," he said. "Except for you not to die," he said, his eyes stinging with emotion.

"Oh, darling, you will always have me with you," she said. "I promise. And I believe you'll feel it. It will hurt terribly in the beginning, but I'll always be with you. You're doomed. You have my genetic material and that won't go away."

He laughed at her words, struggling with a dozen emotions, most of them sad and wrenching. "Is there anything else I can do for you?"

"You've already done it. You've given me this wonderful gift of time in Chantaine. Now live your life," she said. "If you need to take care of business, do it. But don't forget your heart. Never ever forget to have fun and to have heart. Promise?" she asked.

He took a deep breath. "I promise."

She looked wistfully at the pool. "Are you sure you won't let me cheat and take a quick dip?"

"One more day, and you can be a dolphin. But not until."

"You're such a tyrant," Amelie said. "But I'm tired again anyway. Good night, darling. Try to get some rest. You know how cranky you get when you don't get your beauty sleep."

He rolled his eyes. "I'll try," he said and helped her to her feet and walked her to the front door. At that moment, he knew what he had to do. She hadn't asked for it, but there was one more thing his mother wanted and he was damn well going to do it for her.

The next day, Pippa came to visit. She began pulling off her disguise the second she climbed out of the car. "Hate this," she muttered. "Completely and totally hate this."

Even her griping made Nic feel a little lighter. He stepped outside his door and grabbed her from behind. She gave a squeal.

"It's me," he assured. "The gray wig brings out my primal urges," he said.

She laughed breathlessly and turned toward him. "You're insane."

"I do my best," he said. "It's damn good to see you." He took her mouth in a long kiss that made him want far more than a kiss.

"I've been unpacking," she said. "I didn't think I had that much, but I clearly underestimated. Plus, I had nothing in my refrigerator and couldn't ring the chef for breakfast or dinner."

"Oooh, tough break, Your Highness. Sure you don't want to move back into the palace?" he asked. "I know Stefan would take you back."

She shook her head. "There will be adjustments. That's expected. Nothing a toaster and microwave won't cure. Plus I'm told my security detail is retiring at the end of this week. The true beginning of my new life will start then."

"Yeah, just be careful," he said. As much as Pippa's security had been a pain in his backside, the fact that she'd had it had given him a measure of relief.

"Oh dear, you're sounding just a bit like Stefan," she said.

"Cut me some slack. I can be protective, too," he said.

She nodded. "I know. It's not totally bad when not taken to extremes," she said. "How are your mother and father?"

"Dad is getting stronger. Mom is getting weaker. It's going to be tricky keeping my dad occupied," he said.

She frowned. "Do I need to take him on an outing?"

Nic chuckled at the image of Pippa taking his dad to the knitting store or brunch. "Nah, I'll just get Goldie to wear him out with some extra workouts."

She nodded. "And what about you?" she asked and he felt as if she were turning a searchlight on his insides.

"I'm good," he said with a shrug.

"You lie, but I understand," she said and squeezed his arm. "I'm sorry this is so hard for you, but you wouldn't be the man I—" She broke off. "You wouldn't be the man I admire you if it weren't hard for you."

"Yeah, well," he said and picked her up off her feet.

Her eyes widened. "What are you doing?"

"Just checking your weight. Making sure you're not wasting away without a chef."

She laughed. "I'm not suffering that much," she said.

He pulled her against him and slid her down the

front of him. "I'm headed out of town tomorrow. Can you come over tonight?"

She nodded.

He felt a rush of relief. "I'll send Goldie to pick you up. Wear this and you'll be fine."

Pippa groaned. "As soon as my security guy retires, I'm burning the wig."

"Don't rush it. You never know when you'll need it."

"Where are you headed?"

"Back to the States for business and one personal mission. Let's go see my mom. She'll fuss if she knows I kept you from going inside," he said.

Pippa saw the weariness stamped on Amelie's face. Nic's mother tried to hide it, but it was unmistakable. Still, Amelie seemed happy to see her and Pippa promised to visit with her the following day. Not wanting to tire her further, Pippa gave the woman a hug and left. Nic walked her to the dreadful machine that was her covert car.

"I'll see you later," he said, pulling her against him. His strength tugged at her. She didn't know how he kept everything together. She just longed to help him as much as she could.

"Later," she promised and kissed him, then drove away.

Hours later, she ate a frozen dinner and tried to play catch-up with her academic work. First, she waited for her security detail to leave for the evening, then she waited for Goldie's call. Her stomach danced with nerves on her way to see Nic.

The more time she spent with Nic, the more she felt

as if she were making a commitment toward him. With the way her family felt about the Lafittes, she just didn't see how anything between her and Nic could end well. Pippa closed her eyes against the thoughts. She couldn't think past tonight. There was too much to work out and she knew she couldn't do it all at once.

But she could be with Nic tonight, hold him and treasure the way she felt when she was with him, the way she felt in his arms.

When Goldie pulled into the driveway, he immediately got out and opened the door for her. "Your Highness," he said with a dip of his head.

"Thank you, Goldie," she said. "But I already told you to call me Pippa."

"Yes, you're welcome, Your—" The big man broke off and smiled. "Your Pippa," he said.

She smiled. He was such a gentle giant.

"I'll take you home whenever you like," he said. "Enjoy your evening."

Pippa walked the few steps to the guest suite and lifted her hand to knock on the door, but it opened before she had a chance.

Nic caught her hand and pulled her inside. "What took you so long?"

"I waited for my security detail to go home," she said.

"Good for you," he said. "Have you had dinner?"

She nodded. "As a matter of fact, I have."

"Are you going to tell me what you ate?"

She shook her head. "No."

He chuckled. "That tells me enough. Goldie put together some appetizers and he baked a pie."

"A pie?" she echoed. "Is there anything he can't do?"

"Not much," he said. "Have a seat. I'll get you a glass of wine."

They shared easy conversation while they ate the appetizers. Pippa was almost too full for pie.

"The proper way to eat this apricot pie is with ice cream," Nic said.

"À la mode," she said. "But I can't imagine eating a full slice."

"Then we can share," he said and scooped up a bite for her. The gesture was both generous and sensual.

"Delicious again," she said. "What time do you leave tomorrow?"

"We're not going to talk about tomorrow, but I'm leaving around 5:00 a.m."

Pippa gasped. "You should go to bed and I should leave. You need to get your rest."

"I can sleep on the flight, but I like your idea of going to bed," he said, his dark gaze wrapping around hers and holding tight.

She took a last sip of her wine and met his challenge. "Then what are you waiting for?"

He immediately took her hand and led her to the bed. He skimmed his hand over her crazy, curly hair. "I didn't expect to want you this much after the first time we were together," he said, kissing her. "How can I want you more?"

Her heart hammered in her chest. "I hope I'm not the only one who feels this way," she whispered. "It's almost too much."

"I know," he said. "I've never felt this way before."

"That's a relief," she said and tugged at his shirt.

"Maybe for you. It's hell for me," he said, and began to undress her.

They kissed and caressed each other into a frenzy. He made her breathless and she did the same to him. Finally he filled her and they stared into each other's eyes.

Pippa wasn't sure if it took seconds or moments later. She only knew she felt taken all the way to her soul.

"I want you," he muttered. "I need you. I—"

He didn't finish, but she craved the words, the emotion, everything that he was. Her heart and stomach clenched, and she arched toward him as he thrust deeply inside her.

Her climax sent her soaring.

"It's never enough," he said. "I can't get enough of you."

Thank goodness, she thought and wrapped herself around him from head to toe. She clung to him with every fiber of her being, wanting him to draw her strength into him.

"I want you with me," he said next to her ear. "All the time."

Love me, she thought. *Love me just for me, that's all I want.* She wished he would say, *I'll take care of you forever.* The thought took her by surprise. Pippa didn't want to be the one taken care of. She wanted to be the woman strong enough to stand up and take care of her man and give him anything he needed from her.

"I want to be with you anytime," Pippa whispered. "Every time."

They made love again and afterward, Pippa realized that Nic needed rest. He might deny it, but the truth was he needed rest. She knew he needed far more rest than he could possibly get tonight.

Relaxed against him, Pippa fought sleep. "I need to go back to my apartment."

Nic swore. "I wanted to talk you into staying here all night."

"It will be easier for you to rest tonight, then wake up to leave tomorrow without me here," she said.

"Says who?" he said.

"Says me," she said and lifted her hand to stroke his forehead. "You have a tough trip ahead of you. Business and something else you're not telling me."

He leaned his head back and narrowed his eyes. "How do you know?" he challenged.

"I just do," she said. "Besides, you said you had a personal mission, too."

He scowled at her, then chuckled. "I'm going to bring my brothers back. Even if I have to kidnap them."

Pippa gasped, then bit her lip. "Well, bloody hell, if anyone can do it, you can."

He laughed louder this time and put his hands on either side of her hand as if she were the most precious thing in the universe.

"If you get arrested," she began.

"Would you pay my bail?" he asked.

"Oh, yes," she said without a second thought. She squeezed his hands. "Call me anytime," she told Nic.

"I will, unless a police officer does…asking you to make bail," he said and gave a dry chuckle.

"You're a bad, bad boy with an amazing heart," she said.

"That's why you fell for me from the beginning," he said.

She bit her lip. "Yeah, maybe. Just promise me you'll take care of you," she said.

"I will. Spend some time with my mother," he said. "She's on the edge and I have a feeling you could bring her away from it."

Surprised at his belief in her ability, she shook her head. "I'll visit her tomorrow, but you know I can't control her future."

"Yeah," he said. "I think being with you makes things better for her."

"I'll do my best," she promised. "My very best."

Pippa reluctantly dragged herself from Nic's bed and washed her face and pulled on her clothes. Stepping out of the bathroom, she felt Nic step behind her and wrap his arms around her. "What are you doing?"

"Drawing your life force into me," he said.

She giggled. "That sounds ominous if it were possible."

"How do you know it's not?" he asked.

"I'm taking a wild guess," she said, turning in his arms.

"Well, damn," he said.

"Well, damn," she echoed, and they kissed. She caressed his mouth and squeezed his body tight. "Kick your brothers' asses down the street like a can and bring them here to Chantaine."

He drew back to meet her gaze. "That's pretty strong language for a princess," he said.

"Just sayin'," she said.

"How cool are you?" he said. "I'll get the job done.

Thanks for sticking with me," he said with a gaze that held all kinds of crazy emotions she was determined to ignore but couldn't. "I'll see you soon," he said.

She kissed him and headed toward the door. "*Ciao,* darling," she said. "Be safe."

Goldie drove her home even though it was 2:00 a.m. He didn't even blink at the time. Pippa took a deep breath and leaned her head back against the seat. "You're kind to drive me back to the apartment at such a crazy hour."

He shrugged. "Crazy is relative," he said.

"You're quite amazing," she said. "With all your skills. Nic and I ate your appetizers and a few bites of your amazing pie last night."

"Cooking relaxes me. I'm glad you enjoyed the food I prepared," he said.

"It was delicious. Is there anything that helps you relax? You spend so much of your time working," she said.

Goldie took a deep breath. "I'm addicted to yoga."

"Really?" Pippa asked. "Does it make that much of a difference?"

"Yes," Goldie said. "Relieves pain, allows me to relax and sleep."

"Do you go to a special studio?" she asked.

"Sometimes," he said. "Otherwise, I use a DVD or cable on TV."

"What station?" she asked.

He smiled. "Eight. You can DVR it. Meditation and acupuncture can help, too."

Pippa thought about the prospect of having needles

stuck inside her and shook her head. "If you say so," she said.

"Take it slow. You will learn your truth," he said.

"Goldie, what do you think of this whole crazy situation with me, Nic, Amelie and Paul?" she said.

"You're more powerful than you know," he said.

She thought about that for a moment. "I hope so, but speaking of power—you are quite powerful and talented. Why do you stay with the Lafittes?" she asked.

"They are my home," he said. "I would do anything for them."

His resolute statements sent chills through her. "I wish I had your talent and your fortitude," she said.

"You have both," he said. "Don't fear them."

Goldie pulled into her apartment complex, flashing a pass, then driving toward her apartment. "I'll escort you upstairs," he said.

"It's not necessary," she said.

"It is for me," he said, pulling to a stop. Stepping outside the car, he opened her door and walked with her to her second-floor apartment. "I'll wait outside. Knock on the door to let me know you're okay."

Pippa ventured inside her apartment. For just a half beat, she felt lonely and insecure. Then she gave a quick walk-through to her bedroom. She realized she was okay and opened the door. "No one here but me," she said to Goldie. "Perhaps I should get a cat."

Goldie chuckled. "Good night, Your Highness," he said.

Pippa spent most of the next day with Amelie. Nic's mother knitted, chatted and dozed on and off throughout the day. Pippa noticed that Amelie's energy came and went in short spurts. Paul lumbered restlessly on crutches. Nic had been correct about his father's need to release pent-up energy. Goldie stepped in and helped occupy Paul.

Pippa remembered Amelie when she'd had so much more energy. She'd been so lively, engaging. Irresistible. She still possessed her charm even when sleeping. Her stubby eyelashes rimmed her eyes. Her face growing more gaunt every day, full of wrinkles, crinkles, hollows and bones, defined her character. Her stubborn chin told the world she would push it to the max, till the very end. Amelie was nothing if not a fighter.

Pippa felt her throat suddenly close shut at the realization that Amelie was going to die, and it would be soon. She'd known all along that Amelie's time was short, but Pippa realized she'd been in denial. Amelie's time was all too close. Pippa left a little later than she'd planned. Goldie gave her a sandwich and followed her home.

Pippa took a shower and fell into a dreamless sleep. She awakened to the sound of her cell phone beeping. Glancing at the caller ID, she saw that Bridget was on the line.

Reluctantly, she accepted the call. "Good morning, Bridget. How are you?"

"When did you move? Why didn't you tell me? I went to your suite and you weren't there. Stefan won't discuss it, but he's clearly furious. How could you do this to us?"

"I moved a few days ago. It took place quickly because I had to do it before I lost my courage. I couldn't continue to live in the palace. I felt so trapped," Pippa said.

"We all feel trapped," Bridget scoffed. "The key is stealing your freedom whenever you can."

"You're a better fighter than I am," Pippa said. "I needed to finish the big fight so there could be peace for me, for everyone."

Silence stretched between them. Bridget gave an audible sigh. "I want to argue with you, but I can't. I obviously haven't had enough coffee." She gave a growl of frustration. "Maybe I'm just jealous that you got out before I did."

Pippa smiled. "You're right on my heels with your ranch in sight. You have Ryder and your boys. I have… genealogy."

"I still may find a man for you," Bridget said.

"Oh, please. If you love me, Bridget, stop," she said and laughed.

"Everyone deserves a second chance," Bridget said.

"Maybe in five years," Pippa said.

"That was cruel," her sister said. "Don't forget, there's a family dinner tonight."

"Lovely," Pippa said. "I'll have the whole table glowering at me."

"Don't be late," Bridget said. "*Ciao,* darling."

Chapter Eleven

"I want to go to the ocean," Amelie said at three-thirty.

Pippa blinked. "The ocean?" Today had been a duplicate of yesterday with Amelie knitting, chatting and sleeping except for this latest request.

"Yes, I want to swim," Amelie said, standing. "I'll put on my suit."

Pippa followed the woman to her feet. "I'm not sure that's wise. I don't think you're supposed to be swimming."

"Why not?" Amelie asked.

"Well, because of your condition," Pippa said.

"Oh, you mean the draining procedure. I'm permitted to swim after five days. I don't suppose you have a suit. I'm not sure mine would fit. Perhaps I should go by myself."

No. "I'll come up with something. Goldie can help me," Pippa said. "Go change into your suit." She wondered if Amelie would tire before they were able to leave. As soon as Amelie walked down the hallway, Pippa called for Goldie. Somehow she ended up with shorts and a tank top.

With surprising energy, Amelie returned wearing a caftan, the strap of her swimsuit peeking through the shoulder sliding over her too-slim frame. "Ready to be a little fish?" she asked with a singsong tone in her voice.

"Ready," Pippa said. "Goldie said he'll drive us."

Amelie frowned. "But what about Paul?"

"He's already given Paul a good workout. Paul is napping in the extra room," Pippa said.

"Excellent," Amelie said. "Let's go. Another adventure."

Heaven help them all, Pippa thought. Moments later, they trudged through the sandy beach toward the ocean. Partway there, Amelie pulled her caftan over her head and dropped her towel on the sand. She lifted her head to the sun and smiled like a child.

Pippa's heart caught. She picked up her cell phone and clicked a photo and another. She was no photographer, but she hoped the photos somehow captured Amelie's love of life.

"Let's go," Amelie called. "Before the water gets too cold."

Pippa tossed her cell phone into her bag and ran toward the ocean with Nic's mother. The water was already cold. Pippa muffled a shriek. "It's a bit nippy."

"Could be worse," Amelie said. "We're lucky it's not winter. The waves are so calm."

Amelie reached for Pippa's hand. "Isn't it lovely?"

Pippa took a deep breath and looked at the beautiful

blue ocean with the slightest caps of white. Both she and Amelie wore water shoes to cushion them from the rocky ground.

Amelie smiled but her teeth chattered. "I always wanted to be a fish or a dolphin," she said. "Or a butterfly."

"You're all of those in one," she said.

Amelie laughed. Her lips were turning blue. "You're such a lovely person. The perfect princess." Her smile fell. "The one thing I'll miss is meeting my grandchildren. You could have my first grandchild."

Pippa stared at Amelie in shock. "Grandchild?" she echoed. She felt her insides clench. Could Amelie sense something? In fact, she was late with her period, but because she wasn't regular, pregnancy wasn't a concern. Nic had worn protection.

"Don't worry, it will all work out. You'll have a beautiful baby," Amelie said.

Pippa wondered for a moment if Nic's mother was suffering from some kind of delusion. "You've grown cold. We should go back."

"Just a moment longer," she said. "I want to feel the water and the waves a moment longer."

Pippa laced her fingers more tightly through Amelie's and began to count. She was torn between protecting Amelie's pleasure and her fragile health. Amelie stumbled, then dipped her shoulders underneath the water.

"Amelie," Pippa said.

Seconds later, Amelie ducked her head beneath, frightening the bloody hell out of Pippa. She tugged on Amelie's hand, pulling her above the surface. "What are you doing?" she asked Nic's mother.

"It was so nice under the water," Amelie said, beaming. "I feel like I'm nine years old again."

Pippa put her arms around Amelie and squeezed her tight. "Let's get our towels. I want you cozy and warm."

Amelie's teeth chattered as Pippa led her to their towels. Goldie rushed out to help them into the car. "Turn on the heat, please," Pippa said.

"But it's—" Goldie broke off and met Pippa's gaze. Understanding flowed between them. For Amelie, it may as well have been winter. Her body was so thin and she'd become chilled in the water.

"I hope she won't get sick from this," Pippa said, scrubbing Amelie's arms.

"She won't," Goldie said. "You did the right thing, Your Highness. She was determined to go to the sea. We're lucky you went with her."

They returned to the cottage and Pippa helped Amelie into cozy pajamas, then into bed. Only after Goldie's promise to frequently check on Amelie did Pippa agree to leave. As she climbed into cab, she noticed the time. Bloody hell. She was going to be late for the family dinner.

Rushing, rushing, rushing, she took a shower, dressed herself and pulled her errant hair into a bun. Forget cosmetics, she told herself. She drove to the palace and raced up to the private dining room and burst inside. Everyone was there, her brother, his child and his pregnant wife, Eve, her sister Bridget, her husband, Ryder, and the twins. For one stunning moment, they were silent. Damn them.

"Hi," she said, forcing a big smile. "I'm so sorry I'm late. Time got away from me." She sank into the empty seat. "How are you feeling, Eve?"

Eve shot her a look of sympathy. "Better, thank you. How are your studies?"

"I'm getting there," Pippa said and glanced at Bridget. "How's the ranch?"

"Well, if we could get the plumbing and the kitchen straight, we'd be most of the way there," Bridget said. "Why is your hair wet?"

"I just took a shower," Pippa said and reached for her glass of water. She eyed the wine, but remembering what Amelie said, she wasn't sure she should do much drinking. She didn't think she was pregnant, but she supposed it was remotely possible.

Her hand shook as she held the glass of water. *Pregnant? No.*

"What's for dinner?" she asked brightly.

"Beef, rare," Eve said, wincing slightly. "Stefan's favorite."

"Mashed potatoes for Eve and anyone else who wants them. It's the only thing she can eat. That, and bread."

With the help of her screaming niece and nephews, Pippa made it through the meal. She gave a sigh of relief as dessert was served. Bananas flambé served with a flourish. She took a few bites, then discreetly motioned for one of the servers to take her plate.

"This had been wonderful, but I should leave. Back to work early tomorrow," she said and pushed back her chair.

"I'd like a word with you," Stefan said. "In my office."

"Our suite," Eve said. "Stephenia would love a bedtime hug and kiss from her aunt Pippa."

A flicker of irritation crossed his face, but he appeared to mask it with a quick nod. "Our suite will be fine." He said good-night to Bridget and her family, then the four of them made their way to Stefan and Eve's suite. Pippa had noticed Stefan had appeared more remote than usual this evening, but she'd just thought he was either still peeved about her move or his mind was on something else altogether.

Once inside the suite, Pippa kneeled down and extended her arms to Stephenia. "Come give me a big hug."

The little girl rushed toward her, her curls bobbing. Laughing, she threw her little body against Pippa. Her uninhibited expression of joy and complete trust tugged at Pippa's heart. "Now that's a hug," Pippa said and kissed the toddler's soft cheek. "You are such a sweet and smart girl. I bet you've been busy today."

Eve nodded with a wry expression on her face. "There'll be an early bedtime for Mamaeve tonight, too. Come along, Stephenia. You need to pick out your book. And Stefan—" she said but stopped.

Pippa saw the silent communication between the two of them and wondered what was going on. Surely he couldn't still be so upset about her move from the palace.

Stefan brushed a kiss over his daughter's cheek. "Sweet dreams," he said, echoing Eve's frequent nighttime wish.

As soon as Eve and Stephenia walked toward the

bedrooms at the other end of the suite, Stefan turned toward Pippa. "How are you?"

"Well, thank you. And you?"

"Also well. Your studies?"

Pippa resisted the urge to squirm. She'd been forced to put her academic work aside during the last week. "Demanding as always."

"You've been quite busy since you returned from Italy," he said. He pulled out a computer tablet and turned it on.

The uneasiness inside her grew. "Moving makes for a busy time." She hesitated to ask but went ahead anyway. "What is your point?"

"Some photographs of you were posted on a social network just before dinner. I'll be surprised if they don't make the rag sheets by morning." He showed her a series of photos of her holding hands with Amelie in the ocean. "The woman looks familiar," he said in a cool voice.

Her stomach knotted, yet at the same time an overwhelming relief swept through her. "Good eye, Your Royal Highness. That's Amelie Lafitte."

Stefan clenched his jaw. "What in hell have you gotten yourself into?"

Pippa sighed. "I got myself involved with a family experiencing a tragedy."

"What tragedy? I'd heard Amelie had been ill for some time, but if she's swimming, she must have recovered."

Pippa shook her head. "Amelie is terminally ill. She's—she's dying."

Surprise crossed his face. "I'm sorry to hear that."

He cleared his throat. "That said, any association with the Lafittes is understandably forbidden. You must stop your involvement at once."

Pippa shook her head. "Oh, I'm sorry. That's not possible."

Stefan tilted his head to one side in disbelief and disapproval. "Pardon me, of course it's possible. You merely send a message to the Lafittes with your good wishes, but tell them you're unable to continue the association."

"I can't and won't do that. At this time of all times, I would hate myself for pulling away from them."

Stefan's jaw tightened again. "Pippa, after I received these photos, I asked my security detail to investigate the situation with the Lafittes. It has been brought to my attention that you've used family connections to secure a cottage for them. Not only that, Paul Lafitte, whose presence in this country is illegal, is living in this cottage. How do you think your cousin Georgina will feel when she learns you've used her cottage to house a criminal?"

"He's not a criminal," she said, unable to fight a stab of impatience. "He's a man with a broken foot and he's about to lose the love of his life."

"Pippa, this is not up for discussion. What you've done is illegal and dishonest."

"I'm not proud of being dishonest with all of you. I've hated every one of the lies I've had to tell, but your attitude made it impossible."

"I don't think you understand what a black mark this will make on our name. I insist you sever your relationship with the Lafittes," he said. "Please don't force my hand on this."

Pippa fought a sliver of fear, but her anger at his manipulation was stronger. "Are you threatening me? With what? Let's not keep it a mystery."

He paused, then narrowed his eyes. "If you don't stop your association with the Lafittes, I'll be forced to consider revoking your title."

Pippa absorbed the potential loss and made her decision in less than two breaths. "Then do what you have to do. I'll do what I must do. Helping the Lafittes through this painful time is the most important thing I've ever done in my life. If I lose my title over it, then c'est la vie. Good night, Stefan," she said and walked out of his suite.

Her heels clicked against the familiar marble palace floor. It crossed her mind that if Stefan carried through with his threat, this might be the last time she walked these halls. Worse yet, she realized, she might lose her relationship with her family. Her chest tightened with grief. Her hands began to shake and she balled them into fists. As much as her dysfunctional family drove each other crazy at times, Pippa loved them with all her heart. She would never get over losing them.

Deep in her heart, though, she knew that she would hate herself if she turned her back on the Lafittes. Stefan had forced her to make an impossible choice. She prayed she would have the strength to live with the consequences.

The connecting flight from Madrid began its descent into Chantaine just after 8:00 a.m. Nic rubbed his eyes, which felt like sandpaper. He looked at the passengers beside him and behind him. By some miracle, all three of his brothers were on the flight. Alex, his youngest brother, sat beside him gently snoring. Paul Jr., who went by James, and Michael sat across the aisle in the row behind them.

The plane had a bumpy landing. Nic hoped it wasn't a sign of what was to come for the rest of his brothers' visit.

Alex awakened, rubbing his face. He narrowed his eyes at Nic. "Looks like we made it. Are you sure our father isn't in a Chantaine dungeon somewhere?"

"You never know with Paul Lafitte, but he wasn't when I left," Nic said. "Besides, you're not here to see your father. You're here to see your mother," Nic said. "If you're man enough."

Alex scowled, but Nic knew that very same challenge had gotten Alex and Nic's other brothers onto the plane. He'd made a strong, no-holds-barred demand, and thank goodness, his brothers had responded.

"There's a car waiting," Nic said. "When we get to the cottage, you'll have a good meal."

An hour later, the driver drove the limo toward the cottage. The ride was mostly silent, but Nic figured he would be paying the price for the intimidation and manipulation he'd used to bring his brothers to his mother. Despite their anger, their brothers drank in the sight of their mother's island.

"Not bad," James said. "Never visited Chantaine before. Mom always said it was beautiful. She was right."

Alex gave a dry chuckle. "Who says they would have let us on the island?"

"You got on this time," Nic said.

"Because you've donated a ton of money and enhanced Chantaine's economy," Alex said.

"There are worse ways to spend money," Nic said.

The limo pulled into the driveway.

"Quaint," Paul Jr. said.

"A friend helped out," Nic said. He wondered how Pippa was doing. He knew that moving from the palace was a huge change for her. He and his brothers got out of the limo and walked to the front door.

Paul opened the door. On crutches, he looked at his four sons in shock. "Well, I'll be damned."

"We've already done that several times over," Paul Jr. said. "Where's Mom?"

Paul's expression hardened. "She's asleep, and if you can't show her respect and kindness, you can go the hell back where you came from," he said and slammed the door in their faces.

Silence followed.

"Same ol' dad," Michael said.

"Yep, sonofabitch, but he was always protective of her," Alex said.

"When he wasn't in prison," Paul Jr. said.

"This is stupid," Nic said. "Let's just go inside. Dad will have to deal with it. I'm sure Goldie has a great meal for us."

"Who's Goldie?" Paul Jr. asked.

"You'll know soon enough," Nic said and inserted his key into the door and pushed it open.

Paul had apparently hobbled to the back of the house. Nic turned on a baseball game and Goldie immediately showed up with platters of appetizers and sandwiches, along with beer. Beer before lunch may have seemed inappropriate, but in this case, it was for the best. His brothers commented on the food and the game while downing a few beers.

Finally, his mother appeared in the back of the den. "She's here," Nic said, turning off the TV. His mother was gaunt and tired, but clearly delighted to see her sons.

"Am I dreaming?" she asked, lifting her lips in a huge smile.

"Go," Nic said in his brother Michael's ear.

"Me?" Michael asked.

Nic nodded, and half a breath later, Michael sprang to his feet and enveloped his mother in hug. "I'm sorry I haven't—"

"No sorries, no apologies," Amelie said, hugging him in return. "I'm so happy to see you."

A moment later, James rose and pulled her into his arms. "Mom, I've missed you."

Alex finally stood and made his way to his mother. "I'm the worst of your sons," he confessed.

"No," she insisted with a smile. "You are all the best sons any woman could want because you came to see me before—" She broke off, her smile fading. "Before I turn into a butterfly."

Nic's heart wrenched at the sight before him. It had taken an enormous effort to make this happen. He just wished it hadn't been necessary.

His mother pretended to eat and sipped some lemonade while she enjoyed the visit with her sons. Amelie asked each of them about what they were doing. None were married and none had children, much to her disappointment. She encouraged all of them to enjoy Chantaine as much as possible during their visit, but Nic knew his brothers were leaving at 5:00 a.m. the next day.

After a while, Nic could tell she was growing tired. "We should let you rest," he said.

"In a bit. I have something to say first," she said. "You're not going to like this, but I raised you to be extraordinary men, so now's the time for you to man up."

The room turned silent. His brothers grew restless.

"Take a deep breath. Listen. It won't be that long. You can handle it," she said. "The truth is your father broke the rules because he was determined to take care of me. He was determined to keep me in the same way a princess should live because, after all, I could have been a princess. How do you compete with that? How do you produce a lifestyle fit for a princess, even though I didn't ask for it?"

His mother's words sank into him. He'd never realized what a burden his father had taken on when he'd stolen his mother from Prince Edward. It made him think of his current relationship with Pippa.

"Can't deny that was tough," James said. "But he made our life a living hell by destroying the family reputation."

"True," his mother said. "But that was a long time ago. It's time to get over it."

Silence followed.

"Excuse me?" Michael said. "Get over it? His disreputable dealings are the gifts that keep giving. We had to move out of the state to reestablish ourselves."

"Well," his mother said. "It's time for you to get over it. You've reestablished yourselves. Paul is nursing a broken foot. I have two things to ask of you," she said. "Be true brothers. Stand together. Be family. And forgive your father," she added.

Nic felt his brothers close up like locks at Fort Knox. "Love you, Mom," he said and moved toward her to give her a hug.

She embraced him in return. "Thank you," she said. "You made a miracle."

"No, it was you," he said. "I just added a little muscle."

"I'm getting tired. I should go to sleep. Can we get a photo of me with my boys?" she asked.

Goldie took a few photos and his mother went to bed. His brothers sacked out in the guest room and guest quarters. Nic considered calling Pippa, but he was drained. He resolved to call tomorrow afternoon, after his brothers left and he caught up with some rest.

Nic arranged for the limo that took his brothers to the airport in the early predawn morning, then went back to sleep. Hours later, a knock on the door awakened him. Goldie, wearing a tortured expression, dipped his head. "I'm so sorry, sir. Your mother has passed on."

Chapter Twelve

Numb from the news, Nic dialed Pippa's number as he paced his room an hour later.

"Hi. Welcome back," she said.

Her voice was like oxygen to his system. "Thanks," he said. "I have some bad news." He paused a beat because he'd already had to say the same thing several times. "She's gone."

"Oh, Nic, I'm so sorry. I'll be right over," she said.

"Good," he said, feeling a shot of relief that bothered him. Now, more than ever, he needed to keep himself in check. There was just too much to do and his father was a mess.

He made several more calls, unsure what to do about a memorial service. Thank goodness, his mother had made her burial wishes clear in her will. She wanted her ashes spread in Chantaine. Nic suspected his father would fight it.

He heard a vehicle pull into the driveway and immediately went to the door. Pippa stepped from the
car and rushed into his arms. "I'm so sorry. How are
you?" she asked.

Feeling her in his arms was a balm to his soul. "I'm
okay. We knew this was coming."

"But you're never really ready," she said, pulling
back to search his face.

"True, but we were more prepared than most," he
said and led her into the den.

"How is your father?" she asked.

"Not good," Nic said. "He was having some pain
with his foot, so he spent the whole night on the patio.
My brothers were sleeping in the guestroom. I think
my father must have taken an extra dose of pain re-
liever because he didn't even wake up when my brothers left early this morning. Goldie went in to take her
a croissant and some juice. He was the one who found
her. My father was horrified that she died alone." His
throat closed up.

Pippa took his hand in hers. "But your brothers, did
she see them?"

Nic nodded.

"It's almost as if she was waiting to see them again
and that gave her permission. You did a wonderful thing
by bringing them here," she said.

"Trust me, I had to be damn ugly to them to make
it happen," he said.

"And now there are other things to be done. Arrangements," she said. "How can I help you?"

Nic took a deep breath. "I need one more favor. My
mother wanted her ashes spread here in Chantaine."

"And a memorial service, too," she said, her eyebrows furrowing together in concern.

"Yeah," he said.

"I'll do my best. Not sure Stefan is speaking to me at the moment," she added in half jest.

"Why? Is he still upset that you moved out of the palace?" Nic demanded.

Pippa waved her hand in a dismissive gesture. "Stefan's always bothered about something. It's his nature. What about your brothers? You said they'd already left."

"They're on their way back," he said. "I'd like to do this quickly and get my father back to the States. There are too many sad memories for him here and he's going to have to find a new normal for himself."

Pippa nodded. "Okay, I'll go out by the pool area and make a few calls," she said and left him to his list.

Fifteen minutes later, she returned, relief on her face. "I was able to get permission for your mother's service. Because the weather has been good, I wondered if you would like it to take place outdoors. There's a lovely green park on the other side of the island that people use for all kinds of occasions including memorial services. Chairs can be set up for your family."

"That sounds good. Thank you," he said, mentally checking the decision off his list. Nic felt as if he had a million-mile journey in front of him. Pippa made everything feel easier, but soon enough, he would be back in the States and he would be handling everything by himself. Again.

Two days later, Pippa took a seat at the end of a second row of chairs arranged for Amelie Lafitte's memorial service. She didn't want to call attention to herself. By a stroke of luck, or fate, she'd located a minister who had lived in the same orphanage as Amelie. She was pleased that someone who had known Nic's mother would lead the service.

It was a beautiful morning. Amelie would have loved it.

"Excuse me, is that seat taken?" a familiar voice asked her.

Pippa looked up and surprise raced through at the sight of her sister-in-law, Eve, and her sister Bridget. She stood, feeling as if her heart would burst with gratitude. "I don't know what to say," she said. "I can't believe you're here."

"Of course we're here. You're family. This is where we're supposed to be. Stefan didn't come because he didn't want to turn things into a madhouse," Eve said. "But he sends his condolences to you and the Lafittes."

Pippa hugged Eve. "You must have given him a Texas-size lecture because the last I heard, I no longer had a title," she said.

Bridget rolled her eyes. "He's got to make that threat to each of us at some point. He just can't stand not having control sometimes, most times," she added and held out her arms. "Come here. Shame on you for suffering by yourself. Why can't you be more like me and make everyone suffer with you?"

Bridget's remark made her laugh despite how emotional she felt. "I knew none of you would approve," Pippa said. "But I couldn't turn my back on them."

"That's one of the many reasons we love you," Eve said as she took her seat. Bridget also took hers.

Within the next moments, many people arrived, taking seats and crowding around the area. "I didn't know this many people remembered Amelie," Bridget said, surprised at the number of people gathering in the park.

"You would understand if you'd met her. I wish you'd had the opportunity," Pippa said, her eyes suddenly filling with tears. "She was a magical person."

Bridget covered her hand in comfort and the Lafitte men arrived, filing into the front row of chairs reserved for Amelie's family. Seconds later, the minister stood at the front of the group and began to speak.

He delivered a heartfelt message with touches of humor as he described Amelie as a child and how she seemed to have held on to her sense of wonder despite life's trials. Nic then read a message his mother had written for the occasion. The sight of him so strong delivering his mother's last words wrenched at her. She knew he had to be suffering but wouldn't reveal it. Pippa wished with all her heart that she could help him.

As the service drew to a close, Pippa noticed Bebe, the proprietor of Amelie's favorite creperie, move toward the front of the crowd. "Please forgive the interruption, but Amelie was such a joy. We were so thrilled to receive a visit from her a short time ago and she was just as beautiful as ever. Several of us who knew her have asked and received permission to plant some buddleia in her honor. We've planted one already. It's over there," Bebe said, pointing to the flowering bush to the left of the crowd.

Eve gave a loud sniff. "Now that could make even me cry. A butterfly bush."

"And look," Bridget said. "There are butterflies."

Pippa saw the beautiful butterflies fluttering and met Nic's knowing gaze. Amelie had often said she wanted to be a butterfly. In that moment, she felt the bond between Nic and her solidify. They would always remember, together.

Nic asked her to come to the cottage after the service. She had arranged for a catering service to bring food. With all the turmoil of the past few days, Nic, his brothers and his father might have forgotten to eat, but their hunger would remind them soon enough. When she arrived, they were silently eating. Nic introduced her to his brothers and they all responded politely. Moments later, they all scattered except Nic.

"It was a beautiful service. I believe Amelie would have approved," she said.

"Yeah, especially with those butterflies. That caught me by surprise," he said, shoving one of his hands into his pocket. He'd pulled off his necktie and opened his shirt. Dark circles rimmed his eyes. Pippa knew he hadn't gotten much sleep.

"What else can I do for you?" she asked.

He pulled her into his arms. "Oh, hell, Pippa, you've already done more than I could imagine. The rest is up to me. I'll pack up my dad and we'll head out tomorrow."

Surprise rushed through her. She'd known he planned to leave soon, but not this soon. "Tomorrow?"

"Yeah, I need to get him away from Chantaine. I'll send in a team to clean up the cottage," he said.

"I can make those arrangements," she said.

"No, you've already done enough. Too much," he

said and sighed. "When I said fate would bring you and me together, I had no idea it would be for this. Or that it would turn out this way."

Pippa felt a twist of nerves at his words. "What do you mean 'turn out this way'?"

"Well, I've got to leave now. I've got to get my dad straight. There's no one else to do it," he said.

Alarm shot through her. "Are you saying goodbye?"

"No. I'm just saying I'm not free to be here with you right now. When I get my Dad settled, we'll see if you're still interested," he said.

Pippa stared at him in disbelief. "Of course I'll still be interested. Why wouldn't I be?"

"Your family still hates the Lafittes," he said. "In their eyes, I'll never be good enough for you."

"My family is rethinking their stance on the Lafittes. Besides, what's important is how I feel about you, not how they feel about you."

"We'll see, darlin'. You've taken a lot of heat for me. You deserve a break to decide if I'm worth the trouble," he said.

"But, Nic," she began and he covered her mouth with his index finger.

"Trust me. This is for the best," he said and lowered his mouth to kiss her.

Two weeks later when Pippa hadn't heard from Nic, she wasn't at all sure this *break,* or whatever Nic called it, was for the best. Plus, there was the matter of her increasingly regular nausea. When she counted the number of days since her last menstrual period, she broke into a sweat and got sick to her stomach again.

Even though she'd known she was late a couple weeks ago, she figured it was due to stress. After all, Nic had always used protection. So nothing could happen, right? The combination of her symptoms and that strange conversation she'd had with Amelie just before Nic's mother had died gnawed at her.

It took several more days for Pippa to work up the nerve to take a pregnancy test. She even dragged out the old disguise of the hated gray wig and ugly clothes and paid cash at the pharmacy so that no one would recognize her. She nearly fainted at the result. Positive. Perhaps she should get another test. She did, three of them, actually, from different pharmacies. The results were all positive.

She knew she needed to tell Nic, but this wasn't the kind of news she could give over the phone. It wasn't as if she could send a cheery little text saying Guess who's going to be a daddy? She knew he must be terribly busy making up for lost time with his businesses and helping his father create a new life, but the lack of contact from him only fueled questions and doubts inside her.

She and Nic had never discussed marriage, and she really didn't like the idea of him proposing just because she was pregnant. She wanted Nic to propose marriage because he didn't want to live without her.

Pippa rolled her eyes at herself. As if Nic Lafitte would ever allow himself to want a woman that much.

Suffering more and more each passing day, she avoided her family. Her older sister Valentina may have gotten pregnant without the benefit of marriage, but she'd had the good sense not to tell Stefan until she was on another continent. Pippa didn't want to even think about how to break the news to her brother.

She plunged herself into her studies and made progress that impressed even her. At the rate she was going, she could wrap up the last of her dissertation within a couple months. She wondered if she would be showing then. Another week passed and she hadn't heard from Nic. What did this mean? Had he forgotten her? The possibility made her ill. What if this had just been a fling for him? What if he hadn't fallen as deeply for her as she had for him? What if she was truly alone? And now with a baby on the way... Even with all the hours she'd been putting in for her dissertation, she was sleeping for only a few hours each night. She avoided looking in the mirror because she knew she was looking more tired and miserable with each passing day.

Pippa had successfully begged off two family dinners, but when Stefan called for an official meeting of all adult Devereauxs, she could no longer hide. The meeting was held in Stefan's office, which indicated potentially serious business. As Pippa entered the office, she noted the additional chairs. Bridget, her older sister Ericka, who lived in Paris, and her younger brother, Jacques, who'd responded to Stefan's missive by leaving his soccer team mid-tour. Ericka and Jacques were both talking on their cell phones.

"Pippa, there you are," Bridget said, then frowned at her. "Oh, my goodness, you look dreadful. What have you been doing to yourself? You need to let me set up a day at the spa for you."

"I've just been trying to make up time on my dissertation. Burning the midnight oil," she said.

"Well, don't burn any more. How are the Lafittes?" Bridget asked. "I apologize for not calling sooner. I've been so busy with the building of our ranch and both the twins got sick."

"I know you're busy. Nic and his father have gone back to the States. They both had a lot to do after Amelie's death," she said.

"Hmm," Bridget said, her mind clearly whirling. "He's been in touch, though, hasn't he? He hasn't just abandoned you after you helped his family."

"He hasn't abandoned me," Pippa said, even though she felt that way. "He's just terribly busy right now. Do you know why Stefan has called the meeting?"

"No," Bridget said.

"It must be big if he insisted that both Jacques and I come immediately," Ericka said and gave Pippa a hug. "I hope no one is ill."

Jacques turned off his phone and approached his sisters. "We're all here except Valentina. I'm stumped about this one. Stefan can go over the top easier than most, but I don't know—"

He broke off as Stefan and Eve entered the room. His assistant closed the door behind him. "Please be seated," Stefan said, his face, devoid of humor.

Pippa's stomach clenched at his expression.

Stefan gave a heavy sigh and sat on the edge of his desk. "As you all know, our father wasn't perfect. We can be thankful to him for our lives, our positions. Nothing will change that. However, he had a mistress for several years. She was a small-time actress. Her name was Ava London."

Pippa felt a stab of surprise, not that her father had

stepped out on her mother, but that Stefan knew the identity of this woman. She slid a sideways glance at Bridget, whose mouth gaped open.

Stefan gave another heavy sigh. "During their affair, Ava gave birth to two children."

Pippa and her siblings gasped in unison. Her mind whirled at the implications.

Stefan nodded. "According to the advisers, this development shouldn't affect succession. The son, Maxwell Carter, is thirty years old and is living in Australia. The daughter, Coco Jordan, is a—" He cleared his throat. "She's a nanny in Texas."

Pippa felt her stomach roll with the news. She couldn't help thinking about her own unborn child. "What else do we know about them? Did Ava raise them? What—"

Stefan shook his head. "Ava made an agreement with my father. He would support her until her death if she gave her children up for adoption and didn't reveal their existence. Ava passed away two weeks ago and her attorney is determined to follow her wishes, which are to ensure that her children know that they have Devereaux blood."

"Great," Bridget muttered. "This sounds like a public relations nightmare."

"It is," Stefan said. "The two children may also have some rights to an inheritance."

Bridget scoffed. "But they haven't had to perform any duties," she protested. "We've spent our life serving."

"True, but our attorneys have not been able to determine the legalities concerning their inheritance," he said.

Pippa skipped over the money issues. She had tried to be aware of economics ever since Stefan had begun to complain about frivolous costs. Her biggest expense had been the cost of her degree and she'd been fortunate to receive scholarships. "What are they like?"

She felt Bridget stare at her. "What do you mean what are they like? They're illegitimate Devereauxs."

"But they're people, human beings," Pippa said. "She's our half sister. He's our half brother."

Eve met her gaze and smiled, giving her a thumbs-up.

"Leave it to Pippa to bring in the human element," Stefan said and gave a half smile. "Both of Coco Jordan's parents have died. She's finishing her education after taking care of her mother during a terminal illness. Her parents left her no inheritance, so we're not sure how she'll respond to the news that she could gain financially from being a Devereaux. The advisers and public relations staff want to control the release of this information, so we will be inviting her to Chantaine as soon as possible."

"Mon Dieu," Ericka said. "You're going to bring her here? Why will you not pay her off and bury this information?"

"Because in a contemporary media environment, we have learned it's impossible to bury this kind of information. Our goal is to take this distressing news and to somehow make it work for us."

"We call that taking lemons and making lemonade," Eve said in her Texas drawl.

"So what's our new *brother* like?" Jacques asked sarcastically. "Knowing our luck, he's a drug dealer or something."

"Not that bad," Stefan conceded. "His adoptive parents live in Ohio. He graduated with a degree in engineering and has been working in Australia for the past few years." He paused a half beat. "He hasn't responded yet to our communications."

"Has the daughter?" Bridget asked.

"Yes," Stefan said. "But she hasn't yet accepted our invitation to come to Chantaine."

"Do you think this is a strategy to make us give her money?" Jacques asked.

"Jacques," Pippa said, "must you be so suspicious? Maybe this has taken her off guard, too. If she stuck with her mother during an illness, she can't be all bad."

The room turned silent because they all knew that Pippa had just helped the Lafittes during their difficult time. Pippa's stomach continued to churn. The realization that her father had denied his own children hit too close to the bone with her. She hadn't been able to talk to Nic yet. How would he respond to the news about her pregnancy?

Suddenly, her feeling of nausea overwhelmed. "Excuse me, I need to leave," she said and ran for the toilet connected to Nic's office. After she was sick, she splashed her face and mouth with water. Glancing into the mirror, she braced herself for what she would face on the other side of her door.

Taking several deep breaths, Pippa opened the door. All of her siblings were standing, waiting. Bridget crossed her arms over her chest, tapping her foot. "Do you have something you want to tell us?" she asked.

Pippa bit her lip. "Not really," she said.

Eve chuckled and the sound eased something inside her.

Stefan narrowed his eyes. "Pippa," he said.

She sighed. "Eve's not the only one who is pregnant," she said.

Stefan's face turned to granite. "Lafitte," he said in disgust. "I'll make him pay."

Her stomach turned again. "No," she said and raced for the toilet again.

Bless her Texan heart, Eve saved Pippa from a grueling discussion with Stefan. Pippa decided she needed to thank the heavens for Eve on a more regular basis. Eve had come through for her in several critical situations.

Pippa returned home and breathed a sigh of relief. She wished, however, that she would hear something, anything, from Nic. She finally gave in, called his cell and left a message. "Hope you and your father are okay," she said. "I need to talk to you when you get a chance."

Less that twenty-four hours later, she got a return call. When she saw the caller ID, her heart hammered so fast she could hardly breathe, let alone speak. "Hi," she said.

"Hey," he said. "It's been nuts here. My father took too many sleeping pills and he's been in the hospital. He's in rehab right now and I'm working on interim housing for him. How are you?"

How could she top his troubles? "I'm fine. I just thought we should touch base," she said, pacing the small den of her apartment.

A short silence followed. "You sound different. Are you sure you're okay?"

"Yes," she said. "I'm fine."

"I would have called you, but I've been slammed with my dad's issues."

"I understand," she said, adding as much backbone to her voice as she could muster. "I'm sorry he's struggling."

"Yeah. I could have predicted it. The good news is my youngest brother has started checking in on him," Nic said.

"That's wonderful. I know your brothers' relationship with your father has been, well, precarious," she said.

"That's a nice way of saying their relationship with him was in the toilet. Flushed repeatedly," Nic said. "My two other brothers don't appear to give a rip, but Alex is working at it. There's hope anyway."

"That's good," she said. "I'm glad."

Another awkward silence stretched between them. "You sure you're okay?"

"I'm fine," she insisted.

"How are the Devereauxs?" he asked.

"In perfect health," she said.

"Good to hear. Stefan breathing down your throat?" he asked.

"No more than usual," she said.

"I need to go," he said. "I'll call you in a couple of days. I'm glad you called. It's so good to hear your voice."

The call was disconnected and it took several seconds before she began to breathe again. His last words vibrated through her. *It's so good to hear your voice.*

He called and left a message the following day. She missed it, damn it, because she was in a meeting with her professor. Three days after that, there was a knock at her door. She looked out the peephole. It was Nic. Her heart hammered against her rib cage. She felt a jolt of nausea rise from her belly.

"Just a moment," Pippa called. She willed her stomach to calm down. Turning away from the door, she took several breaths and told herself she would get through this. She walked to the door and opened it. "Hi," she said.

"Hi," he said, studying her. "Are you okay? You don't look well," he said.

"It's good to see you, too," she said and headed for the toilet. Moments later, she returned to her small den where Nic stood with a brooding expression on his face.

"You're not sick, are you?" he asked.

"Not really," she said. "I've just had some nausea lately."

He frowned. "That was one of my mother's symptoms," he said.

Her heart softened. "Oh, it's not that. I'm not sick that way, Nic."

"How can you be sure?" he asked.

"I just am. Trust me," she said.

He searched her face for a long moment. "Then what is it?"

She took a deep breath. "Why don't we sit down? Would you like water or ginger ale?"

"Ginger ale," he echoed, clearly disgusted.

"Water," she said and laughed. "Have a seat." She filled two glasses with ice and water and brought them into her small den. Giving one of the glasses to him, she sat across from him. "I didn't expect you."

He took several swallows of water. "I didn't like the way you sounded."

She winced. "How is your father?"

"Okay at the moment. Alex is checking in on him." He set his glass down on a coaster on a lamp table. "What the hell is going on? Something's wrong. If you want to dump me, just say it."

Pippa dropped her jaw in astonishment. "That thought hasn't occurred to me."

"Then why are you acting so weird?" he demanded.

"I wasn't aware that I was acting weird," she said.

"Well, you are," he said.

"We haven't seen each other in nearly a month and we didn't talk for almost three weeks," she pointed out.

"I told you what was happening with my father," he said.

"Yes, but that doesn't change the fact that we didn't communicate for three weeks."

He frowned at her. "You're still not telling me what's going on," he said. "Spit it out."

She took a sip of her ice water, hoping the cool hydration would help calm her nerves. "What made you come to Chantaine?"

"You," he said.

She gave a nod, but didn't say anything.

"And I missed you," he admitted.

"That's good to know," she said in a dry voice.

"What the hell—" He broke off. "What's going on?"

"I'd rather not discuss it at the moment," she said. "I'd rather hear your true feelings for me."

He met her gaze for a long moment, then raked his hand through his hair. "You're more important to me than I had planned," he said.

"What had you planned?" she asked.

He shrugged. "I knew we would be together."

"So you planned for a fling, a temporary affair," she said.

"Yes."

His honest answer, which she'd asked for, stabbed at her.

"What had you planned?" he asked.

His question caught her off guard. "I don't know that I made any real plans," she said. "I just knew I couldn't turn away from you. The situation with your mother made it even more intense. I wanted to be with you. I wanted to be there for you." She closed her eyes and allowed the words to tumble from her heart. "I fell in love with you, and now I'm afraid I'm in this all by myself."

"You're not," he said. "But I don't want to be a wedge between you and your family. You would grow to hate me for that."

"It's not right for you to make that decision for me. Don't you see that in another way you're treating me like Stefan does? You're treating me like I don't know my own mind and heart." She clasped her hands together tightly and voiced her worst fear. "Are you sure this isn't some kind of smokescreen to hide the fact that you don't really love me and you don't want to be with me?"

His eyes lit with anger. "That's the most ridiculous thing I've ever heard you say."

"It isn't at all ridiculous to me, and it occurs to me that if I have to extract a commitment from you, then maybe I don't want it after all," she said, feeling a terrible wrenching sensation inside her.

He pulled her against him. "What do you want from me?"

"Not much," she said. "Just undying love, devotion and adoration."

"You've had that for months," he said.

She was afraid to believe him. "Why didn't you tell me?" she asked, her eyes burning with tears.

"I had to wait for you to catch up," he said and cupped her face.

Pippa finally saw everything she'd been afraid to wish for right there in his eyes.

"I love you, Pippa. I just don't want to make your life a living hell. I want to give you an opportunity to—" he shrugged "—come to your senses."

"Too late for that," she said, laughing breathlessly. "Besides, if being without you means I'm coming to my senses, then I don't want to do that." She bit her lip. "But there's something else I have to tell you."

"What?"

"I'm pregnant."

Epilogue

Nic felt as if Pippa had hit him upside the head with a two-by-four. In a way, she had. It took three seconds before his mind moved into high gear. His immediate response was primitive and protective.

"You have to marry me," he said. "Your brother may want to kill me, but our child deserves a father."

Pippa winced. "That was romantic," she said in a wry voice.

Nic sweated bullets. He couldn't lose her. He had to protect her. He had to protect their child. He had to make her see everything he'd tried to hide. "I love you. I want to be with you all the time. Forever. I just didn't know how we could work it out with your family. Cut me some slack. I didn't plan on falling for a princess."

"That's much better," she said and pressed her face against his chest. "I wanted you to want me for me, not just because I'm having your child."

"That was never an issue," he said, stroking her crazy curls with his hand. He couldn't believe his luck. Pippa was pure gold without her title and somehow he'd managed to win her heart. "So am I gonna need to do the pirate thing and steal you away?"

She laughed and the husky sound vibrated against his chest. "No. I think everything will be okay once you talk with Stefan."

Nic anticipated a rough discussion, but was determined to do whatever was necessary for her and their baby. "I'm up for it."

"My family can be difficult," she said.

"You're worth it," he said and sealed his promise to her with a kiss.

Later that day, Nic met with Stefan. Nic didn't blame Stefan for being protective of Pippa. She was worth protecting. If the situation were reversed and Stefan had gotten his sister pregnant, Nic would have knocked him into next week. Nic admired Stefan's physical restraint and did everything he could to reassure the prince that he was devoted to Pippa. Nic suspected it would take a while to win over Pippa's clan, but he would keep chipping away at it.

Despite their differences, Nic and Stefan had a lot in common. One thing they both agreed on was that Nic and Pippa should get married right away. Three weeks later, he pledged everything including his troth, allegiance, love and devotion to Pippa. He was in it for good and he was relieved that she was, too. Nic hadn't known he could love a woman this much, but he'd never met anyone who brought him so much peace and happiness at the same time. He knew it wasn't possible to be any happier than he was with Pippa.

Until Pippa took him to a level he'd never imagined months later, when she gave birth to a beautiful baby girl. Pippa insisted that they name the baby Amelie and Nic had a feeling that the baby was gonna wrap him around her finger the same way her mother had. He was damn sure he didn't deserve all this joy, but he wasn't giving up the treasure he'd been given for anything. Her Highness was stuck with him, and thank God, she seemed to be just as happy about it as he was.

* * * * *

wires in the same manner. He must exercise positively
the very highest degree of skill with the parts.

One Corps and all, in a general sense, undergoes
changing him, A little at a time, but in a specific rapidity
with important load that may make the plates on the said
his dealt, feeling, and two abreast seem as very but
brought his electric sense try the point. Final. Provided
with some he adds security. 20 the total. All it would
use the no reaction such a energy given to any charge
of the principal. that with her, and dealt it for the
straight to his late, heap, should it be at his position

Dear Reader,

What would it be like to grow up with an identical twin who was nicer than you were? It's hard enough not comparing yourself to others without having a mirror image beside you, doing everything tidier, neater, more precisely.

Except, what if your twin *wasn't* so perfect? What if she'd got herself into a mess and you finally had a shot at pulling the family together?

That was my starting premise for this book.

Some say that splitting from the same egg makes you identical right down to your personality. Every parent of twins I talked to says that's baloney. So I took a free spirit—Vivienne Jansen—and gave her a nurturer as an identical twin. Then I found her a hero.

You may already have met Ross Coltrane, the hero's best friend in *Here Comes the Groom*. The heroine of *Here Comes the Groom* calls him an alpha hole—an annoying combination of asshole and alpha male. Obviously the guy needed a lesson or twenty. What better woman for a Special Forces explosives expert than a firecracker?

Ross is one of a five-strong Special Forces team, only three of whom survived an ambush some nineteen months earlier. Each survivor is dealing with the aftermath in their own way. Ross wants to take the biblical route—an "eye for an eye"—except he's still recovering from his injuries and is struggling to reach combat fitness. The last thing he needs is to be distracted by a family drama that potentially threatens his relationship with his brother. But that's the situation he finds himself in, after Viv's sister-swap forces him to become her reluctant ally.

I love feedback from readers. E-mail me at karina@ karinabliss.com and let me know how the story worked for you.

Karina Bliss

STAND-IN WIFE

BY
KARINA BLISS

First published in Great Britain 2012
by Mills & Boon, an imprint of Harlequin (UK) Limited,
Eton House, 18-24 Paradise Road, Richmond, Surrey TW9 1SR

© Karina Bliss 2011

ISBN: 978 0 263 89464 6
ebook ISBN: 978 1 408 97858 0

23-0912

Harlequin (UK) policy is to use papers that are natural, renewable and recyclable products and made from wood grown in sustainable forests. The logging and manufacturing processes conform to the legal environmental regulations of the country of origin.

Printed and bound in Spain
by Blackprint CPI, Barcelona

To the Pyle women—Judy, Hayley and Debi—who
read every book and say all the right things.
With lots of love.

CHAPTER ONE

"DON'T TELL ME NOT TO PANIC. Any sensible person would panic!"

Vivienne Jansen held the phone away from her ear as her twin's remaining thread of sanity snapped.

"Why the hell did I ever listen to you...I must be crazy."

Seventeen hours into her surprise visit, Viv sat down on the floral couch in her sister's suburban Auckland home, eyed the schnoodle glaring at her through the front door's sidelight and really tried not to take all this unjustified hostility personally. "Of course you're upset," she soothed. "You're about to have surgery, but don't worry I'll—"

"Who talked me into wearing high heels?" Merry demanded. "Who?"

"Stature adds confidence—" Viv crossed her own teeter-high ankle boots "—and you said you needed a boost for the job interview this morning."

"Something *else* I let you talk me into. Except I won't be a nurse here, I'll be a patient with a broken shin." Merry's voice broke. "As if my life wasn't enough of a mess already. Oh, Viv, what will I *do?* They say I'll be here at least a week." Her sister was in Hamilton, an hour south of Auckland and the perfect place, Viv had argued over last night's jug of duty-free margaritas, for a fresh start. The schnoodle barked. "What's wrong with Salsa?"

"Nothing." Returning the white-and-gray miniature hellhound's glare, Viv lifted a finger to her lips. He gave her a "you're kidding, right?" look and barked again. "He's playing in the yard…. Good dog!" *Yeah, right.*

Salsa's begrudging tolerance had disappeared the moment Merry left the house, replaced by low warning growls that frayed Viv's jet-lagged nerves. When she'd discovered him chewing one of her Jimmy Choo UGG boots she'd lured him outside with the second sheepskin boot and the fervent wish that he'd choke on it.

They were not friends, oh, no.

Salsa kept barking, and Viv hurried into the guest bedroom and shut the door. Maybe if he couldn't see her.

Merry started to cry. "Charlie's going to find out I was interviewing out of town…he'll be furious that I'm considering moving with the kids…. Oh, God, he'll use my hospitalization as an excuse to move them to his mom's. Sue for full custody like he threatened when we first separated."

"As if he would—or could—take the kids away from you. Take deep breaths." *Encourage that presurgery sedative into the bloodstream.*

Though, what did she know about custody laws in New Zealand? Not to mention her brother-in-law had been acting completely out of character. Charlie had walked out on the marriage three months ago and was apparently making her sister's life a misery with his onerous demands on visitation.

How could Merry move on when they were constantly doing kiddy handovers, and her estranged spouse was dating their baby's day-care teacher? Worse, Merry still pined for the SOB. It was way past time for an intervention.

"Charlie's at school camp with Tilly for two more nights," she reminded her twin. The four-day adventure camp, organized through school, relied heavily on parental volunteers. "That leaves us plenty of time to come up with a way to spin this."

"But what about my baby?" Merry sobbed. "I'm due to pick up Harry from Linda's at five and—"

"I'll go get him and I won't say a word to your mother-in-law about the accident." Viv opened a window to dispel the lingering mustiness of the spare room and the scent of freesias wafted up from the garden bed.

"He'll be thrilled to meet his auntie." Her nephew had been in bed when Viv made her surprise appearance at 7:00 p.m. and Bad Granny had picked him up early. Viv didn't do early. As a New York–based costume designer, she was a bright lights, late nights kind of girl.

"You're right…of course you're right." Merry gulped in an obvious effort to compose herself. "Look, I'm sorry about blaming you earlier. This is all my fault."

"You have every right to make a fresh start," she said hotly. "And the job's ideal for your new circumstances… school hours five days a week instead of three long grave-yard shifts. And it's not as if you'd be taking the kids to Siberia. It's only an hour's commute, for God's sake."

It had been precisely this defeatism that had prompted Viv to fly home when the cancellation of an upcoming Broadway show freed up her schedule for a month. Plus, she needed to get away from Jean Paul.

"Anyway, I'll pack you a bag, pick up the baby and drive straight to Hamilton. We should be there by the time you're out of surgery."

"No. Harry will need a bath and dinner first." Her sister swung into mom mode. "Do you know anything about looking after a fifteen-month-old?"

"Of course I do, I babysit all the time." Theater divas. But it would be easy enough to find information on the in-

ternet…who was the kid guru again?…Dr. Block…Flock…
Spock.

Merry sounded doubtful. "So you like children now?"

Viv paraphrased W. C. Fields. "As long as they're well
cooked." Her twin didn't laugh. Viv placed a hand on her
heart where it got tangled in the beads. "I promise I'll look
after him as though he were my own…and you don't want
to leave him with the mother-in-law, do you?"

Linda Coltrane was one of those awful women who saw
her son's wife as a rival and had made her people-pleasing
daughter-in-law's life miserable for years. The old bat must
be ecstatic having her son living under her roof again.

Merry seemed to read Viv's thoughts. "You will be
polite, won't you? To Linda? And don't get all caught up
defending me if she blames me for the breakup…just grab
Harry and get out of there."

"You can't be serious, she blames you? Even though
Charlie walked out? Even though he's already dating another woman and—" Viv bit her lip to stop herself from
saying, "was probably screwing her while you were married?"

Meredith refused to discuss the circumstances around
the separation. But last night after the third margarita, Viv
had asked, "He cheated on you, didn't he?" and her twin
had burst into tears. Enough said.

"And don't wear anything too revealing. You know how
conservative Linda is."

Viv looked down at her bare legs—hers and Merry's
best feature—under a short-sleeved, sunflower-patterned
minidress, their length accentuated by kick-ass-high Isabel
Marant boots. Her push-up bra cleavage was all but hidden
under a tangle of thrift-shop beads and phony diamond
strands.

In New York and London her style was called boho chic;

in the New Zealand rural farming community where she'd grown up her vibrant mixing of color, texture and bling had made Viv the brunt of jokes.

She'd forgotten that after a decade of being a costume designer living in cities that embraced diversity. Forgotten that when the other kids teased her, Meredith had always begged her to try to fit in.

"I'll put some jeans on," she said. Her sister was injured and frightened, and hurt feelings were selfish. "What do you want me to pack for you—toiletries, night wear?"

"I don't think you should come in the dark." Meredith was speaking a little slower. The tranquilizer must be kicking in. "You're not used to the left-hand side of the road anymore. Leave in the morning."

She wasn't used to driving anymore, period. "You need someone there when you wake up."

"I've managed without you for ten years. I'm sure I'll survive another night."

Her sister could always guilt-trip her with one pointed comment. And like a pebble in a pond it rippled back to older transgressions Viv could never atone for. Being the greedy twin in the womb and taking more than her share of nutrients—unequal placenta sharing. Asking to be put in a different class on their first day of school. Suggesting at twelve that they didn't share *every* friend.

Merry didn't understand Viv's claustrophobia because she'd always been the twin who embraced family as opposed to the twin who ran away from it.

No, that used to be true. Viv might still be a screwup in her romantic life but everything else was under control— she'd even tossed out the peroxide and let her hair grow. She was so secure in herself, she was relaxed about looking like her twin again. "I'll fix this, Merry. Have I ever failed to get you out of trouble?"

"I can't think…" Thank God for sedatives.

"That's settled then," she said briskly. She should have come home immediately after her sister's marriage broke up. But she was here now.

"Viv, this is important." Merry's voice was a drowsy whisper. "I can't lose my kids. Not them, too."

"You won't, I swear." Before her twin lost the plot completely, Viv got the mother-in-law's address. Then she talked to the surgeon. First he described her sister's condition in terms she didn't understand—like "tibial shaft fracture" and "intramedullary rodding" before using words that unfortunately Viv did.

She sat on the bed and stuck her head between her knees as he described how a metal rod would be inserted down the center of Merry's shin to stabilize the break. He promised to call immediately after surgery with an update.

Viv hung up and dug in her tan slouch bag for her booklet of patron saints. For a moment she couldn't find the right saint to invoke. Her finger went down the list. Roch for knee problems and Servatius for foot troubles…nothing for shins. Finally, she found Mammes, protector of sufferers from broken bones, and said a little prayer.

Thumbing to the kids' saints a horrified thought struck her. Was a fifteen-month-old out of diapers? Rolling off the bed, she opened her laptop and looked up Dr. Spock.

After wasting ten minutes reading a fascinating article on Leonard Nimoy's prosthetic ears, she found potty training information. The news wasn't good. Unless Harry was extremely advanced—and given his father's stupidity in leaving the nicest woman in the world, Viv doubted it—she'd be dealing with diapers. The food thing was more encouraging. Most of what he ate could come out of a glass jar.

She realized she was chewing her very expensive false nails and stopped.

"Get a grip. If you can survive eighteen months as a fur groomer on *Cats*—" her first job "—you can survive looking after a little person for one night until the cavalry arrives." That reminded her—her father and brother didn't know she was in the country yet. Viv glanced at her watch. 4:30 p.m. They'd still be working the family farm, two and a half hours south. She'd call home later.

After hauling on a pair of Sass and Bide jeans she headed to the master bedroom to raid her sister's wardrobe for a sweater. When she'd packed, she'd imagined a New Zealand spring to be a lot warmer. Viv opened Merry's wardrobe, scanned the hangers and sliding baskets and winced. Had they sprung from the same species?

Half a dozen T-shirts in block pastels, far too many pairs of jeans, flat shoes and trainers. Sensible skirts, even more sensible blouses and shorts befitting a Brownie troop leader.

Only one outfit caught Viv's eye, the dress she'd given Meredith on her previous visit home two years ago. Pulling it out, Viv saw it still had the tag on. And she'd tried so hard to channel her sister's tastes, right down to Merry's favorite cherry-red. Maybe the deep V in the back deterred her twin...it wasn't a dress you could wear a bra with. Not that either of them had much to support.

Viv returned it to the wardrobe and dragged out a V-necked green angora cardigan, which matched the leaves on her sunflower minidress. Linda would just have to deal with the cleavage Viv couldn't hide.

Then she called the cab company she'd used last night.

The dog's feathery curly hackles rose the minute she opened the front door. He gave a low, warning growl. Viv put a hand on her hip. "Cut the act, Salsa. I was raised on a farm with working dogs…I'm not scared of a poodle-schnauzer cross with button eyes and a shoe fetish."

Salsa sprang; Viv slammed the door closed.

"Okay I take that back," she called through the mail slot. "You're a fierce and awesome beast. How about we make a fresh start?"

Salsa snarled. His limbs and face were white, his body a darker gray that made him look like he was wearing a cute little jacket. He had a tuft of darker fur between his eyes that acted as a permanent frown. Viv glanced at her watch. "C'mon, mutt, I don't have time for this."

Considering for a moment, she went to the kitchen, donned a rubber glove and picked up the plate of four boneless sirloin steaks defrosting on the countertop. Opening the window closest to the front door a few inches she waved a bloody steak like a white flag. "See this? Yours if you behave yourself. Sit!"

Salsa barked. Once. Twice.

"Tough negotiator, huh? Okay, I can make a goodwill gesture." Viv tossed the raw steak at the narrow opening and missed. It slid down the inside pane, leaving a smear of blood behind it and flopped onto the hardwood floor. "Damn it!" Outside, Salsa leaped up and put his paws against the pane, scratching at the glass. "No…. Don't do that…wait!" Grabbing the meat she shoved it through the gap. It hit the pavement with a wet slap and Salsa fell on it, wolfing it down and then whining for another.

Viv picked up a second steak. "Sit!"

Salsa barked.

"Sit," she repeated sternly, and the dog half crouched on his haunches. "Nice try, mutt, but I can still see air." Reluctantly Salsa sat. Viv tossed him a second steak and worked out her escape plan. When the taxi driver honked, she opened the front door, hurled the two remaining steaks as far as she could across the yard, then sprinted for the gate, slamming it behind her.

Peeling off the bloody glove she dropped it in the neighbor's curbside trash can and smiled at the startled driver. "How fast can you drive?"

CHAPTER TWO

To be nicknamed The Iceman by your peers in the SAS—one of the world's elite military units—was a hard-earned accolade.

And yet Ross Coltrane was close to surrendering his famed self-control. Not because he was under enemy fire. Not because his foe had a territorial advantage and knew how to play him. No, what brought him to the verge of losing his temper was his stepmother's total disregard for civilian casualties.

"It's okay, mate." Pitching his voice gentle, he picked up his baby nephew who'd unexpectedly scooted in on his butt from the lounge where he must have been playing. Tears welling in his big brown eyes and lower lip trembling, Harry looked between his grandmother and uncle. The child hated conflict.

"No, it's not okay," Linda snapped. "It's not okay for you to bully a fifty-nine-year-old woman with a heart condition in her own home."

Still smiling at Harry, Ross said softly, "You should have told me he was here." He'd never have raised his voice if he'd known. Linda, of course, could justify any outburst by saying she was provoked. "What'cha got there, mate, a train?" Harry held it up. Yellow and green and covered in drool. His free hand tugged at his eyelashes. "This kid needs a nap."

"I know that." Linda's high color faded. "Come to

Nana, darling." A waft of expensive perfume, repellent through association, hit Ross as she took the baby. "Yes, that's right," she crooned when Harry pointed to Ross. "Naughty Uncle Ross was being mean to poor Nana…. His mother was supposed to be here forty minutes ago so I didn't bother with his nap."

Was that actually defensiveness? Interesting. Normally Linda didn't give a shit about what anybody thought. It was the only thing he could admire about her.

Ross reached for Harry. "I'll do it." He wasn't leaving until he got what he wanted and that meant getting the baby out of the line of fire.

She spun the toddler away. "You're not going anywhere in this house. God knows what else you'll find that you suddenly decide is yours. Wait here while I put him down."

I'd like to put you down.

She headed upstairs, all bone-and-gristle chic. He thought he'd worked through his hatred of this woman with her acid tongue, preserved face and remorseless jealousy. Ross resisted the urge to yell, "You're sixty-one, sweetheart, the heart condition's a scam and Dad's been dead for four months…there's nothing else to compete over anymore."

Except there was. He looked at the faded sampler hanging above the black lacquered sideboard. Ross wished to God he'd waited for Charlie in the car last week instead of coming to the door. Then he wouldn't have seen it, wouldn't have felt the pressure build until he had to act.

His thigh and knee started to ache, a sign he'd pushed himself too hard at training again. It had been seventeen months since a land mine in Afghanistan had broken the leg in two places. The damn thing should be doing better than this.

Frustrated he paced it out. Linda was taking a long

time…but then she'd always liked to make him wait. For acknowledgment, for attention, for his turn.

Ross stared at the sampler, picking out a line of bible verse, *A time to get*... Maybe he should just grab the damn thing and run. He scanned the hall for something to stand on, dismissing a decorative stool with delicately turned legs. Style with no substance. Like its owner.

He turned at the sound of footfalls. Linda swept down the marble stairs, her gaze hostile as she tidied her gray-blond chignon. *What the hell am I doing here? She's not going to be reasonable.* But he had to try. "Like I said, it has no value, except to me."

When his mother left it to him, Ross had given it to his father, but John had refused to accept it. Said it had been stitched 1924 and Yvonne was set on Ross having it. He'd finally agreed to look after it until Ross was old enough to appreciate his heritage.

Guess he'd finally grown up.

Now Linda didn't so much as glance at it. "It reminds me of John. I can't part with it."

Ross tried but failed to keep the scorn out of his voice as he said, "Don't you have plenty of other things to bond with?" Linda had inherited everything under his father's will and Ross hadn't bothered contesting. His father had made his choice years ago, which family he supported.

He'd ended up with a few of John's personal effects—cufflinks, a watch, photographs—only because his half brother had forced them on him, Ross suspected behind Linda's back.

"Is that what this is about," she said. "The will? You break your father's heart by cold-shouldering him all these years and now you're pissy because he didn't leave you anything?"

Ross refused to be baited. "All I want is that sampler—left to me by my *mother*—which Dad was safe-keeping for me. That's all, Linda." In retrospect he should have asked Charlie to make the case for him.

"You've had your own house for five years and never came to get it. Now John's dead suddenly it's all-important. I wonder why?"

"Call me sentimental." The sampler was tacky and clichéd; a bible verse embroidered in the middle of a border of flowers and birds. Yet Ross couldn't stand the idea of something so precious to his mother ending up with the woman who'd stolen everything else from her.

And she knew that, yes, Linda knew that. She'd always been able to sense what was important to him and had taken it away. He'd only lived with her from the ages of twelve to sixteen when his mother's death gave custody to his dad but she'd very quickly taught him to hide his emotions. God bless her, she was probably responsible for the grit and determination that had got him into the SAS. Certainly his father never had a backbone.

"You don't really want it," she said bitterly. "You just don't want *me* to have it."

A part of Ross could even understand her insecurity. His father had regretted his midlife fling and was talking reconciliation with Ross's mother when his former secretary presented her trump card. She was pregnant. But both Ross and Linda knew John had really loved his wife.

"Please," he said.

Surprise flashed in her hazel eyes. "John and I could have been happy," she said. "If you hadn't made him feel so guilty with your judgmental attitude. And my son would have fought for full custody if you hadn't contradicted my advice. So you know what, Ross? Go to hell."

THE EAST INDIAN CABDRIVER whistled as he drew up outside Granny Coltrane's two-story concrete monolith.

"If the owner was a guy you'd have to wonder if he was compensating for something," Viv commented, making him laugh. "Though, I have to give her credit for the front door."

Ten feet high and fire-engine red, it brought scale and color to the stark design. Shame the garden had the life topiaried out of it. She handed over the fare—embarrassed at not having enough for a tip. Fortunately tipping wasn't common practice here. She'd have to borrow the fare home from Linda. It was too late to stop at a bank and exchange more U.S. dollars for Kiwi. "Now remember my advice, Sanjay."

"Leaving town isn't running *away* from your troubles," he quoted her. "It's running *toward* new possibilities."

"Exactly. If you don't want this arranged marriage, then go hide out with your cousin in Australia."

"Thank you, Vivienne, and I hope your sister's surgery goes well. You wanted me to remind you—"

"To be polite to her mother-in-law. I'm on it." As she hurried down the sweeping circular driveway, Viv practiced. "Hello, Linda! So how about your saintly son cheating on my sister? Guess the apple doesn't fall far from the topiaried tree."

Skirting Linda's Range Rover—she could just imagine that small woman in a big 4WD terrorizing suburbia—she snagged Merry's cardigan on the thorn of a rose and stopped to untangle it.

The front door slammed, Viv pulled the cardigan free. "Linda, how nice to—" The platitude died on her lips as she recognized the powerfully built man bearing down on her.

Her pulse gave a queer little skip even though it had

SAVE UP TO 25%

Subscribe to Cherish today and get 5 stories a month delivered to your door for 3, 6 or 12 months and gain up to 25% OFF! That's a fantastic saving of over £40!

MONTHS	FULL PRICE	YOUR PRICE	SAVING
3	£43.41	£36.90	15%
6	£86.82	£69.48	20%
12	£173.64	£130.20	25%

As a welcome gift we will also send you a FREE L'Occitane gift set worth £10

PLUS, by becoming a member you will also receive these additional benefits:

🌹 FREE Home Delivery

🌹 Receive new titles TWO MONTHS AHEAD of the shops

🌹 Exclusive Special Offers & Monthly Newsletter

🌹 Special Rewards Programme

No Obligation - You can cancel your subscription at any time by writing to us at Mills & Boon Book Club, PO Box 676, Richmond. TW9 1WU.

To subscribe, visit
millsandboon.co.uk/subscriptions

MILLS & BOON

been eight years since she'd hit on her sister's brother-in-law. Eight years since she'd called Ross Coltrane chicken for turning her down.

Time had sandblasted away whatever trace of softness he'd had, and there'd never been much. He was pale, tight-lipped and his gray eyes glowed like titanium after a rocket launch. Instinctively Viv stepped back and her heels sank into the garden mulch. "Are you all right?"

"What do you care?" he barked.

She blinked.

Impatiently Ross gestured for her to get out the way of his car. "Save the startled fawn look for someone who'll buy it."

"I can see you're mad," she said, perplexed. "But why take it out on me? I haven't done anything."

Ross snorted. "What color do you call that new lipstick you're wearing…scarlet? Suits you." His lip curled. "And explains why you're late picking up Harry."

"It's not scarlet, it's poppy-red." Edging past the Range Rover, she held out her hand. "Can we start over, please? Long time no see."

Ross stared incredulously at her outstretched arm. "You're joking, right?" He sidestepped her and went to the driver's side, pulling car keys from the pocket of his jeans.

It took a few seconds for Viv to find her voice. "When did you turn into such an *asshole?*"

The Range Rover's lights flashed as he deactivated the alarm. "About the same time you turned into a tramp."

She gasped.

"What are you going to do," he said, sneering, "go tattling to your big brother again? You know it really grinds my balls that I fell for that all-round nice girl persona you had going."

The penny dropped. He thought she was Meredith. Gentle, wouldn't-hurt-a-fly-or-fight-back Merry.

"You bastard. Where do you get off talking to M…me that way?"

"Yeah, keep playing the victim, you're good at that." Ross folded his arms, planted his muscular legs in a man stance. "Here's an idea, Meredith. Suck it up and accept some goddamn responsibility instead of letting Charlie take the fall with your family."

"Wait a minute…you're defending *Charlie?*" Next this Neanderthal would be telling her that if only Merry had made more effort in the bedroom, her husband wouldn't have strayed.

"Someone's got to. He's running himself ragged making sure the kids see him regularly and staying on top of his business."

"The only thing he's staying on top of is Harry's day-care teacher. Which broke up M…*my* marriage."

His expression hardened. "Is that how you're going to play it in the divorce court? Make false allegations to try and swing full custody? Think very carefully before choosing that route, Meredith."

Viv felt like Bruce Banner must have on the verge of turning into the Incredible Hulk. "Are you threatening me?"

"I'll do whatever it takes to protect my brother's interests."

She raised herself to her full height. "And I'll do whatever it takes to protect my…mine!"

Ross made an impatient gesture and dropped his keys. Impulsively Viv stepped forward and kicked them under the car. That'll make him think twice before bullying her twin again.

He muttered something, but the blood was pounding so

hard in her ears, she didn't catch it. Spinning on her heel, Viv marched to the house. To think she'd once pined for that son of a bitch.

She jabbed at the doorbell, once, twice. Thank heavens she'd never slept with him.

"Get lost!" yelled a woman's voice.

"Relax, it's not Ross," Viv said as she turned the handle, feeling an immediate rapport with Merry's mother-in-law. The huge door cantilevered open. Glancing over her shoulder she saw him kneeling awkwardly on the driveway to reach under the car. Remembering his injury, Viv squirmed.

"You're late." Dressed in black pants, a silver silk shell with chiffon sleeves and black pearls, Linda stood on a spindly stool, straining to reach an embroidery that hung above the sideboard. "But I guess you've thrown away any sense of responsibility along with your marriage."

"It's Viv," she said, feeling her temper spark again. "Meredith's been delayed."

"Brought in reinforcements, has she?" But Linda's tone had softened. She liked Viv. Or rather her success. "Well, Harry's having a nap so you'll have to wait. I'll make tea in a minute." Linda tiptoed to extend her reach and the large diamonds on her outstretched fingers sparkled in the late afternoon sun. "I can't reach the bloody thing."

"You want me to—?"

"I've got it. Here, take these." She thrust a tall aluminum vase of tiger lilies at Viv, who instinctively held out her hands in time to receive a dusting of orange pollen. "Be careful of your clothes, that stuff stains. Wash your hands in the bathroom through the door behind you."

Bemused, Viv placed the vase on the floor against the wall. "You're spring-cleaning?"

"Clearing out old junk." Linda hauled herself onto the

lacquered sideboard. From a kneeling position she un-hooked the picture frame. "I am so going to enjoy burn-ing this."

"Okaaay." Viv went into the powder room, nudging the door closed for a moment's respite. "Everyone's crazy around here," she muttered to her reflection. Twisting the space-age faucet, she began washing her hands. A thud reverberated through the wall. "Everything all right out there?"

Silence. Viv shut off the water, reached for a mono-grammed hand towel. "Linda?"

She turned the handle but the door only partially opened before it hit something solid. Viv ducked her head through the gap. "Lin—" The name caught in her throat.

The older woman lay on her back, arms outstretched, water from the overturned vase soaking her trouser hem. Her chignon had come loose and a thin ash-blond pony-tail snaked over her mouth. Wiggling frantically through the gap, Viv crouched beside her and lifted the fall of hair. Linda's eyes were closed, her skin the color of putty.

With a moan, Viv laid her cheek to the thin chest but heard nothing except the pounding of her own heart. CPR... She could never remember the number of compressions to breaths. Through her panic, she heard the starting roar of an engine. All SAS troopers were advanced paramedics. Shoving to her feet, Viv stumbled outside. "Ross!"

His attention was on the rearview mirror as he reversed the Range Rover down the driveway. Waving and yelling, Viv tore after the car. "Ross!" The radio must be on; he didn't respond. He was going to leave. At the end of the driveway he spun the wheel in a tight turn.

Accelerating into a sprint she dived over the hood, glimpsing Ross's startled face as he slammed on his brakes. In her sister's cashmere cardigan, Viv slid across the sun-warmed metal, rolled off the other side and landed on the road with a soft "Oomph." The driver's door flung open.

"What the—"

"Linda's not…breathing." Viv scrambled to her knees. "Help…her."

He ran, leaving the door open, the engine idling. Viv switched off the ignition and followed him, her breathing a sobbing hiccup.

She found Ross crouched over Linda, checking for a pulse. Sunlight sparkled off the spilled water at her feet and the pearly luster-painted toenails under the black stockings. The tiger lilies lay scattered over the pale marble, their long green stems releasing a faint swampy odor. "Call an ambulance." Tilting Linda's head, Ross pinched her nose closed and began CPR. Viv watched Linda's chest expand.

"Go!" he ordered between breaths, jarring her into action. It took three failed dials before Viv remembered New Zealand's emergency code was 111 and she had to run outside to check the letter box because she'd forgotten the street number. By the time she returned to the hall, Ross was starting chest compressions.

There was something terrible about those powerful interlocked fingers punching into Linda's fragile sternum. Viv lifted her gaze to his face and saw his focus. If anyone could save her, Ross could.

The thought steadied her, allowed her to think. Spying a toy-covered quilt on the carpet in the lounge, she shook the toys clear then wiped the water away from Linda's feet and laid the dry half across her legs.

"Heart attack?" Ross didn't look up.

"No…at least…I don't think so." Viv hugged herself. "I was in the bathroom and heard a thud. …I think she fell."

Dazed, she glanced around for the stool. It had skittered through the open sliding doors leading into the lounge.

Ross kept up compressions. "Check the back of her head."

Viv recoiled. "What?"

"Feel for a contusion."

Swallowing hard, she settled behind the unconscious woman, fighting the urge to cry. Linda Coltrane was a cantankerous woman but she was helpless…needing help. Tentatively she slid her fingers through the silky blond-gray hair. Ross stopped compressions and laid his fingers against the pulse in Linda's neck. His expression was grim. "Well?" he asked.

Because she was looking for lumps and bumps it took a few seconds for Viv to realize what she was feeling was soft and spongy. Cold sweat popped out on her forehead. She closed her eyes, fighting nausea. "Her skull is shattered," she heard herself say. Carefully she withdrew her hands.

Ross sat back on his heels. "Oh, God. Charlie," he rasped.

But Viv wasn't listening. She was staring at her blood-covered palms. Helen Mirren. Yes. Helen Mirren had played Lady Macbeth on Broadway last year. All those phony blood capsules…

Only, with the wail of sirens, the smell of iron, this was real…too horribly, horribly real.

"'Yet who would have thought the old man to have had so much blood in him?'" she quoted, Ross staring at her.

Viv's eyes rolled backward and she fainted.

CHAPTER THREE

SUNLIGHT REFRACTED OFF a chandelier, throwing rainbow splotches of blue, red and green over the ceiling. Pretty, thought Viv.

She was lying down, with her neck supported by something soft. But the ambiance was all wrong for meditation. Woozily she listened to a buzz of urgent voices, a clatter of steel on hard surface.

Viv caught sight of her boots elevated on a sofa arm, tan clashing with aubergine leather and frowned. Where was she?

"My sister-in-law was here when it happened. That's Meredith Coltrane. *M-E-R-E...*"

Viv snapped upright only to fall back on a wave of dizziness. "It's all right, love, you've had a shock," she heard a female voice say. "Take your time." Firm hands helped her to a sitting position and Viv caught a glimpse of a practical countenance and the St. John Ambulance insignia before she was pushed forward. "Head between knees. That's right."

She was sitting on a couch in Linda's lounge. At least that's where she guessed she was because she was staring at a plush white rug. Memory flooded back to her. With a moan she dragged her hands forward...the blood was gone.

"No, don't sit up yet. Another minute."

"Is Linda okay?" Maybe the paramedics had been able to save her, maybe—

"I'm so sorry."

A noise from the hall made her raise her head. Viv glimpsed a second paramedic pushing a gurney through the red front door, black straps holding a blanket snugly in place over the bulge of small feet. Ross, grim and composed, was talking to a cop. The cop was taking notes.

The paramedic caught the direction of her gaze. "He'll need to ask you a few questions when you're up to it. It's only a formality. They always attend in cases of accidental death."

Curling up, Viv faced the couch. "This can't be happening."

The woman patted her shoulder. "Like I said, take your time."

She left to help her colleague, and Viv stared at the fine leather.

"You okay?" said Ross gruffly.

Was she? Through her stage work, Viv had witnessed beheadings, stabbings and strangulation, and had taken a ghoulish interest in how makeup achieved bruised flesh and gaping wounds. But this was graceless, pointless... and permanent. "I was only talking to her twenty minutes ago."

Ross sat beside her and suddenly she was crying into his chest, big shuddering sobs. "I don't know why I'm reacting this way," she managed between paroxysms. "It's not like she ever had a nice word to say for anybody. The only person she's ever cared about was Charlie."

"And the kids."

Viv sobbed harder. "That's right, she and your dad took Tilly to Disneyland last year.... I n-need tissues."

"Ma'am?" said the policeman Ross had been talking to earlier, handing her a handkerchief. Viv sat up. Close up, he had kind eyes under bristling ginger eyebrows, the exact match of his light blue police shirt. He'd taken off his navy police cap, obviously out of respect. "Than-thank you." She blew her nose hard.

"I'm Officer Wright. Condolences for your loss. Can you fill me in on how it happened, Mrs. Coltrane?"

I'm not Mrs. Coltrane. Viv opened her mouth and closed it. Ross had been so menacing about custody…would a clarification right now *really* be in her sister's best interests? On the other hand, was providing false information to the police in *her* best interest?

I can't lose my kids. Not them, too.

"I'd come to pick up my…son." Viv took a deep breath. "He's napping upstairs. I met Ross in the driveway. We—" she faltered but The Iceman didn't flicker so much as an eyelash "—talked. Then I came inside. Linda was standing on that stool, trying to reach a picture." She pointed to the stool on its side near the living room doorway.

A second policeman came in from the hall to examine it. It would take her a while to get used to the absence of gun holsters here. He held up the stool wordlessly. One filigree leg had splayed. "That explains the fall," said Officer Wright. Beside her Ross stiffened and she saw he was staring transfixed at the empty hook on the wall.

"Ross?" Viv took his hand. "Are you feeling okay?"

He pulled free of her hold. "Fine."

Officer Wright cleared his throat. "If it's any comfort, Sergeant Coltrane, our paramedics agree with your assessment. Her head hit the marble first, fracturing the skull. Nothing would have saved her."

"Thank you," Ross said so politely that Viv remembered he was trained to handle worse than a split skull. That he had.

"You were saying, Mrs. Coltrane?"

Viv returned her attention to Officer Wright. "Linda

handed me the flowers so she could climb onto the side-board." Her voice wobbled, she paused to compose herself. Ross disappeared and returned with a glass of water, which she gulped gratefully. "My hands got dirty, I went into the bathroom." Casually the second cop pushed off the door-jamb and disappeared into the bathroom.

Wait a minute. Were they checking her story? Disgruntled ex kills bitchy mother-in-law? Alarmed, she opened her mouth to tell the truth, when she remembered how Linda had looked with the ponytail across her waxen features, the water wicking up her elegant trousers.

Appearances had always been so important to Linda. Merry had never understood that, but Viv did. The woman had suffered enough indignity without adding the element of farce to her passing.

The cop reappeared. "Pollen on the hand towel."

"Linda said it would stain." Viv gathered her scattered wits. "As I started washing I heard a thud. I called out and she didn't answer. The door wouldn't open very far…she was lying behind it." The glass of water shook violently and Ross took it from her nerveless fingers. "I—I ran for my brother-in-law."

"I was pulling out of the driveway when Meredith threw herself on the hood." Ross indicated the scrape on Viv's elbow. She'd noted the burning sensation but hadn't made sense of it. Now seeing the trail of dried blood she grew faint again and had to look away.

"I'm sorry, I'm not normally a wimp."

"Your brother-in-law told us you're a nurse," said the cop who hadn't been introduced. "Why didn't you begin CPR?"

"I froze," she said truthfully. "Panicked. When I heard Ross start his car, all I could think about was stopping him."

Officer Wright jotted a note. "One of our guys did the same thing attending a car accident involving his grandmother. It happens."

"Was she all right?" Viv asked.

"Yeah," said the nameless policeman. "Granny pulled through."

A cry came from upstairs, grumpy and half-awake. Viv swallowed hard.

"The baby," Ross explained to the cops. "I'll get him."

Their first meet couldn't be in public. "No, I'll go." She dug her fingers into Ross's knee to stop him from getting up and he flinched. "I'm sorry, was that your injured leg?" Merry had said it was keeping him from active deployment.

"It's healed," he said coldly. "This is muscle strain."

Obviously a sore spot in more ways than one. Viv had a flash of inspiration. "Land mine in Afghanistan," she said to the cops. Here was a way of confirming herself— Merry—as one of the good guys. "You must have read about it early last year. It got massive press coverage."

"You mean you're the SAS trooper who survived that ambush?" Officer Wright looked toward his colleague. "Remember that shot of the airlift, Bill?"

The second cop forgot his reserve and came closer. "Yeah. You got carried to safety by that other guy...the hero what was his name? Held off an attack until reinforcements arrived."

Viv could tell by his rigid posture that Ross was furious. You don't out SAS *ever,* but she was frantic.

"Nathan Wyatt," she answered for him, listening for another summons from the baby.

"Yeah," Bill interjected, taking a seat. "What did he get again...the Victoria Cross?"

"New Zealand Medal of Honor." Viv glanced between the two law enforcers, as animated as schoolboys, while

Ross gave cursory answers. It had worked, she'd distracted them, but she felt sick. Two men had died in that ambush, one of them—Steve—had been her cousin. Thank God her brother, Dan, hadn't been on duty.

"It's important my identity stays confidential," Ross cautioned the cops. "Meredith shouldn't have said anything." He shot her a glance that caused Viv to shift down the couch. "Do you have any further questions about Linda?"

Officer Wright looked to his colleague who shook his head, but Viv's relief was short-lived. The baby cried again. Imperative, demanding. "Excuse me." Standing, she headed for the stairs.

"Based on the paramedics' assessment—and our report—it's unlikely the coroner will order an autopsy," she heard Officer Wright say to Ross. "In which case Mrs. Coltrane senior can be transferred to a funeral home tomorrow. We'll leave you to contact your brother."

Viv climbed the stairs, thinking fast. Charlie would rush home from school camp with Tilly. Her niece was what… six or seven now? Still a believer in Santa and the Easter Bunny, Viv should be able to fool her for one more day until Merry got transferred back here to Auckland Hospital.

Of course the two of them would then have to fudge the details of her accident and injury—delaying it by twenty-four hours for a start—but Merry worked at Auckland Hospital, there had to be favors she could pull. And Viv could think on her feet. They'd work something out.

Charlie had only known Viv as Monroe blonde but he'd be harder to convince she was his estranged wife so she'd minimize their interactions. And she'd kept her Kiwi accent—it made her unique in the U.S. in a profession where it paid to stand out. She and Merry even had the same enunciation, courtesy of an exclusive girls' boarding school.

She was on top of this. It would be fine.

Tracing the crying to a bedroom at the end of the corridor she opened the door. The wailing stopped and a flushed face peered through the bars of a crib. She took in Harry's appearance: big tear-filled brown eyes, fringed by lashes like a giraffe's—thick and straight; his dab of a nose; and a shock of fluffy golden hair, sprouting in the same pattern that his daddy was losing his.

Viv closed the door behind her. "Hey," she said, approaching with caution. "You're awake." An acrid smell hit her nose and she recoiled. Either someone had left the top off a bottle of ammonia or this guy was sitting in a wet diaper.

He wore a "little man" outfit obviously chosen for Linda's benefit—navy bibbed overalls and a striped collared T-shirt bulged over his diapers and baby belly. His baby fists clenched the bars.

Looking from the crib to the change table, she realized Nana Linda had quite the nursery going here. No wonder Merry had worried about custody. "Good nap?"

Brow furrowed, Harry stared at her.

"It's Mommy," she prompted. Bustling over, Viv picked him up and registered that the kid was a lightweight. Harry continued to eyeball her. Surely he couldn't tell?

"Did you see Mommy...I mean...*Mummy's* cardigan?" Positioning the baby awkwardly on her hip, she waved a green sleeve in front of him but his unblinking gaze never wavered.

"Fine." She lowered her voice. "Since I blew it by saying *mommy.*" She made a mental note to guard against Americanisms. "I'm your auntie Viv but you can't tell anybody. Well, I know you can't because your mo—*mummy* says you can only say seven words."

She paused but Harry didn't offer any of them. Still

making his mind up about her. "Anyway—" she started to sweat "—I'm sorting a few things out for your mummy so go easy on me. And I'm definitely going to need your help with Salsa."

Harry stirred. "Dog?"

"Yes," she said, relieved she'd found the magic word. "We'll go home and see the maniac dog…this diaper's awfully warm and saggy. I'm guessing it needs changing?"

He wriggled to get down. "Dog."

"I'm willing to put it off if you are." She let him go, picked up the diaper bag and the tiny shoes. It hit her then that Linda had taken them off. Viv took a shaky breath, then knelt beside Harry who was tugging on the door handle. "Can I have a hug first?"

Harry wrapped his skinny arms around her neck and planted a sloppy wet kiss on her cheek, obviously well trained. Of course Merry played this trick, too. They'd been brought up by the same emotional blackmailer and split from the same egg. She could do this. Viv turned the handle. Harry trotted ahead to the stairs, spun around and started sliding down on his belly.

Was the blood still in the hall? She broke into a run, taking the stairs two at a time, the diaper bag bouncing off her shoulder. At the bottom, Ross turned, holding a mop. Casually shoving it aside, he picked up their nephew. "Hey, mate, where's the fire?"

He needed a hug, too. She could see it in the way he enveloped the baby, buried his nose into the tiny shoulder. Glancing up, his eyes met hers.

It had been an especially cold winter in New York when his life had hung in the balance. Viv had spent most of it huddled over the radiator in her tiny apartment, sketching costumes for a charity production off Broadway and telling herself she had no right to care as much as she did.

Her relief when he'd pulled through had been disproportionate to their brief acquaintance.

Abruptly he handed her Harry.

"Your son's diaper needs changing."

CHAPTER FOUR

ROSS ITCHED TO TAKE HIS sister-in-law to task for telling the cops he was SAS but the presence of his nephew stopped him. He reminded himself he had more important priorities. Like telling Charlie his mother was dead.

Holy crap, he needed a drink. Heading to the liquor cabinet in the lounge, he poured a finger of whiskey into a crystal tumbler. Despite his father's efforts, this place had never been home. Even now, with Linda beyond caring, Ross felt like a trespasser. Behind him, he heard the diaper bag hit the carpet. Harry on her hip, Meredith held out a hand. "Oh, God, yes, please."

Passing his glass over, he poured himself another. Harry made a grab for his mother's tumbler and Ross distracted him with a shiny stainless-steel cocktail measure.

Meredith raised her glass. "To Linda," she said with a faint tremor in her voice.

Ross wouldn't be a hypocrite so he simply chinked glasses. They tossed back their drinks in one gulp. "I owe you an apology," he said, while the whiskey was still a smoky afterburn on his tongue. Might as well get this over with. "For venting on you after an argument with Linda." Though come to think of it, Meredith had given as good as she got.

"She was angry but not clutching her chest or anything when I arrived," she offered, putting her empty glass on the cabinet. "In case you were feeling guilty."

He glanced at where the picture used to hang and resisted the temptation to pour another shot. He had caused Linda's fall—indirectly. Cleaning up he hadn't seen the sampler; it didn't matter. Ross never wanted to set eyes on it again.

Because of the sampler, his brother would suffer losing his mum and Ross would suffer for him. In the saddest of ways, Linda had had the last word.

Steeling himself, Ross pulled out his BlackBerry. "I'll phone Charlie while you're changing Harry." He considered asking Meredith to call—a woman might break the news more gently—but dismissed it.

His brother was finally getting over his ex, although dating Harry's day-care teacher was just plain dumb. God knows how Harry's baby brain was making sense of it.

But Ross had long since given up pointing out emotional minefields in favor of standing clear. Only once had he stepped over his self-imposed line—deterring his brother from starting a turf war over custody. Women rarely came first in Ross's world but kids always did. He knew firsthand how an acrimonious divorce affected a child.

He waited until she and Harry were out of earshot before punching in Charlie's number. "The cell phone you have called is either turned off or outside the coverage area." Damn it. Ross considered a moment, then snatched Meredith's handbag from the sideboard and went upstairs, following the sound of her voice. She sounded fraught.

"Sweetie, second time's lucky, I promise."

"Meredith."

She jumped and turned guiltily from the change table. Two diapers lay discarded, one used, one fresh. "The tabs wouldn't stick," she said. "This one seems okay." She finished fastening Harry's diaper and stood back. "There." Anyone would think she'd painted the Sistine Chapel.

Impatiently, he lifted her handbag. "I need the number of the camp where Charlie and Tilly are staying."

Her eyes widened, she darted forward to grab it just as Harry dropped the cocktail shaker and started to roll. Ross dived forward and scooped him off the change table before he fell. "Oh, no, you don't." He turned to his sister-in-law. "Relax, I wasn't going to open it." Though now he wondered what she was trying to hide.

She clutched the bag to her chest. "The zip's faulty…. It splits open sometimes and spills everything." She hadn't even registered Harry's near tumble. "The camp is called Findlay Park. You'll have to look up the number."

He gave her the baby. "Where is it?"

There was a long pause. "I'm sorry, my brain's stopped working. I need to get out of this house." She set Harry back on the change table and snapped the domes closed on his overalls. "All I can remember is that tonight they were doing some sort of wilderness camping thing…I've been worrying that Tilly's sleeping bag won't be warm enough."

Typical. She'd always been a helicopter mum. Ross did a search for Findlay Park on his BlackBerry. "Karapiro," he said, "just over two hours' drive away. Did Charlie take his car?"

She had to think about it. "No, everyone met at the school and took the bus."

"I'll drive down, break the news in person and bring them home. Are you ready to leave?"

Meredith picked up Harry, who'd begun to fuss. "I need to call a cab…my vehicle's getting serviced."

Ross looked at his grumpy nephew. "I'll give you a lift." He led the way downstairs. "Where's Harry's car seat?"

"Umm." She glanced around helplessly, clearly flustered.

He tamped down his impatience. Meredith hadn't liked

Linda any more than he did but she had a soft heart. "I'll check Linda's car."

He found the car seat in the garage by the small door into the house, still holding half a cracker from an earlier journey. Picking off the fluff, Ross handed it to Harry, then strapped the happier toddler in the Range Rover while his mother went round the house collecting baby stuff.

When he returned to the front door, she was standing in the hall, looking at the spot where Linda had fallen. "I feel we should say something," she mumbled.

It was a civilian preoccupation, wringing meaning from death, and in this case he had no patience for it. "She was a terrible woman," he said bluntly. "You know it, I know it. We're going to have to pretend otherwise for Charlie but between ourselves we can be honest."

"And yet you worked so hard to resuscitate her." His sister-in-law, normally so reserved, seemed to stare right into him.

For Charlie. "Maybe I just wanted Linda beholden to me for saving her life." It occurred to Ross how much she would have hated that and he smiled grimly.

"Why do you talk like that?"

He shrugged. Death didn't make saints out of sinners even if he'd seen the bereaved reinvent loved ones until they were unrecognizable. And wasn't that the ultimate irony? "I'm sorry she's dead because it will hurt my brother and Tilly. But Linda wouldn't have cried over me and I'm not sugarcoating the truth for the sake of political correctness."

"Whatever she did to you, you need to forgive her," she said.

Ross snorted. "Turn the other cheek? Personally I've always found an eye for an eye works a hell of a lot better."

"You've changed, Ross," she said slowly. "I mean you were always a hard-ass but…" Meredith brushed a loose strand of hair off her cheek and he noticed her nail polish exactly matched her lipstick. Earlier he'd suspected she'd come from a lunch date.

"Yeah, well, I'm equally disappointed in you," he said. Ross did a visual check on Harry in the Range Rover. The baby was happy with the cracker.

Meredith stared at him. "Why would you be disappointed in M—me?"

The innocent act again. "Look, say a few words if you have to, but make it snappy. I've got a long night ahead of me."

She opened her handbag and pulled out a thick gilt-edged book the size of an index card.

"Is that a bible?"

"No, a saints book." Meredith flipped through the pages. "Here's one. Saint Barbara covers sudden death… Oh dear, she also looks after ammunition workers. You can't help but think the two are connected."

Maybe she *was* still in shock. "Meredith, this is a waste of—"

"Found one." Closing her eyes, she took a deep breath and bowed her head. "Linda, there's no point pretending you were a nice person. But without you there wouldn't be Charlie or Tilly or Harry so we thank you for them." Ross found himself bowing his head. "And for their sake, we ask Saint Joseph, the patron saint of happy, holy death, to make a case for you at the pearly gates." His mouth twitched. The timbre of Meredith's voice seemed huskier than usual. *She must really be upset.* "Rest in peace," she finished. "Amen."

He lifted his head and met her expectant look. "Amen."

They didn't talk much on the drive to her house. Harry finished his cracker and began fussing again. His mother couldn't soothe him. "He's hungry."

"Any food left in the baby bag?"

"I'll check." She found a half bottle of milk and Ross caught a faint scent of honeysuckle as she unfastened her seat belt and leaned over the seat back to pass it to Harry. Since when had he noticed his sister-in-law's perfume?

"I've been thinking," she said as he turned onto her road. "If you time your arrival at Findlay Park after all the kids are in bed then Charlie can adjust to the shock before he has to tell Tilly. And she gets a good night's sleep before she has to deal with it. You could drive back first thing in the morning."

Ross examined the idea. "I'll do that."

As they got out of the Range Rover, Salsa started barking, which just showed how long it had been since he'd visited. Any contact with the kids these days was through Charlie.

Meredith unstrapped Harry from his car seat. "Could you…ah…grab the seat while I take Harry?"

"Sure." Dumping her bags in the car seat, Ross picked it up in one hand and opened the gate with the other. "Sit," he ordered the barking dog and, with an apologetic whine, Salsa complied. "Yeah, you've forgotten your manners." Ross bent to give him a rough pat. Salsa's stubby tail wagged at Harry, in Meredith's arms.

"So, Harry's the key to the dog," she said behind him.

"What?"

"Can you hold Harry while I find the key?"

Her cell rang as she rummaged in her bag, with a zippy tune he recognized as "New York, New York."

"Hello…oh…hey." With her other hand she fumbled the key in the lock and opened the door. "I…can't talk right now."

Stepping inside, Ross put Harry down and the baby toddled over to Salsa who was licking a brown-red streak off the windowpane beside the front door. If he didn't know better, he'd say it was dried blood. "No, I'm not putting you off." She glanced over at him. Clearly she was lying and the male caller knew it, too, because Ross could hear his volume rising.

"Look, I'll call you later...yes...we'll talk about this, I promise. Goodbye."

Ross distinctly heard the sound of blown kisses. He folded his arms and reminded himself that it was none of his business that his sister-in-law was a goddamn hypocrite for pretending she was still heartbroken over Charlie.

Meredith hung up. "Telesales," she said brightly.

He raised his brows. "And you're calling them back?"

"Who doesn't need another insurance policy?"

Ross glanced around for Harry and saw he'd wandered into the playroom. "Liar," he said in disgust. "You're still playing doctors and nurses with the guy you screwed Charlie over with." Her mouth fell open. "Don't worry I won't tell my brother. He's got enough to deal with."

"I would *never* have an affair."

"See here's where you and I part ways on our definition of fidelity," he said. "I think tonsil hockey with another man is off the agenda for a married woman. Call me old-fashioned."

Her fury was unexpected. "Who started that rumor... *who?*"

"What are you talking about? You admitted it."

She looked at him blankly. No hint of remorse. Ross felt a wave of protectiveness toward Charlie.

Ross had been twelve when his mother died and he'd had to move in with his father and Linda. Charlie had been six and his mother's baby, which meant he dressed like a sissy and had no practical skills because Linda did everything for him.

Ross had expected to hate him and he did. Hated the kid's homemade sympathy cards, hated how he shared his lame computer games and really hated being told earnestly that even though his mother had gone to heaven, he didn't have to worry, because he still had a brother.

Charlie was like one of those weighted punching-bag toys…bouncing up smiling after every smackdown.

Walking home from middle school his first day, Ross saw his half brother being bullied at the adjoining junior school. He did nothing. Let Mummy sort it out. But Charlie didn't tell Mummy that night. Or Daddy, who spent most of his time working to support his second wife's lifestyle. Instead Charlie said he'd fallen over. Seemed he was accident-prone.

Ross resisted intervening for three days—that's how badly he wanted to protect himself from caring. On the fourth, he told the bullies he'd beat the crap out of them if they ever touched his little brother again.

"But I'm perfect," Meredith protested. "Perfect wife, perfect mother, perfect everything."

Over the past few months, this woman had pummeled Charlie emotionally, and Ross had stood back and let his little brother fight his own battles. Metaphorically it was day four.

He narrowed his eyes. "I don't know what game you think you're playing but I'm not letting you give Charlie any more grief than he's already facing. Pull your head in and behave yourself for the next few days, you hear me?"

"Or what?" She'd lost some of her bravado.

"Your ex is about to come into money, honey," he pointed out. "Imagine the edge that would give him if he renewed his bid for full custody. He listened to me once. I'm sure I can get him to listen to me again."

CHAPTER FIVE

LUGGING HARRY IN HIS CAR SEAT, Viv walked into Merry's room at Waikato Hospital Orthopedic Unit at six-thirty the following morning, her eyes gritty from a three-thirty start. And her brain reeling from Ross's disclosure. Not to mention his threat.

The room could hold two patients but the other bed was empty. One leg in a split cast that ran from midthigh to ankle, Merry was half sitting, staring out the fifth floor window at the pink dawn. With her face as pale as the white hospital gown, her dark hair pulled into a ponytail and her hands clasped, she could be a nun at morning prayers.

She didn't look like a woman who'd cheated on her husband.

"Hey," Viv called softly. "How are you feeling?"

Merry's head swung around. Her first glance went to Harry, fast asleep, then she sank against the pillows. "Why do I have a text from Charlie thanking me for trying to save Linda's life?"

Thank heavens. Breaking the news had been the part Viv dreaded the most. Everything else was reversible. "She didn't suffer."

Brown eyes widening, Merry covered her mouth. "So it's true…she's dead?"

"I'm afraid so." Shrugging off the overnight bag she carried over her left shoulder along with the baby bag, Viv planted the car seat on the floor and stretched out her spine.

"And I always told Charlie his mother exaggerated her heart condition," her twin whispered through her fingers.

"It wasn't her heart." Viv pulled up a chair and filled her in on the accident. Merry cried.

"She was a bitch but…"

Viv reached for her hand. "It's a terrible way to go."

"Poor, poor Linda." Merry's grip tightened. "And poor you, having to deal with her accident. But why would Charlie think I was there, too?"

Viv hesitated. "First, let me say that everything I did was to protect you."

Merry dropped her hand. "What's that supposed to mean?"

"Secondly, there's no time for panic or recriminations. I have to be in Auckland by ten when Ross and Charlie are due to drop Tilly home."

"Tell me!"

Viv took a deep breath. Maybe if she said it fast. "I met Ross arriving at Linda's and he thought I was you and he was so hostile that I went along with it to show him you couldn't be bullied. And then the accident happened and I fainted and when I came to, Ross had already told the cops I was Meredith Coltrane."

Her twin gasped.

"And all I could think was how panicked you were about Charlie finding out you'd interviewed for a job out of town so I—" Viv sucked in air.

"Lied to the police!"

"Didn't correct the misunderstanding." She pinned her twin's gaze. "And it worked. I bought us time to get you transferred to Auckland Hospital and come up with a cover story."

Merry bit her lip. "Go on."

"Unfortunately there isn't an ambulance available for

elective private transfer and the hospital won't consider the backseat of your car as an alternative. But—"

A bitter laugh interrupted her. "I thought telling Charlie I was considering relocating was going to be difficult, but telling him my twin was pretending to be me, a nurse, when his mother needed saving—"

"No one could have saved her, Merry, not even you," Viv said sharply. "You think I planned any of this? That I'm having fun here? Let me tell you how my hell day ended, Miss Ungrateful. I looked after your toddler and ate organic baby food for dinner because I used all the steaks to placate your mad dog. When Harry finally settled I packed you a bag—" she kicked it "—and tried to organize an ambulance, then had a rental delivered so I could drive here in the middle of the night."

The baby stirred in his car seat. Leaning forward she added in an accusing hiss, "Perhaps I wouldn't have felt such an overwhelming need to protect you if you'd just mentioned that *you* were the adulterer, not Charlie!"

Merry pulled the sheet over her head.

"Damn right. Hide your face, lady!" For long seconds there was only the sound of her own breathing as Viv struggled to control her temper, and Harry's soft snores. Then she heard faint sobbing from under the covers.

Viv sighed. "Mere, come out."

Nothing moved.

Viv tugged back the thin bedspread and sheet and her sister covered her eyes with a slender arm. "I'm so ashamed," she wept.

"Oh, honey." Pity dissolved her anger. "Does anyone in the family know?"

"Only our brother." Merry struggled to compose herself. "Ross told Dan." Which figured, the two men were former troop mates and it was through their friendship that Merry first met Charlie.

But Viv was in no mood to be fair. "Bloody Ross Coltrane!" She handed her sister a box of tissues. "Why can't he mind his own business?" Aware her sister was barely coping, she kept his ultimatum to herself. "But don't worry, I have another plan."

Her twin gave a strangled laugh. "Of course you do." She blotted her wet cheeks. "God, I am so sick of being a crybaby. I was coping until Charlie started dating Harry's day-care teacher. I guess I still believed he'd forgive me." Her composure crumbled.

"Here." Unzipping the baby bag, Viv handed her sister a take-out coffee and pulled out her own, along with a couple of chocolate-filled brioches. "Real food, real coffee. Not that chicory crap you have in the pantry. So. Were you in love with this other guy?" Charlie had been Merry's one and only; she wouldn't have betrayed him lightly.

"Luke? No!" Merry swallowed. "But…he thinks he's in love with me."

"Naturally," said Viv. "We're irresistible. It's our curse." She was still trying not to be hurt by her twin's secrecy. They'd never been close, but they phoned every couple of weeks and Viv always pretended her sister's domesticity was interesting just like Merry pretended Viv's work was important. Except it appeared domesticity was interesting.

"We never had sex," Merry said hastily. "There was only one kiss."

Viv frowned. "So who kissed what, exactly?"

For a moment, Merry stared uncomprehending, then blushed a fiery red. "Lips. We kissed lips…. Your mind, Viv!"

"C'mon, Mere, even a stick-in-the-mud like Charlie wouldn't leave over a kiss."

"What do you mean, *even* a stick-in-the-mud like Charlie?"

"Nothing. Your marriage always seemed so happy." In a stage version of their marriage, Viv would have dressed Merry as a smiling 1950s housewife and given her brother-in-law a pipe and slippers to go with his smug expression.

"It was. But you can't imagine how routine kills romance."

"Oh, yes, I can. It's not dumb luck I haven't got hitched. Losing your identity to a couple. It's bad enough being—" Viv took a sip of her coffee.

"An identical twin," Merry finished flatly.

Viv dodged the bullet. "Brought up by unhappily married parents."

"Except our trouble was that Charlie and I *weren't* a couple anymore. We were parents, churchgoers, workers. I was a part-time nurse and full-time soccer mum. Our conversations revolved around kid pickups, clean laundry and what's for dinner? I suggested date nights and Charlie said we were already overscheduled. And didn't being married mean we could quit trying so hard?" Merry gave a small laugh. "I said I needed more intimacy and he thought that meant more sex. Even sex was becoming a chore…another thing to do before I could go to sleep."

Speaking of sleep. Viv glanced at Harry, then her watch. He hadn't settled until ten last night but at some point she'd have to wake him or he wouldn't nap on the drive home. Why did babies have to be so complicated? She'd found a daily blog by a mother who chronicled her toddler's every waking moment from bowel movements to teething to diet. And the woman had been almost hysterical with joy when Viv posted a question. It was like being dragged into a cult.

"Tell me about this Luke." She needed to understand the emotional landscape to pull off Plan B.

"He was a colleague—a doctor—who became a friend. When our shifts coincided we'd lunch together in the staff canteen or later at a little deli a block away from the hospital. At the beginning there was a few of us, then gradually…" Merry began picking at her nails, cut short, unpolished, the nails of someone who never had time for small vanities.

"I knew I was skirting a line," she continued, "but I thought Luke understood there was a line—that we were friends who flirted. When he kissed me, I could no longer pretend our lunches were innocent. I felt so guilty, so ashamed. I went home and told Charlie everything."

Harry woke up, saw his mother and clamored to get into bed with her. Viv positioned him next to Merry's good leg. Half-asleep, Harry cuddled against her with his blankie, sucking his thumb and looking the angel Viv had already learned he wasn't.

"You named him after Houdini, didn't you?"

"What?"

"Never mind. How did Charlie react to the confession?" As if she couldn't guess.

"Angry." Merry swallowed. "And so hurt. He knew those lunches constituted more intimacy for me than crazy monkey sex. He stormed off to Ross's, and moved into his mother's house a week later."

"You mean that was it?" Harry started to squirm in his mother's hold and Viv grabbed him off the bed before he could do any damage, distracting him with her half-eaten brioche. "What about when he calmed down?"

"He refused to discuss salvaging our marriage. You'd think after eight years and two kids I'd earned the benefit of the doubt."

"Of course you'd earned it," Viv asserted. "The way you

used to run after that—" Merry caught her eye and she shut up. "You still love him."

"That's why when he started dating Susan I knew I had to move out of Auckland. I don't want to become a martyr like Mum." Their parents had recently separated and Mum was currently "finding herself" on an extensive tour of Europe with a couple of girlfriends.

"Heavens, no. I wouldn't let you. And you're not throwing yourself on your sword now," Viv added decisively, "which is why I'll keep impersonating you until we can get a transfer. You'll need to stay in Auckland Hospital at least one night to explain the cast to Charlie anyway. But we could say the break's simpler, couldn't we?"

"You be me?" Merry stared at her. "That's crazy."

"Exactly why it will work. It's so insane no one will consider it." When Merry protested, Viv leaned forward. "Think about it, Mere. I haven't been home in two years. There's been no opportunity for comparisons. And nobody knows I'm in the country. Ross saw the person he expected to see, even though I was dressed nothing like you. He was puzzled when I couldn't tell him where Tilly's camp was but all I had to say was something Merry-ish—you'd mentioned you were worried Tilly's sleeping bag wouldn't be warm enough—and we were back on track."

"You might be able to fool Ross but you'd never fool Charlie."

"Normally, I'd agree with you. But your grieving ex is going to be way too busy burying his mother to pay any attention to me—you. And let's face it, you've already acted so out of character by having a flirtation—because that's all it was, Mere, and Charlie's an idiot for thinking otherwise—that you've paved the way for any slipups I might make."

"What about the funeral? You won't know any of Linda's friends and relatives."

"Sweetie, you're the scarlet woman. You'll be lucky if they say hello." Her sister winced. "And Linda being such a tyrant has one upside—none of our family will feel compelled to go if you phone and say you don't want them there."

Merry straightened. "Harry!"

Viv turned to see her nephew break into a trot, crushing her brioche in his fist as he made a break out of the room. She caught up to him in the corridor and he squealed a shrill protest as she scooped him up. "I get exactly how you feel, honey, but Mummy needs us so suck it up." Holding him away from her body to avoid being smeared with chocolate she returned to Merry's room, nudging the door closed with her hip before putting the toddler down.

Harry threw himself on the floor and screamed, ignoring his mother's soothing calls from the bed. A nurse poked her head in to remind Viv that "this was a hospital," then did a double take between the twins. In desperation, Viv gave the toddler her cell.

He beamed at her through crystal tears and held it to his ear. "Dog?"

"Tell that mutt he better not be anywhere near my shoes," Viv requested, and turned to her sister. "You can phone work, ask for a week's bereavement leave. So what do you say?"

Merry was chewing her lip, a good sign. "Tilly will work it out. She's highly intelligent."

What parent didn't say that about their kid? "I'm sure I can fool an eight-year-old." *As long as I remember to say* mummy *not* mommy.

"Tilly's seven! See how little you know about my life?"

"That's why I have you on speed dial… Which reminds

me, we have to swap cells." She tried to ignore Harry gumming hers. "You give me daily instructions and details of who I'll encounter and if I get stuck I'll sneak away and phone you." Viv warmed to her theme. "I even booked a one-way rental so I can drive your car home. And if, by some remote chance, Tilly figures it out I'll tell her the truth and swear her to secrecy."

"You mean that Mummy's lying to Daddy?" Merry folded her arms. "No, Viv, I'm not dragging my child into this."

"It might not come to that, Mere, and look at the alternative. Charlie finding out is not a good thing right now. For him, for you or the kids." She paraphrased Ross. "What if he decides to lobby for custody? With his inheritance, he'll have more resources. I'm thinking of the greater good here."

"By adding lie on lie?"

"Did the truth help when you told Charlie about Luke?"

"No," Merry admitted reluctantly.

"Think big," Viv encouraged. "Whenever I'm stuck it's because I haven't been thinking big enough." She glanced at her watch. "I hate to rush you but if I'm getting back to Auckland by ten, you need to make a decision."

Her twin's cell started to buzz on the bedside trolley. Merry gulped as she checked the caller. "It's Charlie."

"We can do this, Mere."

Her sister shook her head as she picked up the phone. "I have too much to lose."

She'd got that right. "I need to tell you what Ross—"

"Hello, Charlie?" Merry turned away from Viv's desperate gestures to catch her attention. "I'm so sorry about Linda…. How's Tilly taking it?…I don't deserve your thanks…Can I just say…Okay, I'll let you finish first." As she listened, a range of emotions flitted across her sister's face.

"Mere," Viv whispered urgently but her twin ignored her.

"What did *I* want to say?" Merry gulped. She blinked and two tears trickled down her cheeks. "Tell Ross to drive safely. I'll see you soon." Hanging up, she clasped the cell to her breast and looked at Viv.

"I'm a bad person," she said brokenly. "But this is the first time in months he's spoken to me with any warmth."

"So we're doing this?"

"We're doing this." Merry gazed at her son babbling nonsense on Viv's phone. "And God help me if we can't make it work."

CHAPTER SIX

LOOKING IN THE REARVIEW mirror, Ross checked his niece asleep in the backseat. Her mouth was slightly open and the pink faux fur edging Tilly's hood stirred under her breath. Her dark lashes stood out against her tearstained cheeks as pink as the quilted anorak she'd refused to take off for the car journey. Turning down the car heater he indicated a lane change to the motorway exit and nudged his front-seat passenger.

"Nearly there, Charlie," he said in a low voice.

His brother opened his eyes, his normally ruddy complexion pale with grief. "I'm awake." He glanced behind at his daughter, then at the off-ramp approaching through the misty morning rain. The buzz cut he'd adopted when his light brown hair started thinning highlighted his solid jaw and jutting brow, and made him appear older than his twenty-nine years. Today he looked forty.

"You get any sleep?" Ross asked.

"No. I've been thinking about what needs to be done. Drop Tilly off, go to Mum's…" His voice wavered and he bought himself a recovery moment by pulling a pen and paper out of his day pack. "Phone people," he added gruffly, making a note. "Meet with the funeral director, check in at work." As the owner of a small construction company he generally had three builds on the go at any one time.

"Shit," Charlie muttered under his breath. Glancing at

his brother, Ross saw him frowning. "I rescheduled some critical jobs to make time for camp and the Master Builders' conference next weekend." Charlie was on the committee. "At least two will have to be squeezed in before the funeral. That doesn't leave much time to organize the service Mum would have wanted."

Bells and whistles, knowing Linda.

"I can help." Officially Ross was on sick leave for another month. Unofficially he haunted the SAS's headquarters, rehoning what skills he was able to.

Without comment, his CO had begun using him, usually as a guest commentator at instructor classes on his particular area of expertise—demolitions.

Sometimes, like yesterday, he sent Ross home to rest. "More haste, less speed," he'd reminded him. But rest and Ross were incompatible.

"I couldn't ask you," Charlie asked. Ross had made it clear over recent months that family and friends came second to his rehab goals.

"You're my brother." *No matter what I felt about your mother.* "And you're not doing this alone. What's on your list?"

Charlie stared blankly at the notepad. The poor bastard was still in shock. "Ordering flowers, choosing hymns and sorting out catering for after the service." He tried to smile. "Right up your alley."

"I'm on it." Mentally Ross scanned his female acquaintances but none jumped out as a culinary-skilled, flower-arranging churchgoer.

His brother's former neighborhood—where they were now dropping Tilly with her mum—was lined with staked saplings that reflected the age of the subdivision. Aspirational living, according to the real estate brochures. All Ross saw were characterless brick bungalows and crippling mortgages, but hey, each to their own. After the separation, Charlie had moved into his mother's so he could still afford the payments and in turn lessen the disruption for the kids. Ross hoped Meredith appreciated it.

He pulled into her driveway, and turned off the engine but Charlie made no move to wake Tilly.

"Give me a minute," he rasped. "It comes in waves, you know?"

"Yeah." Sometimes Ross sat out on his deck in the dark, cocooned by the surrounding bush and let pain off its leash. It didn't always come back when he called. Seventeen months after the ambush, he found it hard to grasp that his SAS brothers, Lee and Steve, wouldn't walk through the door, clap him on the shoulder and say, "It was a bad dream, Ice. We're the Indestructibles, remember?"

Acceptance was a thousand little daily adjustments—a thousand little deaths. He squeezed his brother's shoulder. "Listen, you want to stay with me a couple of nights, rather than at Linda's?" His place was in Muriwai, a black-sand beach on the coast, a forty-five-minute drive west.

"It's easier being in town but…" Charlie looked up hopefully. "You could stay with me?"

"Well…" Ross would have sworn he'd kept his expression neutral.

"No, stupid idea. Forget it."

"Of course I'll stay," he said. "If you need me to."

Charlie took a deep breath. "Let's get drunk tonight."

"I'll add beer to the list after flowers and hymns." Unfastening his seat belt, Ross got out of the car. "Take your time, I'll handle the bags."

Removing the luggage from the trunk, Ross opened the gate then kicked it closed as Salsa bounded over with a welcome yip. Seemed he and the dog were back on good terms.

As he rang the doorbell he noticed Charlie had hunched forward in the car, shoulders shaking.

Throat tight, Ross turned to the door. Thirty seconds passed. He jabbed the buzzer again and peered through the sidelight. Finally he saw Meredith hurrying down the hall, tying her hair into a ponytail. She seemed flustered. Salsa growled.

Ross glanced down. "Quit that."

Today, she was dressed in her customary jeans and T-shirt, no makeup. After overhearing her conversation yesterday, he no longer believed her harassed-mom act. "Hey," she said breathlessly, as she opened the door. "I wasn't expecting you for another half hour."

"Not interrupting anything, I hope."

"Of course not." Meredith glanced toward the spare bedroom.

Ross pushed past and went to the doorway, scanning the room. No doctor scrambling through the window.

"Don't scare me like that," he growled, then registered the clothes sticking out of the suitcase, half-unzipped on the bed. "Going somewhere?"

"Sorting out summer clothes…" Without bothering to fasten it, she shoved the case under the bed.

"We're barely into spring. And it seems an odd thing to be doing the day after Linda's death."

"I don't have to explain anything to you. Where are the others?"

"Coming." Why was she being so furtive? Surely she wasn't planning a runner with the kids? He'd meant to frighten Meredith into behaving through his throwaway comment on custody, but hell, not this much. Ross told himself to quit being paranoid but every instinct prickled. "Where's Harry?" he said sharply.

"In his highchair eating a—"

Crash!

They heard a faint "Uh-oh."

They both sprinted toward the kitchen, nearly tripping over half a dozen oranges rolling the other way. Harry was leaning over his highchair next to the kitchen counter looking at the upended fruit bowl. He had banana smeared on his chin, a crust of bread in one chubby fist and a carving knife in the other. He greeted their arrival with a two-toothed grin, then the blade glinted as he pointed it at the bread in his hand.

Meredith gasped. "Give me the knife, Harry."

The small chin jutted. "No!" As she stepped closer the baby twisted his body away which brought the knife tip even closer to his tiny thumb.

Meredith stopped.

"Look!" Picking up three of the fallen oranges, Ross started juggling them. "Bet you want one of these." Still juggling, he moved closer. "Go ahead, take one." Entranced, Harry leaned forward, reaching for them. The knife clattered to the floor and Meredith dived for it. Ross handed his nephew one of the oranges and he sank his teeth into the rind. His face contorted as a shudder went through his small frame.

With a reproachful look at his uncle, he threw it. "No!"

Salsa leaped, caught it in midair and ran.

Ross dropped to eye level with his nephew. "Don't play with knives."

The baby offered him his soggy crust.

"Apology accepted." Ross glanced toward Meredith. She'd dumped the knife in the sink and stood with her back to him, shoulders slumped.

"Accidents happen," he reassured her. "Even to good mothers."

She gave a slightly hysterical laugh. "I wish I could say

that made me feel better." She turned suddenly. "So if you think I'm a good mother why—"

"Mum!" Tilly ran into the kitchen and wrapped her arms tightly around Meredith's waist. "Nana Lin's not really dead, is she?"

In her pink tracksuit with her feathery brown bangs clipped back in two garish butterflies, the sturdy little girl appeared like any other seven-year-old. However Ross knew that five minutes in her company was enough to make people remember that on both sides of the family she had uncles in the SAS and grandmothers who could politely be described as strong-minded.

From birth she'd ruled the roost; lately Ross had noticed her dictatorship had become less than benevolent. Apart, her parents had become guilt-ridden putty in her Machiavellian hands. Since he'd started pointing this out to her father, Ross was no longer Tilly's favorite uncle.

Cheek pressed against her mother's waist, she glared at him now, her gray eyes—same color as his—two chips of steely determination over a cute button nose and rosebud mouth. "Uncle Ross is making it up."

Meredith gathered her daughter close. "I'm afraid it's true. Nana Lin really is dead."

"But I don't want her to be," she wailed. Normally that was all it took.

"I know it's hard."

Tilly pulled away from her mother. "You smell funny."

"I...have a new perfume."

"And you look different, too," Tilly accused.

"I put a color rinse through my hair and had it layered." Meredith actually seemed scared of her seven-year-old's disapproval. Ross shook his head.

"Well, I don't like it." The little girl burst into sobs. "I want things to stay the same."

His irritation melted. She'd been through a lot lately; no wonder she was acting out.

"Oh, Tilly," Meredith took her daughter in her arms and rocked her. Seeing Tilly upset, Harry began to whimper. "It's okay, darling," Meredith called, then bent her head to Tilly's. "Can we be brave while Harry's in the same room? He's upset seeing his big sister crying."

Tilly sobbed harder.

Ross released his distressed nephew from his high-chair. "Let's go find Salsa and that orange, hey?" Leaving Meredith to soothe Tilly, he and Harry followed flecks of rind down the hall. Glancing outside, he saw Charlie had stopped in the garden to take a call on his cell.

They found the dog next to the suitcase under the bed in the spare room, chewing on a strappy leopard print sandal with a lacy black G-string tangled around one paw. His sister-in-law was definitely leading a double life.

"Bad dog," said Ross approvingly and Salsa wagged his stubby tail. Then he looked beyond Ross and growled.

"What are you doing in here?" Meredith said behind him, then caught sight of the half-chewed shoe and gasped. "Why didn't you stop him?"

"He already had it." Ross hauled Salsa out by his collar and made him drop the shoe. She was genuinely upset. "Were they expensive?"

Viv stared at the saliva-soaked fang-needled leather on her Christian Louboutin flats—then remembered she was Meredith. "Where would I get the money for expensive?"

Ross gave the dog back her shoe.

She couldn't decide who to kill first. Concentrate, she told herself. There'd been a hairy moment when Tilly had told her she smelled funny but she'd handled it. Like she'd handled their early arrival, scrambling to hide her suitcase, change into Merry's clothes and strip off her makeup between doorbell rings. Two down, three to—

Viv jumped as she heard Charlie's footfall in the hall. Trying to relax, she turned to greet him. In the past two years since she'd seen him, her brother-in-law had added some weight to his gorilla frame. But today he was a knuckle-dragging Kong with red-rimmed eyes and a little boy lost expression that had her moving forward to hug him before she could think about whether it was a smart idea.

"Charlie, I'm so sorry." She never could ignore someone's hurt.

For a moment he stood frozen in her embrace, then his arms came around her in a vice. "I know," he said. "I know you are. I'm glad you were with her...for everything you did." He let her go, struggling for composure.

"Da!" Drawn by his father's voice, Harry toddled into the hall and threw himself at Charlie's shins.

"Hey, little dude." He picked up his son. "I missed you." His voice cracked. Hastily Charlie handed Viv the baby and turned away. Viv was choking up herself. Glancing helplessly at Ross, she saw his face was completely expressionless. How did he do that?

"Go find Salsa," he said to Harry.

"Dog?" Harry wiggled down from Viv's arms and she pulled herself together.

Back still to them, Charlie knuckled his eyes dry. "Where's Tilly?"

"In the garage breaking the news to the guinea pigs," said Viv. She wasn't quite sure what to make of her niece yet. Without an audience she'd recovered remarkably quickly.

"I don't want her seeing me upset."

"You go," she encouraged, gently pushing him toward

the front door. Her brother-in-law may have bought the switch but it would be stupid to spend more time with him than she absolutely had to. "Call me later when you know what's going on. And don't feel you have to see the kids over the next few days."

Charlie stiffened. "I'll always find time for my children, Meredith. They're the most important thing in the world to me."

"Of course." In her hurry to rectify her mistake Viv overcompensated, by adding, "And obviously, if there's anything I can do, just tell me."

"Seriously?" His gaze softened. "I mean I gave Ross some stuff…you could help him with that. Mum liked things done right and you're such a terrific organizer."

Viv exchanged horrified glances with Ross.

"I can handle it," he said tightly.

"Not the feminine touches," said Charlie. He gave Viv a pleading look. "Mere, I know it's a big ask, given our situation. And you and Mum didn't get on. But I need to do this right. I'd be in your debt. I really would."

Oh, hell.

Behind Charlie, Ross frowned and shook his head no.

"Happy to help," she said.

CHAPTER SEVEN

"PE4 IS A CHALKY-COLORED solid plastic explosive with a more rapid detonation rate than C4. We're talking 8210 meters per second as opposed to—"

Turning from the electronic whiteboard, Staff Sergeant Ken Worrell caught sight of Ross who'd paused at the open door of one of the SAS Group Headquarters's meeting rooms. His face split in a welcoming grin. "You wanna answer that one, Sergeant?"

"Eight thousand and forty meters per second." Ross nodded to the SAS's newest recruits. En route to an informal interview with the commanding officer, he'd looked in out of curiosity. A month ago, he'd been roped into the DS—directing staff—basically as a checkpoint monitor during the nine-day selection course. He was curious to see how many of the eighty soldiers had come through.

Those who stumbled exhausted across the finish line were rarely the biggest or fastest or toughest soldiers. Success came to the stubborn bastards who could call on willpower when their bodies failed. And the last day endurance test—a sixty-kilometer walk, with pack, to be completed within twenty hours—had been designed to ensure their bodies did fail.

In the SAS, self-motivation was everything.

He saw six trainees and recognized two. So an above average intake then. And they'd probably lose a couple more during the nine-month training cycle these soldiers had to pass before they graduated. Not for nothing were the SAS called one-percenters.

They returned his nod respectfully. They knew who he was. Just as he'd known everything about *his* superiors when he'd been a raw recruit. And in each man's eyes he saw the same hope he'd had—to emulate, to attain, to prove themselves worthy of the elite badge. Can I do it? Am I good enough?

"Staff," they chorused. If they passed cycle they'd call him Ross. There was no distinction made for rank or background among the SAS.

He also saw sympathy in a few gazes. With a farewell nod to Ken, he continued down the corridor. Despite Ross's distinguished service record, he'd always be known as the trooper dragged unconscious and near death from a burning Dumvee—desert-modified U.S. Humvee—by a decorated hero.

Given that decorated hero was one of his closest friends, Ross could live with that. What he wouldn't live with was the possibility that those injuries signaled the end of his operational career.

His gut tightened, as it always did when he thought of Nate. He could forgive him leaving the SAS after the loss of two of their mates. Just. What he found harder to forgive was Nate trading off that valor medal to get a top-paying job as a goddamn bodyguard for some Hollywood star.

Pausing in the corridor, Ross checked his Heuer. Like most demo guys he had a thing for precision timepieces. Still ten minutes early. Because he didn't want the CO to read nervousness into that he detoured into the History Room. There he tried to distract himself with the displays of past NZSAS operations, from the first in Malaya in 1955 through to Borneo, Vietnam, Bougainville, Kuwait, East Timor and Afghanistan.

He'd been deployed in three of them with Dan, Lee, Steve and Nate.

Grief punched into his solar plexus and momentarily he closed his eyes, forced himself to refocus on the friends who'd survived. Dan was a farmer now and the two men were making scrupulous efforts to avoid taking sides in their younger siblings' imploded marriage. A few months earlier Ross had helped Dan get his new bride, Jo, to the altar. Hell, if a cynic like Ross could play matchmaker surely he could think of some way to help Nate?

For the hundredth time, he searched for a clue to his mate's self-destructive behavior but only fragmented memories of that day remained. Pain mostly…crippling, mind-bending pain mixed with the smells of burning metal and flesh.

"I've done my duty," Nate had said in their last phone call. "That medal's my passport to the easy life."

"That's not you talking," Ross had replied quietly. Nate's passionate loyalty to the SAS had surpassed even Ross's.

Nate laughed. "God, I love your idealism, I really do," he'd mocked. "I guess you're our Black Knight." Ross froze in front of the glass display. The Monty Python guy from *The Holy Grail,* the one who'd had arms and legs lopped off and still insisted he was capable of fighting. Talk about blatant cruelty.

He checked his watch again, then walked through reception. In his life he needed very little. Only to be the best at what he chose to do. And that was being a soldier. As he passed the chunk of lapis lazuli beneath the wall carving depicting the ethos of the NZSAS, he bent to pat it for luck. In the Middle East, the dark blue gemstone shimmering with golden pyrites was thought to have magical powers.

For the benefit of the receptionist he kept his gait sure

as he climbed the stairs to the CO's office on the second floor and tapped on the door.

His superior might be spinning this as a casual chat with a man still officially on sick leave but Ross knew better. Which was precisely why he'd worn the SAS Corps uniform, so the CO knew he meant business. Unfortunately, even with all the weight training and protein shakes the damn thing still hung loose.

He tightened the blue belt then straightened the sand-colored beret. His fingers touched the cool metal of the badge, a flaming sword above the motto Who Dares Wins.

"Enter." The older man's level gaze took in his uniform but the CO offered no comment as he gestured Ross to a chair and came out from behind his desk to take another beside it. "Condolences on your recent bereavement, Ross. We could have postponed this chat. I know it's a difficult time."

"Thank you, but my stepmother and I weren't close."

"I'm sorry to hear that…. Anyway, I'm looking forward to welcoming you back in that uniform permanently next month. Your dedication in regaining your fitness hasn't gone unnoticed, son."

"I'm glad." Ross's voice cracked in relief. Last week he'd taken on some mates in close-quarter battle and managed to win a few. Despite his weak leg he still had a few tricks up his sleeve. The med team had told him to go easy, rest up and let nature take over but Ross had achieved more by doing rehab his way. Who Dares Wins wasn't some token corporate team-building slogan, it was imprinted on an SAS trooper's DNA.

"And counseling. How's your progress there?"

"Working equally as hard in that area." To appear un-emotional, nerveless…The Iceman.

Thoughtfully, the CO scrutinized him and Ross started

to sweat. Finally the sharp gaze shifted to the wall calendar behind his desk. "I'm thinking of scheduling you for a couple more advanced instructors courses early next year. A GPMG—General Purpose Machine Gun—course in January, a Patrol Procedures in February and Counter Terrorism in March."

That was three courses, not two.

"We'll be short of good instructors when Frank retires midyear," the CO continued. "And I've liked your style on demolition. You're an excellent teacher."

"You know my goal is to be available for operations." Ross managed to keep his voice even.

"And these courses don't preclude that, but it's early days to be talking about deployment. According to your physio you're not even jogging yet." His ironic tone suggested he knew differently.

"I've been doing some light training runs," Ross admitted.

"Stop."

So much for informal. "Sir."

"You're a valuable resource…. Conserve, Ross."

"Sir."

"You still have some healing to do, son, mind as well as body."

Ross tightened his jaw. "Did the psych say that?"

"No, you've convinced him you're completely rational."

It was delivered as a joke so Ross smiled. "Sir."

But he'd heard the qualifier. Which son of a bitch had put doubt in the CO's head?

"How much more do I have to lose, Ross?" Charlie had decided beer wasn't strong enough and moved onto spirits. He'd given up on his mother's purple couches— "fifteen thousand bucks each and they're not even comfortable"—and lay sprawled on the living room carpet, head and shoulders resting against a pile of black and white polka-dot cushions. Reminded Ross of dominoes. Strewn around the shaggy white rug lay pictures of coffins.

It was 9:00 p.m. and the only light in the room came from the backlit nooks and recesses showcasing Linda's objets d'art. "First Dad dies, then my marriage and now Mum." Leaning on his elbow, Charlie held out his empty crystal tumbler with an unsteady hand.

Silently Ross refilled it with Linda's cognac, topped up his own glass then returned the decanter to the polished black coffee table.

"Or maybe there's a Coltrane curse," Charlie continued. "It's not as if you've done any better." He hesitated. "Do you miss Dad?" He was drunk to be asking such things.

Ross wasn't drunk enough. "No."

"How about Steve and Lee?" Ross's troop mates who'd died in the ambush.

"What is this, twenty questions?"

Charlie waited for an answer.

He sipped his cognac, felt the burn. "Every day."

Satisfied, his brother lifted his drink, pausing as something under the coffee table caught his eye. Reaching under it, he retrieved a chewed orange plastic *Y* Ross had missed in his earlier cleanup. Charlie put down his glass and turned it over in his hands. "Trust Mum to buy a baby who can't talk, an alphabet set." His face crumbled, his shoulders heaved in a silent sob, before he wiped his eyes with the back of one clenched fist. "How do you do it, Ross? How do you make peace with death?"

"I don't. Grief is fuel to get me where I need to be."

"Which is Afghanistan?"

Ross nodded.

His brother's gaze dropped to his injured leg, then slid

away. Charlie didn't think he could reach operational fitness again—few did—but that didn't faze Ross. It was enough that he kept the faith. No one had expected him to survive his injuries, either, and he'd proved them all wrong.

Returning to Afghanistan drove everything he did from the food he put into his body to the punishing rehab schedule he'd superimposed over the occupational therapist's. No way in hell would he accept being relegated to behind the scenes.

He had to show the bastards who'd ripped apart his unit, killed his two close friends, that they hadn't won. That whatever the ambush had changed, it hadn't been him.

Charlie groped for his glass. "There is something I can take peace from," he said, and Ross shifted uncomfortably. He hated navel-gazing, hated its potential to weaken him.

"Knowing the two people I trust most were with Mum when she died." Charlie knuckled his eyes again and sighed. "Though I guess still trusting Meredith is crazy, given what she did to me."

A prickle of unease ran up Ross's spine. Now was not the time for Charlie to start questioning his feelings toward his ex. For a moment he considered telling him about Meredith's conversation with her boyfriend, except in Charlie's current state that would be cruel. Maybe having to organize funeral stuff with his sister-in-law wasn't all bad. Ross could be a buffer.

He realized Charlie was still waiting for a response. "I don't know what you want me to say, mate."

"Nothing to say." His brother lay back on the cushions and stared up at the ceiling. "Didn't you ever meet a woman who got under your skin?"

"What, like a tick?"

Charlie snorted. "You're such a tool."

"I prefer finely honed instrument." The opposite sex

was a pastime to Ross and he dated women with the same attitude. His longest relationship—six months—had been with a female triathlete. They'd enjoyed the training together as much as the sex.

"Do you miss Terri at all?" Charlie's mind was obviously running the same track.

Ross sighed. "No."

"I still don't get why you dumped her." It had been one of the first things Ross did when he was shipped home to Auckland Hospital. "She was prepared to stand by you."

"Charlie?"

"Fine." His brother reached for his tumbler. "I'll shut up."

The doorbell chime made them both start. Ross looked at Charlie. "You expecting someone?"

He started to shake his head then stopped. "Hell, I forgot. Susan said she'd stop by to commiserate."

The girlfriend. Ross stood up. "I'll make myself scarce." Though he approved of him moving on, he wasn't yet comfortable seeing his brother with another woman.

Reluctantly Charlie rolled to his feet and tucked his shirttail into his jeans. "I wish I'd said no."

"I can tell Susan you're not up to visitors." His kid brother had always attracted nurturers, women who responded to the mommy's boy under Charlie's misleading Bruce Willis exterior. Personally, Ross couldn't imagine anything worse than having his emotional temperature constantly monitored, though his little brother seemed to enjoy it.

Ross didn't let women into his head and the only female allowed in his buddy clubhouse was Dan's new wife, Jo. He enjoyed annoying her by calling her an honorary guy.

"The thing is," said Charlie, "it's not only tonight I don't want to see Susan. I think I only started dating her to get back at Meredith."

"What's wrong with that?" said Ross, only half joking.

"Susan's a sweet woman, she deserves better." Charlie staggered toward the door. "I'm gonna break up with her."

Ross moved into his path. "You're drunk and you're grieving…leave it a couple of days and then see how you feel. There's no hurry is there?"

"I'm not you, I can't be with a woman I don't love." Charlie's expression was mulishly stubborn. Just like his mother's so often was. And his daughter's.

"I get that," Ross said patiently, "but Susan's come over to commiserate. She's probably bought a casserole. Dumping her now would be plain mean. I'll send her away."

As Charlie hesitated, they heard the sound of the front door being opened. He frowned, so did Ross. They both really hated it when people came in uninvited.

"Hello," Susan called. "Anyone home?"

Charlie eyeballed him, and with a shrug Ross stepped aside and surrendered to the inevitable. "In here."

HOLDING HARRY LIKE a human shield, Viv opened the front door at eight forty-five the next morning and yelled into the house, "Come on, Tilly, we're running late!"

"Dog." Chuckling, Harry pointed to Salsa who, torn between conflicting impulses, wagged his tail and growled.

"You were happy to accept fillet steak from me this morning," Viv snapped. She'd left more meat strewn across the countertop defrosting and there was a packet of emergency sausages in her handbag for when she returned. "What is it, anyway? My perfume? Most dogs *love* me…. *Tilly!*" At least she had the mother holler down pat.

Her niece meandered into the hall, chewing the last

morsel of toast Viv had given her half an hour ago. "I'll just brush my teeth."

"No time." How did Merry cope with such a dawdler? "I have to drop you guys at school and day care and make it back for your uncle Ross, remember?"

Tilly had decided to go to school when she'd heard Uncle Ross was coming. "He's bossy," she explained when Viv asked why. "He keeps telling me to think about other people." As she spoke she'd swiped her baby brother's toast and replaced it with a piece she'd already licked the butter off. "It's bad for him," she'd said blithely when Viv protested. "Butter causes heart attacks."

"What about your heart?" Viv had started to wonder if her formidable niece had one. She seemed to have shaken off her grief over Linda and pretty much ignored Harry. Possibly because he was too young to take orders. Viv, on the other hand, had been barked at incessantly. By dog and child.

Strapping Harry into Mere's seven-seater people mover, Viv gave him a toy, returned to the house for his baby bag and Tilly's school backpack then heckled her niece out of the bathroom and into the front passenger seat. Tilly had refused to get in the back. "I can't sit next to Harry, he stinks."

"A little present for Daddy's day-care girlfriend," Viv had muttered.

As Viv shut the passenger door she noticed the Subaru's insignia—Liberty. Ha!

Merry's cell rang and Viv turned away from the car in case Tilly could lip-read. She'd been eyeing Viv suspiciously ever since she'd offered to style her for school. She checked caller ID. Merry. Again.

"Hey—" she injected cheerfulness into her voice "—how are you feeling this morning?"

"As if I've got a plate screwed to my leg," said Merry tightly. "But the specialist is coming at ten, so hopefully he'll up the pain meds. Someone called Jean Paul left three messages on your cell overnight."

"Oh, no, I forgot to return his call," Viv said. Too many other things to think about.

"Should I text him your new phone numbers?"

"Yes…no…too dangerous. I'll phone him when I'm alone."

"His tone suggested he wasn't taking the breakup well," Merry commented.

"I told him I don't get serious," Viv said indignantly. "For Pete's sake, affair is even a French word. It's not like it got lost in translation. I haven't got time for dramatics." Merry snorted. "Except this one," she amended. "Anyway, the only callers who get your number are the big Broadway producer, Cal Muldoon, or his assistant, Sue Bradbury. In fact, it's very important that—"

"I've got it—Muldoon or Bradbury. Listen, I've emailed more tips and lists through to my PC. Make sure you don't leave any printouts lying around."

"I won't." Viv was starting to regret lending Merry her new laptop. With nothing to do but lie in a hospital bed her sister's organizing brain had gone into overdrive. Worse, she'd latched on to Charlie's slight warming as though it heralded the end of the Ice Age. It made Viv nervous. As if there wasn't enough pressure.

"Have you dropped the kids off yet?"

"Just leaving. I hadn't allowed for Princess Dawdle."

"You did get up at six like I told you?"

"Yes." Bleary-eyed and jet-lagged she'd given Harry a bottle and taken him back to bed with her. Woke thirty minutes later to find him trying to crawl through the cat door in the kitchen. Her brain threw up a factoid from Merry's tutoring. Pickles, died aged fifteen, buried in the garden.

The baby banged on the passenger window. "Uh-oh, Harry's spotted the cell. I'll call when I've dropped off the kids." Merry had already given her instructions on location, teachers, mums she might meet and Viv's brain was full to bursting. Had she really only been in the country three days?

"One day at a time," she kept telling her sister. "That's all we have to do." Even if that day felt as long as a week. "I'll call you when I have privacy, Merry." If she could costume all of Henry the VIII's wives, getting two kids to school and day care should be a cinch.

As long as she remembered to stay on the left-hand side of the road. It had been that long.

Flipping her cell shut, Viv turned to see Tilly hanging out the open car window, holding her nose. Her eyes were as wide as saucers.

"Hey," she said weakly. "Guess you heard Mom—Mummy talking to her friend, Merry. Real funny that we have the same name, huh?"

With a gasp, Tilly released her nose. "I'm so gonna tell on you, Auntie Viv."

CHAPTER EIGHT

"WHERE *is* MUM?"

Viv switched on the indicators to signal a right turn and the wipers squealed across the dry windshield. "In hospital in Hamilton…she went to an appointment there and broke her leg but she's fine. She just can't come home for a few days and while she's away I'm looking after you."

"Why are you pretending to be her?"

The traffic lights at Fendleton turned red. Viv braked and turned to the passenger seat.

"It's kinda a game." She tried to win her suspicious niece over with a big smile. "Can you see it could be fun having an identical twin you can swap with?" *Oh, yeah. Fun, fun, fun.*

"No," said Tilly flatly. "I like to be just me. When Harry came things got badder and Dad went to live with Nana Lin."

"Harry has nothing to do with your parents' separation, Tilly. Really, it's not his fault. It's a coincidence."

She didn't look convinced. "Anyway, you hate being a twin."

Viv was shocked. "What makes you say that?"

The small shoulders shrugged. "Everyone says it—Uncle Dan, Nana, Pops…Auntie Jo, Cousin—"

"Okay, you've made your point."

"And Mum," said Tilly.

Viv broke that disconcerting gaze. "Well, we're doing the twin thing now." *Whether we want to or not.*

A car honked impatiently behind her, the lights had changed. She concentrated on the busy morning traffic.

"Would Daddy be mad if he finds out?"

"Yes," said Viv because Tilly had to understand the gravity of telling. Except how did you explain adult screw-ups to a child? Tell her that Daddy might try to take her and her brother away from Mummy out of fear and anger. Tell her that things could get worse, when to her child's mind they were already as bad as they could be.

"Your mum and I made a couple of poor decisions and now we're trying to reverse them, Tilly, without making things worse. Keeping this secret is best for everybody— you, Harry, your mum *and* your dad. Which is why you can't tell anyone. Not Uncle Ross, not even your friends."

The little girl was silent a moment. "Mum wants Dad to come home and live with us again. So do I. That's why not all of me is sad about Nana Lin. Maybe Dad will change his mind now he can't live with her anymore. He doesn't like living by himself. I heard him tell Uncle Ross."

"Oh, honey, don't get your hopes up. But I think if we can keep this secret your mum and dad will be better friends."

"Because he thinks that Mum—you—tried to save Nana Lin?"

Viv winced. "Yes. But remember no matter how they feel about each other, Tilly, they love you. That doesn't change ever."

"And they buy me anything I want now, to make it up to me. And now you have to, too," she added cheerfully.

Uh-oh. "Well, I don't know—"

"I want McDonald's for dinner," said Tilly, and it wasn't a request.

Viv braked at the roundabout, trying to work out who gave way. "I'll think about it."

Another impatient toot, then a BMW overtook her. Now that was definitely illegal. "I have a baby on board, idiot!" She flipped him the bird, New York style.

"I can help you get better at being Mum."

Viv pulled tentatively into the roundabout traffic. "I'm listening."

"Take out those streaky things in your hair."

"Highlights. Sorry, kid, your mum could have had those done."

"And your teeth are too white."

"Laser," said Viv. "I'll drink more red wine."

"And you don't really act the same."

"Okay, maybe this is worth McD's." Viv pulled into the drop-off bay outside the school. "How can I be more like your mum?"

The little girl's brow wrinkled as she shouldered her school backpack. "Don't smile so much. And look sadder."

It was like a punch to the heart.

Tilly opened the car door.

"Does your mum normally hug you goodbye?" Viv managed to ask.

"When I let her."

Viv opened her arms with a pleading expression. "That's more like Mum," Tilly approved. She slid out of the car, landing solidly. "Maybe I'll let you hug me tomorrow." She turned, then swung back anxiously. "Who'll take soccer practice tomorrow, if Mum's not here?"

"It's okay, I can manage a simple training session." Merry was a coach. Not because she was particularly athletic, she'd told Viv, but because there was no one else and she had a chronic problem with volunteerism.

Tilly frowned. "Do you know the rules?"

"A ball, an end zone, touchdowns…" Her niece's face darkened and Viv relented. "It's okay, hon, I'm making a joke. I know there's a try-line."

"You mean a goal," said Tilly.

"That's what I meant to say." Viv made a mental note to check online sites.

Tilly was still frowning. "No more jokes about soccer," she said.

"Yes, ma'am."

Satisfied, the girl walked away, equal parts titanium and vulnerability, sparkly pink scrunchie glittering against the nut-brown hair, the backpack bouncing on her Dora the Explorer velour tracksuit. "Tell me the truth." Viv glanced behind to Harry in his car seat, being ignored as he waved goodbye. "Can your big sister keep a secret?"

"No," he said.

"Of all your seven words you had to pick that one." She turned her cell off because she didn't trust Merry not to call while she was with Ross, then pulled into the stream of traffic. "Let's extend that vocabulary. Say 'rock.'"

"Dog," Harry offered.

"How about 'hard place'?"

"Train," Harry countered.

"You're right, hard place is two words, I apologize."

The day care was only a few blocks away, a wooden building with a sloping sod roof, planted in fat swells of purple and green succulents and swathes of spiky grasses. There was a wide verandah on one side, overhung with an awning.

"So," said Viv. "This is where Daddy's squeeze works."

Harry clapped his hands.

She shrugged off Merry's fawn trench coat and shivered as the cool air hit the skin exposed by the deep V in the back of the sexy cherry-red dress she'd bought for Merry.

Harry stared at it. "Hey, it was in her wardrobe so technically it counts," she said defensively. Merry might want to be civilized about this but Viv was in the mood for a little restorative justice.

Charlie might have been more open to forgiveness and reconciliation if it hadn't been for this rebound opportunist. Viv slipped out of her sister's practical shoes and stepped into some red satin high-heeled mules. Apparently Susan was twenty-one and gorgeous. "Well, Mummy can be gorgeous, too," she said to Harry, unstrapping him from his car seat, "if not twenty-one." She and Merry hit thirty next birthday. "Let Susan be the insecure one for a change." If Viv could throw a spanner in the works, she would.

"Ooose," he said.

"Are we talking about what's in your diaper?" Breathing through her mouth, she checked for leaks then positioned the baby on her hip and picked up his bag. She jumped as Harry's chill hand settled on her bare flesh. "What we do for love, hey? Both of us deep in doozy."

He gave her a drooly grin then laid his head against her breast. "Aww," she said. "Stinky or not, you're gorgeous."

A tall brown picket fence surrounded the center. She unhooked the safety catch, opened the gate and walked into noisy chaos. It reminded her of the chicken house on the family farm a few hours south. Lots of frantic, small creatures underfoot, intent on their business. Something hard slammed into her calves. Viv turned and looked down at her ripped stockings, then at the tiny driver of the pedal car.

"I think we're going to have to exchange details for the purposes of insurance."

"You're on the racetrack," complained the unsmiling tot.

He backed up and pedaled around her.

"You'll be hearing from my lawyer."

Harry agitated to get down and Viv soothed him perfunctorily as her gaze swept the grown-ups for a woman fitting Merry's description. She settled on a curvaceous tousle-haired blonde in a denim skirt and long-sleeved T-shirt who was handing out toys. Jackpot. Viv headed toward her, lengthening her stride so the split in her sexy dress opened wider. Harry pointed. "Ooose," he said excitedly.

"Traitor," she muttered. "Hello, Susan." She coolly traversed the sandpit then ruined the effect by leaving a shoe behind.

The younger woman picked it up and returned it. "Oh, Meredith, how awful about Linda." Her big blue eyes radiated sympathy. "When I heard you were with her when she passed, I added you to my prayers."

Viv blinked. "Yes, well…thank you." Putting on her shoe, she was suddenly conscious that her dress wasn't appropriate for a woman in mourning.

Susan looked at it, too.

Feeling the high ground slipping away, Viv thrust the baby forward and said with an evil smile, "Harry needs changing."

"No problem." Susan brushed sand off her fingers. "Mind carrying him until I can wash my hands?"

The sweetness jarred Viv, and she started toward the building to hide her scowl. Didn't this ditz know Meredith was heartbroken over Susan's relationship with her husband?

"Meredith, did you get a tattoo?" said Susan in an awed voice behind her.

Viv felt her stomach plummet. Calling herself every kind of idiot she said, "Heaven's no. It's a transfer. One of Tilly's fun things to do."

Susan laughed and the sound was all silvery bells. "Of course, you'd never get a tramp stamp." She leaned forward. "Close-up I can tell it's a fake, quite badly done. And how corny, angel wings."

Viv resisted the urge to slap her. Inside the brightly painted restroom where the toilet bowls were leprechaun-size, Susan washed her hands. "I wasn't sure if I'd see Harry today after what happened. It's such a tragedy." Her eyes filled with sudden tears. "I never met Linda and now I never will."

"Don't you think tears are a bit over the top?" Viv couldn't keep the hostility out of her voice. "It's not as though you're family."

Blue eyes looked at her blankly, then widened. "Oh, no. I'm not tearing up over Charlie's mother. That would be inappropriate."

And boinking my sister's husband isn't? Viv bit her tongue.

"I'm upset about Charlie."

"I'm sure he'll be glad of your support." *All 36D of it.*

Taking Harry, the younger woman placed him on the changing table. Viv backed up. This was her second encounter with baby poop and she was in no hurry to repeat it.

Susan sent her a sidelong glance. "I saw Charlie last night."

Viv folded her arms. "Really." So her brother-in-law could find time to seek comfort on Susan's ample breasts but relied on his estranged wife for help with funeral arrangements. Meanwhile Mere was lying in a lonely hospital bed riddled with false guilt.

The younger woman wiped Harry's tiny bottom clean. "Do you want to hear what happened?"

Incredulous, Viv stared at her. "You are some piece of work."

"What?"

"You heard me." To hell with it, the woman needed a reality check. "Isn't dating a client's father breaking the preschool equivalent of a Hippocratic oath? I don't know how you can look at that baby's sweet face—" actually Harry was presenting another part of his anatomy "—and think I want to hear what you and my *husband*—because we're not divorced yet—get up to in the sack."

Susan looked shocked. "As a committed Christian, I don't believe in premarital sex."

Viv narrowed her eyes. "You're waiting until you're the second Mrs. Coltrane, is that it?"

Susan's full lower lip trembled. "You're upset about Linda, that's why you're being so hurtful. And of course you can't know…" Susan put Harry on his feet and the baby scrambled off to play without a backward glance. "Anyway—" bravely, Susan lifted her chin "—I forgive you."

"You forgive…" For a moment Viv was speechless. "If you're the devout Christian how come *I'm* the one having to turn the other cheek?"

Susan burst into tears.

Viv hardened her heart. This sniveling, pathetic victim mentality from the perpetrator was too much. "You hurt M—me and you hurt my kids and you need to accept some responsibility for that."

Susan cried harder. "Charlie broke up with me."

"What?"

"Last night. And you're right, I am to blame. Even when you said you didn't care when I wanted to ask him out, I guessed that was probably your pride talking."

And wasn't that typical of Merry, Viv thought irritably.

Backing off when she most needed to fight. Making it too damn easy for another woman to move in. Susan was still sobbing. Grabbing a roll of toilet tissue, Viv handed it over. "I'm sorry," she said grudgingly.

"No, you're not." Mopping her face, Susan gave her a tremulous smile that made Viv feel as if she'd pulled the wings off a butterfly. "And why should you be? I'm only getting my just deserts. He wasn't ready to move on and I ignored that for my benefit. But when he dropped Harry off after you guys broke up…seeing that big strong man so vulnerable and brave, week after week…he just got to me, you know?" She started to cry again. "And now he's broken my heart."

Viv steered her over to a bench on one wall and sat her down. She'd never been fooled by Charlie's hulking appearance and he'd always seemed to need too many societal props for his masculinity, such as earning more than his wife and being head of the house. "I know it hurts now," she soothed, "but you'll get over it."

"Like you're getting over Charlie?" Susan asked skeptically.

Viv tried to channel, but it was hard. Why did people put everything into a relationship? Her mother had given up her own ambitions to marry Dad and though Pat had tried to make the best of it, her unacknowledged regrets had corroded not just her marriage but Viv's view of it. Not her twin's, though.

"I'm still in love with him," Viv declared solemnly. To hell with Merry's pride, this was too important.

Susan rubbed her eyes. "How you must hate me."

"I don't hate you." No wonder Merry had trouble being mean to Susan, she was so sweet. "Stop crying now. Heavens, someone who looks like you do can win any man she wants. Raise your sights."

Her feelings about her brother-in-law were mixed. She'd learned enough over the past couple of days to sympathize with him, but she was far from empathizing. He was still an idiot for ending his marriage and she didn't approve of him inveigling her—his wife—into doing so much work on his mother's funeral.

Puzzled, Susan lifted her head. "What?"

"There's a whole world of great guys out there. And you're young. Don't be in such a hurry to get stuck with one for the rest of your life."

"I don't think you love Charlie at all," Susan said hotly.

Viv shut up.

"ABOUT TIME," ROSS MUTTERED under his breath as Meredith's Subaru finally pulled into her driveway. She got out, looking flustered and hot, which made it odd that she double-knotted the belt on her trench coat before walking over to the curb where he sat waiting in his SUV. He'd noticed yesterday that she moved differently these days.

He averted his eyes from a flash of leg as she climbed into the car. He'd never been aware of his sister-in-law as a woman before. Maybe being separated was causing her to send out pheromones? Or maybe he'd just been celibate too long. Whatever the hell it was, he didn't like it.

"Sorry I'm late." Settling into the front seat, she reached for her seat belt. "Traffic was a nightmare."

He tried to read her expression, keeping his own neutral. Had Susan told her? Bloody Charlie and his drunken truths. Susan had been pretty upset when she left last night; maybe she hadn't gone to work this morning?

"Everything okay…at day care, I mean?"

"Fine. Why do you ask?"

"No reason."

He started the engine and gestured to the women's

clothes draped over the backseat. "First on our list is to drop off one of Linda's outfits to the funeral director's." Charlie had left at seven to make sure a residential building site was ready for the concrete truck's arrival at nine-thirty. The foundation pour would take until midafternoon.

Meredith glanced over her shoulder, then frowned. "Oh, no. That won't do. Linda can't be buried in a winter wool skirt and summer floral blouse." Unfastening her seat belt she turned in her seat to take a closer look. "And the red and olive color combo…" She shuddered. "Is Charlie color-blind or something?"

"Is that supposed to be funny?"

"What?" She shot him a blank look. "Oh. That's right, he is. Well, you should have weighed in with a second opinion."

"You do remember Linda is being cremated right? Not going to a garden party with the Queen? The clothes don't matter."

"They did to her. Drive back to her place and I'll choose something else because she can't wear *that*." She settled back as though the matter was closed.

"Meredith, there's too much to do without—"

"She died without dignity, Ross." Her expression was raw. "This is one thing I can fix for her." Without another word he did a U-turn.

"Redress," she said with a shaky laugh. "To put it in military terms."

Eyes on the road he gave her shoulder a brief squeeze, and then was annoyed because he didn't want to commiserate with his sister-in-law. Those days were gone. But, yeah, he definitely understood redress.

"By the way, you and I need to get something straight," Meredith said. "I'm not seeing that doctor."

"So who was sending you air kisses?" She hesitated

and frustration got the better of him. "Don't bullshit me, Meredith. What I can't work out is why you've been acting all heartbroken over Charlie and Susan when you've been dating Doctor Dick all this time."

"Luke," she corrected. "And we didn't—"

"So you just wanted to make Charlie feel like a heel?"

"Of course not! Look, it's too complicated to explain. All you need to know is that I'm not having a relationship with anyone."

"So the air-kisser was a one-night stand?"

"You're the most cynical guy I've ever met."

"Is that a yes?"

"Everything's black or white for you, isn't it? It must be so nice sitting in your tower judging the poor idiots who screw up occasionally. Why don't you try seeing the breakup from my side—walk in my shoes?"

He glanced down and said drily, "Those would be the slutty red ones you're wearing."

"God, it's like talking to a brick wall! Okay, leaving my marriage aside, no one could be a more devoted mother than me. You said it yourself yesterday, so why—"

His car phone rang. "It's Charlie," he said, and answered on speakerphone.

"Is Meredith with you yet?" His brother didn't wait for a greeting. "Her cell's switched off and I need to talk to her urgently." In the background, Ross could hear the graunch and grind of heavy machinery and the gravelly whoosh of pouring concrete.

Viv answered, "I'm here, Charlie. Is something wrong?"

"Tilly's school has been trying to contact you. Why did you drop her off when the rest of her class are still at camp?"

Briefly, Ross took his eyes off the road. The expression on his sister-in-law's face was priceless. "I...I guess we both forgot." Ross shook his head and she averted her gaze. "What's the number? I'll arrange to pick her up. Uh-huh… okay. No, I can take care of it. Bye."

Ross cut the connection. "So you were telling me what a good mum you were."

"Hey, you're the one who should be questioning himself," she countered, turning on her cell. "The only reason she went to school was because she didn't want to spend time with mean old Uncle Ross."

"That's because I don't put up with any of your daughter's spoiled-brat behavior," he retorted, swinging onto Stoke St. But her accusation had stung him.

"She has become a handful," she admitted, keying in the school's number. "I'm not sure how that happened."

It surprised Ross that Meredith seemed to be inviting his viewpoint but he wasn't going to pass up the opportunity. Tilly was too important to him for that. "You and Charlie used to be good at setting limits." He slowed to give way to a bus waiting to pull out of a stop. "Since the split, you tend to cave in and give her everything she wants. I know it's to make up for living apart, but that kid's inherited Linda's genes, Meredith. Absolute power isn't good for her."

She nodded. "Thanks, that's helpful." Ross filtered her tone for sarcasm but found none. Normally his sister-in-law was defensive about her eldest.

Meredith phoned the school and talked them into keeping Tilly until morning break so the little girl didn't have to go to the funeral home. It was halfway through the call, that Ross became aware she was studying him.

He pulled into Linda's driveway, switched off the engine and faced her. "What?"

"You won't do it," she said, returning the cell to her bag. "Encourage Charlie to go for custody."

He narrowed his eyes. "Why won't I?"

"Because you won't do anything that will hurt those kids."

Ross frowned. He didn't like being read that easily by a woman he no longer trusted.

"Look, I get it," she added. "You want to protect Charlie and shepherd him through the next few days without any more drama. Believe me, I do, too. And I've got enough troubles without your threat hanging over me. Can we call a truce, please?"

"Maybe I could have been less confrontational," he acknowledged.

"You think?" His sister-in-law wasn't normally this sarcastic. Lips curving, she climbed out of his SUV. She'd changed somehow…was more frank, less earnest…. It was like some kind of straitjacket had been taken off her. Ross hated noticing how much being on her own suited her—it felt disloyal to Charlie.

Helping his inebriated brother to bed last night, he'd seen last year's family photo on Charlie's bedside table. Everyone smiling, even Tilly. Charlie with his arm around Meredith. He'd forgotten what his brother looked like when he was happy.

He followed Meredith. "Charlie broke up with Susan last night." He wanted to gauge her reaction before he agreed to anything.

"Yes, and she's devastated." Meredith turned to level a look at him. So his first instinct was right. Susan *had* told her. "You should have made Charlie wait until he was sober."

"Oh, so now you're feeling sorry for Susan?"

"I feel sorry for any woman who has to deal with Coltrane men."

Using the spare key, Ross opened the front door. "He's

susceptible right now and I don't want him doing anything stupid."

"Like trying to get back together with me, you mean?"
She laughed, as if at some private joke. "I highly doubt
that, but I promise not to encourage him. In fact, I'll try
not to be alone with him for the next few days if it makes
you feel better. Be my chaperone."

She *sounded* sincere.

Thoughtfully, Ross stepped inside. He'd cleaned up after
putting Charlie to bed, too much the soldier to leave the
mess until morning. Realizing Meredith hadn't followed,
he turned. She'd paused on the threshold. It took him a
moment to realize why.

"You okay with coming back?"

Swallowing, she nodded and stepped inside. "How's
Charlie coping with the fact that his mother died here?"

"What bothers him is having people over after the funeral...all passing through the hall." An idea occurred to
him. "Will you have it at your place? The food's going to
be catered, so there'd be no work involved."

"No, it's out of the question."

Her flat refusal annoyed him. "Technically it's Charlie's
house, too," he reminded her. "He still pays the mortgage...
and before you jump down my throat, remember the only
way he could afford payments was by moving in with his
mother. Don't tell me that wasn't a sacrifice."

"No, I won't tell you that," she said. "But think about
what you're asking. It's going to be bad enough seeing his
relatives for the first time since the breakup."

"Yeah, but if it's in your house, they'll be forced to behave
themselves. Say yes and I promise to run interference."

"I don't know."

"You want a truce," he challenged. "Make a goodwill
gesture."

CHAPTER NINE

Viv looked at Ross's implacable face. Rock and a hard place? More like being clamped between two of the earth's tectonic plates. She'd intended to skip the after-funeral get-together, citing a headache, premenstrual craziness, anything. But if hosting Charlie's family got Ross off her sister's back then Viv didn't really have a choice. "And you'll ride shotgun," she reiterated as she held out a hand to shake on it, "stop any lynch party?"

His mouth twitched and his incongruous dimple made a brief appearance. Dang, but the man was hot, even mid-blackmail. She liked making him smile when he didn't want to, liked cracking through that icy disapproval.

Of course, Viv reflected, with her being Merry—the sister-in-law who'd purportedly broken his brother's heart—she should probably refrain from flirting with him. Though it might be worth it just to see his face. As his hand seized hers in a firm handshake, she smiled at the thought.

Ross released her hand abruptly. "Okay, let's get on with it." He gestured to the coatrack. "You can hang your coat here."

Viv's hands dropped protectively to the belt. "I'm cold."

"Really?" He looked at her perspiring forehead and she felt herself flush even hotter.

"Really." She'd allowed twenty minutes to change before Ross picked her up, and had spent thirty comforting Susan. You'd think she'd know by now to factor in the unexpected.

Viv led the way up the stairs then realized she had no idea which room was Linda's and paused at the mirror.

Shaking his head, Ross carried on. His limp was less pronounced today but his footsteps slowed as he approached a paneled door at the end of the corridor. As he opened it, he recoiled slightly before going in. "Can we get this over with?" he said shortly.

"Sure." Curious to see what might have stalled him, Viv followed, stopping at the doorway. It was exactly Linda's kind of bedroom. Restrained ostentation in gold, cream and eggshell-blue with ornately carved French reproduction furniture. Ross was at the window, sweeping aside the cream, brushed satin curtains to open it. It must have been the lingering scent of Linda's perfume—expensive, heavy, floral—that he'd reacted to. Being here was hard for him, harder than Viv had appreciated.

In that case, they'd do this quickly.

The wardrobe ran the length of one wall. Opening the sliding door she cast a professional eye over the clothes, immaculately organized—by season as well as color—with shoes neatly stacked in clear storage boxes. "What would suit her?" she mused aloud.

"A witch's hat and broom?" Ross pushed aside the curtain and took another breath of fresh air. "God, it's good to say that."

"How are you doing," she asked. "With the pretending?"

Ross shrugged. I'm not comfortable with it, but hell, what choice do I have?" Every time he was distracted he unconsciously massaged his leg.

He saw the direction of her gaze and straightened.

"How's the rehab going?" she asked to cover the awkward moment.

"Great."

"Dan said you've been helping out with trainees," Viv

persisted. Okay, she still asked her brother about his former troop mate, she couldn't help it. "Is that something you'll be doing more of when you go back?"

Ross stared at her. "Is that what Dan suggested?" he asked slowly.

"He mentioned it was an option."

"Did he?"

The hair on the back of her neck rose at his tone. "Did I get that wrong? He just said it might be something you'd consider."

A moment passed, he suddenly put up a hand to rub his forehead, shielding his eyes. "No...he'd never do that to me," he muttered.

"Do what?"

"Nothing. Go ahead, choose something."

Baffled, she returned her attention to the wardrobe, flicking through the hangers. "Aqua seems to be Linda's favorite color."

"Yeah, I remember her in a lot of bluey-green."

Taking that as a direction, Viv chose a simple belted dress patterned in swirls of mariner-blue and seafoam-green and laid it on the bed.

Ross looked at it strangely. "She wore that at Dad's funeral."

Viv picked it up. "I'm sorry, I'll change it."

"No." He turned back to the window. "She wore it because it was his favorite. It's probably appropriate."

She could see the tension across his shoulders, like a rubber band pulled tight. "Can I ask you a question...about the day she died? Why were you visiting a woman you disliked so much?"

He didn't turn around. "She had something of my mother's I wanted."

"What was it?"

"The artwork she was taking down when she fell."

"Oh," she said, then the significance hit her. "Ohhh! But that doesn't make her fall your fault. You know that, right?"

He faced her with folded arms. "We done here?"

"No, we need shoes."

"The funeral director said they were optional."

"She has to wear shoes," she said sharply. She couldn't forget Linda in her stocking feet, water pooling under her heels, wicking up her trousers. Suddenly afraid she was going to cry, Viv smoothed out the creases in the skirt.

Behind her she heard Ross move to the wardrobe. He probably thought she was being melodramatic but as the last person to see Linda alive, Viv felt a terrible compulsion to do right by her.

A pair of silver slingbacks landed on the bed. "She wore these with that dress," he said.

"You remember what shoes she wore?"

"It's my job to notice things."

Viv swallowed hard. "Thanks. I was thinking some costume jewelry in turquoise but I'll need Charlie's permission."

Ross pulled out his cell, dialed the number and then handed it to her. Charlie said he was happy to defer to her judgment. "Thanks, Meredith, you know how hopeless I am at this." Viv resisted the impulse to tell him that he'd never get better if he didn't practice because it was something her long-suffering twin would never say, even to her estranged husband.

"I phoned Pastor Fred about taking the service," Charlie said. "He suggested getting some of our church choir. How would you feel about that?"

"It's entirely up to you." *None of my business, Charlie. We're separated, remember?*

"So, can you text everybody? See who's available?"

She blinked. "You want me to organize the choir?"

"It makes sense. Listen, I have to go, the concrete truck's returned with another load."

"Charlie, wait." Both twins sang like caterwauling cats, but maybe church choirs were obliged to be inclusive? Viv tried to recall if Merry had ever mentioned anything, but she drew a blank. "I won't be expected to sing at the funeral, will I?"

"God, no," said Charlie with feeling. "Just your usual job. And we're only talking two hymns, the start and finish of the service—not there, you idiot! Sorry, Mere, gotta go, we'll talk later." He hung up.

What was her usual job? Printing copies of the hymn sheets? Though Merry couldn't sing, she did play an instrument. But Viv was confident the choir wouldn't be harmonizing to a double bass.

"Everything okay?" Ross asked.

"Sure." Clarification would have to wait until her next phone call to Merry. In the meantime, Viv collected a few pieces of costume jewelry, then crossed to the nightstand and picked up a photograph. "We'll give this to the funeral parlor so they can see how to apply her makeup."

It was a studio shot of Linda with her late husband. In keeping with men styled by their social-climbing wives, John Coltrane looked both uncomfortable and immaculate. "Of course Linda would treat her husband like another accessory," she commented. Then remembered. John was Ross's dad, too. "I'm sorry."

Ross shrugged. "He didn't have to go along with it."

Viv returned her attention to the photo. On the few occasions they'd met, she remembered John Coltrane as a nice man, if resigned and sad. "Did your dad ever try and mediate between you and Linda?"

"Probably. But he didn't stand a chance. To Linda I was a surly reminder of a woman she wanted my father to forget. And to me, she was the home wrecker who stole Dad away and broke Mum's heart." He seemed to become aware that he was talking about his feelings, because he stopped. Blinked. "Ready to go?"

He picked up the dress and shoes and left. Conversation ended. But that wasn't Viv's style. Not when she could see he was hurting. And this was one thing she could definitely fix.

Grabbing the jewelry and photograph, she caught up to him at the bottom of the stairs. "Ross, where did it end up? Your mother's sampler?"

"I don't know. I didn't find it in the cleanup. I expect Linda hid it."

"No, she was still taking it off the wall when I went to wash pollen off my hands."

"It doesn't matter," he insisted, and opened the front door.

"I wonder…" Putting down her load, Viv tried to slide out one end of the black lacquered dresser. It didn't budge. "Come help me move this."

He shook his head. "I don't want it."

"Ross," she said impatiently, "you didn't scare her into trying to hide it. When I arrived Linda was taking the sampler down to burn it."

"What!"

"She told me."

He huffed out a breath. "She really was a piece of work."

"So, you going to help me move this or what?"

When he'd hauled it forward, Viv crouched down and slid her arm into the gap. "I can feel something…yes…it's a frame." She pulled out the sampler and held it out but

Ross didn't take it. "Don't you dare feel guilty," she said. "Meanness killed Linda."

His gaze met hers, for once unguarded. The anguish shocked her. "Should I tell Charlie?"

"That his mother was a vindictive horrible woman? I wouldn't," she advised.

His shoulders relaxed and he accepted the sampler. "Thank you," he said gruffly. Smiled.

"Don't mention it." Viv turned to pick up Linda's accessories. Because her reaction to that smile was far from sisterly.

"I'M HUNGRY," TILLY ANNOUNCED as she climbed into the backseat of Ross's Range Rover.

"Say hello to your uncle." Viv dumped Tilly's bag and morning's drawings at her niece's feet.

"HelloUncleRoss." She returned her attention to Viv. "Can we get McDonald's on the way home?"

"That's only for treats, honey. If you're hungry, eat what's in your lunch box. Right now we're going to choose flowers for Nana Lin."

Tilly gave her a meaningful look. "But you said I could have whatever I want, *remember?*"

"That's not exactly what I said." Viv laughed nervously, acutely conscious that Ross had slung an arm over the back of the driver's seat and was *also* sending her a meaningful look. Oh, hell. "Anyway—" she leaned forward to help Tilly with her seat belt "—we'll talk about it *later,* okay?" She launched a meaningful stare of her own.

"But that's not—"

"You heard your mother, Attilla." Ross ruffled his niece's hair and faced the steering wheel. "Let it go now."

Tilly folded her arms and sat back, her mouth set in a mutinous line.

"Good girl," Viv encouraged. Shutting the door on her niece's sulky face she returned to the front passenger seat, hot and sweaty under the coat she couldn't take off. Crisis averted. Ross started the ignition and the SUV rumbled out of the school parking lot.

"Tilly was helping out with the kindergarten class this morning," Viv said brightly to Ross.

"Yeah?" In the rearview mirror, he grinned at Tilly. "So what did you teach them?"

"I read stories and said their drawings were good an' stuff…. Uncle Ross, do you know my auntie Viv?"

Viv stiffened. The little rat.

"I met her at your mum and dad's wedding but that was a long time ago. Why?"

"Just wondered."

"Look." Viv pointed. "A Prius. One of those eco-cars."

"McDonald's recycles," said Tilly.

Ross laughed. "Nice try, kid."

"You can tell me all about it *later*," Viv stressed.

"Did Auntie Viv look the same as Mum when you saw her, Uncle Ross?"

Flipping down the passenger visor, Viv pretended to check her makeup in the inset mirror and glared at her niece. Tilly glared back.

"Not at all." Ross braked to allow a car waiting for a gap in the traffic to pull in front of him. "Her hair was white with pink streaks in it."

Even locked in a stare-off with Tilly, Viv heard the male speculation in his voice. "So you *were* tempted."

"What?" Ross said, confused.

"Nothing." Damn it. She'd blinked. And if Tilly's smirk was anything to go by, she'd read that as victory.

"McDonald's is coming up, *Mum*," she said in a sing-song voice. "Last chance to change your mi-i-ind."

"You know it's the darndest thing—" Viv snapped the visor closed "—I know it's only ten-thirty but I suddenly find myself craving chicken nuggets. Pull in, Ross."

"You're giving in?"

"Don't miss the turn."

Shaking his head in disgust, he swung the car into McD's drive-through lane.

"I don't want drive-through," said Tilly. "I wanna eat in the restaurant next to the playground."

Ross looked at Viv. "We're expected at the florist's."

"What's an extra twenty minutes," she said feebly.

He stared at her, incredulous, then shrugged. "Hey, it's your funeral." The tires squealed as he accelerated out of the drive-through lane and into the restaurant's parking lot.

"No, it's not, it's Nana Lin's," said Tilly, cheerful again now that she'd got her way.

Trying to retrieve the situation, Viv wagged a finger at her niece. "No Coke, though. That's one thing I'm going to be strict about." She only sounded more pathetic.

Ross obviously thought so, too, rolling his eyes as he got out of the car.

"I don't like Coke anyway," said Tilly airily.

Resisting the urge to strangle her niece, Viv grabbed Tilly's hand and hurried ahead. "Our treat," she called over her shoulder. "What would you like, Ross?"

"Just coffee, thanks. Black, no sugar."

"You get a table. C'mon, Tilly."

In the queue she positioned them both so the only view Ross got from the window booth he'd selected was Viv's back. Warm air blasted from an overhead air-conditioning unit, mixing with the heavier mimosa of oil and fries. "Tilly, this isn't a game. This is about keeping people happy remember…your dad, your mum…"

"And me," Tilly said. "I have to be kept happy, too."

The queue moved forward. Over her shoulder Viv glanced at Ross. They didn't have time for this. Sweat trickled down her spine. Surreptitiously, she undid her coat and flapped it open in tiny bursts, desperate for a draft.

"Okay, let's talk a deal," she said briskly. "What will it take for you to be happy?"

"McDonald's every day?" The question in her voice suggested she already knew the answer.

Viv shook her head. "Today and that's it. Your mum would kill me if we ate out everyday." The queue moved forward again.

"I want my friends to come for a sleepover."

"It won't work. First we've got the funeral and then your mum will be home and she'll need peace and quiet. But I will take you and your friends to a movie."

"Laserforce would be better. It's where you shoot people with lasers."

"Done." Viv opened her handbag for her wallet. Why was there a packet of sausages in there? Oh, that's right—Salsa.

"I wanna stay up late."

"What time are we talking?" She had no idea when kids were supposed to go to bed.

"Nine o'clock."

Sounded reasonable. Viv pulled out her wallet, closed her handbag and reshouldered it. "So your normal bedtime is...?"

"Seven-thirty on a school night."

Lucky she'd checked. "Eight," she said firmly. "Okay, that's enough."

"One more," Tilly insisted.

Viv folded her arms. "What?"

Tilly stopped looking like Tony Soprano and turned back into a little girl. "I want to phone Mum every day."

Of course you can. Viv pretended to consider. "And in return for all this you'll keep our secret and behave yourself? No more stunts like you just pulled with Ross?"

"Promise." Tilly held out her hand. "Now we have to shake."

"How do I know I can trust you?" Viv said sternly.

The little girl looked offended. "I'm a Brownie."

So blackmail was okay for Brownies, but questioning their word wasn't? On the other hand, Viv was currently living a lie so who was she to quibble? Sighing, she shook Tilly's hand.

"Deal."

"WHY IS YOUR CELL TURNED OFF?" Merry demanded as Viv was preparing the kids' dinner some five hours later. "I've been calling you for hours."

"I told you I'd phone as soon as I had privacy." Viv navigated the pureed applesauce still splattered around the highchair from breakfast and plonked a new two-liter bottle of milk in the fridge. In total she'd had maybe five minutes alone today, and even then Harry had banged on the bathroom door. According to Tilly, mummies had to leave it open.

"I can't take your calls when I'm with Ross or Charlie," she reminded her twin. "Then I was running la— To pick up Harry, and as soon as we got home we exercised Salsa. He's been shut in the yard all day." Viv hoped Merry wasn't all that fond of her spring daffodils.

Far from being grateful, the schnoodle had stubbornly sat on his haunches when Viv had put on his lead, only cooperating when Tilly took over. Their makeshift family had walked to the corner store where Viv had bought some basics for dinner…milk, ground beef, pasta sauce, spaghetti. Most of it had ended up stowed around Harry's body in the stroller after the plastic carrier bag was needed as a pooper-scooper.

Viv was heartily tired of poop.

"I'm sorry, I shouldn't have snapped," said Merry. "It's just so frustrating being unable to do anything or help... so much depends on you."

About to shut the fridge, Viv paused. "What's that supposed to mean?"

"How would you like to be bedridden and passive when your future's at stake?"

Okay, maybe the comment wasn't personal. It was her low blood sugar; she hadn't eaten since the McNuggets. Grabbing an apple, Viv closed the fridge and returned to the stove. "I'd absolutely hate it," she admitted. "So what did the surgeon say?" She dumped the minced beef in the pan where onions and garlic were already frying. Smelled almost homey.

"He thinks I might have picked up an infection, they've done some blood tests. Anyway, tell me about my kids? Is Tilly coping with Linda's death? Is Harry still constipated?"

The apple halfway to her mouth, Viv put it down. "Harry's constipation is cured, believe me." She heard *brooom-brooom* under the kitchen table where the baby sat in the middle of his circular train track, resisting Viv's attempt to teach him choo-choo.

"And Tilly's coping," she added. "She's drawing a picture now to put in Nana Lin's coffin." Ross's idea. Viv glanced into the dining room where her niece labored with crayons and card, feet swinging on the chair, her tongue out in concentration. There'd been more tears at the florist's as reality hit the child.

She'd resisted Viv's efforts to comfort her until Ross had crouched down and told Tilly that everyone cried when someone they loved died…yeah, even him…buckets and buckets. Mollified, Tilly had allowed Viv's hug, cheering up when her aunt asked her to choose the flowers for Linda's wreath. The result had been a hideous clash of colors but they came from Tilly's heart, and hopefully Linda was in a place now to appreciate the gesture.

"Tell me everything about your day," Merry said. "Did anyone suspect?"

Viv stirred the meaty lumps out of the ground beef. "We had a couple of setbacks but your secret's still safe."

"What do you mean, 'setbacks'?"

"Hang on." Crossing to the dining room door, Viv closed it softly, catching a glimpse of Tilly's picture. Mum, Dad and the kids all together. Her throat tightened. Returning to the kitchen she picked up the phone again.

"Tilly overheard our conversation this morning," she told Merry, "but she's on board—" *at a cost* "—and hanging out to talk to you." The ground beef started to burn, she turned down the heat. "We're all going to Skype you after dinner."

Merry moaned. "My daughter's involved?"

"I know it's not ideal," Viv said, thinking of Tilly's picture. "But we're trying to save your kids more heartbreak."

"Viv, I'm scared. Tell me we're doing the right thing."

She turned off the stove and went and sat down. "We're doing it for the right reasons." Who was she reassuring here? "And Charlie's got enough to cope with right now." They'd passed the point of no return. "Which reminds me… he ended it with Susan last night."

Stunned silence. "You're kidding. Really?" Merry laughed, then immediately sobered. "You're not joking, are you, because this is—"

"It's true. Susan dropped the bomb this morning. Apparently, he regrets leaping into another relationship, told her he's not ready. Did you know Charlie never slept with her?" Not by choice, Viv suspected, but that was beside the point.

"No…gosh…that's the last thing I'd ask either of them." Merry laughed again, with the same giddy lilt of their childhood. "How on earth did you find that out?"

Viv opened her mouth, closed it. Harry *brooom-brooomed* an engine over her feet.

Fortunately, her twin didn't wait for an answer. "Well, then we definitely can't tell him the truth now. Viv, I never dared hope…" Merry's voice tripped over itself in her excitement. "You saw how gorgeous she was, didn't you?"

"Totally gorgeous…and the boobs, Mere." Both sisters sighed.

"And so nice," her sister continued. "I tried to hate her but—"

"You couldn't."

"I even had them getting married…in my mind…but this! If Charlie can walk away from a woman like Susan then maybe he's not over me. Maybe—"

"Don't get your hopes up," Viv warned. "I hate to be the voice of reason but he could change his mind again. He's all over the place right now. Besides, you have choices, too." Briefly, she considered putting this delicately. "Would you really want that asshole back, after the way he's overreacted?"

"It was all my fault."

"Don't talk like that. You're human, Mere, you can make mistakes."

"No, *you* do that. I'm the sensible one. I should have seen the kiss coming."

You're this. I'm that. The personality straitjacket. "These things don't knock on the door and announce themselves." Viv steered the conversation to less dangerous waters.

"Where's the recipe for your raspberry chocolate angel food cake? Tilly wants to make Nana Lin's favorite for the post-funeral reception. It's being held here, by the way."

"You're hosting it at *my* house?"

Viv explained Ross's truce ultimatum and waited for sympathy. "What else did you get yourself into?" Merry said.

"Nothing," she said irritably, "I was very careful. I even made sure you didn't sing in the choir before I agreed to organize it for the funeral. So what do you do with the singers exactly? Hold the hymns? Organize the organist?" Definitely low blood sugar. She was getting silly.

"I conduct it," said Merry. "And I *know* I mentioned that on the phone six months ago when I volunteered!"

Viv started to laugh, then stuck a knuckle in her mouth and bit hard. *Hold it together, one of us has to.* "I'll feign an injury...put a sling on."

"And then I show up with a broken leg and a bound wrist? Why don't we just mummify me and be done with it."

Viv laughed again, letting the hysteria take over. Because this really was very funny. Harry poked his head out from under the table and laughed with her.

"Look, it's okay," Merry said quickly. "Don't panic, I'll teach you. Two songs in, what, thirty-six hours? It'll be easy. We'll practice over Skype. And I'll send you some links. You can do this, Viv. Okay?"

Tilly came in, wrinkling her nose. "I smell onion. I don't eat onion."

"Of course you don't," said Viv, still smiling. "That would be too easy."

"Okay, Viv?" Merry repeated more urgently.

She looked around at her smelly nephew needing a bath,

at the half-cooked dinner full of onions. She still needed to learn the rules of soccer for Tilly's training session tomorrow. Closing her eyes, she took a deep breath. "Okay."

CHAPTER TEN

ROSS WOKE IN THE MIDDLE of an erotic dream about his sister-in-law, as he was untying the halter on Meredith's slinky, satin dress prior to taking her on the starched tablecloth he'd swept clear of crystal and cutlery.

Feeling like one sad, sick bastard, he lay in his stepmother's spare room and waited for his hard-on to subside. Then with a groan he covered his head with a pillow and considered making an appointment with the shrink who'd told him he was in denial about how much the ambush and his buddies' deaths had affected him. Maybe the dream about Meredith was some kind of twisted release of repressed grief? It spoke to how shaken he was that Ross hoped so.

Remembering the dream's setting, he shuddered. A wedding. Not theirs, thank God, because Meredith's dress had been a shimmering pink, more of a bridesmaid's—

Ross jerked upright. "Son of a bitch." He'd never desired his sister-in-law but he'd wanted her twin. Except he'd recognized a live shell when he saw one. No, the very idea was crazy. He shook his head to clear it. Viv Jansen was a spiky-haired blonde half a world away.

But his brain was already respooling the past couple of days—the sexy outfit Meredith was wearing the first time he saw her. Meredith, a nurse, fainting at the sight of blood. The thousand hesitations over details she knew like the back of her hand. Not grief—ignorance. He cursed again recalling the suitcase shoved under the bed. Not leaving. Arriving.

Mind racing, he switched on the light. "Damn it, it's her. It has to be." Grabbing his cell, he rang Dan. The twins' brother, his former troop mate, answered on the fourth ring.

"Ross?" he said sleepily, obviously recognizing his number. "You okay?"

"Everything's fine." Now wasn't the time to grill Dan about the CO's sudden desire to push Ross into a training role. "I need your little sister's cell number."

"In case you hadn't noticed it's two in the morning," Dan complained. "Merry will be asleep."

"But in New York, Vivienne won't be."

There was a long pause. "Now, after all these years, you decide to hit on my sister?" Dan didn't sound happy about the prospect. Ross's report card with women generally read, "Would get better grades if he applied himself."

"Relax, it's strictly business. Have you heard from her lately?"

"Phoned her last week." Ross heard a drawer being opened. "She was about to start work on a new show and dodging some lovesick Frenchman she'd given marching orders." Dan gave him the number. "So exactly what business was that again?"

"When did you last talk to Meredith?" Dan had always been able to instantly tell his siblings apart.

"Yesterday. She said she was helping Charlie out with the funeral and I warned her not to get too involved because things have only just settled down between them."

Ross's certainty faded. "And she sounded exactly the same?"

"How else would she sound? Ross, what's going on?"

"Following a misplaced hunch, apparently. Listen, I'll call you at a civilized hour." He needed Dan's advice on how to deal with the CO. "Tell Bridezilla the alpha hole apologizes for interrupting her beauty sleep."

"Jo says you need beauty sleep more than she does and agrees there's something going on we should know about."

"You're newlyweds. Haven't you got better things to do than pry into my dull life?"

"Come to think of it," said Dan. "Yeah." He hung up.

Ross crumpled Viv's number and went back to bed, making a mental note to call the psych. But he couldn't fall asleep. To hell with it. He got up, smoothed the crumpled note and dialed Viv's cell.

"Hello?" said a feminine voice, and Ross breathed a sigh of relief. He wanted to be wrong. Before he could speak, she added sharply. "Is that you, Viv? Is everything okay with the kids?"

He let her hang, one second, then two, while he made up his mind what to do. "I'm real sorry, ma'am." Ross feigned an American accent. "I got the wrong number."

Cutting the connection, he dressed quickly, then rang his sister-in-law's cell. "I have to talk to you," he told Meredith's semiconscious impersonator coldly. "No, it can't wait until morning, it's about Charlie. I'll be there in fifteen minutes."

VIV FILLED THE KETTLE with water and flicked the switch, ready to cry with tiredness. A yawn caught her, so wide she nearly dislocated her jaw. Enviously, she glanced at Salsa, curled up in his basket in the corner. He'd barely raised his head for a token growl before returning to sleep. Lucky schnoodle.

Had Ross somehow found out? Frowning, she opened a box of tea bags. Except she'd talked to him at ten about the catering choices and he'd been fine. Charlie had already gone to bed, exhausted.

No, he probably wanted to lecture her again about staying away from his brother. She turned away from her reflection, trying not to care that Merry's dressing gown and old-lady slippers were completely unsexy. Thinking along those lines around Ross Coltrane would only get her into more trouble, and Lord knows, she had plenty enough as it was.

She'd gone to bed at midnight after a frustrating ninety-minute conducting session on Skype with Merry.

"We only have time for a monkey see, monkey do approach," Merry had said. "I've chosen two hymns with simple patterns that the choir knows by heart. All you'll have to do is stay with them."

"Oh, is that all I have to do."

"We're identical twins." Merry's tone had been brisk. She'd cheered up with something to do. "If I have a musical ear, *you* have a musical ear."

"I saw a documentary where one identical twin was gay and one wasn't. How do you explain that?"

That hadn't got her out of choir practice.

Smothering another jaw-breaking yawn, Viv dug two cups out of the mound of dirty dishes piled up in the sink and rinsed them clean. Cleaning the house was tomorrow's job.

Headlights flashed into the driveway and she hastened to open the front door so Ross didn't wake the kids by pressing the doorbell, not that he would because Ross seemed to consider the ramifications of his every action, which was a skill Viv wished she could emulate.

He strode up the path without the slight limp that characterized his end-of-day gait. Viv caught herself smoothing her hair and stopped.

"What's so important we have to talk about it in the

middle of the night," she complained, closing the door behind him.

"Confessions," he said so close behind her that she jumped.

"Wh-what do you mean?"

"I haven't been entirely honest with you, Meredith, about why I was so mad when I discovered you were dating Dr. Dick."

She sighed. "Not this again. I told you, I'm not seeing *Luke*."

"I believe you. Now."

"Well, that's good." He was still standing very close and she felt a frisson of unease at the way he was looking at her. Hawklike. Intense. As if he was seeing her for the first time. "Anyway, I made tea…" As she turned toward the kitchen, she found herself spun around.

"You see, Meredith." His grip tightened on her shoulders. "I was jealous."

"Wh-what?"

"God knows, I've struggled against falling for my brother's wife but I can't hide the truth any longer. I'm in love with you." The glint in his eyes wasn't very loverlike but she was too shocked to notice that more than fleetingly.

"You can't be," Viv whispered, then gasped as he released her shoulders and hauled her into his iron-hard arms.

"Give me one good reason why I shouldn't rip off that prudish dressing gown and make mad passionate love to you."

Horrified, Viv planted her hands against his chest as he bent to kiss her. "Ross, this is insane, I'm your brother's wife!"

"Practically ex-wife."

"Yes, but I'm still in love with him!"

He paused, his mouth inches from hers. "So you say," he murmured, "but somehow, you don't sound convincing."

She averted her face as he swooped and his lips brushed her ear. "But remember Viv liked you!"

"Who?"

"My twin!" She couldn't keep the tartness out of her voice. "The feisty, fun one."

Ross raised his head. "Oh, you mean Flea!"

"Flea?" Viv said faintly.

"Yeah, you know…always bouncing around. She's the annoying itch a guy wants to scratch just to get rid of it so he can get back to more down-to-earth women such as yourself. Don't play games, Meredith." His hold tightening until she was plastered against his body. His gray eyes challenged her. "I've noticed the way you've been looking at me the past few days."

This was a nightmare. Her worst nightmare. Viv struggled to free herself but she might as well have been in a straitjacket. "I wasn't…I was…I was…" her brain scrambled for an escape route "…looking at your leg and feeling sorry for you."

He released her so abruptly she stumbled backward. Then he smiled. It wasn't a pleasant smile. "Hey, I'll take a pity—"

"Ross!"

"Fling," he finished. "You make me so crazy, Meredith. There are so many things I'd like to do to you right now." He moved toward her and she darted behind the couch.

"Ross, let's sit down and talk about this!"

"Why talk when we can act?" He circled right, she scurried left. In one smooth movement, he stepped on and over the couch. His arm shot out and he caught the tie on her dressing gown and started reeling her in. "I've got these bondage fantasies."

"Wait," she said desperately. "Ross, please wait."

"Mais, je t'adore," he protested, catching her around the waist.

Through her panic, the language registered. Viv froze in his hold. Her eyes met his. "Why are you talking French?"

"I heard you like it. How do I say, 'I'd like to wring your neck' *en français?*"

"So, Ross, LONG TIME no see," Viv quipped nervously.

He released her in disgust. "Where is Meredith?"

"Not buried at the bottom of the garden if that's what you're worried about." His gaze didn't waver. Okay, nervous humor wasn't helping. "She's in Waikato Hospital recovering from a broken tibia."

"Is she okay?"

His concern steadied her. Ross might slam Meredith but deep down he still cared about her.

"She'll recover, physically." Perching on the arm of the couch, she gestured to the armchair opposite. "Her emotional health now depends on you."

Ross remained standing. "So I guess that brings us to the 'why the hell are you impersonating her?' question."

Viv dug her trembling hands in the pockets of the velour dressing gown. "First of all," she managed to say calmly, "she was perfectly entitled to consider all her options and we never expected the…" She paused.

"Hoax?" he suggested. "Fraud? Deception? Scam?"

"Swap. Never expected the swap to last this long." Viv recalled the Lemony Snicket book she'd read Tilly at bedtime. "What happened was a series of unfortunate events."

His eyes seemed to bore into the back of her skull. "The first being?"

Her fingers found some lint in the dressing gown's left

pocket and she worried it into a ball. "Merry breaking her leg while she was in Hamilton for a job interview."

There was a pregnant silence. His expression darkened. "Did Charlie know she was planning to move away with the kids?"

"It's only an hour and a quarter away…he'd still see plenty of the children. As I said she was exploring her options, and, anyway, she's decided against it."

"So that's a no, then." He swung on his heel.

Viv straightened. "Where are you going?"

"Where do you think?" He strode toward the door.

Alarmed, she sprang to her feet. "Ross, you have to hear me out."

"Actually I don't. Only Charlie does. Unlike you, I stay out of other people's business."

She blocked his path. "Says the guy who browbeat me the other day, thinking I was Merry. Come to think of it," she added on an inspired thought, "if you hadn't been such a bully I wouldn't have impersonated her to show you she couldn't be pushed around, and *none* of this would have happened."

Incredulous, he stared down at her. "Are you saying this is *my* fault?"

"Partly." Viv warmed to her theme. "Actually, more than partly. I told Linda who I was but then she died and I fainted and the next thing I'm waking up to hear you telling the cops I was Meredith Coltrane. What was I supposed to do?"

"Gee, I don't know," he said sarcastically. "Tell the truth, maybe?"

Viv snorted. "When Meredith was terrified of Charlie hearing about her interview and you threatening custody battles?"

"You're right." He slapped his forehead. "What am I thinking? My fault, again."

"Don't beat yourself up." She matched his tone. "If I'd known at the time that Charlie hadn't cheated on Merry I might have been more tolerant of your childish outburst."

They glared at each other. Inwardly Viv groaned. What the hell was she doing? She should be placating him, but she hated being treated like an idiot. Especially when it was deserved.

"That's real big of you to be so forgiving." Two hands clamped on her shoulders, firmly Ross moved her aside. "Let's hope Charlie is as magnanimous."

Viv panicked. "Okay, we've got off on the wrong foot… let me explain—"

"Save your excuses for him." With one hand he jerked open the door, with the other he pulled out his keys.

"Ross." She touched his hand and he suddenly gripped hers, lifting it to the light. Merry's engagement and wedding rings sparkled on her finger. His eyes were so full of contempt that Viv squirmed. She felt exposed and vulnerable, a kid caught in a prank instead of a woman trying—however badly—to save a family from further disintegration.

Humiliated, she nearly let him leave. But Charlie would go ballistic if he found out now and, no matter how much Viv privately wished she'd done things differently, there was no going back. She'd leaped over the cliff—convinced Merry to leap with her—and they were wholly reliant on Viv's wits to parachute them to a safe landing. She'd pulled off the swap for three days, she could do it for three more. But first she had to convince Ross to let her.

And his expression said he wasn't going to do it.

Taking a deep breath, she snatched the keys out of his hand and ran toward the downstairs bathroom. Merry's carpet slippers slapped the wooden floorboards as she fled down the hall.

"And you called *me* childish," he called after her in exasperation.

Salsa woke up as Viv dashed past, and gave chase with a yip of excitement. Viv slammed the bathroom door behind her and turned the lock seconds before Ross turned the handle. The rattle made her jump. How did he get there so fast?

"I don't believe this. Open this now!"

Salsa followed Ross's bark with one of his own. She listened to the scratch of paws against the paintwork. "Quiet, both of you," Viv whispered fiercely. "You'll wake the kids."

The handle rattled again. "I'm giving you thirty seconds."

"Acting in anger was what got me into this situation and I'm not letting you repeat my mistake. You have to listen first."

"I've already filled in the gaps," he said impatiently. "You're pretending to be Meredith until she can be transferred to Auckland at which point she'll make up some cockamamie story about how she broke her leg and you'll swap again, leaving Charlie none the wiser about her job interview in Hamilton."

It still sounded doable. Viv caught sight of herself nodding in the mirror. "And no harm done," she added. "Because she decided not to take a job there anyway."

"And you're expecting me to fall in with this litany of lies."

She frowned. "White lies," she corrected, and dropped to peer through the keyhole. She was eye level with the logo on his navy T-shirt. Obey Gravity, It's the Law. "Believe me, if we thought Charlie would respond rationally to the truth we wouldn't have gone this route."

A snort from the other side. "Sorry, I thought you

mentioned the word *rational*. Charlie's not the crazy one here." At least he'd stopped rattling the handle.

"No?" It was difficult to sound persuasive through a keyhole but Viv did her best. "You think it's normal to abandon your family over a kiss your wife hadn't expected, immediately confessed and apologized for?"

"You know it was more than that. She'd been seeing the guy for weeks."

"Seeing, not sleeping with," she said fiercely, then jumped back as a doggy snout materialized, and hot, meaty breath blasted through the keyhole. Salsa whined excitedly and was pulled away.

"Quiet, boy. You can savage her later, I promise."

She returned to the keyhole. "Look, whatever one-off mistake Merry made, she's a decent person and a great mother who deserves a second chance and, frankly, your brother needs a lesson in how to forgive. It's not as if he's blameless in all this."

"Oh, yeah, Charlie really had it coming." Ross's hands appeared holding a wallet. He pulled out a credit card and Viv's eyes narrowed.

The sneaky son of a…

"In some ways he did." Keeping her tone conversational, Viv unfolded from her crouch and scanned the bathroom for some kind of brace. "Merry was starved for attention… *starved,* Ross." Standing on tiptoe, she carefully removed the old-fashioned brass curtain rail from its holders above the shower and unhooked the curtain. "Merry said she felt invisible for the last two years of their marriage. Whenever she tried to talk to Charlie about it, he'd brush her off, tell her everything was fine." Padding one of the pointed ends of the rail with a towel to stop it from gouging the wood, she angled it between the shower cubicle base and the door. "Because it *was* fine—for Charlie. I mean why would he want to change the status quo? Much easier to let Mere run round after him."

Ross snorted. "And did she once say, 'Hey, asshole, get your own beer...I'm making some changes'? No!" Because Viv was listening for it, she heard the soft slide of plastic as he worked the lock. "Instead, she sighed and kept doing it all, and waited for Charlie to notice she wasn't happy."

"*You* noticed she wasn't happy," Vivienne pointed out.

"That's different." There was a frown in Ross's voice. "I'm trained to be observant."

"Who can't spot an elephant in the room," she scoffed. "Oh, that's right, *Charlie*."

The lock clicked, the handle turned and the door bulged slightly as Ross leaned his weight against it. The brass shower rail creaked but held. "Nice try," Viv said. "But I grew up with Dan, remember?"

He gave a muffled curse. "My point is, everyone knows marriage is hard work. So if you've chosen the shackles, quit whining and get on with it. You're not going to change my mind, so you might as well give me the keys."

"All that cynicism," she said softly. "It's a wonder you can't corrode the hinges with it."

"At least I'm not a pathological liar!"

"*White* lies," she insisted.

"So many you must be snow-blind."

"I'm a very truthful person, but if the greater good is best served by a lie then I'll tell it."

"The greater good being what favors your interests."

"Actually, it's the opposite," she said earnestly. "You can't lie to further your own cause because that's bad karma and you should never lie to yourself because that's self-defeating. If the truth is going to hurt rather than heal, then don't use it."

"So you can lie prescriptively…?" He sounded as if he was thinking about it.

"Yes." She hunkered by the keyhole again. "And, Ross, you just say 'not my business.' It's like the Good Samaritan. If you come across a situation you can fix, then you have an obligation to fix it."

Silence. He was definitely thinking about it. "Damn it!" he said. Viv took that as a positive sign.

Another silence. Another curse. "Okay," he conceded. "I take your point."

Viv curled her fingers around the shower rail bracing the door. "You'll keep the secret?"

"I'll keep the secret."

She removed the brace and let him in. "I'm so glad, I'd hate to be on bad terms with— Hey!"

He'd plucked his car keys from her hand. "I'll be leaving now."

Viv grabbed his forearm. "You bastard, you *conned* me."

"No, I told a white lie for the right reason. To get the keys so I can go tell my brother."

"Yes, let's think about Charlie," she said desperately. "Whatever the rights or wrongs of this are, he's not in a fit state to hear it. Ross, please don't let your need to tattle override what's best for your brother." His eyes narrowed. Oh, hell, she shouldn't have said "tattle." He removed her hand from his forearm.

"Okay, forget Charlie and think of the kids."

"Those would be the kids you're lying to."

"They know who I am."

"They're in on this scam? Oh, this just gets better and better."

"Haven't they been through enough already without having their parents fall apart again?"

He looked down at her with implacable eyes. "Wasn't

it enough that your sister broke my brother's heart without trying to make it harder for him to spend time with his kids? I'm telling Charlie the truth."

Viv watched him walk away. "How did you know it was me, anyway?" She'd failed Merry, she'd failed the kids. "Was it because I was too happy, Ross? That's what your niece said when I asked how to act more like her mom. 'Look sadder.' Please!" Her voice broke. "Don't do this."

For a moment she thought he hesitated but maybe that was the limp because he didn't glance back. She was going to cry and she didn't want him to see it. Swallowing a sob she sought refuge in the bathroom.

CHAPTER ELEVEN

Ross GLANCED BACK when the bathroom door closed behind her and told himself two wrongs—falling in with the sisters' scam—wouldn't make a right. He didn't lie, ever, least of all to his brother. He was so angry with Viv he wanted to shake her. How the hell did she think such a ridiculous masquerade would ever work? Except it had worked for three days…and the only reason he'd caught on was not through his honed SAS instincts, but through his body's reaction to her.

It seemed to delight in betraying him these days. "Shit!" He slammed the doorjamb with his open palm. "Shit, shit, shit."

There was a gasp, so soft, Ross barely heard it. He looked up. Tilly, in pink flannelette pajamas imprinted with black cats, her current obsession, sat on the stairs, clearly shocked. *Shit.*

"Did you hear all that?"

The small throat swallowed, but she didn't speak. Her eyes accused him.

Oh, hell. "You're cold, honey," he said gruffly. "Let's get you back to bed."

She stood obediently, let him shepherd her upstairs. Her bedroom was to the left of the stairs, the walls covered with posters of kittens.

Awkwardly, he tucked her in. "You want to talk about this?"

She turned away and faced the wall. Tilly always got stoic when she was hurt. If Meredith or Charlie fussed over, say, a knee scrape or a bee sting, she'd get mad. She didn't like to cry. Saw it as a weakness, Ross supposed.

"Honey, someone has to tell the truth."

She stared at the wall, very small and still under the duvet. His heart felt like a pump, building pressure in his brain. Since the separation, both he and the twins' brother, Dan, had worked damn hard to avoid fallout on their friendship. Now Viv had thrown a massive spanner in the works through this ridiculous charade. Ross had to take sides.

Until now, he'd believed that was Charlie's side.

Viv was huddled on the couch when he came downstairs a couple minutes later, Salsa glaring at her from his basket. Glimpsing Ross through the banisters, the dog scampered over. Viv lifted a tearstained face, then shoved to a sitting position when she saw Ross and grabbed a handful of tissues from the box beside the couch. "I thought you'd gone." She looked pathetic and sad and Ross didn't care, he was so bitterly resentful.

"I was putting Tilly back to bed. She heard everything."

Her head shot up. "No!"

"I told her I wouldn't tell Charlie."

"Oh, Ross, thank you." She started to smile but he scowled at her.

"As soon as Charlie's over his initial grief and can deal with the truth, Meredith's telling it."

"But—"

"It's not open to negotiation. Understood?"

She eyed him. Did the woman have no sense of self-preservation? "Understood?" he repeated.

Her lashes fell, screening her expression. "Understood."

With that reassurance, Ross became all business. "How are you planning on identifying everyone at the funeral?"

"Merry's briefed me, and Tilly and I have been going over photo albums."

He frowned. "Funerals don't have RSVPs. You can't know everyone who'll be there."

"Then I'll come over all teary...excuse myself."

"You'll have to use them sparingly or they'll look like crocodile tears. Everyone knows Linda bullied Meredith." He paced the living room. "I'll stay close when I can—run defense with Coltrane relatives."

She blinked. "So...are you helping me now?"

"What choice do I have? I've given Tilly my word." He decided he hated Viv Jansen. "You're putting my relationship with my brother at risk. I have to make sure you don't blow it."

"I've done okay so far," she retorted. "I'm not going to fall apart halfway through."

"Except I sprung you, remember?"

Viv sighed. "Fair point," she conceded. "What gave me away?"

Something very close to a wet dream. "I'm SAS," Ross said brusquely. "You can't hide anything from us."

"Then thank God Dan isn't coming to the funeral."

He hadn't thought that far. "And your parents?"

"Mum's still in Italy and Dad's busy helping Dan with lambing. Obviously he and Dan offered—for Charlie's sake—but Merry put them off."

"At least you've got something right," he said grudgingly. Actually she'd got a lot right over the past few days; he could only marvel at her ingenuity. But he wasn't telling *her* that. Except... "Why the hell did you let me talk you into hosting the reception after the service? Your best strategy was a quick appearance and a quick getaway."

Viv gave him an exasperated look. "You think? But if you recall you made it a condition of our truce."

"Damn it. Well…we're stuck with it now, so best thing to do is set up a schedule for the day." He stopped because she was shaking her head. "What?"

"I don't need another person trying to micromanage every detail."

"Is that what Meredith's doing?" He could imagine that; she'd done it with Charlie. Because whatever sob story she'd told Viv, his sister-in-law helped plow her domestic rut. She was one of those wives who complained her husband did nothing in the house, then made him feel incompetent when he did.

Ross remembered Charlie trying to cook dinner while Meredith cleaned up behind him like a super Hoover. She'd taken over walking the dog because Charlie wanted to wait until after the sports news. As a scheduler himself, Ross could appreciate her frustration. As a guy he thought: What's an extra twenty minutes as long as the job gets done?

"I'm not talking micromanagement," he clarified. "I'm talking risk management. Making sure you're on top of all the things under your control so if the proverbial hits the fan, you're better able to think on your feet." He noticed she was nearly falling asleep on hers. "Minimizing close calls."

"That would be helpful." Unconsciously she hugged herself. "I have to admit I've been living the past forty-eight hours on tenterhooks, lurching from one crisis to another. I mean, take a look at the house."

Ross started picking up the toys scattered across the floor. "Go to bed, Viv. We'll go over things tomorrow. When's the best time?"

Her brow wrinkled. "The only outside thing I've got on is running a coaching session for Tilly's soccer team tomorrow after school."

He tossed Garfield and some Matchbox cars into the toy basket. "You know soccer?"

"I'll research the rules online. I figure I can learn enough for training."

Ross resisted offering assistance. He had enough to do for Charlie and damned if he'd make this easy for her.

"Other than that," she continued, "I'll be looking after Harry, trying to walk that unfriendly dog... Oh, I also need to rent some extra tableware...clean the house and learn to conduct."

He lifted a brow. "Electricity?"

"And Tilly wants to make that cake...Nana Lin's favorite."

She hid a yawn and Ross frowned. Exhausted, she'd make more mistakes, maybe even a critical one.

Damn it! "Up until a couple of months ago I took Tilly's team." He'd dropped everything to intensify his training when he realized he wasn't making the progress he'd expected. "I'll meet you at the school, run the training session."

Her face lit up and Ross marveled that he'd ever been fooled. Viv's energy had always been completely different from her sister's. She'd succeeded through a visual perception trick, like those pictures where you either saw the profile of a young woman in a hat or an old hag, depending on where your eye first focused. Cleverly, she'd focused them on Meredith, through clothes, through setting, through sheer bloody gall. Hiding in plain sight.

"I'll phone you tomorrow," he said. "Meanwhile I'll keep Charlie away from you and your small accomplices as much as possible. It shouldn't be hard, he's run ragged finalizing the funeral arrangements in between work commitments."

"Thank you, that would be a big help."

"What the hell possessed you to tell Tilly, anyway?"

"She overheard me talking to her mother." Wearily, Viv raked a hand through her hair. "But that's sorted out now. I turn off my cell so I'm not caught in public by calls."

The penny dropped. "That guy blowing air kisses was your French boyfriend, not Dr. Dick."

"Dr. Luke," she corrected. "Wait! How did you know Jean Paul was French?"

"Like I said, SAS." She seemed too tired to move so he put a hand under her elbow and steered her toward the stairs. "Bed. Now."

"I thought I wasn't allowed to get closer," she joked weakly. Brown eyes lifted to his—half apologetic, half defiant. And physical awareness sparked between them, as it had sparked eight years ago. Dangerously alive with something too close to a connection. At the wedding he'd turned her down because of it.

Now she'd embroiled him in a situation entirely driven by moral and emotional dilemmas, his least favorite kind. If mishandled, this had the potential to alienate him from one of the few people he needed—his brother. Ross dropped his hand from her elbow.

"Let's be clear, Viv. I don't give a damn if your motives are as pure as spring water. You've created an unholy mess and I'm compromising *my* ethics to help you clean it up. When this is over the only Jansen I still want ties with is Dan."

"AND YOU'RE *sure* ROSS won't tell Charlie," said Merry. "Or our brother?"

"He gave me his word, so it's all good."

So why did she feel so bad? Viv sat at the computer nook in the kitchen. A cheerful midmorning sun streamed through the windows, and revealed every smear and scrap of food on the floorboards, except where a basket of dirty laundry cast a mountainous shadow. The Himalayas, she thought, moving her half-eaten cereal into the shade before the milk soured. *Me and a couple of trusty Sherpas, climbing Everest. It's got to be easier than this.*

The kids were at school and day care, and Viv had rushed home for a second Skype session on conducting. "Breathe when you want your choir to breathe and take an exaggerated breath on the beat before any new part is supposed to start. That's in addition to the hand gestures."

She was way too busy to be stressing about last night.

On the computer screen, Merry worried the edge of the sheet. "But *how* did Ross work it out?"

"Omniscient powers apparently."

Merry's brow puckered. "It must have been something you did."

Hurt, frustration and fatigue boiled over like Tilly's morning porridge. "Why? Because everything that goes wrong has to be my fault?"

"I didn't say that," Merry said wearily, and plumped up the pillows. "Only you need to find out what it was and fix it before the funeral."

Her twin's complexion was the same shade as the white pillowcase. Viv leaned forward. Merry's eyes were fever-bright. "Why aren't you looking better?" she said abruptly.

Merry smoothed down her covers. "I needed stronger antibiotics, they'll kick in shortly."

"I'm driving down there."

"No!" Her sister looked up in alarm. "You've got too much to do. Our conducting practice…memorizing names and faces—now there's the choir's names, too, remember? Shopping for cake ingredients…and cleaning, too, if the rest of the house is as dirty as what I can see behind you."

"None of that matters if you need me."

"Viv, I need you *there*."

"At least let me call Dan. He—"

"The kids know, the dog knows, Ross knows." Merry threw up her hands. "Now you want to tell Dan? Soon the only person in ignorance will be Charlie. I'm on the mend, so can we get on with conducting practice, please? I'm scheduled for more tests in thirty minutes."

"What kind of tests?"

"Nothing…more blood work. I'll still be fine for a transfer in a couple of days. Now, 'Abide with Me' is four/four timing." Her pale arms rose in graceful movement. "That's down for beat one, over across the body for beat two, out for beat three and up for beat four."

Halfway through their practice, Viv's cell rang. "It's Charlie," she told Merry. "I should get this." She trusted Ross to keep his promise but was still nervous as they exchanged pleasantries. "Did I confirm the choir?" Viv glanced at her sister who'd made the arrangements.

Merry nodded and held up her hands. Ten fingers, then another five.

"Fifteen are coming," said Viv smoothly.

"Okay if I pick Harry up from day care?"

"Sure, you can pick Harry up from day care," she repeated for Merry's benefit. The sisters looked at each other. Or did he want to see *Susan?*

"And I'll collect Tilly from school, too," Charlie said. "I thought I'd take them for ice cream since I've seen so little of them…what with Mum and everything."

"Didn't Ross tell you? Tilly has soccer training after school. He's offered to take it."

"Of course," he sounded weary. "Why didn't I remember?"

"You have other things on your plate."

"I'm writing the eulogy tonight. Any cute stories involving Mom and our kids come to mind?"

"I'll think about it and phone you," she promised.

"Thanks, Mere." Charlie cleared his throat. "And thanks again for all you're doing. I'm aware that it's a big ask."

"Just trying to do the right thing here." To Viv's horror, her voice wobbled. Ross's condemnation had really knocked her confidence. Horrified, she shot a glance at Merry, but her sister lay back in bed with her eyes closed. "Gotta go," she managed briskly. "Goodbye, Charlie."

Merry opened her eyes. "You did tell me not to get my hopes up. He's going to make up with Susan, isn't he?"

"We don't know that," Viv replied. "Maybe it really is about spending time with Harry. He's only seen him once since camp." She blinked. "Is this really only my fifth day in New Zealand?"

"Which reminds me," said Merry, "Jean Paul left a message overnight. He wasn't happy with a text message instead of a phone call."

Great, something else to feel guilty about. She'd contact him after this—no, the time zone was wrong. Viv suddenly felt swamped by the burden of other people's expectations. "Listen, Charlie wants fun stories about Linda and the children for the eulogy. How about you phone him directly? If you call him at Linda's home number tonight and use the hospital's landline instead of my cell, it should be safe enough. Her phone doesn't have call display."

"That's a great idea."

"I do have them occasionally."

"Don't get prickly. I'm surprised I didn't think of it, that's all."

"Because you're the sensible one." Old wounds, reflex reactions. She'd had therapy for this, damn it. "Forget it, I'm tired…you are, too." She tried to smile. "So Linda actually had a couple of Kodak moments with the kids?"

"Believe it or not, she was a different person with them."

"Is that why she was still getting playdates after your separation?"

Merry shrugged. "With Charlie living there, the children were going to see her anyway. And frankly, I needed a break sometimes…it's hard being a single parent."

"Tell me about it."

Her sister gave her a strange little smile—tight, almost pained. "You know what's funny about this situation? How many times did I beg you to swap places when we were kids? I was so hooked by those books, *The Tricksy Twins*— Tess and Terri. I always wanted to try your life but you never wanted to try mine…and now you're stuck with it."

CHAPTER TWELVE

CELL TO HIS EAR, Ross filled his water bottle from the U-shaped faucet in Linda's designer kitchen in preparation for soccer training, and listened to Tilly's other uncle wax lyrical about his new Ford truck.

"Three liter, four-cylinder," said Dan. "Turbo."

"Farming's paying then?"

"The Ute's an investment."

Ross snorted. "Is that how you sold it to your bride?" He packed the water bottle into the sports bag on the gleaming white marble counter.

"What do you mean?" Dan was all hurt innocence. "Jo helped choose it."

"That explains the reinforced steel cage and bull bars." Ross teased Jo mercilessly about her driving.

His buddy laughed. "Torque peaks at 1800 rpm which gives it great lugging power. Hauls up to 3000 kg."

"If the suspension's tuned for load-carrying, how's the road ride affected?" Ross pulled out his rain jacket, glanced at the overcast sky through the kitchen window and replaced it in the bag again.

"Pretty good. Wishbones and coil springs up-front… solid axle and leaf springs rear."

"Shame the model's got a hood like a storm trooper's helmet."

"You're just jealous."

God it was good to relax his guard. Talk about stuff that

wasn't loaded with moral dilemmas. Ross carried his bag out to the SUV. All day he'd kept Viv's secret from Charlie and all day he'd felt dirty.

Briefly he considered telling Dan—Shep to his former troop mates, short for Good Shepherd. The twins' level-headed sibling would soon toss a nice bucket of ice-cold reality over their harebrained scheme, and Ross would be off the hook. Except he'd given Viv his word. She might have elastic ethics, he didn't.

"So, you get hold of Viv last night?"

"No," lied Ross, hating the woman who'd forced him to it. Dumping the sports bag in the trunk, he slammed it shut. "Guess my friends holidaying in New York will have to pay full price for Broadway tickets like everyone else." He opened the driver's door. "Shep, I have to go but I need you to do me a favor. The boss wants to sign me up for advanced instructors courses."

"Congratulations. Obviously, the old man considers you leadership material."

Ross paused with his hand on the ignition. "Have you been inhaling too much methane on that farm of yours?" he demanded. "I'm a combatant, always have been. You know that. Put a word in for me will you? You were always one of the CO's favorites, he'll listen to you." He turned the key and the engine roared into life.

"Ice," Dan said slowly. One word to hold so much emotion. Regret, apology, defiance.

Ross turned off the engine, forcing himself to articulate the unthinkable. "Except he already has listened," he rasped. "Hasn't he?"

Dan cleared his throat. "Jo and I were in Auckland for a checkup." His bride was a cancer survivor. "I called in to see everybody and the CO requested a word. He asked me if I shared his concerns for you. Did you want me to lie?"

Why the hell not? Your sisters have no trouble doing it!
His lungs felt constricted, he had to struggle to breathe.
"If I was frickin' one-legged, Dan, I'd still be more use on
patrol than any recruit I train to take my place!"

"His concerns aren't about your physical fitness. You
think I'm the only person who's noticed this is about re-
prisal?"

"And if it is? *You* of all people should understand it."
Dan hadn't been with his patrol during the ambush and his
survivor's guilt had nearly derailed his wedding.

"The best revenge is not letting tragedy destroy your
life."

"You needed some kind of emotional catharsis to get you
through, but I don't. Let me make peace with it my way."

"Peace?" There was a snort from the other end of the
line. "Mate, you've been slow-burning with rage from the
moment you regained consciousness in a German military
hospital. Would you arm an angry man and send him back
to a war-torn region where there's already too many angry
men bent on thoughtless, reflexive violence? Is that what
the SAS stands for?"

"So, what are you suggesting?" Ross challenged. "We
walk away with our tails between our legs?" He clenched
his jaw. "Let Steve's and Lee's deaths signify nothing?"

"Going Rambo isn't going to serve you or the future
unit you're assigned to. We don't make war personal."

"What about our friendship...isn't that personal?" He
could barely speak. One of his best friends had stabbed
him in the back.

"Yeah, which is why I can't stand by and—"

"*Screw you,* Dan." Ross cut the connection, slammed
the steering wheel with the flat of his hand. For a long time
he sat staring through the windscreen at the garage door.

At last he stirred.

Lying in a hospital bed, working through rehab, Ross had kept his sanity by setting goals. To stand, to walk. To run. Fight it, fight the futility, the sense of powerlessness. Hopelessness. Find solace in action. In purpose. With a mighty effort he distanced himself again now. What did Dan know?

He needed to do damage control, undermine his former buddy's credibility. Ross glanced at his watch. The CO was still at HQ. He'd go there now. Quickly, he phoned Meredith's cell. Busy. He left a brief message for her impersonator.

"I can't make soccer but I'll come by later to sort things out for tomorrow." He stopped himself from adding, "sorry."

SHE WAS NEVER ever going to rely on Ross again.

The school field was still soft from winter rain and green with spring growth. Mud splattered the kids' trainers as Viv warmed them up with jumping jacks, so she sent her fourteen-strong team on a jog around the field, while she stood in the middle under an overcast sky with the sports kit of balls and marker cones and racked her brain for appropriate drills.

Tilly hadn't seemed surprised when Viv told her Uncle Ross wasn't coming. "He always backs out of stuff now. That's why Mum had to take over coaching. Uncle Ross used to do it."

The kids came back too soon, eager to begin the real stuff and Viv bought more time with yoga stretches. In team shirts obviously meant to be grown into, they were puppy-dog keen and exuberant from being cooped up in class all day.

"Can we get the balls out soon, Mrs. Coltrane?"

"Mrs. Coltrane, do I have to be goalie on Sunday, I wanna be the striker."

"I can only stay for the first half of practice, Mrs. Coltrane, so can we do the practice passes first?"

Viv surrendered to the inevitable and got a soccer ball out of the bag. "Sure, Karl—"

"Kyle."

"Kyle," she amended. "Everyone get in a circle and we'll pass the ball to each other." She hadn't bothered to learn the rules of soccer because Ross was going to be here. Only he wasn't here. One cryptic message as she was leaving the house. And no time to go back to Plan A.

The circle formed and she threw the ball to Kyle, who caught it with a look of surprise. "Pass it on," she encouraged him.

"With our hands?"

Viv looked at Tilly who scowled.

"Only the goalie can touch the ball, remember, Mum?"

"Just seeing if everyone's paying attention," Viv said, and added jokingly, "You're all on the ball today."

They looked at her blankly. Damn Ross.

"We need a few balls for this drill," Tilly prompted.

"Sure." Viv grabbed another couple.

"Meredith."

She straightened to see Charlie crossing the field with Harry. The baby looked like the Michelin man in a padded rain jacket and gum boots with a Bob the Builder logo.

The last thing she needed was a witness to training. "Hey, I wasn't expecting you until later." *Please don't be here to watch.*

"How's the game going, kids?"

Viv said quickly, "Tilly, take over for a couple of minutes while I talk to your dad." Tossing the balls into the circle, she steered Charlie out of earshot. "Anything wrong?"

Harry held out his arms to her. "Iv."

"What's that," said his dad, "a new word?"

"Wind." Grabbing the baby she put him down and pointed to the sports kit. "Go get the balls out of the bag, sweetie." Harry didn't need any more invitation.

"Look, I'm sorry but something's come up at the Sycamore Street job," said Charlie. "The owner's requested an emergency site meeting." In team shirt and track pants, Viv shivered in the wind, wishing she'd remembered a rain jacket. "I can't take Harry to a construction site," Charlie reasoned, "and Ross isn't answering his cell. You'll have to take him."

She stared at him. "I'm training the kids for an hour."

"Thank God you're superwoman then, huh?" Charlie looked at his watch. "While I remember, I told Mum's bridge club there was an open invitation back to the house after the funeral. You might have to order a few more club sandwiches from the caterer...I'd do it but—"

"But it's easier to palm it off on me." Viv curbed her temper. "Look, I understand it's a terrible time for you but stop treating me like I'm still your wife. You left, remember? And frankly, Charlie, you shouldn't have treated me like your personal assistant when we were married, either!"

He blinked. "But you offered to help with the funeral."

"And I am helping. I'll take Harry, if there's no other option, but *you* phone the caterer with your extra requests."

Charlie looked hurt. "It isn't like you to get het up over a simple request."

"Well, maybe you walking out on the family changed me," she snapped.

"I wasn't the one who—"

"Save it, Charlie, I've heard it all before."

"Mrs. Coltrane?" Kyle, Karl, whatever the heck his name

was, ran over panting. "Tilly says I have to drop and give her twenty…do I?"

"No, Kyle, you don't…I really must go back to using my maiden name," Viv added.

Charlie's lips tightened. "I'll leave you to it," he said crisply. "And I'll go write my mother's eulogy."

She refused to feel guilty. "Like I said, I'm happy to help out in this difficult time, but there are limits, Charlie. You set them, not me. The name of the catering company is Bite Delight," she added. "They're in the phone book."

Without another word Charlie turned on his heel. Viv stared after him, then took a deep breath and glanced toward her charges.

It looked like a hostile game of British Bulldog—the team was lined up on one side facing Tilly who'd found a whistle and was blowing it so hard, her face was red with the effort. The little girl opened her mouth and the whistle fell. "You have to do what I say. V—Mum left me in charge."

Oh, great.

And where was Harry? For a moment Viv couldn't see him and her heart stopped with terror, and then she caught sight of a bald head among the soccer balls—he'd climbed into the bag. Viv ran over and scooped him up, resisting the urge to yell at him for giving her such a fright. If anything happened…

He gave her a gummy smile. "Iv," he said.

Ross CAUGHT A DRIFT of choir music as he opened the gate to Meredith's house at five-thirty. It swelled to a hymn as he approached the front door, a blending of angelic voices. He made out the words, "To save a wretch like meeee."

He hoped God was feeling benevolent, because after his afternoon, Ross wasn't in the mood to forgive anyone.

Supporting Charlie through Linda's death was already sucking time away from his rehab schedule. Dan's betrayal meant it would take everything he had to convince the CO he was combat ready. Except the boss was out of town, pressing the flesh in government circles in a bid to avert cuts to the defense budget. Unavailable until next week. Ross didn't need this farce on top of everything else, but Viv had left him no choice.

He was a dangerous man with his back to the wall.

His profession had taught him that preparation was everything so he figured he'd assess Viv's strengths and weaknesses and compensate accordingly. However erratic her behavior, even the chaos theory had some predictability, if not of outcome, then of pattern. That didn't mean he had to like it.

Feeling manipulated, frustrated and aggrieved, he pushed the doorbell.

No one answered. The music was probably too loud. He tried the handle; it turned. The house was a bomb site and as a demolitions expert, Ross knew bomb sites. His sense of grievance grew. In the living room, he found Tilly curled on the couch in her pajamas, her hair wet, reading *1001 Pictures of Adorable Cats.* Harry sat beside her with a bottle.

At least the kids looked cared for. "How was soccer practice?" Ross called above the hymn.

Without looking up from her book, Tilly shrugged.

Harry dropped the bottle and held out his arms, gurgling something indecipherable.

Ross picked him up. "At least someone's pleased to see me."

Tilly didn't respond. This kid could reverse global warming when she had a frost on.

"I'm sorry I couldn't make practice."

She turned the page.

"When I'm redeployed, I'll go back to the way I was, I promise."

She looked at him with a seer's eyes. "No, you won't," she said.

Ross gave up. "Where is she?"

Tilly pointed and, carrying Harry, he followed the music to the bathroom.

"Iv," the baby said proudly.

Ross stopped dead. "No, buddy, now is not the time to learn new words."

"Dog," Harry offered.

"Better."

The door was ajar, he saw a flailing arm and hesitated, but Harry, no respecter of privacy, had already planted his tiny palms against the door and pushed. It swung open. Viv stood in front of the mirror, her right arm swinging like a maniacal metronome.

"Through many dangers, toils, and snares, I have already come."

His heart sank.

"No thanks to you," she said tightly, still marking time. "Down...across, up." She still wore her soccer training gear, and had obviously been caught in a rain shower because both the navy shorts and T-shirt clung damply to her body and her ponytail dripped down her spine. Mud splatters dotted her shapely calves. Through the semitransparent white T, Ross got an eyeful of the leopard-print demibra he'd last seen wrapped around Salsa's paw and made a mental note to lecture Viv about deep cover. At least there was one positive to this mess—he could stop feeling like a pervert.

Viv started to sing along. "We've no less days to sing God's praise—" her singing voice was awful "—than when we first beguuu—" The last strains faded, she finished with a circled flourish and met his eyes in the mirror. "How'd that look, convincing?"

His heart sank. "Tell me you're not conducting the choir tomorrow."

Harry flung himself forward with a delighted gurgle and she caught him, kissing the downy head before she answered. "Okay I won't tell you."

"Then we're screwed," he said.

She leveled a look at him. "We will be if you keep setting me up to fail."

"What?"

"I was relying on you to help with soccer…where the hell were you?"

"Since when am I at your beck and call? I left a message."

"Too little too late." Viv put the restless baby onto her other hip. "Don't encourage people to rely on you if you can't deliver on your promises."

The echo back to Tilly's disappointment stung. "My priorities come first."

"And have done for months, I hear," she countered. Harry started to fuss and she patted his back. "Good luck with whatever's more important than your family."

"You're the one who's going to need the luck!"

"I haven't got time to cross swords with you," she said impatiently. "Tilly's in a snit, I still have a cake to bake, names and faces to memorize, another hymn to practice and I'm worried sick about my sister. If you're in, Ross, then *be* in. Otherwise—" she covered the baby's ears and glared at him "—bugger off."

The only way to save his brother further pain was to make this farce work. Ross sighed. "I'm in."

Viv uncovered Harry's ears. "Then talk nice and trust

me to have *some* sense. Merry's teaching me to conduct
on Skype and if she says I'm doing well, then I must be
bloody fantastic because she's even more critical than you
are."

She swept past him, baby on her hip and a glint of tears
in her eyes.

Ross followed. "What's wrong with Meredith?" he said
quietly.

Viv put Harry down. "She's picked up some kind of infection. Iop…ison-something."

"Iatrogenic cause?"

Her anxious gaze met his. "Yes, that's it."

"It means she picked it up in hospital, through procedures or treatment. More common than you'd think. Is she
on antibiotics?"

"Yes, but I don't see an improvement. Someone should
be with her."

Ross resisted the urge to say Viv would have if they
hadn't pulled this stunt. "What does Meredith say?"

"That she'll be fine and for me to concentrate on the
funeral."

"Then let's do that." God knows, they had enough to
worry about.

"Anyway, I need to make these kids dinner." She started
toward the kitchen. Definitely no spring in her step today.

"Shower and get out of those wet clothes first."

"The kids are hungry."

He began to feel caught in a vice, Viv and her misguided
altruism on one side, his need to disengage on the other. "I
can start dinner," he said grudgingly.

"You can cook? No, don't tell me." He saw a flicker
of returning spirit in her smile. "SAS guys can do everything."

"My mother taught me."

"Well, if you could beat some eggs for me, fry bacon and put pasta on to boil that'd be great. I'll be as quick as I can."

"No hurry. I can handle carbonara."

"Just don't add anything green, including herbs. Tilly's in a bad mood as it is."

"So training wasn't a success?"

She pulled her hair free of its constricting ponytail and rubbed her scalp. "I let her run some of it."

"Let me guess. It was like inviting Captain Bligh back onto the Bounty."

Viv nodded. "We had a mutiny after ten minutes."

"I'll talk to her." Ross caught himself watching her legs as she walked away, and frowned.

Twenty minutes later, the kids were eating and Tilly was pouring her troubles into her uncle's ear. "She can't do anything right, Uncle Ross. At soccer, we hardly even kicked the ball." Tilly was a grade ahead of her age through sheer tenacity but she struggled to match the coordination of the eight-year-olds. She mishit the ball, kicked wildly and then blamed the pitch, the boot, the ball, the pass.... But you couldn't question her fierce and unswerving passion for the game, or her dedication.

Viv, her hair hanging in shiny waves, walked in wearing kick-ass boots teamed with a shirt and jeans too well-fitting to be Meredith's. "I need some 'me' time," she said, mistaking his surprise as disapproval. It wasn't. Seventeen months and suddenly his libido was firing for *this* woman?

Harry opened his mouth to greet his aunt and Ross took the opportunity to shovel in another spoonful. They didn't need to hear "Iv" right now. "Tilly's getting a few things off her chest," he warned.

"And she put onions in the ground beef and then smelly

cheese on top," Tilly continued. "She's just not as good as Mum."

"This isn't a competition, Tilly." Viv's tone was light but it was obvious their niece had struck a nerve. "I'm just filling in. I'm good at other things."

"Like what?" The little girl was genuinely curious.

"Building an international career in costume design," Viv offered, pulling up a chair.

Losing interest, Tilly returned to her carbonara. "Well, Mum has a job *and* she can play soccer *and* cook mac and cheese *and* put the trash out on the right day *and* teach Brownies and drive without saying, 'stay left, stay left' all the time." She paused to suck up a strand of spaghetti. "And dogs like *her*," she finished.

"Dogs like me," said Viv in a small voice. "Just not your dog."

"Attilla, you could help Viv with Salsa," Ross suggested.

She shook her head, sucking up another spaghetti strand. "I don't have to help anyone. I'm a little girl."

"Except how will you be able to do all the things your mum can if you don't practice?"

Viv added, "You don't want to end up like me, do you?"

"No," said Tilly.

Viv's smile faltered.

Ross coaxed another spoonful into Harry's mouth. "Your aunt does have a cool party trick," he said casually. "She can do a cartwheel holding a glass of wine and not spill any." He'd seen it at the wedding.

"Really?" Tilly looked at Viv with new interest.

"I used to do gymnastics when I was a kid."

"I thought you did ballet with Mum…I saw a picture. You were fat then," she added.

"The exploding meringue next to the dainty princess picture? I wish she'd destroy that! Anyway I only lasted in ballet two weeks before changing to gym." She added reflectively, "All those tiny, careful movements made me want to scream. But I always envied your mom her sparkly pink tutu."

As he wiped the excess food off Harry's chin, it occurred to Ross that a free spirit would have a difficult time being an identical twin.

Tilly handed Viv her empty plate. "Mum said you wore it to a party and spilled green jelly on it and the stain never came out."

Viv stood up with the plate. "Gee," she said, "does she say anything good about me?"

"She said you're the fun one." Tilly's tone made it clear she didn't agree with that assessment.

Brat.

Viv turned to the sink.

"If Tilly won't help with Salsa," Ross suggested, "maybe you could look up the patron saint of dogs in that book of yours."

His niece jumped to the bait. "Dogs have a saint?"

Viv dumped Tilly's plate in the sink and dug the tattered booklet out of her back jean pocket. They fitted so snugly Ross was surprised she got a hand in there—not that he was complaining. "Every animal has a saint," she said, thumbing through the pages. "Here we go…Saint Roch. Busy guy. He's helping your mom's knee. And he also covers plagues and pestilence. Hmm, I would have thought Salsa *was* a pestilence."

"You can talk," Ross commented.

She ignored that. "Tilly, you have a saint, too. Saint Agnes watches out for girls."

"Lemme see." Viv pulled a chair close to Tilly's and they bent their heads over the book. Their hair was the same rich brown. Suspecting he might be missing some fun, Harry squealed to get out of his highchair.

"Hang on, mate." Ross cleaned him up with the dish-cloth first.

"Look, Tilly, Joan of Arc has the Girl Guides, which is what Brownies grow into." Viv lifted the baby into her lap. "Girl Guides and soldiers, Ross. Isn't the juxtaposition sweet?"

"Darling."

But Tilly was delighted. "Uncle Ross, the same saint looks after both of us."

"That's cool, honey."

"Here's another patron for your uncle," added Viv. "Elmo."

Tilly gurgled with laughter. "That's silly. Elmo is a toy."

"Let me see that," he said.

She held the book out of his reach. "His real name is Erasmus, Tilly, but his friends call him Elmo and he looks after pyrotechnicians. That's a fancy word for people who enjoy blowing things up."

"So Viv and I share a patron saint, too," he retorted. "Since she excels in destroying the peace. Tilly, if you're done, go wash your hands. We'll make the cake while Viv eats." Tilly scrambled from the table and left for the bath-room.

Viv stared at him. "You made enough food for me?" Her delight made him wonder when she'd last eaten.

"Running on empty leads to mistakes, mistakes lead to discovery." *Nothing personal in it.* He dished up a portion and put it in front of her. She'd used her own perfume… that honeysuckle again. "I figure I've got an hour and a half before Charlie expects me home." Ross held out the cutlery. "Use me."

The remark hadn't been intended as sexual, but their

eyes met and the cutlery clattered on the table as they mistimed the exchange.

"Harry, want an ice cream?" Ross grabbed the baby, plonking him in the highchair, then opened the freezer, tempted to stick his head in to cool down.

It disgusted him that he wanted her. He reminded himself that she was a liar, aiding and abetting a cheater to mislead his brother. That he'd been emotionally blackmailed into this scam. And that *her* brother had just sold him down the river. It helped.

When he shut the fridge Viv was eating, focused on her plate. As if it was her first good meal in days. Ross tore his gaze from her mouth. Making Harry a small cone, he reminded himself she was identical to his brother's wife, and he'd never been attracted to her—but his body didn't buy it. He'd thought after Dan's betrayal today, that his life couldn't possibly get worse. Seemed it could.

Viv cleared her throat. "Was Susan there when Charlie picked up Harry from day care?"

"She does work there." He handed his nephew the chocolate ice cream and Harry gummed it.

"That could have been awkward…their first meeting since the breakup."

He shrugged and picked up the cookbook lying open on the table. "I guess."

Viv cleared her throat again. "Did Charlie mention anything about it?"

"Of course." Ross scanned the cake recipe. "We talk about that kind of stuff constantly. How Charlie could have done things better or differently. Oh, no, wait, I forgot. I'm a man."

"Is he interested in getting back together with Susan or not?" Viv asked impatiently.

He glanced up. "Not. Your. Business. Not my business, either."

As Viv opened her mouth to argue, her cell rang. She checked caller ID. "Meredith," she said to Ross. "Hey, sis."

Ross disappeared into the walk-in pantry where he scanned the shelves for ingredients. When he emerged a few minutes later, Viv was waiting for him with a pensive expression. "Merry rang Dan to reiterate that he didn't need to come to the funeral." Viv saved the egg carton, precariously balanced on the top of the armful he carried and put it on the counter. "He said he's having trouble getting a hold of you and asked her to remind you to phone."

"I'll do it later," he lied. He'd blocked Dan's number.

Viv finished her meal and started unbuttoning Harry's ice cream–splattered bib and pajama top. "He said it's urgent."

"Later," he said harshly, drawing that astute gaze.

"What happened?"

"Nothing, everything's fine."

"Uh-huh." The house phone rang. "Will you get that?" she asked. "Normally I'd let call answer pick up but if you're here…"

It could be Dan. Brown eyes challenged his. She knew it, too. The woman was smart. Holding his nerve, Ross picked up the receiver. "Hello?"

"'ello? This is Jean Paul. May I speak with Vivienne, please?"

"Sure, mate," Ross said easily. "She's just undressing 'arry."

"Excuse me?"

He thought about clarifying and discounted it, figuring any guy stupid enough to take on Hurricane Viv had to be a masochist anyway.

Tilly came back into the kitchen. "Where's my ice cream?"

Ross held out the phone. "The Frenchman."

Shaking her head, she whispered, "I'm not here."

Ross put the phone to his ear. "She's right here, mate, and dying to talk to you."

CHAPTER THIRTEEN

STANDING IN THE DOORWAY, Viv stared bleary-eyed at the empty cell charger, then at Harry who was wandering around the living room, the dog at his heels and her phone pressed to his ear. His diaper hanging in a soggy lump between his skinny bow legs, he beamed at her. Delighted to see her, delighted with his new toy—all obviously right with his world.

It was the morning of the funeral and she'd overslept.

With a moan, she moved to rescue the cell and something crunched under her foot. She lifted it to see crushed cornflakes. Her eyes followed a splotchy trail of milk and cornflakes from the kitchen to the overflowing cereal bowl on the coffee table.

She'd cleaned the place spotless last night. Now the kitchen and living room looked as if there'd been a wild party. And the TV was blaring loud enough the wake the dead—sorry, Linda. And yet somehow, Viv had slept through it. Maybe the alarm had gone off, maybe it hadn't. It was certainly switched off when she'd woken up and stared in disbelief at the time. 9:05.

"I got breakfast for me and Harry." Tilly didn't glance up from the TV where two cartoon Ninjas were balletically beating the crap out of each other. "I'm being helpful, like Uncle Ross said." Eyes glued to the screen, she waved a dripping spoon in Harry's general direction. "Here, Harry," she cooed. Obediently the toddler trotted over, but Salsa and his little pink tongue got there first. Tilly laughed.

"Dog," chortled Harry, and in his glee, threw the cell. It landed with a plop in the bowl.

With an exclamation, Viv fished it out and wiped it dry on Merry's cotton pj's. The battery light flickered and went out.

She tried to find a bright side. "Well, that's all the crazy out of the way early."

Tilly snuggled into the armchair with the remote. "I did good, didn't I, Auntie Viv?"

"Call me Mum, Till, so you don't forget when it's important."

"Mum," said Tilly absently. She'd been captured by the Ninjas again.

Harry toddled over and wrapped his arms around Viv's shins. "Iv," he said.

In between getting everybody dressed, icing the cake in chocolate frosting, staging the house with flowers, and accepting a delivery from the caterers, Viv sang, "Mum-MumMum" to her nephew to reindoctrinate him.

She tried to prepare her niece for the funeral. "It's okay," Tilly reassured her. "I have buried a guinea pig."

Five minutes before Ross arrived, Viv finally found a few minutes to phone Merry and tell her to reroute messages to Ross's cell. "How are you feeling…any improvement?"

"Definitely on the mend." Viv took her word for it, she didn't have time to go on Skype. "I talked to Charlie last night," her twin added.

"Really?" *Please, Charlie, don't have brought up our argument yesterday.* "About anecdotes for the funeral… he was really offhand. I think he's back with Susan."

"I'm sorry, Mere." *God, I'm so sorry.* But if the guy

couldn't stand hearing a few home truths then her sister was better off without him.

"Yeah, well, you told me not to get my hopes up," Merry said tiredly. "Let's go over the chorister names again."

"Barry the balding baritone. Cindy the frizzy-permed alto—"

"Cindy's a soprano. Concentrate, Viv! If you mess this up—"

"Thanks for the vote of confidence."

"Of course you can pull this off," Merry said unconvincingly. "It's just there's—"

"A lot at stake. I know." Viv couldn't keep the sharpness out of her tone. "You don't have to repeat it. Ross's SUV is pulling up. We need to go."

"Good luck."

"Shouldn't that be break a leg?"

"I know you joke when you're nervous but *don't,* Viv, there's too much at—" Merry caught herself. "Do what I do. Chew your nails."

Except she'd cut them short yesterday. "Are you kidding, acrylic nails are ten dollars apiece." Yuk, Yuk, Yuk. Oh, yuk.

She commandeered Ross's cell as soon as he walked in and waited anxiously while he checked her appearance. A black Polo dress—Merry always chose clothes half a size too big because she didn't like showing off her figure—with a matching plaited belt. Viv had teamed it with one of Merry's carry-all handbags, low black pumps, a fine gold chain and small gold hoop earrings. She'd pulled her hair back into Merry's customary ponytail and her only makeup was lip gloss and eye shadow. Merry wore blue, instead of the brown that suited their coloring.

In one way, at least, Viv figured she'd perfected Merry. Drawn, tired and drained of confidence.

"Perfect," Ross approved, and tears sprang to her eyes. Encouragement had been in short supply. Viv blinked hard.

"Attilla?" Ross touched their niece's shoulder. "Go put your brother in the car seat, hey? And you can choose the music for the ride to the chapel." Tilly loved being in charge of in-car entertainment.

"You okay?" he said when they'd gone.

She resisted a sudden urge to lay her head against his broad shoulder. "I will be." Viv fished the saints book out of Merry's bag.

"You use that thing like crack." Ross took it away from her. "We're relying on preparedness, remember?"

"And I'm covering all the bases." Grabbing it back, she flicked through the pages. "Saint Jude's our man. He looks after desperate situations and lost causes."

Ross reconfiscated it. "Where'd this come from, anyway?"

"I dressed the production of *The Sound of Music* last year and the producer gave me a thank-you gift of crystal rosary beads. The saints guide came with it. I started reading it as a curiosity and now I don't go anywhere without it."

She made a grab for it and he held it out of her reach.

"You can pull this off."

"I've got melodies, posture tips and names all jumbled together in my head," she admitted. "I don't think I can keep everything straight."

"You've done the work, the information will come when it's needed."

"Harry keeps calling me Iv."

"Damn. I'd hoped it was a one-off." He thought a minute. "Okay, it's short for 'give' as in 'gimme.' Whenever he says it, hand him something."

"Yes." She felt a rush of relief. "That could work."

"If things get too dicey, pretend you're overcome and start crying."

"Now *that* I can do."

His mouth softened, Ross's equivalent of a smile. He handed over the saints book. "And I've got your back."

"Think you can resist the urge to put a knife in it?"

Ross shepherded her through the front door. "A British prime minister, Lord Melbourne, once said he wanted men who would support him when he was in the wrong. Today, I'm your guy."

And tomorrow? Viv paused on the doorstep. "How's Charlie doing this morning?" Obviously he hadn't mentioned her outburst to Ross or he would have lectured her by now.

"Holding up. He'll be glad when this is over."

"Won't we all."

They walked toward the SUV. "Right about now he's picking up Aunt Agatha. Who is…?"

"Linda's older and only sibling from Wellington," Viv said without thinking. "Short, straight gray hair, walks with a cane. Never married, two cats…Fifi and Flo. Merry— I—get on well with her. She and Linda had periodic feuds but were speaking prior to her death."

He reached to open the passenger door. "As I said, you're ready."

She stopped him with a hand on his arm. "If it all turns to custard, I won't implicate you in any way," she said awkwardly

"Failure's not an option, Viv."

Guess the reassurance part was over. If one more person told her what was riding on this… She inhaled deeply. "Not Viv," she reminded him. "Meredith."

That softening of his lips again. She was starting to look out for it. "Meredith," he repeated. In the car he swung around to look at the kids. "Attilla, I want you to stare at this woman and say Mum ten times."

"Mum, Mum, Mum, Mum…"

Harry clapped his hands. "Mummmm."

"Good to go." Ross started the engine and pop blared over the speakers.

"Uncle Ross, you only had dumb stuff," said Tilly, "so I brought my Justin Bieber CD."

"I was hoping for the battle theme from *Apocalypse Now*," Viv murmured and Ross laughed, startling her.

"You're enjoying this, aren't you, soldier boy?" she accused. "Impending danger, the adrenaline overload, relying on your wits."

Ross blinked. "Certainly not."

"Now who's the liar?" Viv opened her bag, found her conducting notes and concentrated on key changes, entrances and cut-offs. Fifteen minutes later the SUV pulled into Puriri Cemetery's sweeping gravel driveway.

Overhead its namesake evergreens butted massive heads, their glossy dark green canopies dotted with incongruous bursts of rose-pink flowers. Viv half expected to see Jane Austen's Pemberley appear through the trees. Instead she found herself staring at a modern chapel, flanked on two sides by rows of cremation plaques. "If I don't make it," she murmured to Ross, "sprinkle my ashes at sea…this place is too regimented for me."

"Meredith would love the neatness of it," he reminded her. "Remember what we talked about last night. Soften your expression, don't hold eye contact more than three seconds and lessen that hip sway when you walk."

"You really do have an eye for detail, don't you?" she marveled.

"Tell me about it," he muttered cryptically.

Because she'd been so busy, Viv hadn't reflected on

Linda's death but as she got out of the car and saw the mourners she had to swallow a lump in her throat. Poor Linda. And poor Charlie. He stood somberly on the chapel steps, greeting people Viv recognized but hadn't yet met. She could only imagine how he must feel. She shouldn't have yelled at him yesterday. They were both doing their best under difficult circumstances.

Unclipping Harry from his car seat, she pointed him in Charlie's direction. "Go give Daddy a hug."

Charlie's expression eased as he caught sight of his son toddling toward him. He picked up the baby. Over the heads of the crowd he thanked Viv with an unsteady smile. Guiltily she turned to close the car door and caught Ross's eye over the hood. For the first time she understood conflicted loyalties.

"I'm sorry," she said, "for dragging you into this. I only wanted to help my sister."

Without reply, he flanked her, positioning Tilly on her other side. Viv picked up her niece's hand.

Showtime.

As they walked toward the small crowd, she saw ambivalence on some faces, embarrassment on others. She was the estranged wife, the loathed or sainted daughter-in-law, depending on people's relationships with Linda. She caught malevolent stares from Linda's bridge and golf partners, Marsha, Caroline and Bettina.

Obviously Linda had embellished the story of how Merry had cheated on her blameless boy. Viv lifted her chin, grateful Merry wasn't here to endure this. Noticing their disapproval extended to Ross—of course, the wicked stepson—she squeezed his arm reassuringly. He looked down, amused. "I'm used to it," he murmured. "But you're not. Chin *down*, Meredith."

She did as he asked, and immediately Charlie stepped

forward to welcome her in a demonstration of public allegiance that deepened her guilt. It was easier to justify her actions when she'd thought he was an asshole.

Following his lead, other mourners came forward to commiserate. Some tried to coax the gory details of Linda's death out of her but she deflected all questions. So, she noticed, did Ross. She guessed very few genuinely liked Linda, most were here for Charlie—workmates, squash partners, friends from church.

Only once through the meet and greet did she draw a memory blank, on a bald old man, craggy as an eagle. The dog collar helped. Pastor Fred.

"The choir is inside, waiting for you, my dear." She tried to smile. "Now who's looking after the children during the final hymn?"

"Ross," she said. "Or Charlie."

"Aren't they both carrying out the coffin?"

She hadn't thought about that. From the blank expression on Ross's face, neither had he. Single, childless…why would they have factored in those last five minutes?

Viv hesitated. Tilly would be okay with virtual strangers, Harry wouldn't.

"I'll do it." Viv heard the familiar voice behind her and froze. A masculine hand landed on her shoulder. Instinctively her gaze went to Ross for help, but stony-faced, he was glaring at her brother. Viv cleared her throat, drawing his attention, and telegraphed an urgent message. *He'll know.* Unlike Charlie, her brother wasn't in a haze of grief. Unlike Charlie, who rarely saw Viv, her brother had had a lifetime to differentiate the twins. Immediately Ross stepped to obscure her from her brother's view as Dan moved past her to embrace his brother-in-law. "Charlie. I'm so sorry, mate."

"Dan, I didn't really expect any of Meredith's family to come...given the separation." He was obviously choked up.

"Dad would have been here, too," Dan said, "but one of us had to stay behind for lambing. He sends his condolences." Her brother turned around and Viv ducked farther behind Ross.

"And we need to talk later," he added to Ross. "So, Mer—"

Viv steeled herself for the inevitable exposure.

"Uncle Dan!" Tilly stopped playing with some remote paternal cousin Viv couldn't immediately place and raced over, Harry trotting behind. Viv spun to scoop him up. Her back was now to her brother.

"Hey, pumpkin," Dan greeted his niece. "You've grown so big, give me a kiss.... Mere?" Puzzlement entered his tone. "No hug for your big brother?"

Keeping her head down, Viv passed Harry to Ross and buried her face in Dan's shoulder. It had been two years. Why the hell hadn't he told anyone he was coming? This was so like him. Always catching her doing what she wasn't supposed—

He started to pull away and, panicking, Viv tightened her hold. Out of the corner of her eye she glimpsed Ross steering Charlie and Tilly toward another well-wisher.

"Mere? You okay?" In a low voice he murmured, "I didn't expect you to take Linda's death this hard."

She pushed him, forcing him to take a step backward. Pushed again. If she could get him out of earshot. At three steps he balked.

Viv lifted her face.

"WHAT THE HELL ARE YOU playing at?" Dan demanded as Viv dragged him down the side of the chapel.

Conscious they could be interrupted any minute, she

gave him the abridged version. "All you have to do is pretend I'm Merry."

"And Mere actually agreed to all this?"

Viv hesitated. "You can't hold her accountable for her actions right now. She's been so devastated by Charlie's dating Susan. And she's feverish, unwell."

"So that's a yes," her brother said drily.

"This is my fault, Dan. You know I can talk her into anything."

He looked at her with exasperated affection. "Jeez, Viv...I thought you'd grown out of this stuff."

"So did I." She gave a short laugh. "Coming home always throws me into regressive mode."

"Is that why you rarely visit?"

"Listen, I suspect Merry's underplaying this blood-infection thing," Viv said, ignoring him, "so she can still be transferred to Auckland tomorrow."

"I'll visit on the way home to Beacon Bay, then phone with a full report." The deviation would add an extra hour to his two-and-a-half-hour drive but was at least in the same direction. "So how is the switch back supposed to work?"

"Merry's going to sell it to Charlie as a simpler bone break to explain a minimum time in hospital. Once the swelling goes down, they'll put a closed cast on anyway. By the time Charlie returns from his three-day conference, she'll be home and I'll be gone. She intended asking Dad to come stay for a week. We didn't factor in lambing season."

"I'll hire extra help." He put a hand on her shoulder. "You do know that at some point Merry has to tell Charlie the truth, don't you?"

"How can she?" Viv asked. "We haven't just burned bridges, Dan. We've blown them up behind us."

He shook his head. "However scared Merry is of making

things worse, if she's still chasing reconciliation with Charlie she has no choice. Without honesty, they've got nothing. No trust."

"You're wrong, Dan. This way no one gets hurt. And, anyway," she added when her brother shook his head, "it's nearly over. Merry will be home tomorrow and Charlie none the wiser. After that, it's up to them."

"You know you could have called me about this, Viv. I am on your side."

She'd hurt him. "I know." Lightly, Viv knuckled his cheek. "Why didn't you tell anyone you were coming today? You nearly gave us all away."

"All?" His gaze sharpened. "Wait a minute, Ross is in on this?"

"Yes," said Ross calmly from behind them. "*Meredith,* the choir's waiting for its conductor. Dan, you're in charge of the baby."

Charlie came around the corner carrying Harry. "What's the problem? Pastor Fred's hunting for you, Meredith. Ross, we ready?"

"Yeah, mate." As Charlie hurried away, Ross looked at Dan through hostile eyes. "Whose side are you taking this time, Shep?"

Startled, Viv looked between the two men. Something was happening here. It wasn't good.

Her brother's jaw tightened. "Yours," he said, "same as always."

Ross snorted and the three followed Charlie.

For once Viv didn't ask. She could hear the strains of the organ and was resisting the urge to run.

THE CHAPEL COULD HOLD OVER one hundred and fifty mourners but today only half that number filed in. From her position in front of the choir to the left of the altar, Viv decided it was still seventy-five too many. Nervously, she watched people take their seats, their first glance going to the mahogany coffin, bedecked with Tilly's mismatched wreath of pink, orange and red blooms.

Charlie sat in the front row, flanked by Tilly and Ross. Tilly sat with hands piously pressed together, a hymnbook open in her lap and her attention a million miles away. Linda's death hadn't really hit home for him yet. Maybe it never would. Beside Ross, Dan sat with Harry on his knee. Their nephew had already commandeered his cell. The tension between Dan and Ross was palpable.

Sunlight blazed through the large plate window behind the altar, momentarily blinding Viv as she faced the choir. Fifteen choristers looked back expectantly, ten short of the normal choir, but a wonderful turnout, Pastor Fred had enthused, considering the short notice. In their white robes, they could be the twelve apostles waiting for her to lead them to the promised land. No, that was Moses—

Pastor Fred coughed. "When you're ready, Meredith." Heart beating a tattoo against her ribs, Viv nodded to the organist and lifted leaden arms and was amazed when they drew out the first soaring notes of "Amazing Grace."

By the third line she knew the pace was off, the choir galloping ahead of the organist. "I-once-was-lost-but-now-am-found-Was-blind-but-now-I-seeee." Over O-shaped mouths, their eyes wide, they looked to her for direction. Viv started to sweat. She was hitting all the right beats with her hands, taking an exaggerated breath on the beat before any new part started. Of course, they'd matched their breathing to hers as she mimed the words. She dragged her panicked breathing back to normal and they hit the right tempo.

The second verse passed without mishap and some of the awful tension went out of her shoulders. After the third, euphoria started to build. "Through many dangers, toils and snares, I have already coooome…" Yee-ha, she was doing this!

The sound swelled and thundered off the walls, the choristers faces red with effort. "'Tis Grace that brought me safe thus far…." her exuberant gestures were encouraging crescendo—abruptly Viv reined in her gestures and the voices faded to a soulful poignancy "…And Grace will lead me…" she closed her eyes, her left hand drawing out the last note "…hooooomme."

Flip the pancake. Palm down. Stop. In the silence, Viv bowed her head. *Thank you, God.*

"How's Dad really coping since Mum left?" Viv asked. "He doesn't give much away when I phone." She and Dan had finally managed to snatch a couple of minutes alone in Meredith's kitchen while she waited for the rented urn to boil for a second round of tea and coffee. Dan was leaving early so he could spend an hour with Meredith.

"Dad's still shell-shocked," Dan said.

Herman should have been launching his retirement on a three-month tour of South America and Europe with their mother. Instead they'd separated on the eve of Dan's wedding and Pat had gone with girlfriends. Viv was torn between supporting her mother and disapproval that she'd abandoned Dad.

"Jo and I made him move back to the farm…he needs company right now." Their parents had a town house in Beacon Bay while Dan had taken over the farmhouse— and the farm—a couple of months ago.

"You're a good son." Viv hugged him. When she and Merry were little Dan had been the shoe-buckle fastener, the bug catcher, the protector. This guy was to blame for her fix-it complex. He made it look so easy.

"And what about *you?*"

Her brother had been restless the whole time he'd been here. Twice Viv had seen him approach Ross, and twice seen Ross turn to talk to someone else. She stepped back to inspect him properly. Sun-streaked hair, gold-tipped eyelashes and a killer tan hinted at his new all-weather profession of farmer. Made the former lady-killer even more rugged and gorgeous. "How's married life?"

His swift grin held a pervasive joy that caught her by surprise. Jo had been his lifelong friend and she'd assumed their match had been based on pragmatism rather than passion. Like Viv, her brother was a love atheist, now his expression held a born-again fervor that was a little unsettling.

"Yeah." His grin grew sheepish. "It amazes me, too. I hope you'll have time to come stay before you return to New York?"

"Three weeks...if I get the job I'm waiting to hear about." Actually she should have heard two days ago, but Viv was still hopeful. "Otherwise I'll be forced to go home early and campaign for business." The urn boiled and she poured water into the giant teapot, laid out clean cups on a tray. Tilly's high-pitched laughter came from the lounge. Ross's gravel baritone was distinguishable amidst the murmur of conversation. Dan's somber gaze went to the door.

"What's going on between you and Ross?" Viv asked abruptly.

"Funny, I was going to ask you the same thing."

Viv laughed. "Why, because I made a pass at him eight years ago? He turned me down, remember?" She started pouring tea, the steam rising to scent the air with Darjeeling. "He's hardly going to be interested now that I'm causing him so much trouble."

"Uh-huh." His blue gaze was like a laser. "Your eyes follow him, did you know that?"

Viv paused with the teapot and frowned. No, she didn't. "Okay," she admitted, filling the last cup. "Maybe the guy's still on my bucket list."

Dan frowned. "He had a girlfriend at the time of the ambush," he said. "Terri arranged leave from her job to nurse him back to health. The first thing he did when he was transferred to a New Zealand hospital was cut her loose." He looked at her with troubled eyes. "Ross is one of my closest friends, Viv, but he's obsessed with getting revenge for Lee and Steve. He's forgotten what balance is. Keep a safe distance."

"Well, at least you're consistent," said Ross from the doorway. "You bad-mouth me wherever you go."

CHAPTER FOURTEEN

"MY SISTER HAD MANY FAULTS but her worst was coming between you and Charlie," Aunt Agatha told Viv as she accepted a piece of angel food cake. "Of course no woman
would have been good enough for her boy." She paused for
a bite, and then sighed. "I'll miss her, though. Did I tell you
we had a real doozie of a fight over Mum's pearls after she
died?" She laughed.

Ear cocked to the kitchen, Viv missed her cue to reply.
It didn't matter. Having lived so long alone with her cats,
possibly the older woman didn't need a response. Taking
a deep breath, she launched into her anecdote, leaving Viv
free to return to worrying.

Dan had asked her to leave and, embarrassed that Ross
might have overheard her admission of interest, Viv hadn't
argued. She forced her attention back to Agatha. Before this
crisis week she enjoyed meeting new people. As Merry,
there was always the specter of making a mistake. Ten minutes later she was dispensing angel food cake and neither
man had reappeared. Through the window she saw that
Dan's new Ute was still parked on the street. She'd give
them five more minutes before she intervened.

There was a tug on her dress. "Iv," said Harry, who had
chocolate icing smeared across his chin.

Aunt Agatha paused in her reminisces. "What did the
baby say?"

"Give," she replied. "He wants more cake." This was

his third visit. A fast learner, was Harry. Handing Agatha the platter, she picked him up. "Excuse us while I find another distraction."

Threading through the mourners she carried the toddler to the laundry where Charlie had banished Salsa after the schnoodle inhaled a plate of sausage rolls.

"Dog?" said Harry.

"I think Salsa's done enough penance, don't you?" During Charlie's reprimand, Salsa had gazed up at his former master with big doleful eyes that spoke of heartbreak, betrayal, remorse and undying love. His expression had haunted Viv ever since. Of course when she opened the door, those same doggie eyes held mistrust, dislike and suspicion. "No, really," she said, "don't thank me."

Salsa's claws skittered on the checkered linoleum as he made his break for freedom.

"Dog!" Viv put Harry down and the baby followed.

She stayed to empty the dryer, not because she was superwoman, but because she'd take any excuse for a respite. The fluffy towels were warm and fragrant with fabric softener and she laid one across the back of her neck and felt some of the tension ease. Okay, now she was ready to deal with Dan and Ross.

"Meredith."

"Charlie!" She yanked off the towel. "I was just… What do you need? Another round of tea?"

"No, I came to let Salsa out." He looked tired and drawn.

"That's okay, I just did."

"I overreacted, didn't I?"

"I'm sure he'll forgive you. Well—" she returned the towel to the heap of laundry "—we should check on the guests."

Charlie cleared his throat. "Thanks for that photo display of Mum that you put together…. You've been terrific."

And a liar and a cheat and a fraud. "Anyone would have done the same."

"I'll have to make sure I keep bringing out Mum's photos for the kids…so they don't forget her." His eyes shining with unshed tears, Charlie picked up a towel and started folding it badly. "Losing Mum like that has made me think about what matters in life, about the things you should hold on to…and the things you should let go of, like anger and bitterness and—"

"Charlie." He wasn't telling her this, he was telling Merry. "We should get back to the others." She looked past him to the door, but he didn't take the hint. Instead he kept folding towels, piling them up in a misshapen heap.

"Susan told me you said you still loved me," he blurted. "Do you?"

Lord. Why did Susan have to be so *nice.* Penance, this was penance.

"You don't want to answer that," said Charlie when she remained silent. "And who can blame you for protecting yourself. You were right to challenge me at Tilly's soccer practice. I was the one who walked out on the family. I need to take responsibility for that." He took a deep breath.

"I turned down your attempts at reconciliation because I wasn't ready to forgive you…and I know that makes me immature. But I was so hurt, Mere." His gaze flicked to hers, then away. Sweat beaded on his forehead as he tried to articulate his feelings. He'd probably prefer to be buried alive in one of his concrete slabs than do this.

So would Viv.

"Charlie, I really think we—"

"I couldn't stand the thought that you might be looking at that doctor the way you used to look at me. Like I could walk on water if I wanted to." He bowed his head, his big hands fisting in the fluffy pink cotton. "How did it happen, Mere?" he asked quietly. "How did I shrink from a person you could look up to and respect into another kid that needed looking after?"

Momentarily Viv forgot her role. "That's exactly how Mum treated Dad."

"I guess she did." Charlie wiped his forehead with one of the towels. "Mere, I have to say this now while I've got the courage. I want to come home...if you'll still have me."

"What?" Viv said faintly.

"I want us to try again." His eyes met hers. "I love you, Mere and—"

"Charlie, we can't rush into this," she said desperately. "With Linda's death and everything we should take a couple of days to think this through."

"You don't trust me after the way I've acted. I expected it—"

Viv squirmed. "It's not that, I—"

"—which is why I've asked Pastor Fred to counsel us. To prove I'm serious and to stop falling into the old patterns. You loosening up about schedules and chores, and me, not taking you for granted."

How could she have been so arrogant? Charging in and blithely casting Charlie in the role of villain. She knew nothing. Nothing. "I'm not necessarily saying no but I feel a couple of days—"

"Hey, I'll agree to anything," he said, "but give me some hope." His crooked grin faded and he held out a hand. "Please."

The door opened. "Oh, I'm sorry." One of the mourners stood there. Linda's friend Bettina. "I was looking for the bathroom."

Viv had never been so glad to see anyone in her life. "Let me show you." She ducked under her brother-in-law's arm. "Charlie, I'll let you know about that proposal."

"Today, Mere, even if it's an agreement in principle."

"Today." In the hall, she pointed Bettina in the right direction, then darting a glance over her shoulder, hurried through the house to the toolshed in the backyard. Among the cobwebs and the bags of compost, she pulled out Ross's cell. Her twin answered on the first ring.

"Viv, at last. I've been on tenterhooks—"

"No time. Charlie's asked for a reconciliation. What excuse can I give him?"

"What! This isn't one of your jokes is it, Viv? I mean—" her voice rose to an excited shriek "—really?"

Viv held the phone away from her ear. "Really."

"You don't need an excuse, the answer's yes! Yes, triple times, yes! I can hardly believe it." She started to laugh. "And you're the most wonderful sister *ever,* talking me into this swap. I had my doubts but—"

"Merry, quit fizzing and think! I *can't* say yes. Charlie will expect to jump straight back into the marital bed. At the very least, he'll try and kiss me."

"Don't you *dare* kiss my husband."

"Of course I'm not kissing him, you idiot. Listen, Dan thinks you're going to have to come clean to Charlie."

"How does our brother come into this?"

"He showed up at the funeral and recognized me." Glancing out the shed window, she saw him standing by Dan's 4WD talking to an increasingly unhappy Ross and felt a surge of fierce protectiveness. Unfortunately it wasn't for her brother. "Don't worry. I swore Dan to secrecy. He's calling in to see you on his way home to Beacon Bay."

"There's no way I'll get Charlie back if I tell him the truth now. My family reunited…it's the best possible outcome." Her twin's voice radiated a passionate intensity. "*Promise* me you'll keep Charlie in a holding pattern until I get there."

Viv paused. Charlie wasn't some actor in a Broadway play to be manipulated into happiness. He was a real man with complicated feelings. But Merry was relying on her. Approving of her for the first time in their lives. Ruthlessly, Viv quashed her doubts. "Okay, I'll make this work somehow. Anyway, I've got to go. I'll phone when everyone's gone." Frowning, she returned to the house. She was reasonably confident she could hold Charlie at arm's length for a couple more days. Heaven knows she'd had enough experience discouraging earnest lovers. What worried her was Ross's reaction when he found out about Viv's new role as proxy wife.

She suspected he wasn't going to like it.

"WHAT DO YOU WANT ME to say, Dan?" Ross demanded. "That it's okay for you to screw me over? Tell the CO behind my back I'm mentally unfit?" The noon sun glinted off the white hood of his former friend's new Ute, forcing him to shield his eyes.

"So what, we're done?" Dan challenged him. "More than a decade of friendship and it's over because I'm calling it as I see it?"

Ross set his jaw. "If you're not part of the solution, you're part of the problem."

"For God's sake, don't you get it yet? It doesn't matter jack shit how many of the enemy you annihilate or how many platitudes you hide behind. Nothing will bring Lee and Steve back."

"I know that but I refuse to become the third victim." Shutting down the pain came automatically now. "I can be the man I was."

Dan looked at him with an expression that made Ross feel like a child. "None of us will ever be the same. Nate, me, you. Steve's wife and son. Lee's fiancée. The ambush blew every one of our lives sky-high and dropped us places none of us wanted to go. Chart a new course and move forward."

"Accept that those who can't, teach?" Ross sneered.

"Yeah, because a lot of second-raters teach in the SAS!"

"That's not what I'm saying. They chose that path. You and the CO are trying to force it on me. Just because you've opted for a quiet life doesn't mean I have to."

Dan stiffened. "Is that what you think? That I've gone soft?"

"I think you'll feel your choice is vindicated if we all link hands and start singing 'Kumbaya,' yeah."

Dan shook his head. "Everything's filtered through your own warped revenge fantasy. As your friend I'm telling you straight. However stubborn you are, you can't bulldoze your way past the CO. And until you accept that you're using anger to avoid grief, you're jeopardizing any future you have with the SAS."

"Thanks." Ross kicked the heavy-duty tires. "Thanks for being on my side."

"I am on your side, dickhead. That's why I'm doing this."

"Yeah? Then why did I catch you warning your sister off like I'm some kind of leper?"

Dan hesitated. "You need to get your shit together before you get involved with anyone and we both know Viv's always had a soft spot for you."

"And I might take advantage?"

"I think at the moment you might do anything," retorted Dan. "Hell, I've pissed you off…you might consider it as payback against me."

Ross wouldn't have felt so outraged if the idea hadn't already occurred to him. Dan must have read his guilt because he stopped playing with his car keys. Their eyes locked.

"You have thought about it," he said slowly.

With an exclamation of disgust, Ross turned and walked away, every molecule of his being concentrating on not limping.

ROSS WAS SO INTENT on getting away from Dan before he hit him that he forgot the house was full of mourners. Thankfully the hum of conversation registered before he marched blindly into the sea of black.

He stopped abruptly on the doorstep, in no mood to be polite, emotions churning in his gut like rancid butter. Behind him, he heard the roar of an engine, then the squeal of tires as Dan released his frustration on a floored accelerator.

Unfortunately Ross couldn't desert Charlie. Not during Linda's funeral. Which left him stuck there.

Accept that your anger is really grief and you have a future with the SAS.

He realized he was grinding his teeth and struggled to bring his temper under control. He was The Iceman, goddamn it, and master of his fate. Yeah. Right.

He was at the funeral of a woman he loathed.

He was deceiving his brother, the only person loyal to him.

He faced being cast adrift by the unit he'd devoted his career to.

And he'd been betrayed by one of his best friends.

Screw the breathing. In fact, screw everything. He'd make some excuse to Charlie, go back to Linda's and get drunk on the bottle of whiskey Agatha had given them in lieu of flowers.

From a defensive position in the hall, he scanned the crowded living room for his brother. Feeling a nudge on his knee, Ross glanced down and saw Salsa holding a ball, doggie eyes begging him to throw it.

"Go find Tilly." Looking up, he saw Viv heading his way, dressed like a nun in her little black mourning dress, lashes lowered demurely, but with that unconscious sway to her hips that she couldn't get rid of. His temple started to throb. She was plotting something again, he could tell.

"We need to talk," Viv murmured urgently.

"The funeral's over." Ross didn't bother to keep his voice down. "There's no longer a 'we.'"

She propelled him into the hall. "We'll talk when Charlie takes Agatha to the airport. The kids are going, too, so we'll have privacy."

"Didn't you hear what I said?" he demanded. "I'm leaving."

"If you're not here when Charlie brings the kids home, how will I stop him kissing me?" she asked reasonably.

"What?"

But she'd already returned to the protection of the herd. The woman was as cunning as a weasel. Salsa dropped the ball and growled in the direction of Viv's swiftly retreating back. "Stand in line," Ross snarled.

By the time everyone had left and Charlie's taillights disappeared around the corner, Ross was in serious danger of wringing Viv's neck.

Returning inside, he found her in the lounge pouring two stiff Scotches. She offered him one. "That went well, I thought."

Ross folded his arms. "Spit it out. Why would Charlie kiss you?"

Holding his glass, Viv gulped a swig of her own. "He asked me for a reconciliation."

For a moment he didn't think he'd heard right. "Who... *you!* You're not even his wife."

"I knew you'd see the funny side."

He stared at her. "Do you take *nothing* seriously?"

"Easier to laugh than cry."

Ross grabbed his drink and took a slug. "And how did you answer Charlie? No, don't tell me. I'll just think what a sane person would do and then choose the opposite. You're going to stall until Meredith gets home."

She nodded.

Ross scowled. "Where's the cell I lent you?"

"Charging. What are you going to do?"

"Enough's enough, Viv." He bent to the power socket and yanked the charger out of the wall.

"Charlie's driving. With Agatha and the kids. You'll cause an accident."

"No more stall tactics." He checked his cell for a signal. Damn it, the batteries were still too low. "Even if you were Merry, it's not as if a reconciliation is a good idea." Ross tried to make the call anyway. It didn't work.

"How can it not be a good idea? For heaven's sake they both want it and—" She broke off. "Wait a cotton-pickin' minute," she said slowly. "When Merry told Charlie about the kiss she said he came home from staying with *you* and asked for a separation."

He didn't like where she was going with this. "Charlie's his own man."

"That's bullshit. He looks up to you."

Surely Charlie hadn't taken his drunken philosophizing that seriously? "The only thing I said was Charlie should ask himself if he could ever trust her again."

"Oh, is *that* all you said." Viv's eyes kindled. "And all this time you've been pretending to be neutral bloody Switzerland and lecturing me about interfering." Her chest expanded in an outraged breath. "And now it turns out that most of the blame lies at *your* door…it was just a kiss, Ross, one kiss!"

"One kiss, sure, but Meredith had been meeting this guy for weeks. If nothing else, she was unfaithful in her heart."

"I didn't know you were such a romantic." Her sarcastic tone was really annoying him.

"No, I'm a realist. Better that Charlie man up to the truth now than face another disappointment further down the track. Cut his losses while he still had his self-respect."

"Good God, it's just like *Pride and Prejudice,*" she exclaimed. "You've gone and Darcy'd my sister's marriage. Stuck your nose in where you have no expertise, no insight, no bloody clue!"

He scoffed. "And *you* have? You run to the other side of the world when someone mentions commitment."

"Don't try and deflect this onto me." She jammed a finger into his chest, obviously needing this argument as much as he did. "One lousy kiss—not even initiated by Merry—and you wrote off eight years of marriage between two wonderful people!"

"You didn't think my brother was so wonderful last week when you were encouraging your twin to run away with his children."

"And I was wrong," Viv shot back. "At least I'm big enough to admit my mistakes. Now admit yours. You shouldn't have interfered in their marriage."

"My interference doesn't come close to yours, lady. I'm not the person impersonating my sibling."

"Yes, but I'm only interfering out of *absolute necessity.* Cleaning up your mess, in fact."

Unbelievable. Her knack of shifting blame was un-friggin'-believable. "Fine." Ross held up his hands in surrender. "I've learned my lesson. I'll never interfere again. Starting now."

"That's not the lesson, chucklehead," she said impatiently. "Do you really want our niece and nephew shuttled between an unhappy, pining mom and dad?"

"Emotional blackmail won't work on me."

"Oh, please, any appeal to your feelings constitutes emotional blackmail."

"You want to know what I really think? Okay. Your sister should have thought about her kids before she succumbed to flattery or a good listener or whatever the hell she thought she was getting when she kissed that doctor. And frankly, I have no patience for her throwing up her hands and whining, 'But I'm a nice person and I didn't mean for this to happen.' The mess made by nice people is the worst kind of mess."

"I hope you're not drawing parallels between Merry's one mistake and your father's infidelity," Viv said slowly.

"No," he retorted, "*you're* doing that." But she was right, he realized even as he denied it. His childhood had influenced his views.

"You helped break it, Ross, and you have to help fix it," she insisted. "All you need is a little resolve. Anyway, isn't that what the SAS are meant to do? Serve and protect?"

Ross lost the urge to argue. *Who am I if I'm not a soldier?* "I'm leaving."

She stepped in front of him. "What did I say that hurt you?"

He was heartily tired of this woman evoking feelings he didn't want to deal with. "Get out of my way, Viv."

"Not until we've sorted this out."

"Yeah? How are you going to stop me? Steal my keys again?"

She pulled his head down to hers and kissed him.

It was an angry, frustrated, circuit breaker of a kiss. Ross threaded his hands through her hair and pushed her against the wall so their bodies fused from breastbone to thigh.

Her mouth was soft, moist. Screw accountability. And screw Dan. Ross owed him nothing.

They broke apart for air, both breathing hard. "Well, I feel better." She impaled him with one of her frank looks. "How about you?"

"What the hell are you doing?" he demanded.

"Kissing it better."

Shit. Ross stepped back. This was pity. "That's right. You're drawn to rescuing the weak and feeble."

"If only they all looked like you do."

Ross felt a strong temptation to kiss her again. Instead he took another step back and clasped his hands behind him. "The last thing we need right now is anyone seeing me making out with my brother's wife. Besides, didn't Dan tell you? I need fixing."

Standing on tiptoe, Viv kissed him again. "Once you're fixed I'll have no use for you. Our family tomcat Boo Boo was never the same after."

Something knotted and painful released in him. "Yeah, well, unlike Boo Boo I know how to protect my assets." He felt a strange sense of loss as he looked at her. "We can't do this, Viv," he said. "We're on different sides." Though he knew she'd do her utmost to ensure he wasn't implicated, this whole situation still had the potential to blow up in his face. He couldn't lose Charlie. His little brother was all Ross had left.

She turned away to pick up their drinks. "Are you going to turn us in, Ross?"

Shit. Ross gulped his whiskey. He couldn't dispute that in his personal life Charlie let stronger people take charge. Guess that was a side effect of being brought up by a control freak like Linda.

"I guess I can keep my mouth shut for another couple of days," he said grudgingly. "Give your brother time to talk Meredith round—what?"

Skepticism flitted across Viv's face. "He might do it," she said neutrally. Placating him.

"With no help from you?"

"No," she admitted, then took a swig of her own drink. "I have to stand with Merry on this."

Ross drained his glass. "And to be clear...I'm only doing this because, unlike the Jansen twins, I accept responsibility for a mistake as soon as I realize I've made one. I shouldn't have broadcast my feelings about marriage to Charlie." Viv cleared her throat. He hated it when she did that because it always heralded more bad news. "Now what?"

"Merry phoned. The hospital won't authorize a transfer until her blood infection clears up. You might have to keep your mouth shut for another week."

Ross took a full minute to respond. Possibly because he had trouble unlocking his jaw. "In the morning I'm returning to my beach house as planned," he said coldly. The funeral was over, Charlie none the wiser. Dan could run interference from here; maybe that was Ross's best revenge. "And I don't want to see you or hear from you unless there's such a monumental crisis that you can't handle it alone. Am I clear?"

She swallowed. "Crystal."

He caught sight of the schnoodle, glaring at Viv from under the coffee table. "And I'm taking Salsa with me. That dog is the only creature in this house whose integrity you haven't corrupted and I'm not abandoning him to a coronary because you're trying to bribe your way into his affections."

Viv lifted the decanter. "Another Scotch?"

"Not funny." Ross whistled for the dog.

"Don't call me, I'll call you?"

Her tone stung. "What did you expect me to say, Viv?" he challenged. "Let's forgive and forget…all pull together? One kiss and I'm supposed to fall into line?"

"Why not? You thought one kiss was enough to end a marriage."

CHAPTER FIFTEEN

"TURN RIGHT IN FOUR HUNDRED yards," said the tinny, electronic voice of Viv's GPS.

"Uh, but *is* it a turn, Shel?" she queried. "Or are you— once again—confused by a side road on a sharp bend?"

Sheldon voiced no reply. So far their relationship had proved fractious, chiefly because Sheldon's favorite advice was, "Perform a U-turn where possible."

The plug-in GPS had been couriered to Merry's home yesterday. No return address, no note, but Viv knew who'd sent it and felt a relief disproportionate to the gift. Ross wasn't abandoning her entirely.

Now at 12:30 p.m. on Friday she was following Sheldon as if he were a trail of sonic breadcrumbs from the airport—where she'd just dropped Charlie—to Harry's day care.

Charlie was flying to Christchurch for his Master Builders' conference and wouldn't be back until Monday night. All going well Merry would be home to greet him.

Viv should be kicking up her heels. For the past two days she'd been torn between relief that she no longer had to deal with her unsettling attraction to Ross and an urge to phone and find out if he was okay.

Who was she kidding? She missed him.

"Turn right in one hundred yards," said Sheldon.

Viv flicked on her indicators and pulled into the turning lane.

While it was a huge relief to have Charlie gone for a few days, it couldn't have come at a worse time for Tilly with her end-of-season match pending. She needed a parent around. Of course, as far as Charlie was concerned, she had one.

"If we don't win, I'm gonna tell," she'd threatened over breakfast.

"That would be breaking your word."

"You broke your word. You said you'd take me to La-serforce with some friends."

"And I will, honey, as soon as I can find a sitter for Harry, and learn all your friends' and their families' histories."

"You're not the fun one," Tilly muttered. The kids were really missing their mother now, despite the daily Skype calls.

Merry fretted over being apart from them but wouldn't let Viv change their routine for fear of triggering questions from Charlie. With reconciliation on the table, she was paranoid, absolutely paranoid about him finding out.

She'd had a new cell delivered to her hospital bed and now handled all calls with her husband, volunteering only the sketchiest information Viv needed for her brief encounters with Charlie around the kids' schedules.

"I told him we had to start over, lots of talking without the distraction of the physical," she'd said vaguely. "So he won't be bothering you that way."

Except there had been heat in her brother-in-law's eyes when he'd said goodbye at the airport drop-off, and he'd murmured that he found the new rules a turn-on. Viv had a horrible suspicion they'd graduated to phone sex.

"Turn left in three hundred yards."

"Thanks, Shel, I can take it from here." Viv switched off the GPS, then frowned as she caught sight of the ambulance parked on the street outside the day care, its flashing light sweeping the building's fence like a searchlight. There was an office block next door to the center, it was probably attending someone there. Parking the car, Viv grabbed the flowers she'd bought for Susan from the passenger seat. The bright verbenas of burnt orange and yellow rustled in their cellophane wrapper as she hurried to the gate, arriving at the same time as another mother—a pretty redhead wearing a business suit. They exchanged anxious smiles.

"I'm sure it's nothing."

"But we worry anyway."

Viv unlatched the gate and pushed it open. Mothers stood in small groups, clutching their kids, and talking in low tones. They glanced over when the two women arrived and Viv's blood froze. The message couldn't have been plainer. *It's one of ours.* Beside her, the redhead moaned. Blindly, Viv scanned the playground for Harry.

All the kids had been taken outside the main building and were cheerful enough, playing, oblivious to the muted distress of the grown-ups. They were under the supervision of one teacher, a middle-aged woman, who stood when she spotted the new arrivals and began threading her way toward them. In her panic, Viv couldn't remember her name.

"Iv."

At her feet, Harry crawled out of one of the playground's big concrete pipes. With a whimper, Viv fell to her knees, dropping the flowers and grabbing the baby in such a tight hug he squawked a protest and squirmed for freedom. She loosened her hold but didn't release him, kissing his little cheek again and again.

He was safe. Her panic subsided and she felt guilty for her joy, ashamed.

Glancing up, she saw the ashen redhead being

shepherded into the building. What could she do to help? Still clutching Harry, she staggered to her feet on legs that felt like they'd run a marathon.

The flowers lay on the ground. When she'd steadied herself, Viv picked them up with her free hand and hurried to the nearest cluster of moms.

"What happened, can someone tell me?"

Jiggling her fretful child on one ample hip, a blonde nodded. "Johnny Campbell had an allergic reaction. Fortunately Susan recognized the symptoms quickly and ran for the epinephrine shot. His allergy's so severe they keep it on hand."

"Will he be okay?"

But the other woman was looking past her. Viv turned and they all stepped back as the ambulance officers came down the path with the stretcher. The redhead walked beside it. Johnny Campbell turned out to be the bombastic little guy who'd driven into Viv's shins the first day she'd dropped Harry off. His small face was waxen, he whimpered, clinging tightly to his mother's hand. Viv's throat constricted.

The small convoy passed by, oblivious, gripped in their private drama. The gate clicked shut behind them.

"I don't understand," murmured the blonde. "We all know not to send anything containing nuts to day care. They remind us every week in the newsletter. How the hell could this have happened?"

"He'll be fine." Susan came out of the center, dispensing reassuring smiles. For the first time, she looked plain. "A day or two and he'll be right as rain." Her gaze lit on Viv and her smile lost its soothing quality. "Meredith, can I have a private word?" Taking Harry, she handed him to another teacher and steered Viv into the tiny office near the kids' locker room and closed the door.

It felt like being back in the headmaster's classroom at the tiny elementary school at Beacon Bay, only this time Viv hadn't done anything wrong. She'd put Vegemite—the vegetable extract beloved of Kiwi kids—on Harry's sandwiches this morning, same as always. "Are you okay?" she said to Susan, remembering her own shock and bewilderment after Linda's accident. "Can I get you anything…a glass of water, a sweater?" The younger woman's hands trembled as she pulled out a chair.

"No, thank you. Meredith—"

"Here." Viv remembered the flowers. "I brought them as a thank you for promoting M—my cause with Charlie." Susan didn't take them, so she laid them on her cluttered desk. "You've certainly earned them."

"I need to talk to you about what you put on Harry's sandwich," Susan said gently.

Viv relaxed. "Vegemite," she said. "Same as every morning." She could see herself putting the knife in the jar, spreading it on the bread, not too much…. "Harry only likes a little. Tilly on the other hand, can eat it by the spoonful. Personally I find the whole idea of yeast extract disgusting, never have got the taste for it." She stopped. "Wait," she said slowly. "We were out this morning. I went to the pantry…the jar was empty. I told Tilly off for putting it back empty." Her hand crept to her mouth. "I put peanut butter on instead."

"Johnny took a bite before he realized. Normally he's very aware of avoiding any food but his own, but they started playing food monsters. And you've always been so careful with Harry's lunch, the supervisor didn't think to check."

Over her hand, Viv stared at Susan, a dozen excuses springing to her lips. *It's not my fault. I'm only pretending to be Meredith. I had no idea we weren't allowed to send peanut products to day care.*

Except…she'd initiated the swap, she'd swept Merry's protests aside, she'd been confident of bluffing her way through every situation that might arise.

"It's my fault," she rasped. "No one else's…I'm so sorry."

Numbly she remembered what she'd said to Dan at the funeral when she'd argued against Meredith telling the truth. *This way no one gets hurt.*

A child could have died.

Viv grabbed a shoe box of crayon drawings from the desk and upended it. The drawings fluttered to the floor in a spread of vivid color.

Then she vomited.

"THREE KILOMETERS TO MURIWAI," said Sheldon, and Viv's hands tightened nervously on the steering wheel.

The first drops of an incoming squall spat against the windscreen as Liberty navigated the narrow winding road that led down to the tiny beachside community where Ross lived.

Sheldon said something she couldn't quite catch. Viv turned down the volume on The Wiggles and got a squeal of protest from Harry in the back. "Okay, okay." She cranked "Nicky Nacky Nocky Noo" up again. "Tilly, can you stop kicking the driver's seat, please?" The kicking continued. Glancing in the rearview mirror she saw her niece had her iPod on.

She could yell louder or she could put up with it. Exhausted, Viv put up with it.

Through a gap in the native bush, she caught her first glimpse of the rugged coastline and pulled into the lookout, where she idled the engine and gazed out over the sea.

Wind-honed land formations forged into the wild surf like the prows of battleships, extraordinarily beautiful. Even the sand had attitude, an uncompromising black. Long rolling dunes, lightly tufted with spinifex and rangy grasses, stretched away to the horizon.

"Why are we stopping?" Tilly complained. "I need to pee."

"Okay," said Viv, but delayed releasing the hand brake. If she got out, stood on the cliff's edge and opened her arms, the wind might reshape her like the dunes into something new and clean.

She didn't know how to make her peace with this.

Susan had been very kind.

Buoyed by his recovery, so were Johnny's parents when Viv stopped by the hospital to make a personal apology.

It made her burden of guilt so much heavier.

Ross had to take over the kids until she could pull herself together. With Charlie in Christchurch there was no one else.

His house lay on a ridgeline above the beach, hidden from the road by a narrow unpaved driveway planted either side with a tangle of drought-hardy native shrubs. Elevated to catch the sun, the house was a modest split-level building with salt-silvered board and batten, and a triangulated roofline of blue corrugated iron.

Native bush fanned out from the hardwood decks, which had been built around mature nikau palms, some of which thrust through the deck itself like natural sun umbrellas—an unexpected touch of whimsy. And beyond, she saw jaw-dropping views of a rain-bleached sea.

The shower became a deluge as she unloaded the children. Lightning flashed across the sky.

The kids' feet clattered on the decking as they beelined for the door. Tilly pounded, Harry hammered. Viv wiped damp palms on Merry's brown poplin skirt. No one answered the door. Peering through the adjacent window she saw a monastically furnished living room with a cozy wood burner in the corner. "He isn't home."

Stupidly it hadn't occurred to her to phone first, which was precisely why she needed to off-load the kids. She wasn't thinking straight. She could make another terrible mistake.

Frustrated, Harry rattled the handle, while Tilly jiggled from one foot to the other. "I need to pee *now*."

"Give me a minute." Standing under the overhang, staring out at the rain, Viv gathered her scattered thoughts. There must be a public restroom at the beach. "Everyone back in the Subaru." It was still pelting down as they left the restroom ten minutes later. They took shelter in the car where Viv let Harry stand in the driver's seat playing with the steering wheel while she sat in the front passenger seat and considered their options.

Ross could be anywhere and he wasn't answering his cell. There seemed nothing for it but to turn around and drive the forty-five minutes home.

All she wanted to do was give up. It took her a minute to realize that; despair was such a new sensation for her.

Tilly drooped quietly against the rear passenger door. She shook her head when Viv offered her a chicken sandwich. Her niece's unhappiness brought Viv to her senses. She was all the parent these two had right now and here she was indulging in a meltdown instead of giving them what they needed.

Viv straightened in her seat. "Okay, who's ready to go to the beach?"

Harry forgot about the indicator lights and scrambled over. "Iv."

"But it's raining," Tilly protested.

"So? We all have extra clothes." She'd expected to drop them at Ross's so she'd packed them an overnight bag. And there were sweats for her in Merry's sports kit. "C'mon, it'll be *fun*."

"No, it won't, I'm gonna stay in the car."

"Suit yourself."

Harry was already tugging frantically at the door handle. Viv opened it for him and he turned to hang his small legs over the abyss before dropping to the ground, blinking owlishly in the rain. She smiled. "Go, baby."

With a grin, he toddled to a nearby dune and dropped to his haunches, picking up fistfuls of wet sand.

"He'll get dirty," Tilly warned.

"He's allowed to," said Viv. The rain hit her as she stepped out, not cold but nearly, the gusty wind forcing it down the back of her neck. Didn't matter. This was all about the kids. "Go ahead, Harry, knock yourself out. We'll splash it off afterward."

Tilly sat up. "You're going in the sea with your clothes on?"

"Yep, since we don't have swimsuits." It was clear from the little girl's face that she found the idea more outrageous than swimming naked.

Harry staggered over, propelled by a gust of wind, and with a chortle threw sand at Viv. It splattered her cheek, across her T-shirt.

Tilly gasped.

Harry's grin faded to apprehension. "Iv?"

She looked down at the T-shirt, one of her own, which could pass—just—as belonging to Merry. "I bet you didn't mean to do that," she said seriously.

"He did, too," ratted his older sister.

Harry thought about it. "No?"

Viv kept a straight face. "Well, I'm going to give you

the benefit of the doubt." She picked the biggest wet lump off Marilyn Monroe's beauty spot. "Like you're going to give me the benefit of the doubt when I do *this*."

Carefully, she tossed some wet sand in his direction and it plopped square on his round belly.

Harry looked at his T-shirt and then up at her with such utter astonishment that she didn't have to feign this smile. "Uh-oh," she prompted.

Tilly giggled, that giggle kids got when adults stopped pretending to be grown-ups.

Chuckling, Harry picked up another fistful and threw it at Viv. She replied in kind.

Tilly scrambled out of the car. "Can I play?"

"Sure, anywhere but faces."

Tilly bent and scrabbled for sand, turned with a cunning expression. Splat. Viv struck first. "Now tell me I'm not fun," she invited.

Harry squealed.

Splat. Tilly got her revenge.

"Run, Harry, run." Grabbing his hand they broke into a toddler-paced trot down the beach. Splat on Harry's bottom. Splat on Viv's. Harry shrieked.

Their joy was balm to her wounded spirit.

Splat. Lacking the coordination to miss faces, Harry hit her right in the kisser. Spitting out a gritty mouthful, Viv grinned and returned to the battle.

CHAPTER SIXTEEN

As Ross crested Otakamiro Point after jogging the goat-steep track up from Maori Bay, he paused in the downpour, letting the blustery easterlies refill his lungs with salt-tanged air, and looked down to Muriwai Beach. Some five hundred meters below, the tiny figures of an adult and two kids crouched next to a sodden sandcastle, near the edge of an incoming tide.

Some lunatic had taken their kids to the beach in the rain.

Sheets of rain buffeted his naked torso and plastered his running shorts against his body, trickled into his trainers. It had been showering when he'd started forty minutes ago—who's really the lunatic?—so he'd seen no point in wearing a T-shirt. His leg throbbed with an ache like a tooth abscess.

Massaging it impatiently, he looked for Salsa and spotted a soggy blog of disconsolate gray-white picking its way up the hill. Damn Viv and her food bribes and damn the dog for his stubborn refusal to let Viv exercise him. Even absent the woman could still make Ross's life difficult.

Salsa's tail started to wag as he caught sight of Ross. Giving an apologetic yip, he broke into a trot for the last few meters. Suppressing his irritation, Ross bent to pat the wet head. "Home stretch, dog."

As he did every time he visited, Salsa cast a wistful look toward the gannet colony lying just below a viewing platform to their left. The schnoodle never gave up hope of finding a way to the birds, and there was always the prospect of barking at the fur seals occasionally basking on the rocks below. "Trust me, no one's sunbathing today. C'mon." Turning downhill, Ross broke into a jog, Salsa following reluctantly.

Rain slicked the trail and made rivulets down the edges. Traversing one of the wide steps, his left foot shot forward on the slippery clay and he fell backward on his ass. A jolt of pain shot up his weak leg, so sharp that he jackknifed forward over his knees with a gasp. "Son of a—" Ross waited for it to pass, cursing the weather, cursing his infirmity, cursing his luck.

He was so tired of fighting the odds.

Anxiously Salsa licked his face. "I'm okay, dog." Ross levered himself to a standing position and tested his leg. On a pain scale it was about an eight, only two higher than normal.

He'd expected his life to recalibrate when he cut free of family distractions, disentangled from Viv Jansen's intrigues and came home.

He'd always been good at compartmentalizing. Unfortunately Viv wasn't staying in her box.

Stockholm syndrome he told himself. He'd been trapped in his mad captor's world for so long she'd brainwashed him into caring what happened to her.

Gingerly he walked out the limp, picking his way downhill, the wind dropping as he descended to the shelter of the bay.

He'd also been suffering through Charlie's enthusiastic updates. "Merry was right," his brother confided at lunch in town yesterday. "Putting the physical aside really helps us concentrate on communication. We were on the phone an hour and a half last night. I think this is going to work, Ross."

Was Ross's silence about the twin swap setting his brother up for a bigger fall? He found his sister-in-law's new cell number on Charlie's phone when his brother went to pay the bill and called her as soon as he reached his car.

"I know what I'm doing," she said. "Anyway, my blood tests show the infection is clearing. I'll be home before Charlie gets back from his conference." The truth or wishful thinking? Ross could only ask Viv or Dan and he wasn't talking to either of them.

Frustrated, he'd cut to the chase. "Eventually you have to tell Charlie the truth, Meredith."

"And risk everything I've regained," she'd said sharply. "Would you?"

"Yes," he'd replied without hesitation.

"Let's give this context, Ross. If withholding one fact was the only thing that stood between you and active service would you tell it?"

He was silent.

"You have your obsession, I have mine," she said. "We were good friends once, so please, let me do what I think is best for my family."

The ground leveled out, sandstone became beach and the ache in his leg eased up. Sweet relief. Gritting his teeth, Ross forced himself to resume jogging, but the heavy wet sand was hard going. Enough, he told himself, that you're doing it. Enough today, that you're not giving up. Beside him, Salsa caught sight of the lunatics and tore off down the beach with an excited bark. "*Now* you find your second wind," Ross grumbled, picking up his pace. Some kids were scared of dogs.

Drawing closer, the figure holding the baby resolved into a woman. Her skirt clung wetly to her legs, an olive T-shirt was plastered to her upper body. She was splattered with black sand. The older of the two children frolicked in the shallows, racing away from the white-water of an incoming tide and shrieking like a banshee.

A bigger wake took the woman by surprise, surging and foaming around her thighs, lifting the skirt so it floated around her like brown seaweed. She held the baby high, all of them oblivious to the rain, as wild and primitive as the weather and the setting. Ross grinned, a grin that faded as he recognized her.

SPECIAL FORCES SOLDIERS had a presence...a charisma that was almost palpable, even at a distance. So Viv knew, even before her pulse kicked, that it was Ross jogging toward them. As he drew nearer she noticed his gait, jarring and not graceful. He shouldn't be doing this.

It hurt to see his struggle, hurt to sense the desperation behind it. It must be terrible to be a soldier who couldn't fight.

Above a pair of black running shorts, his torso was bare, glistening with rain and she found herself drawing a quick breath. His body was like this landscape, without softness or compromise.

Harry straightened in her arms. "'Oss." Harry pointed. Another new word. Their nephew would be writing dictionaries at this rate.

"Uncle Ross, Uncle Ross!" Tilly galloped out of the surf and tore along the waterline toward her uncle, who'd slowed to a walk. "Look, I'm swimming in my clothes!"

Harry squawked and, backing out of the tide, Viv put him down to stagger after Tilly, sea-soaked nappy hanging below his knees.

Closer still and she could pick out detail. Scars like leopard markings crossed his ribs and abdomen where metal shards had sliced into the flesh. A deep scar crisscrossed his right thigh, ragged and as ugly as a shark's bite, purple-red against his pale skin.

His recovery to date was extraordinary. She could only marvel at the will that had got him this far. But Dan had told her everything—Viv suspected to deter her from pursuing an affair. He needn't have worried. The kiss had already sent Viv's own early warning system into hyperdrive. However impulsive she might be in other areas of her life, she didn't go near love. Not with the example of her parents' marriage behind her.

Ross bent to scoop up Harry and laid a protective hand on his excited niece's shoulder. His gaze met hers, wary, unwelcoming.

"You said if there was a crisis I couldn't handle alone...." The morning's events crashed down on her like a wave. Hoping he'd mistake her sudden tears for rain, Viv bent to pat Salsa, received a warning growl and withdrew her hand. "If you could take the kids tonight," she managed gruffly, "I'll pick them up in the morning."

She waited for him to argue. Instead a key appeared in front of her. "Salsa and I will meet you at the house."

"Thank you." Blinking hard, Viv took a bedraggled Harry and turned toward the parking lot.

"I'll walk with Uncle Ross," Tilly announced. She grabbed his hand and the pair continued along the beach. "Uncle Ross, you have to help my team with soccer on Monday after school. Dad's not here for the final or Mum and you *have* to. Please!"

Even when she was asking a favor, Tilly couldn't quite take the command out of her tone. "As long as Viv doesn't mind an assistant coach," he hedged.

"I think I can put my ego aside!" she called over her shoulder. Her doubts about coming here fell away. What was it about this taciturn, disapproving guy that fostered in her a sense of security?

Tilly's voice came faintly down the beach. "Uncle Ross, after we change can I use the weights machine?"

"They're not toys, Attila."

"I know that! I'm building muscle."

By the time everyone had showered and changed, the kids were hungry. They ate canned soup and toast around the white oak dining table, while Tilly chatted about soccer plays.

"I'll get going, then." Viv took her bowl to the kitchen counter.

"Til," Ross said casually, "Go put on the SAS CD you like—take Harry."

He had every right to an explanation if she was dumping the kids on him. Steeling herself, Viv told him what happened, sitting at the table, looking at her hands, the ragged nails, trying to control the tremor in her voice. "I've been so arrogant," she finished. "Assuming that I can bluff my way through any crisis...if that child had died, Ross." Her throat tightened, cutting off the words.

She jumped as he put a hand on her shoulder. "Don't give me sympathy," she said. "I don't deserve it."

"You didn't deserve what happened, either."

She closed her eyes and leaned against him, felt his hand, gentle against her hair. He wore jeans and another ThinkGeek T-shirt. She'd sent Dan one a year back and he'd mentioned that Ross was hooked. This one read Resistance Is Futile—If < 1 ohm—and smelled of shampoo and pine soap. Having used his shower, so did she. Silent tears ran down her cheeks. She buried her face against him and cried.

He didn't offer any platitudes, didn't try to make her feel better, he simply let her cry it out. And Viv was grateful.

"C'mon, Uncle Ross," Tilly wandered in from the living room and Ross turned to shield Viv from their niece's view. Hurriedly, Viv wiped her eyes with the sleeve of her sweatshirt. "Let's all go work out."

"I'll bring Harry in a minute," Viv said. It was ten before she'd composed herself enough to follow, splashing her face with cold water and fingercombing the tangles out of her hair.

Something had changed. She just wasn't sure what.

THE FIRST THING HARRY did when Viv carried him into the basement weight room was bang on a cupboard door until she opened it. He rolled out a Swiss ball bigger than he was and prodded it around the carpet with a toothy grin. Under Ross's supervision, Tilly was busy adjusting the setting on a rowing machine.

"These two know how to make themselves at home," Viv commented. She was feeling a little shy since her crying jag. People expected her to be upbeat.

"Charlie used to come stay weekends with them when he and your sister first separated." Ross gave Tilly a thumbs-up and she hauled on the "oars."

A series of framed photographs lining the back wall caught Viv's eye and she wandered over for a closer look. The first was of the guys sitting in a Dumvee, sharing a casual moment of camaraderie. Ross, Nate, Dan, Lee and Steve. Young and smiling. Gently, she touched her late cousin Steve's face. "How did you become interested in the SAS, Ross?"

"Mum and I had an elderly neighbor—George—who'd been in the Unit. After her death, I begged Dad to let me move in with him. Naive, really." Absently, Ross stood back from the rowing machine and massaged his knee. "We stayed in touch."

"Is your injury paining you more than usual?" Viv asked quietly. "You've been favoring it since you took Salsa for a run."

All expression disappeared from his face. "If you think I can't keep up with that fat dog—"

"Salsa prefers 'big-boned.'"

Ross raked a hand through his hair, still slightly damp from the shower.

"I slipped and fell," he admitted. "Not badly but there'll be a bruise on my hip in the morning."

Want me to kiss it better? Lust was interfering with her risk radar. Viv returned her attention to the other photos for fear he'd read her eyes.

Ross, Dan and Jo at her brother's wedding, the best man holding the bride's ring finger out to the camera showing the beer tab that had been her last-minute wedding ring. Work commitments had stopped Viv from attending. Merry had arrived without Charlie and finally confessed he'd left her. Ross had kept his mouth shut, didn't want to ruin his friend's wedding.

A picture of Nate, ripped from some celebrity magazine. All macho chic in a plain black suit and wraparound shades, some Hollywood starlet on his arm, and the azure-blue of an L.A. swimming pool behind him.

Lee and his fiancée Jules…Steve and Claire holding their newborn son.

The photographs were a constant reminder of what Ross had lost and why he was doing this, she thought with a flash of insight. When you opened your heart to so few people you couldn't afford to lose any. Ross had lost two and considered himself betrayed by a third. She suspected Ross knew he couldn't make this better. What he was really struggling with was accepting it.

The Swiss ball came rolling toward her, Harry an unseen

propellant behind it and she stepped aside as he staggered past, palms planted against the juggernaut, teetering on the edge of balance.

"Save the sampler, Viv," Ross called. In Harry's path, the frame sat on the floor, leaning against the wall.

"Got it."

She had the leisure today to examine it, and again she noted the quality of the stitching—wool silk threaded on linen. The fabric had yellowed with age but the colors in the silk hadn't faded, vibrant reds and greens. She glanced across the room to the weight bench where Ross was helping Tilly grasp the pull-down bar. The little girl's face was flushed with exertion, her expression fiercely focused. "I can do it, myself," she warned, hauling down the weight-free crossbar.

Viv held up the sampler. "Why haven't you hung this?"

"No time." It bothered her that he couldn't find five minutes from his training schedule.

"Why don't we hang it now? Unless…" she hesitated "…you're still ambivalent. Because of Linda?"

"No." He paused. "Thanks to your pep talk at Linda's. I'll find a hammer."

She watched as he tapped the wall for a stud, lined up the frame and hit the nail home with one sure stroke. "Safe for another generation," she said lightly.

He'd be mortified to know how well she'd pieced together the scraps he'd let drop of his personal history. His father's betrayal, his mother's death, Linda's unkindness to a lonely teen—all leading to a painful retreat into self-reliance. Being Ross, he'd taken it too far, of course.

Maybe that explained her growing compulsion to kiss that arrogant mouth, strip that soldier's hard body naked and warm him all the way through to that battered heart.

A time to keep silence, and a time to speak. "Interesting

how different parts of the verse resonate every time you read it," she said. "At Linda's I saw, 'A time to be born, and a time to die.'"

He hung the sampler on the wall, stepped back to check the alignment, then made the adjustment. "What do you see now?"

"A time to embrace," she said without thinking, and Ross's hands stilled on the frame. Viv glanced at the kids but they were happily absorbed with the equipment. Her curiosity got the better of her. "Tell me honestly," she said in a low voice, "did you ever wonder—imagine—what it would have been like if you'd said yes at the wedding?"

He might have turned her down but he'd liked her...she wasn't confident enough to hit on guys who didn't. The words came from a long denied part of her, "We could still find out, Ross."

For what felt like forever, Ross stared at the sampler. Finally, he stirred.

"Who wants milk and cookies?"

Mortified heat swept up Viv's cheeks.

"Me! Me, Uncle Ross." Tilly came running over.

"Me," echoed Harry.

"I'll make us coffee." Awkwardly, he touched Viv's shoulder in passing.

She closed her eyes. I am not going to be embarrassed about this. I'm a twenty-first-century woman. I have a right to be sexually assertive.

With that bracing reminder she followed, but her steps faltered as she approached the kitchen. She couldn't meet his eyes, yet. The open-plan kitchen/dining area was partially separated from the living room by a solid wall with a built-in bookcase at the end. She paused to scan the shelves.

"You read," she called inanely.

"I prefer it to watching TV."

Her humiliation subsided, she was able to notice how cannily the bookcase was built, each cubicle sized for different shaped books from coffee table tomes to paperbacks. So orderly and precise, she suspected Ross had made it. "I love the design of your bookcase, it's giving me storage ideas for my sewing materials."

See this wasn't so hard.

A couple of the cubbies held framed photographs— one of Ross and an older woman who must be his mother, another of Ross and a woman who definitely *wasn't* his mother. Viv peeked closer. A shapely blonde dressed in running gear with a number bib on her tank. Laughing into the camera, she gripped a gold medal and Ross equally possessively.

Viv remembered now—he'd dated a triathlete before the ambush. This woman looked perfect for him. Blonde, athletic, stacked…probably had to Vaseline those puppies to avoid runner's chafe. *Stop being a bitch, Viv, because you're feeling rejected.*

"Coffee's ready."

Steeling herself, she went into the kitchen where she found the three of them sitting around the table munching biscuits. "We should get going after this, kids."

"I thought you wanted us to sleep over?"

"I wasn't feeling very well before, Til," Viv rushed to answer, "and thought I might not be able to look after you properly but now I'm fine."

"Then why don't we all stay?"

Because your uncle knows I want to jump his bones and probably thinks this was some kind of setup. Viv shot him a look but his expression was unreadable. "Uncle Ross wasn't expecting us anyway, and we have to be home to Skype Mum."

"We can phone her from here instead."

"I don't have pajamas." She looked to Ross for backup, but he was looking out the window with a frown.

"Uncle Ross can lend you some," Tilly persisted.

"The weather's not improving anytime soon," he noted. "I guess you'll have to stay." He sounded like he was agreeing to a root canal.

"Yay," said Tilly.

"Thanks," Viv said tartly, "but we don't want to put you out."

He turned his frown on her. "And I don't want to worry about you driving winding roads in this weather."

His attitude was really starting to piss her off. "Get over it," she snapped. "Let's leave now, kids, so we're not driving in the dark."

"All I see on that sampler is 'a time to heal,'" said Ross abruptly. "It's all I can allow myself to see. If I came across as rude it's because I wish it could have been different. I'm sorry."

"What could have been different, Uncle Ross?"

"Have another cookie, honey. You've only had three." Still looking at Viv, he pushed the plate over.

Mollified, Viv folded her arms. "There, was that so hard?"

His mouth twitched. "No."

Harry squawked and Viv gave him another cookie, too. "I'm not going to go into a decline because you keep turning me down."

"Turning you down for *what?*" Tilly mumbled through a mouthful.

"I'm sorry," Ross said again. "Please, Viv, I'd really like you and the kids to sleep over."

"Yay!" said Tilly.

Viv held up a hand. "What's for dinner?"

The rare dimple appeared. "Steak, chipped potatoes,

fresh beans. I could probably rustle up some kind of dessert."

"Okay, we'll stay."

"Thank you," he said humbly.

Tilly giggled. "Maybe you are fun," she said to Viv.

CHAPTER SEVENTEEN

"I DON'T GET WHY HE STILL doesn't like me. Dogs like me!" Viv complained after Ross refused to let her feed Salsa the fat off the raw steaks.

"It's because you're an imposter."

"But how can he tell? I wear my twin's clothes. I even wear the same deodorant. We're exactly the same."

"You're nothing alike, not really." Ross thought about it. "You radiate a different energy from your sister," he said. "I never look at Meredith and want to—" He concentrated on turning the steaks on the barbecue.

Viv finished chopping up a second chicken patty for Harry who'd demolished the first in record speed. "Wring her neck?"

"That's right," Ross said easily. He was barbecuing under the overhang of the deck. Harry and Viv sat at the trestle table using a sun umbrella to protect them from the rain. Harry was in hog heaven, shoveling down bits of chicken patty with one hand, the other thrust outside the umbrella, palm up to catch raindrops.

Engulfed in Ross's black leather jacket, collar upturned to frame her face Viv looked as sexy as hell as she took every opportunity to spoon peas into Harry's mouth. Ross forced his attention back to the barbecue.

He wasn't sure how they'd ended up here. Except when she'd cried, he'd had to comfort her. Regardless of how he felt about her actions, her motives were always pure. Purer than his.

"You were pretty keen on wringing my twin's neck at Linda's," she reminded him.

"Any neck would have done. Your sister's happened to be the closest."

The sound of gunfire drew his attention inside. Tilly was engrossed in watching another of his SAS DVDs. Viv followed his gaze. "Have you told her that selection isn't open to women?"

"Hell, no. I'm too scared." He checked the steaks and turned them. A jet of flame roared through the grill as fat dripped onto the gas burner. "Why don't you encourage her into your line of work," he suggested. "It seems cut-throat enough to suit her."

Viv laughed, "Ain't that the truth." Ross raised an eyebrow. "I've been on the shortlist for a remake of *Kiss Me, Kate* starring Anne Hathaway and Johnny Depp. I'm ninety-nine point nine percent sure I've missed out on the job."

"Only ninety-nine point nine percent?"

"The producer said they'd notify the successful applicant by the fifth." She shrugged. "That was four days ago." She accepted raindrops from Harry's cupped hand. "Thank you!"

"So phone. Find out," Ross suggested.

"In our industry, it's very much a matter of don't call us, we'll call you."

"I said that," he reminded her. "And you ignored me."

"No." Viv shook her head. "Phoning now smacks of desperation. I'm supposed to be the much-sought-after Vivienne Jansen."

"Which makes it even more impressive when you ask

how you can improve your chances next time. I'm guessing you want there to be a next time?"

Viv accepted another raindrop from Harry. "You're right," she said at last, "and it stops me fretting about it. Watch the baby?" Retrieving her cell from her jeans, she keyed in a number. "Hello, Sue. It's Viv Jansen. Listen, I realize you must have chosen someone else for the Depp/Hathaway project but…" Her voice faded as she disappeared inside the house.

"Iv?" said Harry.

"She's coming back, mate." Harry offered Ross a raindrop with a big smile. Chicken patty dotted his face like smallpox.

Ross returned the grin. It *was* good seeing the kids, good seeing Viv, now they'd finalized boundaries.

He plated the meat. "C'mon, mate, let's go inside. It's too wet to finish a meal here."

"No."

"I can hear a helicopter on TV…"

Harry held out his arms. Ross cleaned him off, scooped him up and took him inside with the meat platter, dumping him by his sister. "Dinner's ready in five, Til." He found Viv sitting at the dining table. She glanced up, dazed.

"Sue said she's been calling. Merry gave her the cell number last Tuesday but of course I've had a new one since the cereal bowl incident." She frowned distractedly. "I don't understand why I wouldn't have got the emails, though, the address was correct."

"Have you checked your spam folder?"

"When have I had a chance to do that?"

"Well, at least you know now." Ross put the meat on the table. "I'm sorry, Viv."

She stared at him blankly, then laughed. "You don't understand. The reason they've been trying to contact me so urgently is because I've got the job."

He grinned. "You're kidding."

Her face wreathed in smiles, she stood up. "They were about to give up on me because they hadn't heard from me. Ross, thank you!" She made a slight movement toward him then stopped, obviously wary of another rejection. So he hugged her, a brief hard embrace that he tried to keep detached from and couldn't.

"Congratulations."

Tilly was impressed by the news. Though she couldn't imagine anything worse than being a princess like Anne Hathaway in *The Princess Diaries,* "other than having an army." She'd loved Depp as Willy Wonka in *Charlie and the Chocolate Factory.* "D'you think he'll still have chocolate left, you know from the movie—I still have Easter eggs 'an it's September."

When they sat to eat, Viv hardly touched her meal, she was too excited…relating funny anecdotes of off, off, off-Broadway stage productions from her early days. And Ross could tell she was itching to text everybody. "It would be bad etiquette at the table," she said when he suggested it.

Ross laughed. "Yeah, and we're really worried about etiquette tonight. Harry's covered in custard, your niece is chewing with her mouth open and you're feeding Salsa under the table…don't think I haven't noticed."

"No, the virtual world can wait," she said firmly. "Right now, I'm celebrating with you guys."

Ross hesitated. "I have a bottle of champagne somewhere," he said. "I'll get it."

"Not if you're saving it for something special."

"This is special enough."

Excusing himself, he went to the kitchen. At the back of a cupboard he found the Krug he'd put aside to celebrate the day he officially rejoined his unit. "Not chilled," he told Viv on his return, "and we'll have to drink it out of wine-glasses but it is champagne."

"Can I have some?" Tilly said.

"Sure." He poured a tiny sip for her.

"Me!" said Harry. "Me."

Solemnly, Ross handed Harry his water.

Tilly giggled. "But that's just—"

Ross raised his glass. "To your clever auntie."

They all chinked glasses, Viv helping Harry, a sparkle in her eyes.

Tilly choked on hers. "But this is horrible," she said, dismissing his $180 wine, then looked at her goblet and brightened. "Auntie Viv, you can do your party trick! The one with the cartwheel."

"After dinner," Viv promised. "I'll need to limber up first. Ross, this is delicious. What is it?"

He refilled her glass. "Some import."

They used the cartwheel as leverage to talk Tilly into an early bedtime, Ross rolling back the rug in the living room, while Viv did stretches. The kids sat on the couch, wide-eyed in their pajamas. It had stopped raining, but there was enough of a chill in the air to warrant a fire and it cast a warm glow on their expectant faces.

Tilly had supervised the refilling of the glass to three-quarters because she wanted to make it tricky but not too tricky, she'd informed them solemnly. After two glasses of Krug, Viv seemed to be finding it hard to drum up the necessary gravitas. Ross joined the kids on the couch, mimicked a drumroll and got an elbow in the ribs from his niece. "Shush!"

Her aunt choked down a laugh.

"Here we go," she said, and holding the glass steady,

did a perfect one-handed cartwheel around it, her long hair sweeping the floor through the turn.

She landed neatly, and Tilly scrambled out of the couch to check the level in the glass. "None spilled," she announced, and everyone clapped.

The firelight caught Viv's eyes as she laughed, her flushed cheeks and disheveled hair, and Ross realized that even an iron will could be challenged by laughter.

VIV WALKED INTO the kitchen where she found Ross settling Salsa on a blanket in the corner. "The kids are waiting for a good-night from you."

"Coming." With a final pat for the dog, he handed her the glass of champagne Viv set down after her cartwheel.

"Are you trying to get me drunk?" she asked. *Friends, just friends.* But she was happy and relaxed and a little high from the alcohol and Ross was so gorgeous she kept forgetting not to flirt with him. Still, he'd made it plain she was safe and she'd switched off her danger radar.

"It's not as if this stuff keeps," he said, disappearing down the hall. "I'll have a glass, too."

Viv looked at Salsa. Salsa looked back. "I don't suppose you'd let me pat…" The dog stared her down. "No, of course not."

Pouring Ross's champagne, she nearly dropped the bottle when she noticed the Krug Grand Cuvée label and realized how kind he'd been. Reminding herself he wasn't interested, Viv returned to the living room. The first thing she noticed was that he'd already laid out bedding for the pull-out couch. Unconsciously she sighed, then put the glasses on the bookcase and stoked the fire since it was plainly the only thing going to keep her warm tonight.

As she picked up her glass again, her gaze fell on the spine of the book behind it. *Overcoming Impotence.*

Viv froze. No, it must mean something else. Impotence in the boardroom perhaps or impotence in the kitchen? With a quick check over her shoulder she pulled it out of the bookshelf. *Coming to terms with Erectile Dysfunction.*

"The kids want you again."

Viv pivoted, fumbling to hide the book behind her back.

"Find some bedtime reading?"

"No!" Her hands tightened convulsively on the paperback. She summoned a smile. "Go tell those brats to quit stalling."

Instead he came closer. "What have you got there?"

With a terrible sense of inevitability she realized there was no avoiding this. "I do have a book but…well…this is a little awkward." *Why* had she said that? Cheeks hot, she brought it forward.

Ross's attention went to the cover and his face lost all expression.

"Of course it's probably not yours."

"It's mine."

Viv wished the floor would open up and swallow her. "If I'd had any idea, Ross, I wouldn't have kissed you…or propositioned you earlier." Now she sounded like a sexual predator. "Would you want to…talk about it?"

His cool gaze lifted. "Not much point, no pun intended."

A nervous laugh bubbled up in her and Viv bit her cheek and tried to think of puppies dying. "It would only have been a disappointment anyway."

Realizing what she'd implied Viv added hastily, "The reality could never live up to my eight-year-old fantasy." Damn the champagne for loosening her tongue. In trying to save his feelings, she'd only exposed her own.

"You've fancied me for eight years?" he said.

"I'll go check on the kids." All thumbs, she jammed the paperback into the bookcase and left the room. She settled the children quickly, not wanting Ross to think she was embarrassed and hiding. Viv scrambled for an innocuous subject as she returned and her eyes fell on the champagne bottle. "Ross, I had no idea you'd opened a Krug…let me reimburse you for it."

"Viv, relax. I'm impotent, not impoverished."

"Right, yes. I wasn't suggesting—"

"Let's just enjoy it."

"Good idea." She took a large sip, then another. He didn't look ill at ease, lounging on the couch, glass in hand, gazing into the fire.

"I'm glad my condition's in the open," he said. "We can relax now."

"Yes." She settled in the armchair. "Is it—"

"But we won't talk about it."

"No."

So they discussed her new job.

Was the impotence permanent or temporary?

Talked about a possible design for a specialist bookcase.

The result of his injuries from the ambush?

He told her about Muriwai's gannet colony.

Is that why his relationship with the blonde ended?

For a wild moment, Viv wondered if she could help Ross overcome his disability, but common sense told her that someone nervously prone to laugh at awkward moments when empathy and encouragement were called for, wasn't up to the job, no pun intended.

Besides, she didn't have any expertise in being a patient lover. Uninterested in the softer emotions, sex was strictly for fun and she was perfectly happy with a mutual gallop to an orgasm. Viv didn't want to be held afterward, or re-assured or cherished. And she didn't expect—or encourage—lovers to make the experience any more meaningful than the enjoyment of an excellent meal or a good movie.

Still, by the time she'd drunk another half flute of champagne she was nearly brave enough to try. Nearly.

Ross leaned forward and threw a log on the fire, then adjusting the cushions and stretched full-length on the couch. "When you asked in the weight room if I'd ever imagined what it would be like?" He watched the dancing shadows on the ceiling. "You meant the sex."

Viv snapped upright. "If I'd known—"

"Yeah," he said. "I did imagine."

A smart woman would stop him now. Viv remained silent.

"We'd leave the wedding separately to avoid gossip, even feigning surprise when we met in front of the hotel elevators. While we waited, we'd exchange small talk but as soon as the elevator door closed, I'd pull all the pins out of your hair—because I'd seen you tug at them through the service—and then I'd draw you close and kiss you."

Viv held her breath.

"The kiss starts slow as we learn the shape of each other's mouth, find the perfect fit, and then gets deeper." His voice dropped to a husky timbre. A shiver went down her spine. "I push down the straps on your girly bridesmaid dress and peel the bodice down to your waist and take my time getting acquainted with your breasts."

She struggled to breathe. "In the elevator?"

"You'd trust me to slide it up again before we reached our floor," he said, a smile on his lips. "Anyway, you wouldn't be worrying about that because you'd be focused on how good my mouth felt tonguing your nipples and wishing my hands would slip under the satin skirt and find skin."

Her nipples hardened. She stirred restlessly on the chair.

"In your hotel room—" Ross put one hand behind his head, and his T-shirt revealed a tantalizing strip of iron-hard muscle "—we'd lose the dress and that cute little pink

G-string I caught a flash of when you did your one-handed cartwheel."

"I didn't think the skirt would fall that far," she confessed.

"And I'd get you naked, except for the stilettos, which make your legs even more incredible than they already are. We'd stop being polite with each other," he said slowly, "and get a little wild."

Viv stopped breathing again.

Ross turned his head, and his silver-gray eyes gleamed in the firelight. "You need a refill."

It was so not what she expected him to say that Viv blinked. "What?" Dazed she looked at her empty glass. She'd drained it.

"Let me take care of that for you." Swinging his legs off the couch, Ross picked up the champagne bottle and emptied the dregs into her glass, so close she could almost see a second hand on his five o'clock shadow above that lush, full mouth, so close she got a hit of his scent, pine and male. She made a helpless sound in her throat and swayed closer.

"This isn't too difficult for you, is it?" he asked. "My therapist said talking without any pressure attached to performing might help."

Viv sat back, digging her nails into the armchair. "No," she rasped. Grateful for the loose sweatshirt that hid her nipples.

He stayed where he was, elbows resting on knees, within reach, as he gazed into the fire. She was helpless to look away.

"Where was I?"

She swallowed. "We were getting wild."

"Oh, yeah." His eyes darkened. "I imagined touching

you, everywhere, and you touching me." She could see them vividly in her mind's eye.

"And maybe my fingers would be a little roughened through soldiering," he said, "but I'd be gentle, taking my time." She nearly whimpered. He smiled at some private thought. "So much time that you'd get impatient because you're a 'want it when I want it' kind of girl, used to being in charge. But with me, you'd want it to last, want the slow, sweet, torturous buildup to penetration, want to wait until I whispered, 'Part your legs for me.' And when it happened, when I finally slid into you—"

Viv shot to her feet. "Ross, I can't talk about this anymore," she said in a strangled voice, unable to look at him. "I'm sorry, I'd love to be helpful but…"

If you keep talking like this I'll spontaneously combust.

"…the kids get up so early and it's late."

"Viv."

Reluctantly, she met his limpid gaze.

"Did I turn you on?"

"No, I mean, yes, but it's my fault. I'm obviously insensitive or very sensitive depending on how you…" Her voice trailed off.

"I'm so sorry." With a contrite expression, he pulled her onto his lap and she felt his body heat through her jeans and suffered another painful surge of lust. His breath tickled her cheek as he stroked a strand of hair off her face. "How can I fix it? A mug of cocoa, maybe?"

Viv shifted to get comfortable and suddenly registered *why* there wasn't as much room as there should be. Instinctively her hand sought verification. He was hard, hot and definitely primed to go.

Ross looked into her eyes. His own gleamed. "It's a miracle," he said humbly.

"You bastard!" Viv shoved hard on his lap to stand up, but though he winced he didn't release her.

"It was a present from your new sister-in-law, Jo. Long story."

She shoved again—harder—and he let her go.

"You tortured me as a joke."

"No. I used a white lie as foreplay."

"A white lie's not supposed to benefit you!"

"So you got nothing out of it?"

She crossed her arms. "Nothing."

"Then come over here and I'll make sure you do."

She could hardly breathe when he looked at her like that, firelight shifting across his lethal smile. Dangerous. Too dangerous?

"We're on different sides," Viv hedged.

"Yeah."

"Charlie…Merry…Dan…no one will like it."

"Which is why we won't tell them."

She had a pang of disquiet. "Is this about paying Dan back, Ross?" she asked quietly.

"No," he said. "It's about how you can charm me with a one-handed cartwheel. You've been screwing with my concentration, my brain and my sleep for days and it's got to stop. So I figure if we can't defuse the bomb we'll detonate it under controlled conditions."

"But—"

"You know, if you keep throwing up objections, you'll spoil the moment."

"What moment?"

"This one," he said, and smiled.

Viv started to say something flippant, then stopped. Something in Ross's eyes made her feel exposed, even vulnerable.

He registered her sudden disquiet. "Or we can say good-night."

Viv wavered. Who was she kidding? She wanted him. She'd always wanted him. What harm was there if she was leaving? A small inner voice started answering that question and she shut it down. Like he said, don't spoil the moment. "In my fantasy," she said, "you weren't wearing anything."

Ross smiled and stood up, sweeping off his T-shirt in a graceful movement that lifted his ribs and tightened his washboard stomach.

Oh. Soldier.

Tossing it aside, he unzipped his jeans, let them fall, stepped free and kicked them aside. He stood there in his navy boxers. Viv's knees went weak and she gripped the back of the chair for support. Hooking a thumb over the waistband of his shorts, he cruised in the direction of his bedroom. In the deep shadows away from the firelight, she caught a glimpse of prime male ass as the boxers hit the floor outside the door.

Viv sucked in a deep, deep breath. They were really, truly, finally going to do this.

On unsteady legs she followed and found Ross propped on one elbow on top of the covers, the bedside lamp providing all the light a woman needed to find her way. "Yep," she managed. "Just like my fantasy."

His lips curved. "Then what happened?"

"I was naked, too." With clumsy hands, she pulled off the sweatshirt, unfastened her jeans. As a costume designer she was comfortable with nudity, as a woman she was acutely conscious that she was revealing herself to a man whose body was his temple and who'd once dated a woman with abs. Her figure might be slim and toned from yoga but it wasn't muscled and on a menu her breasts definitely fit under the appetizer category.

She'd never cared about this stuff before and, annoyed that she did now, Viv adopted a clichéd pose, hand on one out-thrust hip, and said, "Ta-daaa!"

"Oh, baby," he said, "where've you been all my life?"

Viv forgot her pose and smiled.

And it was easy, so easy to walk to the bed, and lie beside him, not touching, but close enough to exchange body heat.

He leaned forward to kiss her but she drew back. "And then," she whispered, "in my fantasy I touched you." Lightly she ran her fingertips across his collarbone, down to a pec, circled around a nipple and watched it harden. "I followed my hand," she said huskily, "with my mouth."

His eyes darkened. Leaning forward, Viv pressed her lips to his warm flesh and dotted kisses over the sparse silky hair of his chest until she reached a nipple. Ross's ribs swelled in a sharp inhale as her teeth closed gently over it. Viv lifted her head. "How's my fantasy working for you so far?"

He made a sound between a groan and a laugh. "It's working."

Her fingers brushed across his ribs to navel and belly, tracing his scars with tenderness, following the arrow of hair to his groin. She closed a hand around him. "Definitely cured…and of course where the fingers go, the lips follow…"

Viv kissed her way down each rib, teased his navel then lay her cheek on his abs, mere inches from his erection, pulsing in her hand. "Ross?" she said, making sure he felt the heat of her breath.

"Viv?" he ground out.

One last gentle breath of air then she released her hold

on his cock, and nipped her way up his body to smile into his dazed eyes. "Mine was a revenge fantasy—for making me wait eight years, you son of a bitch," she said sweetly.

His gaze cleared. With a chuckle he hauled her on top of him and kissed her until she forgot payback fantasies. And Ross touched where he said he'd touch and the skin on his fingers *was* rough, but his caresses achingly gentle. And she cried out as she came under his exquisite exploratory touch, and then again around his heat, an orgasm that was savage and fast for both of them.

Ross rolled off her and they eyed each other sheepishly across the pillows, and then Viv started to laugh. The release of tension after all these years of wanting him was so breathtaking, so splendid, such a hilarious anticlimax after such an astonishing climax.

Her laughter ignited his and they ended up laughing so long and hard they had to use the sheet to wipe away tears. "In my defense," Ross said when he could speak, "it has been more than eighteen months since I last did this."

"You've been celibate that long?" Viv suffered a pang of unease because it gave their lovemaking more meaning than she was comfortable with. So the blonde in the photo on the mantel was Terri? The one he'd been dating at the time of the ambush and unceremoniously dumped, according to Dan. But Viv suddenly knew exactly why he'd cut her loose.

"How's your ex-girlfriend doing on the triathlete circuit?" she asked casually.

"First place in the world champs last year," he said proudly.

"I hope you take some credit for that," she said, and felt him tense as he realized the trap she'd laid for him.

"If you want to make it as an elite athlete, you have to

be single-minded," he said testily. "All I did was free her to make the most of her opportunities."

"Speaking of opportunities, I'll give you ten minutes' recovery and then we're doing it again."

Under her cheek, the muscles of his chest relaxed as Ross chuckled. The Iceman figured his reputation as a hard man was still intact, but Viv knew she'd never think of him the same again.

"I only need five," he said.

CHAPTER EIGHTEEN

A SOUND WOKE Ross from a deep sleep. Rolling over he caught a pale gleam of skin in the corner of his bedroom before Viv shrugged on her sweatshirt, covering the tiny angel wing tattoo on her back. She already wore jeans.

"What time is it?" he murmured, and she jumped, then glanced over her shoulder.

"Sorry, I was trying not to wake you. I'm just heading to the sofa bed."

They'd fallen asleep with the bedside lamp still on. He glanced at the clock beside it. Two in the morning. "We've got a few hours before the kids wake up. I'll set the alarm for half past five if you're worried."

"It's not the kids," she said. "Actually, I have this kind of rule."

Rule? Viv? Curious, Ross propped himself up on one arm. "Let's hear it."

"I don't sleep over with guys I have sex with."

"To stop them getting ideas?"

"Not that it's an issue with you," she hastened to add. "But it's become sort of a habit of mine…like Salsa turning three times each way in his basket before he settles. I hope you don't mind."

If anything he was intrigued. Fluffing up the pillows, Ross cupped his hands behind his head. "And all your lovers happily go along with this?"

Viv frowned. "We're not talking a cast of thousands."

Her gaze drifted to his biceps. "But, yes, they do. Normally, I make sure it's covered off before we do the deed—you caught me by surprise."

He was very glad to hear it. Ross patted the empty space beside him. "Best fill me in on how this works going forward. I wouldn't want to inadvertently infringe on any of your regulations."

Her eyes narrowed. "Are you making fun of me?"

"Hell, no." Ross feigned hurt. "I'm all about structure and forward planning, you know that."

"That's true," she acknowledged. "You are rather anal."

She'd pay for that. Maybe Ross was a stickler for rules but he always established their value first. As she approached the bed, he moved over—ostensibly to give Viv more room and the sheet fell to his hips. Decent only if you didn't look.

Viv dragged her gaze to his face.

"So," he prompted. "Your rules."

She perched on the bed. "The reason I broke it off with Jean Paul was because he didn't understand that I need my freedom."

The Frenchman who needed his head read for getting involved with the woman Ross had just taken to bed and potentially risked his relationship with Charlie for. The situation stopped being quite so funny.

"I generally emphasize that any relationship with me is transitory," she explained. "The truth is, I'm not all that hot on living up to people's expectations, so by spelling that out at the start, no one gets hurt."

"I've already learned to have no expectations where you're concerned," he said. "You only confound them."

She gave him a femme fatale smile, the one irresistibly mixed with mischief. "Good."

Reaching out a hand, Ross traced that smile. "So what do you usually do the morning after?"

"I'm not there the morning after," she reminded him.

"Then let me tell you what *I* would do if a woman stayed over. I'd make her breakfast…because she'd need her strength built up and the only reason you're smiling now is because we didn't get to round two yet because we both fell asleep."

He slid a hand under her sweatshirt, stroked it over the swell of her breast and felt the nipple peak. "Of course, you could leave *before* breakfast but I don't think Attilla and Harry or Salsa would be too happy about that. And I did promise to take the kids to see the gannet colony before you went home, but I'm sure they'll understand that the Cinderella rules come first."

He moved his hand to her other breast, watching her gaze become unfocused. "Except—darn it—in the afternoon I've been suckered into helping with Tilly's soccer training, but other than that I'll be sure to keep a respectful distance."

Viv pressed against his hand. He loved her sexual confidence. "Okay, in this context maybe the rules sound a little ridiculous," she conceded, her own fingers starting to explore. "But you must appreciate the intent. You've spent the last week nagging me to be careful."

Ross nuzzled her neck, breathing her in. "You being careful," he said, "is a major turn-on." Usually he was the one with the exit strategy. "And I completely respect your autonomy, but right now I'm also extremely interested in getting you naked again."

She shivered under his kisses, pushing him onto his back. Her jeans rasped deliciously against his cock as she straddled him. Her eyes were dark, her hair tumbled around the faded sweatshirt and under it her nipples were tight peaks in his palm. Ross experienced a moment of disquiet. He felt like a snowman feeling the first thaw of spring, surely this kind of heat didn't bode well.

He caught Viv's hips and stilled her sensuous movements. "Maybe you should be passing on some of your rules for self-restraint to your twin," he said. "Did you know she's been having phone sex with her husband? Charlie told me."

"I suspected as much when I dropped him off at the airport this morning. I only just stopped him from kissing me."

Ross didn't like that; didn't like his brother ogling her.

Viv sobered. "Ross, after what happened today, I'm going to try and talk Merry into telling Charlie the truth. To be honest, I've been having second thoughts since Charlie asked for a reconciliation. I ignored them because Merry was so desperate to keep the swap going and," she pulled a face, "I'm a sucker for my sister's approval. But also because I couldn't see a way of fixing this without someone getting hurt."

"And now you have a win-win for everybody?"

She nodded. "For Merry, Charlie and the children. Assuming she agrees."

"Go tomorrow," he said, relieved. "I'll handle the kids and Tilly's soccer training."

"Can you spare the time?" He liked how she took his rehab schedule seriously.

"I need a rest day from running." His leg still hurt from this afternoon's jog. "And the kids love playing in the weight room."

A slow smile curved her lips. "I'd kinda like to play in the weight room, too, some time," she teased. "I've always had this fantasy…"

"Yeah?" He pushed up between her thighs, watched her

register his hardness. "Hot, sweaty gym grunters do it for you?" He imagined her under him on the weight bench, spine arched as he thrust into her. Lost a little more self-control. His hands tightened around her hips. "What the hell am I going to do with you," he asked half-seriously.

Smiling, Viv pulled off her sweatshirt. "Taking my jeans off would be a good start."

VIV DIDN'T WARN MERRY she was coming, strolling into her hospital room at about two with a big smile, a steely determination and a sinking heart.

"Surprise!"

Her twin's head jerked around and Viv saw she held a cell to her ear. Merry's eyes widened in unmistakable dismay, and then she held a finger to her lips. "Uh-huh… Listen, I've just seen our little guy heading for the cat door…have to go…" She glanced away from Viv and lowered her voice. "You know I do. Enjoy the next conference session."

She cut the connection. "What's happened?"

"Nothing, the kids are with Ross." She decided not to tell Merry about the accident at day care. That was Viv's burden, not her sister's. "How's my husband?"

"Fine. I tell you now, Viv, if you've only come to repeat Dan's arguments you can save your breath."

"And hello to you, too."

Merry had the grace to look sheepish. "Sorry." She opened her arms. The sisters embraced. "I keep forgetting you're on my side. And thank you—" Merry's arms tightened "—for all your awesome miracle work over the past week."

"Make this harder, why don't you?"

"What does that mean?"

"Nothing, it's great to see you."

Stepping back, she gave her sister a critical once-over. "Pink-cheeked, certainly more pep, shine back in your hair...you must be having phone sex."

Merry blushed. "I have no idea what you're talking about."

"Uh-huh." Viv chanced a quick look at the surgical scar in the open cast and shuddered. "I'm assuming that's a better color?"

"I'm getting a closed cast tomorrow. Finally, Viv, it's all coming together. I just told Charlie that I'm cleaning the gutters on the garage. Cue a fall from the ladder, and he'll return from his conference to find me recuperating at home."

"Won't he think it strange that you didn't phone him immediately?"

"I'll say I didn't want to distract him from his committee responsibilities during their conference."

Viv cleared her throat. "About responsibilities."

"I need you to talk Ross into saying he took the children when I had my fall and then kept them overnight," Merry continued. "It will seem odd if he's not involved. Oh, and I've checked—there's a flight to the States at noon on Monday. I figure the kids and I can manage alone for a couple of hours until Charlie arrives home."

Too bad if Viv wasn't ready to go. But she'd already made up her mind to do this. When the swap began she didn't have a vested interest. As she'd told Ross at the time, her motives were pure. Lately, she'd been letting her need to bond with her twin override her conscience. It was time to practice what she preached.

Merry was still talking. "You won't be able to come home for six months at least—as a safety margin—and you'll need to dye your hair again. Looking the same as me is too dangerous." She paused to take a breath, and Viv seized her opportunity.

"Mere, I agree with Dan…you have to tell Charlie. No, don't pull a face and get all prickly. I think I've earned the right to an opinion, don't you?"

"Yes," Merry said grudgingly. "Just don't go sensible on me now."

"Actually," Viv smiled, "I've been sensible off and on for years."

"How would I know if you've changed? It's not as if we've spent much time together over the last decade."

"Now tell me how I stole all the nutrients in utero again."

"What?"

"Not important." Viv pulled up a chair. "Did it ever occur to you that you might be eaten up with guilt once the euphoria of being back together fades? Eventually you'll blurt out the truth to Charlie. But the longer you wait, the worse the repercussions will be."

"Except—"

"Let the best-sister-ever-whose-advice-you'll-never-doubt-again finish."

Merry nodded reluctantly.

"At the same time," Viv continued, "I think Ross and Dan are crazy expecting you to come clean without a plan to minimize the fallout. Surely if the two of us are smart enough to sell Charlie a lie, we're smart enough to sell him the truth?"

Her twin folded her arms. "Go on."

"The guy loves you, Mere." Viv watched her sister's face soften. "I've learned that these past few days. And Linda's death has given him a new perspective. I really believe he'll come around, particularly if we convince him this is all my fault." She hadn't told Ross this part of her plan because she suspected he'd disagree with it. Viv wasn't too fond of it herself.

"It is all your fault."

"That's what I said. Of course you have a teeny tiny bit of culpability in letting me believe Charlie was the cheater, hence my initial rush to defend you against Ross, but let's not split hairs. So, here's how we sell it." She ticked the points off on her fingers as she said, "I talked you into going to the interview, I talked you into the deception, and you played along not only to protect Charlie in his time of grief but because your painkillers—" Viv made a mental note to check whether the hospital used medicinal marijuana "—left you dazed and confused. In short, you had impaired judgment. Now your medication's been reduced, your head has cleared and you're understandably horrified by what you've been a party to and… Why are you shaking your head?"

"Except Charlie and I have been talking…a lot over the past few days. He knows I'm lucid."

That's right, the phone sex. She'd forgotten her sister hadn't stuck to the plan. "Damn it, Merry, why couldn't you have played it cool like we agreed."

"You don't understand how it feels to be crazy in love."

"You're not the only one with something to lose here," Viv said quietly. "Charlie's going to hate me. I'm risking access to your kids, access to Ross."

"What do you *mean* access to Ross?" Her twin's gaze narrowed. "Viv, you didn't!"

"I admit the timing's not—"

"And you called *me* irresponsible," Merry interrupted, her eyes kindling. "*Now* I understand why you're here." She laughed bitterly. "Silly me for believing this whole sisters-standing-together speech. Trying to persuade me to tell Charlie is all about getting on side with your old crush!

You've always ditched me when someone more interesting came along."

"That is too ridiculous to grace with a reply!" Viv gathered in air to fuel one. "What the hell do you think I've been doing this past week other than being there for you?" How could Merry not understand what it was costing her to make this offer? "But that doesn't matter, does it? Because there's always some guilt trip you can lay on me from our childhood." The closeness Viv had fondly imagined they were building was a sham. "And yes, actually, I *did* prefer other people's company to yours and you know why?" She leaned forward. "Because I didn't have to worry about them running to tattletale back to Mum and Dad every five minutes to reinforce their position as Goody Two-shoes favorite!"

Merry gasped. "Maybe I *tattled* to stop you getting into even worse trouble...did you ever think of that?" she snarled. "And I was a Goody Two-shoes because I knew our parents couldn't handle any more pressure than Hurricane Viv was already giving them."

"I am so *sick* of everything that went wrong in our family somehow being my fault!" Viv shot back. "As long as I was there to take the blame, none of you had to deal with your own issues. Like Mum and Dad being married to someone they shouldn't be, or your anal-compulsive need for approval." Momentarily she stalled. Hadn't *she* just struggled with that? No, they were nothing alike.

Viv stood up, and the chair toppled backward. "Maybe my acting out was a release for the tension of living with unhappy parents, ever think of that, Miss I'm-so-sensitive? Honestly, if it wasn't for Dan, I would have gone crazy. And I may be a screwup but at least I don't have to bring someone else down! Everyone you love has to meet the same impossible standards you set yourself or be crushed by your disappointment! Charlie said as much when he asked for another chance." Viv mimicked her brother-in-law. "'How did I shrink from a person you could look up to and respect into another kid that needing looking after?' The poor bastard doesn't understand yet that nothing he ever does will be good enough for you."

"What would *you* know about maintaining a relationship?" Merry snapped. "You can't even commit to three-minute noodles. You can't even commit to a weekly phone call to your twin. No, I get to talk to you twice a month if I'm lucky, if I do all the work. So don't act as if it's going to be a sacrifice giving up contact with Tilly and Harry. You've never shown more than a cursory interest in them or anyone other than yourself."

Hot tears stung Viv's eyes. She blinked them away and fell back to a defensive childhood position. Pretending not to care. "Fine," she said coldly. "It's my bad. It's always been my bad. Make me the scapegoat like you've done all our lives. But do it alone, Mere. I. Am. Done." Grabbing her bag, she stormed to the door, nearly colliding with the irate duty nurse.

"What on earth is going on here? We can hear shouting at the nurses' station."

"My twin's reverting to type," Merry said bitterly. "Abandoning me to sink or swim."

"Oh, I have no doubt you'll float," Viv retorted. "Just use your overinflated sense of superiority."

Ross HEARD MEREDITH'S ELECTRIC garage door rumble open at eight, thirty minutes after he'd put the kids to bed. He'd already guessed that Viv wouldn't want them seeing her upset, which was why she'd returned home so late.

He switched off the TV remote. Having talked down one distraught woman, he fully expected to need to soothe another, but Viv entered the living room with a bright smile.

"Sorry I'm later than expected." She dropped her keys and bag on the coffee table. "How was Tilly's soccer game? Did Harry go down okay?"

Ross didn't do preamble. "Meredith's been phoning almost every hour."

Still smiling, Viv met his gaze. "Of *course* she has." The ancient Greeks constructed their shields by overlapping layers of hardened leather, left unpainted if the owner was an exile. Her eyes were exactly that impervious brown. "So," she added lightly, "you're up with the play then."

Maybe preamble was a good idea. "I saved dinner for you."

"I'm not hungry."

"Tea?"

"I'm not thirsty."

"Then let's talk about this."

With a humorless laugh, Viv kicked off her twin's sensible shoes. "Hey, you have Merry's side of the story. That's all that counts. I'm self-centered, egotistical and unreliable." Hauling her hair loose from her ponytail, Viv flicked her fingers through it with short, sharp strokes. "Thank God she reminded me before I did something stupid like ruin my life for her." She strode down the hall toward the spare room.

A minute later, he heard the squeak of suitcase wheels. Ross went to the doorway. "So that's it, then? Vivienne Jansen is giving up."

"Yep." Pulling the red suitcase, she marched past him. "I gave it my best and it's still not good enough. Well, I'm done. I'm leaving her to it. There's an eleven o'clock flight to L.A. I'm sure I can pick up a connection to New York."

He followed her into the master bedroom, where she

flung the suitcase on the bed. Unzipping it, Viv pulled out some of her own clothes, then started to strip. Off came her sister's easy fit denims, the pink collared shirt. Folding them carefully, she hurled them into the open wardrobe. The underwear had to be Viv's own, a matching set of black lace and red velvet stripes, which he suspected had been intended for him when she'd come home to change this morning. Ross tried not to let it distract him.

"This is crazy."

"Running true to form then. You can tell Charlie the whole sorry saga, or phone Dan to come and take over the kids…I don't care what happens anymore." Roughly, she tugged on black denim leggings, then shrugged on a gray mohair-knit sweater. "Tilly needs to take a permission slip for a school outing tomorrow. Harry only likes the sippy cup with a hippo on it. His backup blankie's in the dryer." She clipped a thin gold chain around her hips as though donning armor but struggled with the clasp.

"Viv," he said.

"Stow the guilt straight into the suitcase," she instructed. "There's always room for more, according to my sister. Apparently I'm responsible for everything that goes wrong in her life." Sitting on the bed, she yanked on a knee-high suede boot.

Argument would be useless until she'd calmed down.

She glanced up suspiciously. "What, no lecture?"

"I didn't think you wanted my opinion."

"I don't." Viv yanked on the other boot and stood, all despair and hostility.

He folded his arms. "That's what I figured."

"Good!" She emptied the bureau drawer, stuffing fistfuls of underwear down the sides of the suitcase. "Merry will work something out, and if she doesn't you or Dan will…I refuse to feel guilty about this."

Moving between the en suite bathroom and bedroom, she gathered toiletries and makeup. "I'm twenty-nine years old. I don't need to take this crap from my twin anymore."

She grabbed one of the lipsticks, crossed to the mirror and applied it with slashing strokes. Ross recognized the shade as the one she'd worn at Linda's. Poppy-red. The lipstick smudged. "Damn it!" Angrily she reached for a tissue and scrubbed at the mistake. "Anyway, the kids will be so much better off without my subversive influence. Hell, I've already corrupted *your* ethics so my work here is done."

"And an excellent job you did, too. Let me know if you need a reference."

Her gaze met his in the mirror, bright with defiance and unshed tears.

The defiance won. "Dang, I'm good. I even taught you how to crack jokes at inappropriate moments." Tossing aside the lipstick, she dug in a jewelry case.

"If you're such a bad role model," Ross commented, "Why is Meredith raising her daughter to be just like you?"

"Is that meant to make me feel better?" Viv pulled out a pair of large hoop earrings.

"Independent, a free-thinker, opinionated, resistant to social pressure."

She didn't reply but her hands started trembling so she couldn't thread the metal catch into her ear and she shoved the earrings back in the case.

Ross persisted. "Is it really unfixable? Meredith doesn't think so."

Viv snorted. "Only because my leaving jeopardizes her precious plans for Charlie!"

Digging in the suitcase, she dragged out a black jacket, scarf and crumpled hat. She punched the latter into shape, a gray felt cowboy's Stetson with a black hatband, put it on and tilted it on a jaunty angle. Under the brim her eyes were bleak. He hated seeing her hurt like this, hated being shut out.

"So is this the end of the affair?" he asked quietly.

"Technically, we didn't get past a one-night stand."

He didn't reply and a blush stained her cheeks. "Anyway, you should be glad to see the back of me," she said gruffly. "I've made your life tougher, taken you away from training, jeopardized your relationship with Charlie…and at least my leaving will force Merry to come clean."

"And yet I don't want you to go," he said. "I guess you really have brought me over to the dark side."

She dropped her gaze, hiding her expression under her hat brim, but her throat swallowed convulsively. "Please don't make this harder."

"I won't lock you in the bathroom if that's what you're worried about."

With an attempt at a smile, she picked up her coat and slung the scarf around her neck. "I would only have climbed out the window anyway."

"Then it's clear you've made your choice."

That brought her head up. "This isn't my choice," she insisted. "Merry's made it impossible for me to stay…you must see that."

What he saw was a woman who'd regret this when she cooled off. "*Impossible* isn't in Vivienne Jansen's vocabulary."

She straightened the glossy black beads on the scarf's tassels. "I can't let her affect me like this anymore, Ross," she said in a shaky voice. "It's taken years to stop being guilty for wanting my own life and she's never going to forgive me for that, so what's the point? I don't have any reserves left." She reached for the suitcase handle and he put a hand over hers.

"I'll take it."

"Thank you."

He didn't move his hand. "Will you ask yourself one question for me?"

Her fingers trembled under his. "What?"

"Disregard what Merry thinks. Disregard what I think. Instead find a way past all the hurt and anger and bitterness and ask yourself how much resolving this matters to *you*."

Viv didn't answer until she was sure she wasn't going to burst into tears. For long minutes she struggled with a lifetime of walking away as an escape from hurt and pain and things she really believed she couldn't cope with.

"It goes back to the womb, Ross," she finally rasped through a constricted throat. "She even blames me for making her malnourished, for God's sake." Her hand turned to tighten convulsively on his, then released. "I'm sorry, but I've got to protect myself."

"At least you know," he said.

"I'll phone for a taxi outside." Blindly, she wheeled her suitcase past him to the front door and opened it. "It's been fun!"

Ross bent to kiss her goodbye and she moved her face so his lips brushed her cheek because she'd be a fool to make this harder than it already was. Which was why she wasn't going near the children. Ross caught her in a hug so hard she thought he might crush her heart. "It's okay," he said. "I get it. Goodbye, Viv."

CHAPTER NINETEEN

OUTSIDE, SHE LEANED against the door and the tears she'd been holding in streamed silently down her cheeks like warm rain. A small yip at her feet made her look down. Salsa peered up in the dark. She half laughed, half sobbed. "At least I'm making someone's day by leaving." The schnoodle whined. "Go ahead—" Viv used the end of her scarf to wipe away tears "—escort me off the premises. I expect you're dying to."

Salsa sat down and presented his paw. Trust him to be a sucker for a distressed female. A sob escaped her. "Don't you *dare* start being friendly now!"

Wheeling the suitcase down the front path, she closed the gate on the schnoodle, sat on her suitcase and called a cab. "Go away," she said, trying to ignore Salsa's whine for attention through the gate. "It's too late."

The dog barked. Ross would come out at this rate and Viv didn't want him to see her a blubbering mess. "Fine, you can wait with me but I am *not* patting you." As she opened the gate she glanced at the house, but there was no one at the lit windows, no one having second thoughts about stopping her doing this.

All week, the guy had been only too happy to give her the black and white and lay down the law. Now when she wanted someone, anyone, to point her in the right direction, he'd been reasonable and left the decision to her.

Keeping a tight grip on Salsa's collar, Viv returned to

her perch on the suitcase and wished the taxi would hurry up. Maybe Sanjay would be driving. *Don't think of it as running away from your problems, think of it as running toward new opportunities.*

But the words rang hollow. When had she let these people sink their hooks into her? Salsa whimpered and she started crying again. "Doesn't Merry realize that by alienating me she'll have to shoulder the blame alone?" She demanded. "Suffer the consequences alone?" Salsa barked and she averted her face. "Not my problem," she told him.

Are you sure it's unfixable? Merry doesn't think so. "Anyway, Merry's olive branch isn't about me, she only cares about Charlie finding out. Well, she should have thought about that before she called me Hurricane! God, I hate that nickname."

"Hurricane lives in her own world and it's not the real one."

"Our Hurricane Viv's like Mr. Magoo…blind to risk."

"Don't trust Hurricane with anything you don't want lost or broken."

All said with great humor and affection. And all true—until she turned twelve and grew up a bit.

Unfortunately by then her parents had gotten into the habit of giving Dan and Merry responsibility for anything that mattered. With a 550-hectare beef and sheep farm to run, they didn't have the luxury of a margin of error.

Salsa nudged her hand and she gave in and patted him, running her fingers through the feathery coat.

Until she went to boarding school at fifteen, Viv had honestly thought her unreliability was some kind of congenital condition that couldn't be cured. Then she discovered teachers who didn't know her history actually had expectations of her.

"In a family crisis," she told Salsa, "Dan is still first

call, then Merry." He licked her hand with a warm, rough tongue. She was never expected to provide practical or emotional assistance and it was turned down when she did. So Viv stopped offering. Pulled back, pretended she didn't care.

In her twenties that had been easy. Why take on the burden of care with an international career to build? But on the cusp of thirty she was tired of being left out of the loop. Dan, Merry, Mum and Dad—they'd all experienced personal crises over the past year. Not one of them had called on her for support. And that hurt. Coming home had been a conscious effort to change the script, and discovering her competent twin in dire need had seemed a heaven-sent opportunity.

"So much for that." She fondled Salsa's ears. Within twelve hours she'd catapulted herself straight into a situation that reinforced her childhood reputation. "I wanted to make up for not being the sister she needed." Wearily, she laid her head on the dog's warm coat. "But don't worry. Ross will clean up my mess."

Only, who would clean up after Ross when it finally hit home that he'd never be deployed again? He'd cold-shouldered her brother and Charlie couldn't see past his hero worship. Nate was on another continent.

She stood as the cab arrived, the taxi light a beacon.

The cabbie wound down his window. "Sorry, lady, we don't take dogs."

Viv realized she was gripping Salsa's collar. That she couldn't seem to let go.

How much does resolving this matter to you? Damn Ross. Even his non-judgment was judgment. Talking as though she was capable of making a different choice when they both knew she was Roadrunner through and through.

Where was beating his head against a brick wall getting him? Nowhere.

But he hadn't given up.

"Lady? Did you hear what I said?"

She looked at the driver helplessly. "I think I've changed my mind."

He grumbled, so she gave him a few dollars, then picked up her suitcase and let the dog through the gate. It clanged shut behind her like a prison cell's door.

Inside she flung the suitcase away so that it toppled with a dramatic bang, then realized there was no one to hear it. The room was empty.

Ross hadn't even waited until she left before moving on. Viv raced to the window in time to see the taxi's red taillights flicker out like the bulbs of a Christmas tree as it rounded the corner.

"You came back."

She spun around to see him at the top of the stairs.

"Obviously I can't leave now that you've made me feel it would be a cop-out." She cloaked her panic under an accusation. "So congratulations, you're stuck with me a bit longer."

"Okay."

She put her hands on her hips. "And frankly I can't believe you were prepared to just let me go like that. It's completely irresponsible. Haven't those kids suffered enough disruption? Did you forget that Tilly's game is tomorrow and neither of her parents are going to be there? Not to mention I'm the coach."

"Aren't I the new coach?"

"Assistant coach. Don't get ideas."

"I'm sorry," he said meekly. He came down the stairs and the light caught his dimple.

"This isn't funny, Ross. I hate my twin right now and I

have no idea how this will turn out or where we go from here."

"We still have another two days before Charlie gets home. We'll come up with something."

"And if you expect me to apologize to my sister then think again. Make sure you tell Merry that."

"I just got off the phone after telling her you were leaving."

"Couldn't wait to break the good news, huh?"

"She phoned me."

Viv resisted the urge to ask what she'd said. "Well, you can ring her back and say I might still be here but I'm not speaking to her until I receive an apology."

"How can she give you an apology if you won't talk to her?"

"She can write one, email one…Tweet it or post it on Facebook. Yes, Facebook. I demand a grovel through a public forum."

He smiled at her and Viv suddenly realized the magnitude of what she'd taken on by staying. Her legs gave way. She sank onto the couch, more scared than she'd ever been in her life. She didn't just leave before people relied on her too much. Viv looked at Ross. She left before she relied on them.

"I should have gone," she said. "You could have fixed this…you or Dan. And the kids don't really need me. Harry's baby brain would have forgotten me in a couple of days. And Tilly's going to turn off my life support when I'm an old lady, and have my body converted to bio fuel."

Ross laughed.

"She's your next of kin, too," she reminded him.

"Look on the bright side," he suggested. "At least we get to have sex again."

"You don't decide that," she cautioned. "I do. And

frankly I don't enjoy being taken for granted. Where's the gratitude, where's the reverence? Take a number and stand in line, buddy."

Still, he smiled. "I see how this works. You've had your way with me and I'm no longer a challenge. So you're casting me aside like that poor bastard Jean Paul."

"You knew the score," she blustered.

He sat beside her and stretched an arm along the couch. "And what if I'm not ready to be cast aside?"

An anticipatory shiver went up Viv's spine at the delicious contrast between the lazy drawl and the glint in his eyes.

She'd gotten so accustomed to Ross resisting her that she hadn't considered what would happen if he decided he wanted her. And of course, she realized with a thrill of dismay, he *had* decided. Last night.

Okay, this had to stop now. "I don't want to fall in love with you," she said baldly. "And if we keep going like this there's a risk I might." It was painful admitting the truth, but the alternative—heartbreak—was worse. He recoiled almost imperceptibly, but enough to confirm her survival instincts were spot-on.

"I can't consider a serious relationship at the moment," he said. "My focus is resurrecting my career."

"I know I'm not a priority," she said. "I'm not asking to be."

"And you live on the other side of the world."

Where there's a will there's a way.

He grew unnerved by her silence. "And you're as career-focused as I am," he reminded her.

That didn't preclude a life.

Viv put them both out of their misery. "Ross, we don't need to have this conversation, because I already get it. I hold the world record for speed dating, remember? So we're pulling back and no harm done."

She walked him to the door. "Will you phone Merry for me?" she asked. "I can't talk to her tonight. I'll visit her in the morning. And ask her for her sitter's number...I'm guessing you've had enough of the kids?"

"I have something on in the morning. I'll meet you at soccer after school. Say, thirty minutes early for a warm-up?"

"Sounds good."

They ran out of small talk and stared at each other. She knew the scent of him now, the taste, the warmth. And he was out of bounds.

With a nod, he walked to his car.

And that, thought Viv, was that.

IN THE END VIV TOOK the kids with her to visit Merry. It seemed odd to consider them a civilizing influence but at the very least their presence would remind the adults to behave like grown-ups. And she and Merry would have something to look at instead of each other. A mirror image was the last thing she needed when she felt bruised by Merry, and confused about Ross.

She sent the human shields in first. Tilly charged into the room yelling, "Surprise!" while Harry made a beeline for the levers on the hospital bed frame that he'd discovered last visit. Merry wasn't there.

"She's getting a new cast," said the ward sister, a thin middle-aged woman with the name tag Florence. "Which is just as well or I wouldn't be able to tell you apart." She swept a jaundiced eye over the children. "I don't want them wrecking the room."

"That's okay, I can supervise," said Viv.

"I doubt that." Florence folded sinewy arms over her

starched uniform. "I hear every time you show up there's a verbal skirmish and I'm telling you straight, there'll be none of that on my shift." She picked up her clipboard. "Who's picking your twin up tomorrow?" Merry had been in hospital for so long she was well enough not to need an ambulance transfer.

"Our brother, Dan Jansen," said Viv. After dropping Merry in Auckland, Dan intended to head to Ross's beach house. He'd had enough, he said, of being ignored. Viv was staying out of that one.

Florence made a note on her clipboard. "Not too early," she warned. "Mrs. Coltrane can't be discharged until after the surgeon makes his rounds."

"I'll let Dan know." Viv glanced nervously down the corridor. Still no sign of Merry. "How nice to have a name that fits your profession," she said, trying to fill time. "Is your surname Nightingale?"

The other woman didn't so much as flicker an eyelid. "It's Hore."

"C'mon, kids, let's get out of Florence's hair."

They went and waited in the room, which smelled of freesias and disinfectant and scrambled eggs. Tilly started to fret. "Mum can't be too long. We can't be late for the game." The whole drive she'd been torn between joy at a reunion and anxiety they wouldn't make it back for kick-off at two.

"I'll allow plenty of time, I promise…hey…look who's here!"

Merry was wheeled in by a young male orderly, leg stretched out in a new cast.

"Mum." Tilly raced over and hugged her mother, while Harry tried to clamor awkwardly onto her lap. "Surprise! Are you surprised?"

Merry's eyes filled as she gathered her children close.

"Oh, you both feel so good. Yes, honey, I'm surprised. It's so great to see you." She looked nervously over at Viv. The atmosphere thickened like an Atlantic fog.

"Wow," said the Maori orderly. "You have an identical twin, how cool is that!"

"Iv," said Harry helpfully.

"Did you hear that, Mum?" Tilly tugged on Merry's hospital gown. "Harry can say lots of new words. Go on, Harry, say other stuff."

The baby looked at the smiling stranger behind the wheelchair and buried his head in his mother's lap.

"Say 'Ross'…say 'car,'" Tilly coaxed. "He can, Mum, honest. C'mon, Harry!"

The toddler lifted his head. "Iv," he repeated.

"Iv, that means Viv," Tilly explained. She crouched beside her brother. "But you're not supposed to call her Iv, Harry, you're supposed to call her Mummy."

Viv and Merry's eyes met briefly and then Merry concentrated on stroking her baby's head. The puzzled orderly looked at Viv. "Shall we get my sister resettled?" she suggested brightly.

Tilly inspected the cast after he'd gone. "When can we sign it?" she demanded.

"When it's properly hardened. Give me another hug, it's so good to see you. But why are you wearing your soccer boots?"

"We're going to the field after this and I wanted to be ready in case we run out of time. But I haven't put my shin pads in yet, that would be silly." Viv could only marvel at her niece's sudden loquaciousness. She'd obviously missed her mum. Tilly paused for breath. "Are those chocolates yours? Can I have one?"

Harry forgot about cuddles and hugs with Mummy. "Me!"

"Just one, Til, then hide them where your brother can't see them."

Viv saw her opportunity. "Tilly, why don't you and Harry go offer them to the nurses at reception." Tilly loved playing Lady Bountiful. "I need a private word with your mum."

"Not to the mean one," Tilly said decidedly. "C'mon, Harry." He looked at the chocolates she cradled and didn't protest when his big sister grabbed his hand. Viv waited until their footsteps faded and took a deep breath.

"I'm sorry." They said it at the same time, smiled and said, "Snap," then smiled again. It broke some of the awful tension. But not all of it.

"We both said some pretty harsh things last night," Viv began tentatively.

Merry waved that aside. "Let's just forgive and forget," she suggested. For an instant, Viv was tempted. But then nothing would change.

And it had to change.

"You were right," she said, "I hate being a twin." Merry's smile grew fixed. "But it wasn't about pushing you away. It was about avoiding comparisons. You sailed serenely from home to school to community, leaving no wake." She pulled a face. "Extreme water-skiers only dream on my kind of wake. Whenever I looked at you, I could see the person I should be…and how far I fell short—no matter how hard I tried."

There was a short silence. "It hurt, Viv," Merry said finally. "Particularly when we went to boarding school and you got caught up with new friends and new projects and I hardly ever saw you. I was so homesick I used to cry myself to sleep every night."

Viv moved to the side of the bed. "I didn't know that."

"I didn't want you to. I was ashamed that I couldn't

embrace boarding school as the great new adventure you did. I wanted home and Mum and Dad and knowing everyone again and being safe…. Pathetic, huh?" Merry fiddled with a loose thread on her new cast.

"But now you're strong and independent and successful," Viv insisted. When her sister shook her head, she added with a touch of impatience, "I've lived your life, Mere, I've seen how much you do. How many people rely on you."

Merry yanked the thread on her cast free. "I thought about what Charlie said to you all last night."

"I shouldn't have criticized your marriage."

"No, but you did." She stopped playing with the thread. "When my marriage started going stale I tried to show Charlie I was indispensable, that no one could do things as well as me. Except it backfired. He wanted to spend less time with me, not more, which only pushed my panic button because I'd already gone down that road…with you." Her eyes were full of painful uncertainty. "What's wrong with me, Viv, that the people I love outgrow me?"

"Oh, Mere." With a gulp, Viv scrambled onto the mattress and the two sisters hugged each other. "That's not true. I never outgrew you. I'm totally in awe of you. Intimidated by you. It was easier to pretend I didn't want what you had than compete. I'm the one who's pathetic."

Gently Merry freed herself, fumbled for a box of tissues and handed one to Viv. "The children can't see us like this," she said, and they both blew their noses. "Why do we always have to compare ourselves," she added. "It's exhausting."

Climbing off the bed, Viv pulled up a chair. "Maybe because our lives have taken such different paths we're constantly wondering if we chose the right one?"

Merry gave a watery laugh. "Gee, part-time nurse and full-time suburban mom or international theatrical success…it's a tough choice. C'mon, Viv, you can't possibly desire mine."

"Can't I?" She was conscious of feeling wistful. "Hard as it was, I enjoyed being you." She picked up her twin's hand. "I liked being the sensible one, the dependable one. I liked hearing about Tilly's day at school and soothing your toddler when he was cranky and not eating alone every night over a sketch pad or sewing machine. And I'm completely envious of how much your husband loves you."

Merry swallowed.

"And, God, I love your kids." Viv dabbed at her eyes again.

"Not too much, I need them back." Merry returned her grip. "Whatever happens, you're in their life, Viv. I promise…. They're perfect, aren't they?"

Somewhere down the corridor, Harry let out a piercing shriek. "Someone tried to take the chocolates from him," Viv guessed. "I should go get them."

Merry's fingers tightened on hers. "In a minute… I'm completely jealous of your verve and your style, I love your optimism and your gutsy approach to life and I'm tired of being the one who cautions everyone to be careful. I want to have more fun in my life, Viv. I've had a lot of opportunity to think, lying in this damn hospital. I want to find a passion that's only mine and I want to be as generous in spirit as you are."

"You have to tell Charlie, Mere."

Her twin bit her lip. "I know."

"He only took the kiss so hard because you've been encouraging him to judge you by the ridiculously high standards you set yourself. But he's weathered the initial shock and bounced back. Yes, the truth will be a severe jolt, but he'll get over it like he did the kiss. And if you keep doing something outrageous with me on a regular basis, we'll soon have the man so desensitized you'll soon be able to dance naked on a bar and he won't bat an eyelash."

"See," said Merry half laughing, half crying, "that's the kind of attitude I need more of."

Viv was struck by a revelation. "God, we're fools, Mere. There's no reason we can't take the best of each other's worlds. We've got the same genes after all."

"You said it didn't work like that. Remember one twin gay and one straight."

"I was using *gay* in its historical sense of being happy."

"Liar!" Merry smiled but she was plainly terrified. "What am I going to say to Charlie?"

"That's easy, tell him you need him. It's all he cares about."

"I *do* need him."

Then you've got it covered, haven't you?"

Merry squared her shoulders. "I'll tell him as soon as I can do it face-to-face," she said. "What else did you like about my life?"

"That your day holds a whole lot more variety and excitement than mine," Viv said. "I don't want to end up on my deathbed surrounded by designing awards. They have to be on one side of the deathbed, sure, but I'd like family on the other. Maybe even my own family." She looked at her twin. "You have no idea how scary it is to admit that."

"Yes, I do. Because it's the only area in your life where you're a yellow-bellied coward. Come to think of it," she added, "so is Ross. That must make the courtship interesting."

Viv frowned. "We're cooling it off."

"I thought I could see the whites of your eyes."

"Anyway, all Ross cares about is getting fit enough for redeployment."

"It *used to be* all he cared about," Merry agreed. "Before

you came we saw him maybe once a month, if we were lucky. Since our separation, Charlie's been spending weekends at Ross's with the kids. But I think Ross only tolerated it because Charlie needed a refuge. How much time has he spent with *you* this week?"

"To protect Charlie's interests, help organize the funeral—"

"And the sex contributes to that how? No, there's a lot more to it."

Viv shook her head. "You're wrong, Mere. Last night, when I told him I was developing feelings for him he backed off so quickly he left tire marks. He's horrified by the idea."

"So? You're horrified, too. Why should Ross be any different?"

She had a point. "Anyway, I don't want to fall in love with him."

"Face it, Viv, the only reason you're panicking is because Mum's convinced you marriage is a prison. Not that I've been the greatest advertisement for the institution lately. But Ross is perfect for you. He's career-driven himself so he won't be threatened by your success, or fazed by a long-distance relationship. Everyone deployed in the SAS accepts regular separations as normal."

The kids appeared, marched in by Florence and looking delighted with themselves. "Supervise, huh?" she said to Viv. "I found them working their way through a box of chocolates with my nurses."

"It's no good," said Tilly matter-of-factly. "This lady's just mean."

Narrowing her eyes, Florence left them to it.

Merry looked at Viv as Tilly and Harry clambered on the bed. "And best of all he knows exactly what he's letting himself in for with the Jansen family."

"Didn't you hear me?" Viv stopped the baby playing horsey on her sister's cast by resettling him on her lap. "The guy's not interested in getting serious."

"What's that got to do with anything?" Merry smoothed her daughter's hair. "If we waited for men to be ready, the human race would be extinct by the time they made up their minds. All you have to decide is whether *you're* interested."

CHAPTER TWENTY

ANYONE WHO COULDN'T PASS the basic RFL—required fitness level—test was considered nonoperational. And part of that test was running two and a half kilometers under ten minutes.

Ross had done the calculations in his head a thousand times. He did them again now in the shower before the time trial, running the water as hot as he could stand to warm the scarred muscle.

Two and a half kilometers broke down to covering two hundred and fifty meters per minute. Or two hundred and sixty-four yards—he knew the sums in metric and imperial. Hell, he knew them in Swahili. Once Ross would have finished with minutes to spare; now he'd need every precious second.

He massaged out the knots in his thigh on autopilot, as used to the ritual as he was to shaving or cleaning his teeth.

The test would have to be done again officially, with the option of a do-over two weeks later if he failed. But Ross knew what his physical therapist and specialist didn't. He'd reached the limit of what his body could achieve. This was as good as his mangled limb was going to get in terms of performance and he'd only got this far through sacrificing pretty much everything else—social life, family life, coaching Tilly's soccer team. His body couldn't sustain this level of intensity. Or the resulting pain.

The irony of course was that once he was back on patrol

he'd be sitting in a Dumvee ninety percent of the time. But it was his speed under fire, the explosive ten percent that mattered.

Turning off the shower, he dressed quickly in running shorts and a T-shirt. His leg hurt, but then it always did. Yesterday's so-called rest day looking after the kids had proved a major workout. He'd been caught up in the sisters' drama, and then unceremoniously dumped.

Viv's common sense in pulling back before they got too deep should have come as a relief. It hadn't and that bothered the hell out of him. He hadn't slept well. Not that he was sleeping well anyway since his argument with Dan. He needed to do this trial today. He needed to know.

Filling a water bottle, he headed out to the truck. Ross had deliberately waited for low tide so that he could drive along the beach—permissible at Muriwai—to a favorite secluded haunt.

The weather had settled overnight but the surf had grown through a subantarctic storm some thousand miles south and spray misted the shoreline, salting the air.

Waves rolled in like juggernauts, peaking to a perfect arcing wall of green water. Each hung on the cusp of falling before toppling in thundering white water, strewing clumps of brown seaweed the length of the beach.

He parked the SUV at the edge of the dunes and walked first, easing the tension out of his muscles and concentrating his will. Two and a half kilometers along the beach lay his finish line—weather-silvered driftwood.

When Ross first bought his plot at Muriwai he'd talked his friends into helping him clear it—no easy task, it bristled with gorse and wild blackberries. They'd attacked the scrub with machetes and axes on a scorching summer day, not a whisper of breeze to bring relief and the cicadas creating a deafening cacophony around them.

After dark the five of them—Lee, Nate, Steve, Ross and Dan—made camp on this section of beach, using the driftwood to shield a fire, drinking beer, stargazing and planning their blazing trail to glory.

Ross only needed to close his eyes to conjure their faces, burnished by firelight—Steve, the Jansen's cousin. Assured, laconic, already married to Claire, their anchor and leader. Lee, the youngest, a cocky extrovert, impulsive in matters of the heart. Both dead now.

He didn't dwell on Dan's face because he was too close to hating him right now and Ross didn't want to cross that line. And it hurt too much to picture Nate. The affection was there but the respect was gone.

Someone had to be the last man standing, but Dan didn't understand that, and it grieved Ross. It upset him that Dan and Nate had moved on from the SAS. It seemed a betrayal of Lee's and Steve's memory. Remaining staunch was a matter of honor. Of respect. Of duty. Of will.

Who am I if I'm not a soldier?

Muscles loosened, he took a slug from his water bottle, chucked it into the SUV and locked the vehicle, putting the keys in his pocket. His starting point was a tussock of toi toi—white feathery pampas grass. Lining up beside it, Ross set the alarm on his Heuer for ten minutes. He'd decided he wouldn't look at it, simply run as fast as he could toward the driftwood and try to beat the alarm.

His heart was already racing. Fine, he could use the adrenaline. Ross took a few deep breaths, readied himself then punched the start button on his watch and kicked into a run. His injured leg didn't have the same stride as his good one so he'd evolved a rolling gait, light on the left, heavy on the right. It wasn't pretty but it worked.

The pace started to bite and he sucked in more air, imagined the oxygen like good oil flowing through every limb and muscle. His leg started to protest; he ignored it. He glanced behind to check the position of his SUV, annoyed that he hadn't marked halfway. Ahead he could pick out the driftwood, the silver stump gleaming through the sea mist. Fixing his gaze on it, Ross dug deep. His heels crunched into the hard-packed sand.

The X factor that made an SAS trooper a one-percenter wasn't strength, skill or toughness. In selection all of that was deliberately stripped away. So that when your muscles were screaming to the point you could hardly put one foot in front of the other and you were so sleep-deprived you'd lost any sense of when this torture would end, the only thing that would get you over the line—and into the elite corps—was how bad you wanted it.

Ross didn't just want this. He *needed* it.

The fire in his leg radiated up and down the left side of his body, pulsing so white-hot that spots appeared before his eyes. The driftwood was maybe half a kilometer away. Gritting his teeth he started pumping his arms like pistons. Unable to help himself he glanced at his watch… three minutes left. He could do this. Five hundred meters, four hundred. His breath hissed, his lungs burned. But he was going to make it. He was—

His knee gave way so fast Ross didn't have time to throw out a hand. Instinctively he rolled, but his left temple and cheek hit first, and he landed jarringly on his side. Dazed, Ross touched his face. Blood. His leg was a continuous scream of agony.

His leg. Hauling himself to a sitting position he stretched it out gingerly, then hunched forward and rode out the nausea. His eye watered trying to get rid of the sand.

The alarm on his watch emitted a shrill beeping. Ross tore it off and threw it against the weather-hardened drift-

wood. But the damn thing was impactproof, waterproof…
idiotproof.

Everything burned, his eye, his leg, his heart, the graze
on his cheek. He hobbled down to the ice-cold surf and
ducked his head under to rinse the grit out of his eye and
wash away the blood.

When his limbs were numb with cold he stumbled out
and lay on the shoreline and let the hiss of water roll over
him. He could drown. For a split second Ross considered
it. Rough swells, strong rips, swimming alone: His family
would never guess it wasn't an accident.

But Dan would.

Teeth chattering with cold, he shoved to his feet, one
hand instinctively going to support his injury.

And if Dan knew, then Viv would know.

The SUV was two and a half kilometers south. A couple
of hundred meters into it, he found a piece of driftwood
and used it as a cane.

VIV STOOD ON THE SIDELINES, Harry at her feet, sucking his
way through the halftime orange segments, watching her
soccer team getting thrashed on the school field in front
of her.

The Under Nines soccer league played on a quarter of a
soccer pitch, in mixed teams. Viv's team, the Selwyn Pri-
mary School Small-Stars had only been on the field for ten
of the eighteen-minute first-half and were already two-nil
down.

Beside their coach were her substitutes, Emma, Cameron and Tilly, who was anxiously scanning the car park
behind them. "Where's Uncle Ross?" she demanded for
the twelfth time. "We *need* him."

"He must have been held up. I'm sure he'll be here soon,
hon." Privately Viv was starting to worry that Ross had

been in a car accident. He hadn't phoned to say he was delayed, which was unlike him, and his cell kept clicking to call answer. On the other hand, he'd let her down before.

The ball bounced out of play and, stemming her growing disquiet, she waved to get the referee's attention. "Substitute, please, Ref! Emma?" She turned to her forward. "Go swap with Neil and tell your teammates to calm down and stay in their positions."

At the junior level, players tended to forget their practice drills and all chase after the ball like a pack of over-excited puppies. Viv winced as the opposition's star player kicked his third goal into the net and punched the air in victory. Blondie, Viv called him, for his flying yellow hair and Hollywood showmanship. Or should that be showman-up-manship.

"Awww, that sucks." Tilly stamped her foot and the studs on her soccer boot stabbed indents in the turf.

Neil, the kid who'd been subbed, came off the field panting. "He's such a bighead!"

"Sportsmanship," Viv reminded everybody, and clapped politely.

"Uncle Ross is here!" Tilly ran to meet him. "Uncle Ross…we're losing. You've gotta fix it."

"What's the score?" he asked as he stopped next to Viv.

No explanation, no apology. Now that she knew he was safe, Viv embraced the luxury of annoyance. "Why didn't you phone?"

"Something came up, Meredith."

"The score's three-nil." Cameron, whose red hair seemed permanently charged with static, pointed to Blondie. "That guy's nine, he shouldn't even be playing but Mrs. Coltrane said he could, 'cause they had no one else."

"I might have been conned," Viv admitted, putting her irritation aside. "Blondie's ball-handling skills leave everyone else's for dead. Our only advantage is that he's not a team player. When he gets the ball, he ignores his teammates and makes his own run for glory."

"Who hasn't gone on yet?"

"Cameron and Tilly in the second half." Only seven players were needed but the Small-Stars rotated three substitutes. "What happened?" she added, concerned as he turned his head to follow the play. "You have a graze on your cheekbone."

"It's nothing." Ross continued to follow the action. "We need all our best strikers on the field. Cam, that's you next to Emma. Neil, I'm putting you on midfield in the second half, swap with Sasha."

"And me," said Tilly. "I'm a striker."

"Offside, Ref," Ross yelled as Blondie slammed another one into the net.

The thickset official hesitated, then blew his whistle and disallowed the goal. "I suspected as much on the first goal," Viv exclaimed. "But I wasn't confident enough to call it."

"Awww, Dad!" Blondie complained. Now Viv knew why the man had a problem seeing infringements from his star player. Each team's coach refereed a half, which was supposed to ensure fairness.

Viv might know the basic rules but she didn't have the nuances needed for officiating. Another reason she was glad to see Ross. She frowned as he bent to ruffle Harry's meager hair in hello. He left his bad leg straight. "Are you up to running around the field? Ross, are you hurt?"

"I'm fine." He limped down the sidelines away from her and yelled an instruction to Cory. The kid managed a raggedy pass to Emma who hovered in the goal-mouth and couldn't miss it—though she did her best to. Four-one. The Small-Stars and their supporters broke into wild cheers.

"I *knew* he'd fix it," Tilly said fervently.

Staring after Ross with a worried frown, Viv didn't reply. He could hardly bend his knee. The whistle blew for halftime and the kids piled off the field, thirsty and disconsolate. Between making sure everyone had a water bottle and bringing out a packet of gummy snakes to replace the orange segments, she lost the opportunity to question Ross.

He gave a pep talk, calming the kids down, then talking them up until they were smiling. He was so good at this—motivating. She'd already heard how great training had been yesterday from the kids, and they'd all been disappointed when he hadn't appeared for the pregame warm-up. Viv had done her best but she wasn't a teacher. It was clear Ross was. And he'd known exactly what to say to stop her from running home to New York.

Viv realized she hadn't told him the outcome of her visit with Merry yet. That he hadn't asked. She gave herself a shake. This apprehension had nothing to do with Ross, it was all about her. Merry's rousing call to action still rang in her ears and she hadn't yet decided what to do about it.

"Isn't Tilly going on?" she asked as the kids ran onto the field, leaving her niece on the sidelines.

"We'll try and get some goals on the scoreboard first." Ross hooked the whistle around his neck, gave her the stopwatch to time-keep. "She's cool with it."

Tilly was retying the laces on her boot and Viv couldn't see her face.

"Okay." She hesitated. "Just to tell you," she said in a voice too low for the kids to hear, "I sorted things out with Merry and she'll tell Charlie. And she and I...Ross...we're okay again."

"That's great," he said. "Start the stopwatch when I signal you from the pitch." Their eyes met and Viv's blood froze at his indifference. Good or bad they always had a connection. Now it was like looking into a black hole.

"I should get onto the field," he added. "The other coach is tapping his watch."

"Sure." Viv folded her arms, so shocked she barely registered what was happening on the field until Tilly tugged on her sleeve.

"Shouldn't I be going on now?"

Dazed, Viv checked on Harry, now absorbed in unraveling one of the bandages from the first aid kit, then her stopwatch. Six minutes in. "What's the score?"

"Five-three to them…that guy's gonna be too good. They *need* me."

Even in her confusion, Viv smiled at her niece's unshakeable confidence. Truth was, Tilly was a lousy player and probably only in this grade because Merry was the only parent willing to coach.

"Ross has probably lost track of time." Viv waited for a gap in play. "Sub, Ref?"

He looked over and held up three fingers. "Three minutes," Viv told her niece.

At two minutes, the Small-Stars scored. Tilly was hopping from one foot to the other, more and more anxious. Viv called out again. "Sub, Ref."

Ross lifted his hands in a time-out and limped over. "Do you want us to win, Til?"

"Yeah."

"We stand a chance if we keep the best players on. How do you feel about staying off today?"

Viv's stomach plummeted. "What are you doing?"

"But *I'm* one of the best," Tilly said in confusion. The two subs behind her sniggered and she faltered. She looked at her uncle with her heart in her eyes. "Aren't I?"

Viv waited for Ross to reassure her. "No, honey, you're

not," he said. "I know it's hard to hear but you still need to grow into your game. Right now, you're the team's weak link."

Unable to believe her ears, Viv stared at him. "What are you doing?" she repeated.

Tilly stuck out that stubborn chin of hers. "I'm playing."

Ross stared their niece down. "You can do what's best for the team and stay off the pitch or you can be selfish and insist on playing. It's up to you."

"Stop this," Viv said sharply. "You know everyone plays. You can't leave Tilly off, she's been looking forward to this all week."

His face was pale, stony. "Make your choice, Tilly."

Tilly's mouth started to tremble. She bowed her head. "I'll stay off," she said in a small voice.

"You are *not,*" Viv said. "Ross—"

"Good girl." He limped back onto the field.

Openmouthed, Viv stared after him, then down at Tilly who stood like a soldier in front of a firing squad, arms by her side, expression rigid, and two large tears rolling down her cheeks.

"No," Viv said fiercely. "No, damn it. This is not right! Watch your brother."

She strode out onto the field just as Ross blew the starting whistle. Waving her arms, she yelled, "Time out, time out!"

"What the hell is this, Grand Central?" The other coach jogged onto the field, and Viv turned on him.

"If you hadn't cheated by bringing in a nine-year-old, we wouldn't be in this position, so wait!" He retreated to the sidelines. "Take five," she yelled to both teams. "There are enough gummy snakes for everybody."

"What the hell is wrong with you?" Ross demanded.

"What the hell's wrong with *you?*" Grabbing his arm,

she swung him around so they had their backs to the intrigued spectators. "You're the one who told me that this was all about fun, and everyone gets a turn and building the kids' confidence and—"

"In a fair contest I'd agree with you," he interrupted impatiently, "but it's not a fair contest. Not with David Beckham playing."

"What matters isn't winning or losing, it's about how you play the game."

"Life doesn't play like the manual, Viv, and the sooner Tilly learns that, the better off she'll be."

"Whatever kind of downer you're on today," she replied angrily, "doesn't give you the right to traumatize children. Give me that whistle, I'm firing your ass. You've humiliated and destroyed our niece—"

"Quit being so bloody melodramatic," he snapped.

She shoved him around to face the sidelines. "Look at her! *Look* at her, Ross."

Viv didn't glance at Tilly—she couldn't—she watched Ross. Saw his jaw set as he struggled to remain unmoved.

"What happened to you today?" she asked, bewildered. "Tell me!"

Ross turned away from the spectators, rubbed his forehead with a shaky hand. "I did a time trial this morning… a run. Not only did I fail, but I've knocked back my return to the unit—by a month at least, the doctor said. My CO will be frickin' thrilled. He told me not to train. Whatever hope I had of deployment's permanently shot. I'm screwed, Viv."

Her heart broke for him, but he'd never forgive her for pitying him and they had a devastated little girl on the sidelines.

Ross took off the whistle. "Tell Til I'm sorry. Take over. I thought I could put a lid on this, but I can't. I can't."

"Don't walk away," she said. "Only you can fix this with Tilly."

"I can't even fix myself," he said harshly.

Viv took a deep breath. "You know your pity party is getting *really* old."

"What?"

"Life's chosen another path for you, so suck it up and quit blaming my brother and the unit for not letting you play out your revenge fantasies," she said brutally. "Steve's and Lee's deaths were tragic, but using anger to fill the void left by their passing won't solve anything. Deal with your grief, Ross."

His gaze met hers. "Who am I if I'm not a soldier?"

She had to dig her hands in the pockets of her sweatpants not to touch him. "You're still a soldier," she said crisply. "It's only your mission that's changed. Quit serving The Iceman's ego and serve where you're needed. And right now, that's here."

He wavered.

"Tilly needs you, Ross," she added quietly. "Follow your own advice and do what's best for the team."

He dug his fingers into his scalp. "Okay."

They found the teams mingling, gummy worms doing more to reconcile the teams than any lecture on sportsmanship. Harry was right in the thick of it, being oohed and ahhed over by some of the girls, a rainbow smear around his clownlike mouth. Tilly stood apart.

"Can we start now?" the other coach called sarcastically as they approached, shooing his team back onto the field. "If it's not *too* much trouble."

"Five more minutes," Ross said, and gestured the Small-Stars into a huddle. Tilly stayed where she was. "Guys, I had some bad news this morning," Ross said, "and I took it out on Tilly and I want to apologize to her in front of you all. She's got guts and heart and even though she's willing to step aside, I'm not letting her. In this team everyone has a place and we encourage each other first and worry about winning second. Are you all with me?"

The children broke into a chorus of enthusiastic yeahs.

"Everyone on the pitch…Neil, you come off for Tilly."

Their niece shook her head. "I don't want to play if I'm not any good," she said.

"You are good," said Ross. "Terrific for a seven-year-old. I'm so sorry, honey, please go on."

"No. I don't want to be the weak link." She looked down at her boots. "I don't want to be a loser," she whispered.

Ross wasn't going to be able to repair this. Viv swallowed hard.

Stretching out his left leg, Ross sat down on the damp grass to bring himself closer to her level. "You have a skill no one else has," he said. "But you won't like it."

Tilly shot him a sidelong glance. "What?" she asked sullenly.

"It's not a glory job but I need a defender," he said. "Defense takes a special person. Someone stubborn and persistent, who can work against great odds." Viv recognized a phrase from Ross's SAS DVD.

Tilly said nothing—too scared now of being hurt again—but Viv could tell she was intrigued.

"See that Blondie kid?" Ross pointed. "He's scoring all the goals because no one's marking him. I need someone who'll make it hard for him to get to the ball."

Tilly eyed the much taller bigger boy. "And you think I can do it?" she said doubtfully.

"You're Attilla," said Ross as though that explained everything. And actually it did.

Tilly looked thoughtful. "You stick to him like glue," Ross continued. "Forget about trying to get the ball. Don't even watch the ball. You watch him and you stay with him. When he gets mad, just pretend you don't hear. Will you do that for me?"

The little girl's chin lifted and she rubbed her eyes. "Yes," she said. Ross gave her the ball and she ran onto the field to join the others.

Genius, the man was a genius, and Viv finally acknowledged that she loved him. Completely, irrevocably and for always. Loved him. God help her.

Ross held out his hand and she helped him up, resisting the urge to throw herself into his arms and beg him to love her back.

CHAPTER TWENTY-ONE

ROSS HANDED VIV the whistle. "You'll have to take over as ref, Meredith. My leg's not up to any more running and we're not letting the other coach ref again. If you get stuck, I'll cue you."

"Aye, aye, captain."

As Viv marched off, Ross turned to the three subs. "You guys are the support crew," he said. "I want you to run up and down the sidelines yelling encouragement when it's needed."

Their faces brightened and they tore off. Briefly, Ross closed his eyes. God, that was close. For a moment he thought he'd lost Tilly for good. If that had been on his conscience... Ross shuddered. The whistle sounded and with a glance at Harry, who was stacking the soccer cones, he refocused on the pitch. Viv needed his eyes.

He found himself drawn into the game, yelling instructions where needed. Cameron managed a successful header, equalizing the score.

Back and forth the ball went, from one goal area to the other, possession equally divided now that Tilly was marking their star out of the game. Scowling, the older kid tried everything to shake her—feinting, ducking and sprinting down the sideline. But Attilla chased him down. Ross grinned.

A pass meant for Blondie bounced off the back of her calves. His scowl darkened and the boy stopped in the

opposition's goal area to snarl something at Tilly. He tow-
ered over her by at least six inches. About to intervene,
Ross saw his niece's eyes turn flinty and prayed she didn't
deck the kid. Blondie's goalie drifted forward to listen to
the argument.

He glanced at his watch…one minute to go. They might
just get a draw out of this.

Midfield the ball deflected off an opposition player and
soared toward the Small-Stars goal. Seeing the danger,
Blondie stopped arguing with Tilly and ran forward to in-
tercept. His goalie scampered back to defend. By the time
Blondie regained control of the ball, Tilly was in his face
again, two feet in front of him. He kicked the ball as hard
as he could toward his goal line—straight at her.

Tilly scrunched her eyes closed and stood her ground.
The ball smacked her square in the forehead and rebounded
forward into the Small-Stars goal, taking the other team's
goalie completely by surprise. Hell, it took everybody by
surprise, including the scorer.

"Does that count?" Viv yelled, but the kids were already
answering, screaming in excitement while Tilly stood astonished, a big red circle forming on her forehead. A grin
split the girl's face.

"I scored!" she hollered. "I scored the winning goal!"

Choking up with pride, Ross wondered how one of the
worst days of his life could hold one of his best moments.
"Cycle of life, buddy," he told Harry, who—perplexed by
all the screeching—had drawn closer to his uncle.

Tilly was going to be insufferable tonight.

She came running over. "Did you see me, Uncle Ross,
did you see me do that header?" He laughed. Is that what
you called it?

"Yeah, honey, I saw…Meredith wants you."

The teams lined up to shake hands, the other coach

standing aside. Ross watched as Viv strode over and forced a handshake out of him, still showing the kids good sportsmanship.

If she hadn't challenged Ross…if she'd let him walk away, the outcome would have been so different. Thank God for Viv, he thought fervently. And she was right.

It was up to the survivors to coax meaning from Lee's and Steve's deaths. His role was behind the scenes now, preparing other one-percenters. Building instead of blowing up. That was a bitter pill to swallow, but it was time to suck it up.

Ross looked at Viv. He breathed deeply. It felt like the first breath in seventeen months that had oxygen in it. How could he not love her with her insane courage and her capacity to push him in every direction he'd resisted going…?

Hadn't he always been a sucker for punishment?

"MEREDITH."

After eight days, Viv responded easily to her sister's name but she continued to pack the trunk because it was Ross and she needed a moment to brace herself. With the teams dispersing and Harry and Tilly strapped into the car ready to go, she was technically alone with him.

Guess it was her turn now.

The trunk was full of the detritus of a soccer mom. Dirty boots, damp socks, a shin guard, a first-aid kit with Harry's unraveled bandage bulging out of it, a plastic bag with a soiled diaper tied up securely and ready for discard, the clean diaper bag, towels, snacks, extra drink bottle, umbrellas, anoraks, sunblock—

"Viv," Ross said quietly, and the weight he gave to her name made her heart kick like a scared rabbit's. By acknowledging she loved him, Viv had handed Ross a gun.

"Viv." Reluctantly, she turned.

"You wanna come back to our house, Uncle Ross?" Tilly yelled through the open passenger window. "She's gonna do her cartwheel again 'cause it's such a big celebration."

Oh, dear, God. A blush burned her cheeks. "Ross is probably too busy, honey."

"You don't want me to?" Surely that wasn't nervousness in his voice? She eyed him warily.

"If you want to, you can come," she ventured. "But don't feel you have to." She shrugged. "If you don't want to." She had no idea how to act around a guy she loved.

"Til?" Ross called. "Can you ask your aunt if she still likes me?"

Viv blinked. "What?"

"When a boy likes a girl and he's too scared to ask if she likes him," Ross said seriously, "he gets a friend to do it for him. Ask her, Attilla."

"But I already know the answer," came the airy reply.

"I don't," said Ross. He hesitated. "Have I blown it, Viv?"

"Can you be more explicit?" she said cautiously.

His eyes crinkled as he smiled. "Wouldn't you prefer to wait for more privacy?"

Did he intend that as a double entendre or did she just have a dirty mind?

Viv looked at him helplessly and, with an exclamation, he pulled her into his arms and kissed her. He'd kissed her before of course, but always with an element of self-control.

This kiss had none of that. It was even a little clumsy, as though it mattered terribly to him, as though Ross was investing everything in it. Enthralled, Viv wound her arms around his neck and matched his passion.

Ross jerked backward so fast he yanked her hair, which was tangled in his fingers. Viv's eyelids flew open and she found herself staring into Charlie's blazing eyes before he turned and slammed his fist into Ross's stunned face. "You bastard," he roared as Ross fell. "How long have you been sleeping with my wife?"

Charlie bent to grab Ross's T-shirt and raised his fist again. Viv dived forward and seized her brother-in-law's arm. "Charlie, no!"

With Viv hanging off his arm, he swung his foot toward his brother's ribs, but Ross rolled free. "It's not what you think, mate."

Tilly and Harry were screaming in the car, and blood streamed from Ross's nose as he grabbed the tow bar and hauled himself to his feet.

"And, you!" Charlie yanked his arm free of Viv's restraining grip. "How could I have trusted you again? How…?" His voice broke. With another bellow he lunged at Ross, who wrestled his brother into a bear hug.

"Charlie," he shouted, "she's not Meredith, she's Viv!" Blood from his nose splattered across the other man's business shirt.

But Charlie was beyond hearing. With a grunt of effort he started to break out of Ross's hold. In desperation, Viv jumped on his back, so all three were locked in a grotesque hug. "You're terrifying the kids, Charlie," she yelled in his ear. "Not in front of the kids."

He stopped struggling. Viv slid off his back and nearly fell over. One hand on the car for balance, she stumbled around to the passenger door to comfort the hysterical kids, waving reassurance to other parents and kids.

"It's okay," she called automatically. "It's a mistake… I'm not Meredith. Everything's fine." Tears poured down her cheeks. "Kids, it's okay," she wept, wrestling the upset children out of their seat belts and soothing them with hugs. "Everything's going to be okay."

In Ross's arms, Charlie started to sob. "How could you do this to me...you're my brother."

Ross tightened his embrace. "She's not Meredith," he repeated helplessly over and over again, ignoring the metallic taste of blood every time he opened his mouth. "Charlie, she's Viv, not Meredith."

At last the message penetrated. Charlie pulled back, his face smeared with Ross's blood and his own tears. "Viv?" he said, dazed.

"It's Viv, buddy, I would never make a move on Meredith, you know I wouldn't."

"But Viv's in New York."

Ross shook his head. "She's here. Now."

Pushing free, Charlie buried his face into his shaking hands. "Oh, God," he rasped. "What have I done?" He raised his head. "When I got out of the taxi and saw you locked in each other's arms, I..." He frowned. "But why is she wearing Merry's soccer-coaching uniform?"

CHARLIE TOOK MERRY'S CAR, he took the kids. He didn't look back.

Ross found a towel in his gym bag and, using the faucet in the kids' playground, cleaned off the blood as best he could, refusing Viv's help.

As soon as he'd walked out of her sight, he'd slammed his fist into the wall of one of the prefab classrooms. Now his hand hurt, too, along with his leg, his nose, his cheek, his bruised eye. Ross still couldn't believe his friggin' stupidity in giving in to his feelings for Viv in a public car park, while she was in character as Meredith. Some covert operator he was.

Charlie had caught an earlier flight to surprise his daughter at her big game. Instead he'd found his brother lip-locked with his wife.

Now Ross had blown it for everybody…himself included.

Not only did Charlie intend to start divorce proceedings against Meredith, he never wanted to see Viv again and he never wanted to see Ross. It had been like looking into Linda's eyes. He saw the same chilling hostility, the same ruthless rejection.

"You're no longer my brother."

"Here," said Viv, and he lifted his face out of the towel to see her holding out a packet of frozen peas. "I found some money in your console and bought them from the convenience store across the road."

Neither of them had said much since Charlie drove off. Both were too shell-shocked.

"Thanks." Ross pressed the package to his nose and wished it could numb him all the way through. He seemed to have experienced more emotions in this single day than he had over the rest of his life, and he was spent.

"I've been thinking about how we're going to fix this."

Peas held to his swelling eye, he stared at her with his good eye. Somewhere in the skirmish, her ponytail had been knocked sideways, giving her a skewed look. She was pale, tearstained and disheveled in Meredith's track pants. And the oversized white Small-Stars T-shirt was rainbow-stained from gummy snakes.

She still had the whistle around her neck and he loved her so much his brain hurt.

But seeing that evangelical fervor in her brown eyes—a fervor that had led to this mess, that had just cost him his brother—was too damn much. Right now, he wished Viv Jansen a thousand miles away.

"Don't look at me like that," she said. "You're with me on this, aren't you?"

"Don't you get it? There's nothing left to save, Viv.

We've screwed up everyone's life—your sister's, my brother's, their kids'." He pressed the peas to his face. *Charlie.* "Haven't we done enough damage?"

"So, what? We walk away and leave them at Ground Zero? You must see that's not an option."

"All I *see* is someone who never frickin' learns her lesson."

"Ross—"

"No," he said. "Neither of us is interfering again."

"Neither of us," she said dangerously.

He wasn't in the mood for diplomacy. "Let me rephrase that. If *you* want to go screw something else up, *you* are going on your own." A low blow. They both knew she had no car, no money and no choice but to go home with him.

Viv's eyes narrowed. "Fine," she said tartly. "That's how I prefer to live anyway. Alone." She marched off, her crooked ponytail swinging like an angry cat's tail.

Oh, for God's sake. "You can't walk to Hamilton," he bellowed after her.

"I've got a thumb," she said. "I'll hitchhike as soon as I get to a main road."

"Don't be so bloody silly, woman."

She used other fingers to give him the bird.

Ross cursed until he'd colored the school grounds blue. Goddamn it! If he wasn't so furious with himself, with her, if he wasn't so gut-wrenchingly sick over Charlie he might have seen the funny side.

She was walking the wrong way.

Storming back to the SUV, he climbed in, tossed the peas into the passenger seat and turned the air-conditioning on full. Tempted as he was to leave her to it, he knew he'd given up that choice half an hour ago. Ross started the engine. If this was love he didn't like it.

He caught up to her at the intersection of Flower and

Main, and curb-crawled beside her with the driver's window down. "Okay," he called. "You win—I'll help you. What are we doing?"

She stopped and Ross pulled over. "We'll take Merry home, grab the kids and leave her and Charlie to thrash out the issue alone," she said. "See, I *can* stop interfering." She looked pissy and defiant and so endearing with that ridiculous ponytail.

"It's a good plan," he said quietly. "Hop in."

"Move over and I'll drive. Coltrane, you're a mess."

Ross hated being driven. Dan's wife, Jo, thought he had a thing against being driven by women, but he got twitchy with anyone else in the driving seat. He'd been the patrol's driver, behind the wheel when an IED—improvised explosive device—detonated under the Dumvee, throwing Lee into the path of the enemy and trapping Steve in a fiery death.

He looked at Viv and moved over without protest. It was one of the hardest things he'd ever done and she didn't even register the sacrifice. She jumped in the driver's seat, graunched the gears... "I'm used to automatic"...and immediately pulled onto the wrong side of the road.

"Left-side drive," Ross reminded her, and she veered over to a cacophony of horn blasts from oncoming traffic.

Reclining the passenger seat, he lay back with a towel and covered his face with the frozen peas.

"Wake me up when we get to Hamilton."

CHAPTER TWENTY-TWO

Staff Nurse Florence Hore's eyes were the prettiest color, the blue of spring skies. Trapped in a glare-off, Viv only noticed the darker shards embedded in the iris.

"The fact that you're embroiled in yet another argument, this time with my patient's husband, doesn't remotely interest me," she'd said when Viv had rushed in and demanded her sister's immediate discharge. "Until the surgeon has given Mrs. Coltrane her final clearance and signed the discharge papers, I'm not authorized to release her."

"So let's phone the guy, get him out here. As I've already explained—twice—it's a family emergency."

Viv might as well have suggested dragging the Pope away from holy mass. "We do not," Florence said, "call out our specialists for anything but an emergency."

Viv glared. "This *is* an emergency. My sister's kids—"

"*General Hospital* called," Florence said. "They want their melodrama back."

Viv blinked first. "Damn it. To hell with this. You know what, Nurse Ratched? We're leaving anyway, with or without your permission."

"In that case…" Florence picked up the phone and punched in a number. "Security?"

Viv leaned forward and cut the connection. "Fine—you win. We'll wait until tomorrow." She added bitterly, "You probably miss the old days when surgery was performed without anesthetic."

"And we were allowed to call people like you lunatics…
yes."

Frustrated, Viv returned to her sister's room, where she
found Merry trying to pace on crutches. She looked up
hopefully but Viv shook her head. "We'll have to wait until
tomorrow…. How about you, any luck getting hold of Charlie?"

"He's not answering…his cell, Linda's phone, our phone.
Tell me the truth, Viv, how upset were the kids?"

Merry read the answer on her face and paled. "Why
didn't I tell him earlier," she said, and burst into tears. "My
poor babies."

Viv swallowed the lump in her throat. "To hell with
this," she repeated. "We're breaking you out of here."

"But the specialist—"

"You're a nurse. Is there any medical reason you can't
go home now?"

"No."

"So it's bureaucracy and Florence on a power trip. We
just have to work out how we'll do it without alerting her.
Get dressed and put your hospital gown over the top. I'll
go find Ross." Parking was notorious around the hospital
so he'd dropped her off while he circled the lot.

"He's not going to go along with this."

Was she right? Viv experienced a resurgence of doubt.
True to his word, he'd fallen asleep en route to Hamilton—
how could he have slept at a time like this? On the other
hand, he'd needed to. He'd looked terrible.

"Do you think he'll help?" Merry looked skeptical.

"I don't know," Viv said honestly. The kiss in the parking lot seemed a lifetime ago…. "All I can do is ask."

"So that's the situation," Ross told Dan. Cell pressed to
his ear, he stepped aside to let two ambulance officers

push a stretcher bed carrying an old man into Accident and Emergency. Pale, blinking to clear his vision, disorientated. Probably a stroke. "Basically," he said to Dan, "it's all turned to shit."

"You need me there?"

"Not at the moment, we'll take Meredith home and see what happens. I'll keep you updated." He changed the subject. "Listen, you were right with your concerns about my redeployment."

"Ice, they weren't concerns about your redeployment, they were concerns about *you*. No," he amended, "they were concerns about *me*. I need you alive."

"Yeah, well, I'm sorry. For behaving like an asshole."

"That's okay, I'm used to it. Anyway, we'll sort this out, buddy. It's not fair that you stand to lose Charlie because of my damn sisters."

"We're playing the one for all and all for one card now." Gingerly, Ross touched the bridge of his nose. The peas had reduced the swelling substantially. Enough to establish it wasn't broken. "So, while I have you on the line, tell me how to sweet-talk Hurricane Viv. It's become kinda important."

"You seriously think I'm going to help you nail my sister?"

"Actually I've already nailed her." Ross checked for the women's orthopedic ward on the board beside the elevator. "I need advice on talking her into some kind of commitment."

There was a long silence. "You want to marry my sister?…No, Jo, there's no way I'm handing over the phone now."

"For God's sake, Shep." Frowning, Ross pushed the elevator button. "Don't mention the *M* word around Viv or you'll scare her off. But…maybe…" He tested the idea.

"Eventually." It began to have appeal. "Actually, yeah. Possibly a long campaign," he added thoughtfully, "unless I catch her in a weak moment, but I have a few tricks up my sleeve."

None of which were suitable for sharing with big brothers. Impatiently he jabbed the elevator button again. "So do I have your blessing?"

"Hell, no!" His best friend sounded appalled. "You need to prove yourself first. I need a history of stability…at least six months."

"I'm glad you don't approve," Ross reflected. "That would have made it too easy."

"Ross!" Jo came on the line, possibly after a struggle because she sounded out of breath. "Is it true? You want to marry Viv?"

He grinned. "You hate being left out of the loop, don't you, journalist?"

"You know it."

"I suppose you want every juicy detail."

"Yes…. Wait a minute. You're going to hang up on me, aren't you?"

"No. You owe me a favor for helping you kidnap Dan and I'm calling it in. Keep your overprotective husband out of my wooing."

"You've got it," she said, then coughed delicately. "Alpha Hole, you do know wooing isn't just dragging Viv off by her hair, don't you?"

"*Now* I'm hanging up on you," said Ross, and did. The elevator finally arrived and disgorged its occupants, including his intended. His target. Whatever. Her anxious frown lifted as Viv caught sight of him.

"The duty nurse won't allow Merry to leave until tomorrow and has security on speed dial if we try." Catching his arm, she hustled him away from the elevator and lowered her voice. "We're going to have to smuggle her out."

He sighed. "Of course we are."

FROM MERRY'S HOSPITAL BED, Viv glanced over at her twin who stood behind the heavy swing door, holding it open in one hand, her crutches in the other. She wore street clothes, the pencil skirt and blouse she'd left the house to interview in a week earlier.

It was lucky, Viv thought inconsequentially, that her sister always wore half a dress size too big for her. The skirt fitted over her cast…just. "Ready?" she asked.

Merry swallowed. "Ready as I'll ever be." She hid behind the door. Placing a pillow over her left leg, Viv tented the sheet over the bulge, straightened the hospital gown to hide her soccer T-shirt and pressed the call button.

Florence showed up five minutes later. "Yes," she said crisply.

"I just wanted to apologize." Viv bit her lip as her twin did when she was stressed. "For the fuss my twin made earlier."

"Humph." Florence folded her arms.

"You see, my sister is so passionate about perceived injustice…" Out of the nurse's view, Merry crept out from behind the door—at least as much as a person with a cast to their thigh could creep "…she can say things she later regrets." Viv tried not to watch as Merry used her crutches with exacting slowness to inch out the door.

"Your sister," said Florence with volcanic heat, "has anger management issues and needs psychiatric treatment."

She started to turn away. "Wait!"

Florence paused. Behind her, Merry froze. "Something's wrong with the adjustment thingie on my bed." What was wrong with it was a folded piece of cardboard jammed under the lever to stop it depressing. "It won't recline and I'd like to nap now."

Merry disappeared from view. So did Florence, down the side of the bed. The frame rattled as the staff nurse struggled with the mechanism. "I don't understand...let me try wiggling it the other way."

Viv imagined the action outside. Ross waited in the hallway with a wheelchair. He'd scoot Merry to the elevator, which she'd take to basement level. There she'd wait to be collected. All Viv needed to do was keep Florence occupied until she heard the distinctive ping of the elevator.

"*Here's* the problem." Florence stood with the chocolate box fragment in her hand. "Who on earth would have put that there?"

"I wonder if my daughter did it yesterday? She's such a kidder."

Still no elevator ping. "Do you have children, Florence?"

"Too scared they'd turn out like yours. Now, if you'll excuse me, I need to get back to the nurses' station and organize meds for Mrs. Pearson."

"Could I ask you to pour some water into a glass for me before you go?"

The older woman's eyes narrowed. "It's well within reach, Mrs. Coltrane. You need to practice independence if you're going home tomorrow."

Still no ping.

Unable to think of another excuse, Viv watched her march toward the exit...and collide with Ross in the doorway. He put his hands on the nurse's shoulders to steady her. "I'm so sorry...I wasn't looking where I was going."

Florence straightened her bib and looked at Ross's face—the grazed cheek, the red-bruised eye and his slightly swollen nose—then stiffened. "You're not the outraged husband, are you, come to cause more trouble?" She thrust out her arms to secure the doorway, obviously with the intention of protecting Merry, and Viv forgave the woman everything.

"I'm not married," Ross said truthfully. "And I'm hunting for X-ray."

Florence relaxed her guard. "You're on orthopedic… X-ray's one floor down. The elevator's right out here."

Ross reached out to clutch the door frame. "Give me a second," he said. "I'm feeling dizzy."

"In here." With brisk efficiency, Florence steered him into Merry's room, sat him on the chair by the door and shoved his head down. "What's wrong with your leg?"

He'd favored it, sitting down.

"That's what the X-ray will tell me," he replied smoothly.

The elevator door pinged.

Ross lifted his head. "I think I'm okay now…. Thanks for your help." He looked at the name badge. "Florence." He made the word sound sensual and followed it with a smile that would have made Viv need to lie down, if she wasn't prone already. Even Florence blinked.

"You're welcome." She cleared her throat. "Here, let me help you." She tucked an arm in Ross's. "Lean on me if you need to."

"Thank you," he said meekly. "I'll do that."

As soon as they left, Viv flung back the sheet, leaped out of bed and stripped off the gown. At the mirror she yanked her ponytail off center, then pulled the curtain around the bed and sauntered down the corridor. Florence—the flirt—was chatting to Ross as he waited for the elevator. Catching sight of Viv, she scowled.

"I thought you'd left?"

"Just about to." Viv nodded politely to Ross, suddenly reminded of his fantasy. *We'd meet casually by the elevators.* Another ping and the door opened. The half-dozen people inside squeezed together to let them in. So much for that fantasy.

Florence smiled at Ross. "You take care now." Ignoring Viv, she sailed back down the corridor. Viv jabbed the button for the basement.

"Halfway there," Ross encouraged, as the door closed. Unfortunately the second part of Operation Reconciliation didn't go as smoothly.

Charlie refused to let Viv in the door.

"I can't wear these now, can I?" Viv fanned out her soccer T-shirt and pretended to shiver. "All I want is my suitcase, Charlie…some clothes aren't too much to ask, are they?"

Her brother-in-law's hostile gaze went past Viv to his brother, sitting in the SUV at the curb. Merry lay concealed in the backseat. "Tilly said Ross only found out the day before the funeral. Sounds like his hands were mostly tied so I'll let him come in to collect it. Not you."

Except Viv was supposed to keep Charlie occupied while Ross helped Merry inside. Past Charlie, Viv saw Tilly hovering at the end of the hall. She smiled encouragingly, received a tremulous one in return. "It's going to be fine, hon. Hang in there."

Charlie stepped into her line of sight. "Don't make out as if I'm the bad guy," he snarled. "You take responsibility for this."

"I do. Total and full responsibility. Don't punish Merry."

"She went along with it. To hell with this. I'm not talking to either of you." He went to close the door and Viv jammed her foot in it.

"I know you're hurt but please, Charlie, Merry loves you so much, give her a chance to fix this."

"Charlie." In the heat of the exchange neither of them had noticed Ross's approach. "Meredith's in the car," he said without preamble. "Go talk to her." Forcefulness wasn't part of the plan. Viv opened her mouth to soften the order and Ross gave her a look that made her close it. He knew his brother better than she did.

Charlie looked over to the SUV where Merry now sat in plain sight and his jaw tightened.

"We're done here."

Ross said in a tone too low for Tilly to hear, "After scaring the crap out of your children this afternoon, you have to reassure them that you don't hate their mother—even if you do. You're a parent first…outraged husband second. You know this, I shouldn't have to remind you."

"Charlie!" They turned to see Merry trying to swing herself out of the passenger seat of Ross's 4WD but the seat was too high off the ground. "I don't expect forgiveness, I just want to tell you why I did it. For our kids' sake, will you listen?"

The weight of her cast started to pull Merry forward and she grabbed the door frame. Instinctively Charlie started forward, then stopped. Viv remembered his gallantry at the funeral when he thought his wife was being snubbed.

"She needs help," he said to Viv, jerking his head in Merry's direction and jamming his hands in his pockets.

"Not me." Viv folded her arms.

Ross glanced between Charlie and Merry. "Not me," he said.

"Someone," Merry called plaintively.

Ross held out his keys. "Go somewhere you can talk in private. We'll watch the kids."

"Seriously needing help here, guys," Merry called.

Charlie snatched the keys. "This isn't agreeing to anything."

"I get that."

Charlie hurried to help his wife, stony-faced as he

resettled her in the passenger seat. Merry's apprehensive gaze met Viv's.

"Good luck," Viv mouthed. Tilly crept to the door, and seeing her, Charlie's expression softened. "I'm going for a drive with Mum," he said huskily. "You want to say good-night to her?"

Viv felt a spark of hope.

Tilly scampered over to hug her mother. Charlie embraced his daughter. "I'll be home *soon.*"

"Okay, Dad." She skipped back to the house much happier.

The first thing Viv noticed when they went inside the house was an open suitcase, half-packed with the children's belongings. She and Ross exchanged glances but with Tilly there, they couldn't say anything. Harry was curled up on the couch, the dog beside him, engrossed in watching a DVD of The Wiggles. "Ub," he said, pointing at the TV screen. At least one of the kids wasn't going to remember this.

"What do we do now?" Tilly asked.

Viv fondled Salsa's ears. "I vote McDonald's."

Her niece brightened. "Really?"

"Great idea," said Ross. "Just let your aunt and I grab a quick shower first."

The vision that evoked…. "Do you have any clean clothes?" she asked. Ross had covered up the bloody T-shirt with a windbreaker.

"I'll borrow a shirt of Charlie's."

They managed to show the kids a good time. At seven-thirty, Tilly went to bed cheerfully, fully expecting that her parents would come home together. Viv hoped to God that she was right.

Ross was pensive when she returned to the living room after settling the kids but she resisted the urge to ask what he was thinking. Viv had no idea where they went from here and she suspected he didn't, either.

She waited for him to say something...anything that would clue her in. He picked up the *TV Guide*. "There's a rugby match on the sports channel."

The disappointment was crushing. "I'll put the kettle on."

So was the relief.

ROSS FLICKED FROM ONE channel to the other unable to settle, and completely frustrated with himself.

Whatever happened with their siblings' relationship, he expected Viv to come home with him later, but did she?

And if so, in what capacity—as a friend, lover, girl-friend? He wanted to talk about a future but he didn't know where to start. How the hell was he going to convince Viv she could still be independent in a committed relationship when he had no experience of making one work?

He needed to ask but the very idea made Ross squirm. What if she'd had second thoughts since their kiss this afternoon?

And why was he worrying about her having second thoughts when she hadn't given any indication that she'd had first ones yet? One quick snog in a parking lot didn't mean she returned his feelings. *Feelings*.

The Iceman broke into a sweat. For a wild moment, he considered waking his niece and asking Tilly to ask Viv how she felt about him.

She brought in the tea, put his mug on the table and took the chair when she could have joined him on the couch. Left the scent of her perfume...honeysuckle. "What do you think?" she said. "Is it a good sign they haven't come back...or has your brother murdered my sister? Is he now burying her body under Linda's topiary?"

"I don't know." Ross didn't give a damn about his brother or his wife right now.

"No need to snap." Viv picked up her mug and looked at the screen. "What's on? Anything good?"

He realized he'd been watching *Romeo and Juliet* and flicked to the sports channel because *Romeo and Juliet* had had it too easy with their families. They should try the Coltrane–Jansen combo sometime.

"Okay with rugby?"

"Sure." She sounded resigned.

He was making a complete hash of this.

"Oh, for God's sake." Disgusted, Ross threw down the remote. "I love you," he said. "Practically, I think we can make it work, if we want to." He glared at her. "Do you... want to, I mean?" *Do you love me?*

Viv blinked, opened her mouth. Ross's cell rang.

He ignored it.

"You should answer that," she said. "It's probably Charlie."

Impatiently he answered it.

"We're working it out," Charlie said, and Ross gave Viv the thumbs-up.

"That's great, Charlie. Goodbye."

"Wait...can you stay with the kids overnight. Merry and I—"

"Yeah, that's fine."

"You don't sound very happy about it."

"I'm frickin' delighted, okay...but right now I'm trying to talk Viv into marrying me and—" Shit. He'd mentioned the *M* word.

"Marry Viv?" Charlie sounded stunned. "No, Merry, you can't talk to him.... Ross, I don't want you to—"

"Tough." He cut the connection and stared at Viv who

was staring back like a possum caught in the headlights of an oncoming car.

"Marriage," she said slowly. "Ross, you never said marriage. We've only known each other a week."

"Eight years and a week," he reminded her.

"You don't believe in soul mates."

He sighed. "I know."

"I don't, either," she said.

"I love you, Viv. Marry me," he said. "I'd get down on one knee if I could. You're everything I never thought I'd find in one woman…adventurous, independent, loving, loyal. Hell, didn't I let you drive?"

Viv stood and wandered to the window. Salsa left his basket and followed her, but she was gazing out distractedly and didn't notice him. Looking for an escape route? Ross swallowed and waited.

"I've never seen marriage and kids in my future," she said at last. "I think because I never thought I could do it perfectly…like Merry seemed to. But I've learned she's not perfect and never was, except in my imagination."

Hope propelled him to his feet.

"And I've discovered," she continued, "that marriage—and kids—is a messy, complicated, think-on-your-feet exercise and since I've had a lot of experience in that area…" She stood in front of him. "I'm extremely worried that I'm overqualified."

"That's okay," he soothed, drawing her into his arms. "I'm a novice so it'll balance out."

"What about practicalities?"

He smiled against her hair. "It's such a turn-on when you talk all sensible."

Viv persisted. "You're based in New Zealand, I'm based in New York. While we can juggle schedules and I can do some design work remotely, it's still one hell of a commute."

She'd already thought about this. A lot. *Excellent.* "Skype sex?" he suggested.

Viv pulled back, concern in her eyes. "I want you to be sure about us because it won't be easy." She laid her palm against his cheek. "Charlie's going to take a while to forgive me."

Always trying to protect. He turned his head and kissed her palm. "We'll sic Attilla on him," he reassured her. "And Jo's got your brother covered. You and I will retreat to New York and wait until the dust settles." Ross had always had the option of easing himself back into the Unit. Now he had a reason to. "And if we come back married…"

She frowned. "Hey, I only said I loved you. I never said I'd marry you."

Actually this was the first time she'd said she loved him, but Ross was learning that stealth, not resistance, worked best with his future wife. He loved a challenge. Loved being challenged. "I'll try not to get ahead of myself."

Appeased, Viv raised her face for his kiss. "I love you."

"That's all that matters." Ross lowered his lips to hers.

Salsa growled.

"You have *got* to be kidding me," Viv said.

Ross laughed and kissed her anyway.

He considered himself a simple man. All he needed was to be the best at what he did. And soon—way sooner than Viv imagined—that would include being a husband.

* * * * *

A sneaky peek at next month...

Cherish™

ROMANCE TO MELT THE HEART EVERY TIME

My wish list for next month's titles...

In stores from 21st September 2012:

❏ The Valtieri Baby – Caroline Anderson

& Slow Dance with the Sheriff – Nikki Logan

❏ The Tycoon's Secret Daughter – Susan Meier

& Bella's Impossible Boss – Michelle Douglas

In stores from 5th October 2012:

❏ More Than One Night – Sarah Mayberry

& Royal Holiday Bride – Brenda Harlen

❏ The Last Single Maverick – Christine Rimmer

& Puppy Love in Thunder Canyon – Christyne Butler

Available at WHSmith, Tesco, Asda, Eason, Amazon and Apple

Just can't wait?

Special Offers

Every month we put together collections and longer reads written by your favourite authors.

Here are some of next month's highlights— and don't miss our fabulous discount online!

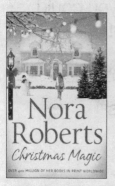

On sale 5th October

On sale 5th October

On sale 5th October

Save 20% on all Special Releases

Find out more at
www.millsandboon.co.uk/specialreleases

Visit us Online

1012/ST/MB387

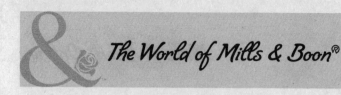

The World of Mills & Boon®

There's a Mills & Boon® series that's perfect for you. We publish ten series and, with new titles every month, you never have to wait long for your favourite to come along.

Blaze®

Scorching hot, sexy reads
4 new stories every month

By Request

Relive the romance with the best of the best
9 new stories every month

Cherish™

Romance to melt the heart every time
12 new stories every month

Desire™

Passionate and dramatic love stories
8 new stories every month